SACRAMENTO PUBLIC LIBRARY.

828 "I"

Sac

I0436940

LIBRARY

EMERGENCE

C.J. CHERRYH

THE FOREIGNER UNIVERSE

FOREIGNER
INVADER
INHERITOR

PRECURSOR
DEFENDER
EXPLORER

DESTROYER
PRETENDER
DELIVERER

CONSPIRATOR
DECEIVER
BETRAYER

INTRUDER
PROTECTOR
PEACEMAKER

TRACKER
VISITOR
CONVERGENCE

EMERGENCE

THE ALLIANCE-UNION UNIVERSE
REGENESIS
DOWNBELOW STATION
THE DEEP BEYOND Omnibus:
Serpent's Reach | Cuckoo's Egg
ALLIANCE SPACE Omnibus:
Merchanter's Luck | 40,000 in Gehenna
AT THE EDGE OF SPACE Omnibus:
Brothers of Earth | Hunter of Worlds
THE FADED SUN Omnibus:
Kesrith | Shon'jir | Kutath

THE CHANUR NOVELS
THE CHANUR SAGA Omnibus:
The Pride Of Chanur | Chanur's Venture | The Kif Strike Back
CHANUR'S ENDGAME Omnibus:
Chanur's Homecoming | Chanur's Legacy

THE MORGAINE CYCLE
THE COMPLETE MORGAINE Omnibus:
Gate of Ivrel | Well of Shiuan | Fires of Azeroth | Exile's Gate

OTHER WORKS:
THE DREAMING TREE Omnibus:
The Tree of Swords and Jewels | The Dreamstone
ALTERNATE REALITIES Omnibus:
Port Eternity | Wave Without a Shore | Voyager in Night
THE COLLECTED SHORT FICTION OF CJ CHERRYH

C. J. CHERRYH
EMERGENCE

A *Foreigner* Novel

DAW BOOKS, INC.
DONALD A. WOLLHEIM, FOUNDER
375 Hudson Street, New York, NY 10014

ELIZABETH R. WOLLHEIM
SHEILA E. GILBERT
PUBLISHERS
www.dawbooks.com

Copyright © 2018 by C. J. Cherryh.
All rights reserved.

Jacket art by Todd Lockwood.

Jacket designed by G-Force Design.

DAW Books Collectors No. 1778.

Published by DAW Books, Inc.
375 Hudson Street, New York, NY 10014.

Book design by Stanley S. Drate/Folio Graphics Co., Inc.

All characters and events in this book are fictitious.
All resemblance to persons living or dead is coincidental.

The scanning, uploading, and distribution of this book via the Internet or any other means without the permission of the publisher is illegal, and punishable by law. Please purchase only authorized electronic editions, and do not participate in or encourage the electronic piracy of copyrighted materials. Your support of the author's rights is appreciated.

First Printing, January 2018

1 2 3 4 5 6 7 8 9

DAW TRADEMARK REGISTERED
U.S. PAT. AND TM. OFF. AND FOREIGN COUNTRIES
—MARCA REGISTRADA
HECHO EN U.S.A.

PRINTED IN THE U.S.A.

To Jane, as always.

Table of Contents

EMERGENCE

1

The rainy day in Port Jackson brought a cool breeze from the open balcony doors. It was quite a lovely balcony, though Bren Cameron's atevi security, watching from across the room, didn't want him to cross that threshold.

The doorway, however—theirs being a third-floor suite in an isolated mansion on the highest hill in town—still afforded a spectacular view of the city, and Bren stood leaning on the door frame, enjoying the moving air. Tall buildings of the present century stood on the right and left. The lower rooftops of the gracious old homes and shops of the prior century barely showed below, descending toward the harbor, with a wide gray gap. One couldn't quite see the harbor from here, but the center of that gap was the sea—the strait that divided the human island of Mospheira from the vast megacontinent that belonged to the atevi, the world's native inhabitants.

Bren's brother Toby was out there on his boat, possibly the safest man on the planet, anchored as he was next to an atevi naval vessel. In his own way, Toby had become as much a bridge between human and atevi, as Bren himself. Toby had carried secure messages both ways across that strait during the Troubles on the mainland, and more than once provided a quiet and safe passage for people and goods, the most recent being his delivery of Bren and his entourage to the island.

Bren's work here was, technically, complete. He'd made his reports, convinced the necessary officials that the answer to the overpopulation in the station orbiting above was to get the refugees from Reunion Station down to the world and integrate them into Mospheiran society. More, he'd set the right people into place to accomplish that deceptively difficult task.

Only one job remained, and that was to be here when the next shuttle landed—to greet the three young people so singularly important to the aiji's son, Cajeiri, and to see to their safe and secure settlement into their new life.

That, however . . . was still days ahead. And meanwhile—Bren and his bodyguard remained out of touch with the mainland, cut off from information, more isolated from doings over there than they had been on the space station. A phone call could reach the station. He had that, which could inform him on doings up there, and he could ask what the station knew—but the station itself would have nothing on the things that worried him. If it had—it might have called him. But it had not.

Toby might know something. A single call right now, and Toby would come into that harbor. Toby might not speak that much Ragi, but he could at least ask the naval escort for news—if the navy itself was told anything beyond its mission, which was to keep Toby safe, to keep one Bren Cameron safe, when he chose to come back across the strait—and to provide the human government of Mospheira a visible earnest of the attention of the aishidi'tat, the Western Association, which was to say, the government of the mainland.

That was the outward face: the aishidi'tat is watching. The paidhi-aiji has the aiji's strong support in his presentations, and in his demands.

But there had been no word about goings-on inside the aishidi'tat, nothing to explain the uncommon goings-on around Cajeiri, the unprecedented appearance by the nine-year-old heir, not just on atevi national television, but feeding over to the island as well. The aiji's family simply did *not* appear on camera, but there had been the aiji's nine-year-old son boarding the train, talking about a visit to his great-uncle Tatiseigi. Alone—

give or take his bodyguard. No sign of the aiji-dowager, who ordinarily would have been with him. Not going *with* Lord Tatiseigi, but going alone to visit him—when Lord Tatiseigi had been under strong pressure by his own party. Conservatives were trying to throw their weight around now that other crises had, in their opinion, abated. Had they gotten the old man that upset?

Other crises were *not* that abated. And the Conservatives getting their way could bring one of those crises alive, with all that went with it.

They had just saved the planet from calamity, for God's sake. Could the Conservatives not let the situation lie quiet for a season?

Unfortunately—Tabini-aiji himself would not. Tabini had presented the Conservatives new worries. A treaty with an alien power? That didn't greatly concern them. The fact that two Conservative lordships lay fallow with the next legislative session looming, and Tabini was proposing to fund the landing of more humans from the heavens, to land at their own space-port, while the aiji was flinging precious cargo down from the station to light gods-knew-where on the hallowed soil of the mainland? They were upset. They had harried Tatiseigi to help them fill at least one of the vacant lordships, and get back a vote that could possibly slow Tabini's plans.

Tabini had made a countermove. The nine-year-old heir had just been moved into public view, sent to bolster his great-uncle, with the aiji-dowager, his usual guardian, nowhere in sight?

What was he up to?

God, he wanted information.

But calling Toby in just brought too much attention to Toby, the phones were absolutely not to be trusted, even if they spoke Ragi, and focusing the Mospheiran news agencies onto events on the mainland, at a time when focus on the next shuttle landing best served the *Mospheiran* political process . . . and the future of five thousand human refugees . . .

No. His need to know was not paramount. His finishing his job here—was. A good appearance, a good impression, and focusing Mospheira on its own peaceful future—that was the best use of the paidhi-aiji. The agreements had to be kept, for the sake of the refugees, and for the stability of the aishidi'tat. Tabini-aiji did not commit himself to unprecedented favors and then have the recipients decide they'd changed their minds.

Banichi came to stand by him companionably—senior of his aishid, black-skinned, golden-eyed, a head and shoulders taller than a tall human and wearing a uniform, Guild black, that he'd likely worn every day since he was a teenager. Banichi was likely asking himself what the paidhi found out there of such interest, given a misting rain and an impenetrable gray in the direction of the homeland.

They'd been together long enough, however, that Banichi needn't even ask the question.

"I am remembering the city," Bren answered. "I wonder how my brother is faring out there on the water, and what he knows that we do not." Two questions begged the felicitous number, three, to settle the universe in order. "I wonder why the young gentleman is traveling alone. And I am becoming very anxious to be home."

Home. It was curious to stand here on the island of his birth and say that, but it was true. Beyond any doubt he had had left, it was true.

"We might have flown," Banichi said. "We still might, at any hour, and easily return to Mospheira for the landing."

"We might have," he said. "We might. But one hesitates to excite the news folk with distracting questions. I take it there is no news from the mainland?"

"Nothing," Banichi said. Guild communication was necessarily by radio, secure in its codes, but apt to raise curiosity when used here, and scant of the very sort of detail they might most want to know. "We have indicated our concern. We have communicated with the aiji."

"And I dare not." There were phones—but phone service to the mainland involved the Messengers' Guild, which was not to be relied upon, even yet. There was also, somewhat more secure than what passed via the Messengers' Guild, a communication link via Lord Geigi's office up on the station. But Geigi had thus far sent them nothing regarding any problem.

And if he did involve himself in something the aiji had not seen fit to communicate to him, he could be seen as putting himself in play, which could ratchet up a situation on the mainland that they, crux of his problem, imperfectly understood. Quiet on this side of the straits served one interest; quiet on the other presumably served the aiji, or the aiji would have said something.

He had not gotten a call from Tabini-aiji—only one from his own apartment staff, that had been far from clear.

"Your aishid has a theory," Banichi said, "regarding the message from staff."

He looked at Banichi, all attention.

"Staff said," Banichi said, "that 'uncle,' which has to be Lord Tatiseigi, has found a 'replacement.' Replacement for what, we ask. We imagine two possibilities. One, that Lord Tatiseigi has declared his own heir, a successor for the Atageini Clan. This would be a great relief, but would not bear on our business here, and it would not be something for staff to mention to you under these circumstances—unless the chosen heir were the young gentleman; and that certainly cannot be the case. The situation is likeliest that the Conservatives are stirring to life, and that the aiji has sent his son to keep *them* at bay—"

That certainly made sense. For other lords to call on Tatiseigi at home while he was hosting the aiji's son as his guest would be a serious breach of protocol. The aiji-dowager as a guest would bring Conservatives flocking to the doorstep: she was political to the hilt. But the boy, a minor child? Absolutely the opposite.

"But this replacement," he said.

"—Is puzzling," Banichi said. "We do not think this was on the horizon when the aiji made his plans. We take it to mean that Lord Tatiseigi has, in fact, named a *viable* candidate for the Ajuri lordship."

"Is not tradition *against* his nominating again?"

"Absolutely against it. Therefore we think, granted he has made such a move, that this must be a significant candidate. The Conservatives pressed him hard to make a serious nomination before the upcoming session; and he deliberately chose from the bottom of the Conservatives' list in absolute confidence that Tabini-aiji would veto it. We surmise he exercised that veto with fair rapidity, in fairness to the person thus named. Now if Lord Tatiseigi has, in fact, broken tradition to name another candidate, something has changed, and by all we can determine, the young gentleman is still *with* him, while the aiji-dowager is still at the opposite end of the continent—so she is not likely the source of the candidate."

"Are you *sure* where she is?" Ilisidi was the one individual who could move Tatiseigi to make a radical change, and she had a habit of being wherever her great-grandchild was. When she was not—it was worrisome.

"We are quite sure. She has not budged from Malguri. She went there deliberately to quiet the Conservatives and keep them away from Lord Tatiseigi, and whatever has happened since, she has not acted."

The dowager *was* a conservative power. So was Tatiseigi. But the dowager's presence in any situation suggested to observers that whatever happened was her idea, and that assumption only complicated a complex maneuver. Tatiseigi's move did seem to be his own, regarding a Padi Valley situation, in which the dowager was an outsider, an Easterner, whose presence in western politics was problematic. The Conservatives were desperate to restore a vital, traditionally conservative Padi Valley lordship *before* the next legislative session. With *two* Padi Valley seats vacant, both Ajuri and Kadagidi, both neighbors to Tatiseigi, with Tatiseigi himself heirless and elderly, and with, in the Conservatives' view, a very critical legislative session looming, the Conservatives wanted something done about the vacancies. Fast.

There were problems with that haste—one of which was that there were so few candidates of the traditional bloodlines left alive. Ajuri clan had killed off *its* eligibles, and all the eligibles in Kadagidi clan were under taint of legal action. The aiji-consort was eligible for Ajuri, but by no means would Tabini have his wife take that post. Damiri's children were both eligible, but one was Cajeiri, Tabini's nine-year-old heir, and the other was a babe in arms, so it could not be either of them. It was a potentially lethal honor, if one went strictly on history.

"Who would be eligible?" he asked. "More to the point, who would *want* it?"

"We have compiled a very short list, but we cannot reconcile any of those with such a change of mind, not from Lord Tatiseigi. Certainly the acting lord would never have Tatiseigi's approval."

"Or the aiji's," Bren said. The acting lord was Cajeiri's great-aunt Geidaro, a detestable woman—and possibly complicit in the murder of the last lord, Cajeiri's grandfather. Oh, wouldn't solid proof of *that* misdeed make life easier for everyone?

"The aiji has reinforced the young gentleman's bodyguard, which we knew he would do soon. We attributed the intent to the young gentleman's new status as heir. However, in that the aiji has both attached that guard and sent the young gentleman under these circumstances—we are reasonably confident the young gentleman's presence has political purpose. Now—we ask ourselves whether *Tabini-aiji* may have asked Tatiseigi to make some specific move, and arranged the dowager's absence and the heir's presence in order for him to nominate outside the bloodline."

That—was about as convolute a piece of politics as one could imagine. The conservative dowager was not inclined to step aside on request, and the other— "One cannot envision the aiji dropping his son this deep into Padi Valley politics."

"One cannot envision it," Banichi said. "Which leaves us to imagine that whatever is going on in Lord Tatiseigi's house was not in the plan, and that something has come up rapidly since the heir's arrival."

"What could? Lord Tatiseigi's health?"

"If *he* were ill, or if there were any crisis with the young gentleman, no order would prevent the dowager returning."

"That is certainly true." He laid his fist on the door frame, gazing out into the gray of the sea and the weather. "One desperately wishes there were word."

"If we were needed back in Shejidan," Banichi said, "or at Tirnamardi, the aiji would surely call."

It did not seem the crisis, if crisis there were, lay in the capital. Not so likely. Tatiseigi's sprawling flatlands estate of Tirnamardi was strategically poised between the sprawling flatlands of Ajuri, Cajeiri's mother's clan; and the vacant Kadagidi manor, which lay just a short drive up the road from Tirnamardi. Currently Ajuri was held by the detestable great-aunt, but at least had a sort of administration; but the Kadagidi, caught in the same misdeed, were in worse state. The Kadagidi manor was under Guild occupation, its lord in utter disgrace and demoted to a factory job in the remote mountains, while Guild administrators and accountants went over the records. Ajuri and Kadagidi had been central to the conspiracy against Tabini—while, between them, Tatiseigi, in his ancient hedge-girt manor, had stood off armed intruders during the Troubles, too powerful and respected a lord for the usurpers to dare take down.

So was Tatiseigi now to give way to a committee of upset political allies?

Not likely. He could sit there until the legislative session began, robbing the Conservatives of yet one more essentially Conservative voice, at which point they would *beg* him to come back.

It was what made this sudden breach with tradition *and* Tatiseigi's own strategy so puzzling.

And the boy traveling by himself? The heir's appearance in full view of news cameras, in that consideration, made perfect sense—if the aiji wanted to signal his support of Tatiseigi despite the impending veto, and make it very clear to the Conservatives that politics was off the menu while the boy was visiting.

But how did Lord Tatiseigi, having received that guest, now reverse course and nominate another candidate?

They could indeed fly back to the capital, as Banichi suggested. He had come over to Mospheira by boat, a slow way, trying to decompress and get his mind sorted back into Mospheiran politics. But they could fly out tomorrow morning, spend a few hours in Shejidan getting acquainted with the changing situation on the mainland, and be back on Mospheira again for supper. It would rouse questions, but he could contrive a dozen sensible explanations that *didn't* involve the Padi Valley nomination.

"Bren-ji?" Jago quietly joined the two of them at the edge of the balcony. "We have a call from Gin-nandi. She asks to speak to you."

Gin Kroger. Newly-assigned stationmaster on the human side of Alpha Station. Gin, calling *him*, and not the President, to whom she was supposed to report.

That wasn't alarming, but it certainly wasn't ordinary.

The heavens themselves were not behaving as expected.

2

Dinner was set for sunset, and the tall hedges that rimmed every horizon of Tirnamardi had some time ago hidden the sun. Cajeiri was dressed for dinner, lace cuffs and neckpiece, clothing not designed for wear out of doors.

But he had tested his permissions, and his personal security, including the senior part of it, had agreed it was all right for him to go out to the stables, at least for a little while, under close guard, considering Uncle's own guard on the house roof, and considering the electronic perimeter. . . .

And that meant he could at least visit Jeichido.

He had to be extra careful of his clothes—he poked his cuff lace inside his sleeves, to keep it white—this shirt being only one of two choices for a formal dinner with Great-uncle. He had brought mostly his country clothes, expecting to go riding every day of his stay at Tirnamardi.

And he *had* gotten one glorious day of riding, and learned so much from Uncle—before the Ajuri relatives had shown up and everything had closed down again.

He had thought he might have to ask the grooms to give Jeichido the treats he had brought. But his own young aishid and the senior team Father had set to guard him said nothing to stop him when he climbed on the saddling-pen fence—carefully choosing the smoothest and cleanest of the age-polished railings. His bodyguards offered not even so much as a caution when he climbed all the way up, threw a leg over, and sat on the top rail of the saddling pen. His younger aishid did move close below and behind his lofty perch—because a hasty dismount was a possibility. But the seniors, seeming unconcerned, stayed back by the house door, talking casually to the stablemaster.

"Open the gate," Cajeiri called out to the grooms. "Let Jeichido into the pen, nadiin."

Mecheiti were scary up close, taller than a grown man at the shoulder, their heads way above that—one never realized how tall until one was up close. And they made a frequent low rumbling that was scary in itself. It was dangerous to walk into the herd—and there were nine of them in the pen, including the herd-leader, who was Uncle's favorite. The grooms, however, who worked with them every day, could walk out with just a quirt and a lead rope to bring a certain mecheita out. The rest of the herd was in the south pen with the gate still open, but if that middle gate should start to shut, the herd would move to unite, with all sorts of commotion, and the mecheiti *would* get where they wanted to be, quirts and objections and all. So one had to be aware of that gate, and the possibilities.

That was the way mecheiti were—torn between man'chi, that made them all keep the herd-leader in sight no matter what, and the driving ambition, among the strongest, to *be* the herd-leader, which could unbalance everything and have rails down and all sorts of mayhem on the instant if the wind swung the gate—or if one of the usual contenders decided to make trouble on a certain day.

Once the herd-leader went under saddle and had a groom up directing the herd-leader's movements, the rest would behave better, so it was all right to go out in the herd then, if one moved briskly and mounted right up.

He was not actually afraid to do that. And a quick mount the way the grooms could do it, even without a saddle, just getting a mecheita to put out a leg and drop a shoulder—that was his current ambition, but he was sure being taller and stronger would help.

Even once one was perched up atop, one had to take care very quickly, because another mecheita might take advantage and nudge the one being handled. Though peace-caps were on the upright tusks, which were as long as a man's hand, that great long neck could flex in almost any direction, and if you went down, those slender forefeet had claws that never quite drew in.

Time was, mecheiti had been trained to war . . . but there was very little encouragement needed for that. If a strange rider came onto Uncle's grounds, it would go very badly for the intruder. Only the most expert riders could manage the peaceful meeting of two herds by managing the herd leaders.

He hoped to be that expert someday. Great-grandmother was. Uncle was. And of course the grooms were. He really envied them.

But right now all he could do was establish himself with Jeichido as her rider, and that meant she had to learn his voice and his commands. The way to begin that was to call her into the saddling pen, and the way to do *that* was to have a pocket full of treats such as jerky and sweet grains—which he did. He perched on the top rail—he was big enough now to hook his toes firmly behind the second rail down, while sitting on the top rail. Antaro and Jegari, of his younger bodyguard, who were Taibeni and well used to mecheiti, waited right behind and underneath him, just in case, and Jegari obligingly handed him up a quirt, which was a point of safety.

Jeichido had to learn to come to him. She had to *want* to come, which meant he would be a fool to use the quirt at her approach at all unless he had to, but he would also be a fool ever to let her swing her head at him, and his bodyguard was right, it was a good idea to let her see he had the quirt as well as the treat.

"Jeichido!" he called out, and made that call the grooms used, while a groom held the gate open. Jeichido heard him, ears lifted, head up. She was, Uncle said it, ambitious, someday apt to challenge the herd-leader—a day on which he did not want to be on Jeichido. Uncle planned a new stable around her—over near Diegi—and Uncle wanted to give it to *him*. It was a handsome, handsome gift. He so wanted to live up to it, and to learn everything he needed to know, and not to be a fool.

"Come, Jeichido!" he called, patting his pocket.

Jeichido did come, and as she passed the gate, the groom waved off the handful trying to follow. She came up to him, her lofty head on a level with his. She turned that head to regard him with one golden, pretty eye, and the peace-capped tusk on that side was right by his face. She could do wicked damage, and he could be scarred for life, but anyone who intended to work with mecheiti could not be bluffed or threatened by them. He already had planned what he would do if she swung her head at him, which was to fall backward off the high fence, trusting Antaro and Jegari to catch him. But he also did exactly what he needed to do, keeping the hand at his pocket moving, to extract a treat and to offer it, so Jeichido knew there was a treat, and that he was not wasting time in giving it to her.

A delicate upper lip took it from his flattened palm. He took the chance to touch that velvety skin and let her smell him over. She shifted just a little, crowding him, and he pushed her head back with the hand that held the quirt, immediately reaching for the second treat, which she took.

He went further, gave her a rough chin-scratch—lighter might tickle; but he did it right. One never laid a hand on the top of the nose. That would get an instinctive head lift, which would not be good. He scratched just the right spot, that spot under the jaw a mecheita could not reach, and heard the rumbling that was a happy mecheita.

"Good Jeichido," he said. "Pretty Jeichido." He was not yet to the point of doing the bridling and saddling himself, even if he had the time and were dressed for it. The visit was just to let Jeichido know he was a giver of treats, *her* giver of treats, and to fix his smell and his sound in her memory. Since he was allowed outside this far, he resolved to keep renewing that acquaintance every day from now on. He could do that much.

He was surprised by the senior Guild his father had set to watch him, that they had gone along and just stood by his venture. They seemed not at all worried. Veijico and Lucasi, the other half of his junior team, held back a little . . . not quite so confident; they had only ever ridden with him, which was not that often. But they were trying to learn. Antaro and Jegari were Taibeni clan, which was to say, riders from before they were born.

He gave Jeichido the last treat, then, and gave the "Su-su-su," command that said she should go, now, unhooked his toes from the rail and swung over it to drop down to the ground.

Jeichido simply turned and went out the gate and back to the herd, to shoulder another mecheita sharply.

He felt rather pleased with himself. Ground training, Uncle called it, explaining why it was important, because either one worked with the mecheiti, or one forever depended on the grooms to do the bridling and saddling and grooming. And that would never do.

"Well done, Jeri-ji," Jegari said.

"The grooms surely have worked with her."

"She remembers you," Antaro said. "And if some stranger sat up on that rail, she would not be so compliant, not that one."

They walked toward the house, and joined up with the rest of his aishid—Rieni's gray-haired team, waiting patiently: Haniri, Janachi, and Onami. The senior unit had brought their rifles out with them, just as a matter of course—added protection, if it had been needed. It had not been.

"One appreciates the outing," Cajeiri said quietly.

"Yes," Rieni said. They could have advised Uncle. They could have called Father if he had been far out of line; but they had let him have his little visit, and quietly taken precautions they saw as necessary.

They had been sensibly obliging to him, not knowing whether he would be obedient or not; and his reliance on them went up another notch with that. He and his younger bodyguard would have been five fairly rowdy young people suddenly out on their own, traveling alone by train, staying together in a beautiful, historic guest suite together with a spoiled parid'ja in a cage, and suddenly they had four gray-haired senior Guild *instructors*, of all things, who had to watch over their behavior. He had expected—

Well, he had expected the trip to be grim. Just grim. He had feared his *life* might be grim, forever, if the new aish:d became permanent. He had feared a sudden, enforced growing-up, since Father had named him officially as his heir this summer. He had already had to attend functions and meet old people and be on his best manners.

But the new team was working out far better than his fears. Rieni and his unit turned out to have a good sense of humor—a fairly wicked sense of humor, at that—and did *not* seem inclined to phone Father every time he stepped out cf routine, though he had no idea what they communicated to the Guild by their own systems. His younger aishid was definitely staying on their best manners in their company, but Onami (who everybody said had been left on the Assassins' Guild's doorstep in a cardboard box—he still was not sure of that story) had gotten them all laughing last night. It was—

Well, what had started as an unwelcome and uncomfortable shift in their lives was decidedly looking more pleasant. It felt more like acquiring four more uncles, fairly forgiving ones, at that.

Now *they* had to get the rifles back upstairs, and *he* had to get to the lower hall servants' bath very quickly, and wash his hands before he dared touch his cuff lace, and become presentable for dinner.

"Bren." Gin Kroger, stationmaster of the human half of the station, was all business in the phone call, and she sounded tired. *"I've put together a documentary of the recent events— that I'd like you to view, before I take it public."*

Mospheirans had had absolutely no concept of the desperate state of affairs up there. A handful of photos, the official reports, simply failed to convey the horror that had almost happened. Releasing security takes on that was a political move and it definitely had to be a political decision. "I trust the President is seeing this."

"*Definitely. But you were there. And part of this vid is atevi.*"

"Then I do need to see it."

"*People on the ground need to see what happened, Bren. God, they need to see it. They need to know what these people have been through. They need to know how atevi damned well saved their collective skins up there. And they also need to see the Heritage Party's new darling in full flower.*"

The Heritage Party's new darling would be Mikas Tillington, Gin's predecessor, who'd heated up a centuries-old resentment between the Reunioners and Mospheirans to justify restrictive measures against the Reunioners and, in the process, catapulted a difficult situation for the Reunioners into a hellish mess because he *hadn't* dealt with repairs in the mothballed 'old section' and then needed the area functional, among other misjudgments involving planning, cargo requests, and food distribution. Conditions up there were changing rapidly, thanks to Gin, but supply was still short and there was no quick and easy fix for the emotional damage.

Three kids were coming down to Mospheira, a known quantity, children, least likely to rouse resentments. But ultimately five thousand Reunioner refugees who had their own culture had to integrate with a ground-dwelling population that had very different ways. Different traditions. Mospheirans had never met human strangers. They 'lived with atevi, but were restricted from meeting them.

No, Mospheirans couldn't envision what the Reunioners had already been through—not the destruction of Reunion Station, not the long voyage under guard, not the miserable conditions they'd lived in since. Mospheirans had believed everything up on the station was going smoothly. They'd understood that the two halves of the station, the atevi half, under Lord Geigi, and the Mospheiran half, under Mikas Tillington, had done heroic things, keeping Alpha station going, feeding their own populations despite terrible problems during the Troubles that had overthrown the atevi government. They believed they'd been cooperating with each other up there, as Mospheirans on the ground had done everything to help atevi solve their political problems and get Tabini back in power, which alone would get the shuttles flying again.

Heroic, well, yes, maybe they were. Certainly the efforts had been heroic on Geigi's part: he'd launched communication satellites and landed base stations, while Mikas Tillington had gone on a building binge, constructing expanded living facilities for the human population, when he should have been concentrating wholly on food production. Tillington had bet everything on somebody settling the problems on Earth and getting the shuttles back in operation.

And then *Phoenix* had come back bringing them five thousand refugees, who had been promised paradise.

Paradise definitely hadn't been the situation on the station when the refugees arrived.

Tabini *had* taken the government back, and the shuttles *were* flying again. But resumption of shuttle flights and slow correction of the situation on the ground during the last year hadn't fixed the situation that had been simmering up in orbit ever since the Reunioners' arrival. Tillington hadn't wanted the Reunioners. The ship couldn't go on holding them: it had reached the end of its resources. Tillington had treated the Reunioners as potential hostiles, denied them employment, settled them in an antique, barebones area of the station that had been scheduled for complete reconstruction.

And tensions on the human side of the station had reached critical when the alien kyo had shown up.

"I've included," Gin said, *"footage of his meltdown on the bridge."*

One felt compelled to say . . . "The man was stressed, to be honest. Short of sleep."

"He wasn't short of sleep when he ordered those section doors shut. And he wouldn't have been short of sleep if he'd followed protocol and made the shift with Lord Geigi."

"Undeniable."

"We've found things, Bren. He's tried hard to operate from house arrest to get rid of evidence, but we have the records and we have evidence. I know who he's been corresponding with. He definitely has close friends on Earth."

Friends on Earth.

In that context, Heritage Party. In the initial setup of the station, Mospheira had screened its half of the station population carefully to keep violent politics and prejudices out of play up there, above all being sure there would be no conflict with the atevi.

Station workers and science personnel had been screened. But corporations had sent their officials unscreened. And the stationmaster and his supporting staff had all been political appointments, outside the screening process.

All Mospheirans descended—in both senses of the word—from a strayed colony, quite thoroughly lost and desperate when they'd arrived in orbit around the atevi world. When the ship *Phoenix* had left them—deserted them, in the minds of many—they'd dropped down to the world. The native atevi had given them a foothold, let humans trade technology for peace, and finally afforded them this one island for their own, separate and safe so long as they didn't test their tolerance for each other too far.

Humans had done all right for themselves on Mospheira. For one thing, it was no small island, even for the modern population. And in the passage of time, the abandoned space station had become just a two-hundred-year-old curiosity, a star in the skies of a world that *atevi* had always called, sensibly enough and in their own language, Earth. Dirt. Ground. Home. *Their* planet.

The Earth of humans? *Phoenix* had unhappily misplaced that in the original disaster that had sent the ship so thoroughly off course and stranded them. *Phoenix* had spent the last two hundred years working their way along the track they *believed* would get them home—but things had gotten . . . complicated. Another intelligent species, this one spacefaring, had taken exception to *Phoenix*'s invasion of their territory, and had objected particularly to the *other* station *Phoenix* had built—right on the kyo's back doorstep.

Which was why *Phoenix* had returned to the atevi Earth, still lost, short of supply and more desperate than they had wanted to confess to anybody at the time. The ship had wanted the station occupied again, wanted, in effect, fuel, food, and a place remote from troubles. In return, they would give the world the benefit of their presence—and hand over their ship's technical archives . . . which might have let Mospheirans overwhelmingly outpace their atevi hosts, except for one thing. The necessary mineral resources and the manpower to get the station up and running—were all on the atevi continent.

So Mospheirans had joined with atevi in a massive campaign to get up into space, to build shuttles and to reopen the space station to serve the ship. And once the station was up and running, human and atevi would live and work as equals on that neutral ground—half the station human, half atevi.

Only after their ten year investment in time, money and delicate social adjustment, did the *hidden* truth behind *Phoenix*'s retreat come out: the possibility of survivors aboard that distant station. Some ship's officers had known it. The ship's crew hadn't. There were questions—deep, angry questions among the crew. *Phoenix* had made the run back to Reunion to answer those questions, and found the Reunioners, the same people now at the center of the current crisis, holding on by their fingernails in the remains of the station.

"Tillington's riding his heroics during the Troubles," Gin said, *"and the inclination is to say, well, he just went momentarily off the edge when the Reunioners came in. But the records tell a consistent story from the moment* Phoenix *left on the rescue mission—deals under the table, promises made that he had no right to make, and some very slippery dealing with corporate interests trying to get past Lord Geigi, especially after the atevi government had its Troubles. He's operated up there as if nobody would ever check the records. He's dealt with corporate officers, claiming that the Reunioners are here to take over and that Sabin and Jase Graham are behind it all, in some deal with you."*

Sabin and Jase were two of *Phoenix's* four captains, the ones who'd taken the ship out and rescued the Reunioners.

"He's crazy."

"Crazy enough can be more plausible to some. The public needs to see this man without the varnish on. They need to see the people in the Reunioner sections using buckets for a water supply. This is overwhelmingly important, Bren. They have to understand."

The Reunioners were descendants of former administrators and management who had, in the story that had come down to modern Mospheirans, *abandoned* them and gone off with the ship. Integrating the refugees into the Mospheiran population would be a delicate piece of work even without that ancient issue made active.

"What's your timeline on releasing this vid?"

"Hope to broadcast it before the kids come down. Allow time for the storm to settle. The President likewise has a copy."

"I'll give it a close look." Having Shawn's eyes on it as well as his made him feel much easier.

"Another thing," Gin said. *"Since the young gentleman recently appeared on the newsfeed on Mospheira, I've dared to include some footage of his and the dowager's visit to Central, and a little of their dealing with the kyo. I think the evidence*

of their help to humans reads extremely well. Appreciate if you could clear that with the atevi, if possible. I can edit it out. I'd rather not. I think it's critical."

"I'll take it on my own head if it needs to be." Footage of the aiji's family was generally *not* permitted, except on state occasions. But there were judicious exceptions. The young gentleman's first independent outing had been one such. Tabini himself had arranged that just in the last number of days. The paidhi-aiji might have to make an executive decision.

"You're such a useful guy, Bren."

"I try."

Who would have thought, two hundred years ago, that the paidhi's function would include vetting a documentary on a crisis in space and making sensitive decisions regarding the aiji's own family?

For two hundred years, humans and atevi had managed not to kill each other on Earth, two hundred years during which each side had kept its boundaries and prospered, due in no small part to atevi willingness to keep their bargains and the fact that humans had been careful what technology they turned over and at what pace.

For two hundred years, the paidhi had been the fulcrum of that exchange, the translator to decision-makers on either side of the channel. Thanks to those conservative and careful decisions, technology had advanced slowly but steadily, not radically disrupting atevi culture, and atevi *and* human culture had slowly shifted, accommodating each other in a civilized way.

That controlled rate of advance had run amok once the ship had come back, urgently wanting the station back in operation. It had threatened to upset the balance of power, and atevi—controlling the vital resources—had finally pulled up equal with Mospheirans in technology—even passing them, where it came to computers and weaponry.

The nature and extent of those changes in relative power had brought him here to Francis House, the seasonal center of the

Mospheiran government and the residence of the Mospheiran President—brought him here not as a Mospheiran citizen, not even as Mospheira's representative to the atevi court, which was what he had been—but as the official representative of Tabini-aiji, head of the Western Association, the aishidi'tat.

That was to say, he now arrived in atevi court dress and spoke for the *atevi* government.

He had, moreover, brought his armed *atevi* security and two of his *atevi* household staff with him, and he had settled in to explain to the Mospheiran government precisely what the aishidi'tat would and would not accept in the solution regarding another shipload of humans arriving on the planet.

It was a decided contrast to his previous visits, as a mere employee of the Mospheiran State Department.

"Well, then. I'll leave it in your hands. Should have down-loaded by now. I'm for bed, but I won't sleep well till I hear at least your initial impressions, so let me know soonest, please."

"Soonest," he said.

The line went dead. He put down the phone and turned to the expectant faces of his aishid.

A documentary on the station situation had the potential to blow a lot of historic misconceptions into dust, with absolutely unpredictable consequences. And Gin was counting on him to pass judgment on its effects.

God. He hadn't bargained for any of this.

But who else *could* do it?

A flying trip back to Shejidan to consult, just for an hour? That might have been remotely conceivable an hour ago. Now it was definitely not going to happen.

"We have a complication," he told those expectant faces. "Gin-nandi is arranging a broadcast. She will show Mospheira the situation on the station. She will show them why these people have to come down now, as rapidly as we can manage, and why Tillington is under arrest for his actions. The Heritage Party has been organizing a public campaign of objection to

Tillington's dismissal. Gin's broadcast will show the public in general things that will upset their understandings about the Reunioners. And they will see what conditions Tillington created. It will not be a pleasant experience for Mospheira and it will not be without repercussions. People will, for one thing, actually *see* the kyo in this broadcast. And there is, for good reason, a request that the young gentleman and the aiji-dowager be seen in this record. They were there. Much of our best visual record of the kyo includes them as participants. And they were, indeed, present and lending authority to Lord Geigi, lest anybody doubt where Tabini-aiji might stand on the matter. Gin-nandi's intent is to show atevi dealing with the kyo and rescuing the whole world from threat."

Sober looks. What Gin asked went entirely against tradition. "The paidhi-aiji will decide," Banichi said. "And we will back him."

"With advice," he said. "With your advice and your good sense. I think the communications storage may have brought this thing down by now, nadiin-ji. We need to view it."

3

The stairway down to the servants' bath was empty, which was not surprising, it being almost dinner time.

Uncle—he was Great-uncle, actually, but Uncle seemed closer and kinder, so that was what Cajeiri called him—Uncle had three formal meals a day even when Uncle was the only one in residence at Tirnamardi, but somehow that seemed appropriate. The manor that presided over Atageini clan was a marvelous place full of traditions. Uncle had his own museum in the basement, a treasure house of wonderful things. He had a grand library of beautiful old books. He had his stable of mecheiti, one of the two best lines in all the world.

Uncle lived all alone in this great old house, with just his bodyguard and his staff. He had no close relatives except Mother, who was his niece, and she never visited, not in all the time Cajeiri could remember.

But lately Uncle had had him, and from early this summer, there was his new baby sister—real blood relatives, which meant a great deal to Uncle.

And for three days now, Uncle had had another guest, Nomari, a cousin, so Nomari said, on Cajeiri's Ajuri side, and related to Uncle only remotely—and through an infelicitous marriage, at that. Nomari wanted to be the next lord of Ajuri and had come here to get Uncle's support.

Nomari had sneaked in, more like, but Nomari had

reason—assassination being the fate of every lord of Ajuri for generations.

Ajuri was a very tiny clan, and it held lands just beyond the border of the Atageini, Uncle's clan. But, along with its internal bloodshed, little Ajuri had murdered its way to a power and influence far exceeding its size—all under the guidance of a terrible old man, Shishogi, who had been another great-uncle, and also Ajuri. Walled away in a messy little office in the Assassins' Guild's headquarters, sitting as master of Assignments, Shishogi, it had turned out, had been killing people for years, forging authorizations, moving Guild about the map, spying, ordering not legal assassinations, but outright murders.

Shishogi had tried to kill Father and Mother, and *had* killed Grandfather, beyond any doubt Cajeiri held. Shishogi very likely had killed other lords and would-be lords of Ajuri before that, when they tried to cross his plans. Oh, never *personally*. It was doubtful if Shishogi personally had killed anyone . . . but his murders were a long, long list, not even counting those dead in the coup, innocent people, like old Eidi, who had used to be Father's major domo and who had died trying to defend the apartment.

Shishogi had created a Guild inside the Guild, an association they called the Shadow Guild, people positioned to bring down the government and kill people who might stop them. It had managed to put the government into Kadagidi hands, briefly, under a man named Murini, who had, after all, been all hollow. The real power had been the Shadow Guild, and that had been far harder to root out.

Shishogi was gone now, which was a good thing, but if his influence and the thing he had created remained anywhere at all, the ragtag end was very likely down in the Marid, and extremely likely—in Ajuri itself. It was Shishogi's longtime supporters inside Ajuri that Nomari feared—quite reasonably so. And the process that looked set to appoint a new lord for Ajuri was why, Nomari had said, he had *had* to come to Uncle, not just for himself, but for all those other Ajuri who dared not speak out. It was, as they saw it, a last chance to put an Ajuri into the Ajuri lordship. They did not want any more Shadow Guild, but they did not want somebody from outside given power over Ajuri.

Nomari was an average-looking young man, rough and poorly dressed when he had arrived, having nothing of lordly polish about his manners, either. His hands were rough and scarred with heavy work, and his face, though pleasant enough, was habitually cold—though it could light into an engaging humor. Cajeiri found Nomari more than interesting, and interesting, too, the fact that Uncle seemed to approve of him and his associates—all of whom, over sixty in number, were currently camped on Uncle's front lawn. Nomari's people had arrived mostly empty-handed, without baggage, so Uncle had offered Nomari, if not the seventy or so people who had shown up to support him, the hospitality of the house—and provided the tents the estate maintained for hunting season to shelter the people outside. Uncle had also set his tailor to work and provided an indoor coat and several nice shirts for Nomari, so that Nomari, representing these people, need not appear in the house at any disadvantage.

But while Nomari had an invitation to stay in the house, where it was certainly warmer, he chose to spend nights and most of the daylight hours in the tents with his associates. Cajeiri approved of that decision—*assuming*, as seemed likely, that Nomari really was who he said he was.

But if he were in Nomari's place, he thought, he would choose to stay with his associates as well, rather than stay alone in the big house with a lord with whom he had neither relationship nor agreement, no matter the promise of warmth and safety. One's people were one's people.

The relationship between Ajuri and Atageini had fractured when Mother was born. That was when. Mother was why.

Mother was why so many things had happened.

Because Mother, who was Uncle's sister's daughter, had been born in a Contract marriage, intended to be raised Atageini and become Uncle's heir. But Uncle's sister had died suspiciously just after Mother was born, and Mother's Ajuri father had stolen her away, to be brought up Ajuri instead.

And that, Cajeiri truly believed, had *also* been Shishogi's doing, to gain a claim on Atageini clan, while Uncle had no heir.

Nomari and his associates had risked everything to come to Uncle's gates. Nomari had needed to speak directly with Uncle, and coming to Tirnamardi when Uncle was here was the only way he could do that—because Uncle was a great lord and difficult to approach when he was in Shejidan, in the heart of the Bujavid. Uncle always spent a good part of the year in Shejidan, in the Bujavid itself, living on the same floor as Father, and Great-grandmother and nand' Bren—that was how important Uncle was in the government, and how thick security was about him. Uncle was very important among Conservatives in the legislature, and right now he was the most important lord still surviving in the Padi Valley Association—since Ajuri had no lord, Grandfather having been assassinated, and Father had yet to approve anybody to replace him. Kadagidi clan, right over the back hedges, was *also* lordless: Father had banished the Kadagidi lord, who had stood only as a puppet for Shishogi's agents—removed him from lordly rank forever and sent him off to a little mill to work, with one chance to stay out of trouble forever.

So Uncle, lord of the Atageini clan, was the most important voice left in what was the oldest association in the whole aishidi'tat. There was a list of people the Conservatives in the legislature wanted Father to choose from, to be the new lord of Ajuri, and they had wanted Uncle, as their spokesman, to recommend someone from the top rank of it. Nomari was not on that list—nobody, in fact, had even known Nomari existed, and Nomari, being in hiding, could never have gotten through to Uncle so long as Uncle had been in Shejidan.

But when Uncle had come home to Tirnamardi, Nomari and his associates had come here, hoping to tell Uncle their side of what had happened in Ajuri and hoping at best to get Uncle's influence behind Nomari as the best candidate to represent Ajuri. Uncle had not yet taken a stand on their appeal, but he seemed to be at least leaning toward believing Nomari.

But the question that had not come up, so far, at least in the discussions to which Cajeiri had been invited, was where Nomari stood on those issues so important to the Conservatives . . . and where he stood on issues important to Uncle.

And those answers might just make a difference.

If Nomari just said what he thought Uncle wanted to hear and not what he truly believed to be best for Ajuri, Uncle would see right through him. Uncle was no fool. And Nomari did not have to agree in every point. These days, Uncle himself did not agree with all the Conservative notions—if he ever had.

Cajeiri might be only fortunate nine years of age, but he had gotten to understand Uncle better and better. His first memory of Uncle Tatiseigi was as a grim and scary old man, *instantly* critical of any breach of tradition . . . but he understood now that Uncle, *being* a very powerful Conservative, had to defend the traditions, because they meant everything to the people he represented. Uncle had started out extremely suspicious of nand' Bren's influence on Father, but that had all changed.

And while Uncle still disapproved of television and airplanes, he was reasonably approving of the starship.

Uncle, for one thing, supported proper manners, and thanks in no small part to the coup, a lot of young lords had taken over clans with less preparation in the traditions than they needed. Manners were in danger—and traditions were threatened, which were a strong issue among Conservatives. But they were not the only issue, and some of the issues the Conservatives backed set them apart from the townships. A few years ago, Uncle might not have entertained people on his lawn and listened so seriously to a candidate even younger than some of the lords who tried Uncle's patience.

Ajuri and its townships and villages desperately needed a lord to represent them—and a lord strong enough to sort out the internal mess Shishogi had created for them. They needed a lord who would represent the ordinary people and do things the way a lord should. *Mother* was in line to inherit the lordship of Ajuri—and the fact that no Ajuri lord had died of old age for at least five generations was why Father did not want *Mother* to step in—but then, the Conservative lords did not favor Mother as lord of Ajuri, either. They remembered how she had flitted between Ajuri and Uncle's house more than once and they called her unpredictable, for one of the kinder names, married to the aiji who had pushed for television and the shuttles and the space station, which they entirely distrusted.

The Conservatives had pressured Uncle to make a nomination off their list, and grown quite noisy about it. That was why Uncle had nominated somebody he *knew* Father would veto, someone down in the Honors section of the list. That was Uncle's opinion of the matter—or as Uncle put it privately, he did not dislike any of the people at the top of the list quite enough to name them to the office, so he named a fine old man just for the honor of it, confident that Father would veto the nomination, then retired to Tirnamardi to have peace and quiet—since it was unprecedented to offer a second name in nomination after the first was refused. So without violating tradition, the Conservatives would have to pester someone else into making a nomination, someone Father would probably not hesitate to refuse with less politeness. It was like chess, threatening with a Rider, on the oblique.

And just to keep the gossipers entirely off-balance, Father had sent *him*, heir of the aishidi'tat, to pay a family visit and support Uncle Tatiseigi, making clear to everybody that Uncle was not in any disfavor with Father, that the old scholar Uncle had nominated was in no disfavor, either, and that Father would veto the old man for reasons not to do with his character or Uncle's actions. Father, one understood, would instead assign the old scholar to some prestigious honor, an academic status that he could enjoy without doing much work at all.

Politics was just crazy sometimes. A year ago he could never have understood the maneuver Uncle had made, and he would not have understood *why* Great-grandmother had gone off to Malguri, not touching the situation at all—more simply, she was another powerful Conservative leader, and Malguri had no phone system, so *she* could not be pestered, either.

What it all had led to was him being here, and Uncle being honestly delighted to have him as a guest.

And on the very first day he had been entirely happy, too. He had really, truly expected a holiday to spend riding his mecheita and being fed far too much north country food and talking, really talking with Uncle, without mani or nand' Bren or any other adult to bring him back to the present day. That would have been almost the best time in his life.

But then of course Nomari had shown up—and right after Nomari, Great-aunt Geidaro had arrived on Uncle's doorstep saying ugly things about Nomari, demanding to have Uncle nominate *her* choice for Ajuri instead and throw Nomari out.

Great-aunt Geidaro was an unpleasant woman. She was always unpleasant. That was no change. And she surely had not expected Uncle to do anything she asked, since they hated each other.

But in that moment, seeing her claim to speak for Ajuri, uninvited, under Uncle's own roof, and acting as if she really were in charge, he had realized she could be dangerous.

She might have been Shishogi's hands inside Ajuri. *She* could have been, and possibly directly, involved in the murder of Nomari's family. It was certainly because of Shishogi's people in Ajuri that Nomari had been forced to flee and take up a life working on the railroads. And it was even possible Great-aunt had had something to do with Grandfather being killed, while pretending to be sympathetic to Mother.

That made him mad. That made her *his* enemy. Personally.

So thus far in what should have been his riding vacation, he could only slip out to the stables with his aishid right before dinner, and then had to go back indoors again. He was not as upset about that situation as he might be, because what was going on really *might* produce a reasonable lord of Ajuri.

And that might settle a great deal that was wrong. It might get Great-aunt Geidaro set down for good . . . maybe retired to a nice village somewhere in the cold mountains.

So he found Nomari interesting for *all* those reasons, but almost more important to him, *almost*, Cousin Nomari knew things from inside Ajuri that he desperately wanted to know— not just stories, though some stories that Nomari could tell about his working in the Transportation Guild were interesting enough. No, the questions he wanted answered were *serious* things. Things about Mother—because Nomari had known Mother when she was young. And there was a *lot* of her life that Mother never talked about. There were some words one could not even mention without adult doors suddenly being closed. There were secrets Mother kept about Ajuri, and there were years of her life that Mother had never, ever talked about, maybe never even with Father, like the reason she had run away from Ajuri and then run away from Tirnamardi.

Nomari might know things about Mother as a little child, and about what had made her leave Grandfather, and about all the nastiness that had gone on in Ajuri, when the Little Old Man, Shishogi, was alive.

Uncle Tatiseigi had already told him that Mother had been *stolen* from Tirnamardi by Grandfather just after she was born, and that Mother's mother had died under very suspicious circumstances, in a riding accident, when she had had no business riding at all.

Mother had lived in Ajuri until she was mostly grown, then

run away to Uncle's tent during a festival in Shejidan. Then she'd gotten mad at Uncle and run away again and met Father, and they had gotten married—permanently married, not just Contracted, which nobody in Father's family had ever done. It had apparently surprised the whole court.

But there was so much about Mother even Uncle *did not* know, the things that had gone on in Ajuri, and he wanted to know about all that. He desperately wanted to know whether it really was an accident that had killed Grandmother, and what had made his mother so suspicious and angry and so inclined not to talk about herself at all.

"Jeri-ji?" Antaro's voice cut into his thoughts and he realized suddenly that he was standing, just standing and that servants had come and were waiting politely, but a bit nervously, for him and his aishid to move so that they could go about their business.

He felt his face go warm. "Nadiin," he said politely, and nodded. They bowed, and motion in the hall went on.

He duly went to the washroom, scrubbed his hands, then took the servants' corridor to the central stairs, and ascended the steps to the big hall.

Shots of the halls on the human side of the station.

Shots of little restaurants on human-side, which operated on credit chits, and were the gathering places and the food distribution system, a genteel sort of operation that let people imagine they were on a suburban street on Mospheira. People sat in cafes on that make-believe street and talked, with apparent title to stay there and take their time. The walls had vid available. Music played.

"Mospheiran workers have food included in their stipend. The restaurants are designed to look like a street in Newport. You slip your card in, you punch buttons to put in an order, choice of five items. The menu changes daily. The computer tracks your orders, estimates your caloric intake, dispenses

appropriate supplements. Choice of beverages, even alcohol. The population is mostly young, mostly single. Children are not permitted on station. No provision was made for them."

His aishid was interested, never mind the narration: it was an aspect of station life they hadn't seen.

Contrast that, sharply, with people in rumpled clothes, standing in double lines to receive a recyclable bottle and an unwrapped sandwich. Contrast the restaurant tables with people carrying water buckets, and sitting on decking in small groups, including babies in arms, eating and drinking, not happy or animated.

"This, by contrast, is life in the Reunioner section," the voice-over said. "This is food distribution, one choice. This is life in the Reunioner residential sections even before the section doors were shut. People arrived from Reunion with no station credit, no certifications, and no papers. Station established them on a marginal existence and generally gave them nothing. They have no jobs, or have temporary employment, which affords some station credit. There is no special provision for children on the station, but Reunioners arrived with children, some of them un-escorted and simply assigned, for administrative purposes, to the nearest adult on the rolls."

The image flashed to a small, orderly two-room apartment, a few pictures on the walls, photographs of home.

"This is the current standard of living for a Mospheiran on station."

Then a shot of a very bare cubby with molded-in furniture, no cushions, laundry hanging, a sort of wall-tap of uncertain use, and a stretched tarp for a privacy screen. "Reunioners have been assigned to a section of the station unused and shut down since the construction. While many things in space don't age as they do on Earth . . ."

Shot of a puddle on the floor.

". . . seals do age. Water leaks in the system have been a problem and a safety issue in the Reunioner section, especially

when combined with electricity. These are the conditions Mo-
spheiran station residents don't ever see. Five people—a family
of three and two unrelated men share this space, in shifts."

Shot of one massive section door, with a group of people
standing near, providing scale. *"The Tillington administration*
shut this huge door as an alarm sounded, warning residents
they had fifteen minutes to clear. People were caught out sep-
arate from families. There were serious injuries as people tried
to reach relatives. This only happened in the two Reunioner
sections. The rest of the station was merely given an advise-
ment to shelter in place.

"Once the doors shut, things got markedly worse.

"And Stationmaster Tillington issued a statement on the
situation."

One minute into Tillington's speech, Bren realized he'd made
a mistake. He should never have allowed curiosity to win out
over prudence. It was nearly time for dinner and this vid was
not a dish to consume hot, but rather ice cold . . . and well-
tempered with brandy.

"Supper is due to arrive soon," he said, and tapped the pause
button. "We've ordered in the fish and it will be here shortly.
There is no need to have Tillington-nadi spoil our supper."

Multiple sets of golden eyes lit up in anticipation. Fried fish,
in the style of Mospheiran street vendors, was his aishid's favorite of the new flavors they'd discovered on the island. Humans
had to be so very careful with atevi food and drink—alkaloids
were an issue in some items—but the converse was not true.
Dinner had been a nightly experiment. His aishid and his staff
tried everything.

And when, a moment later, the phone rang, Bren picked it up
himself, his staff not admitting any facility with the Mosphei'
language. It was, as expected, the guard station downstairs, advising them that dinner was coming . . .

And that a large envelope was coming up with them.

"Thank you," Bren said, mildly. His temper was already up,

after the video. An envelope had arrived. And waited. Yes. It had waited.

He'd spent a tedious, idle afternoon waiting for that envelope. So Francis House security had stopped a packet he could have been working on. Probably they'd only let it wait for the expected dinner delivery, so it was one easy trip up the stairs for somebody. Possibly it *hadn't* been a long delay at all.

Entirely reasonable, if one was Mospheiran. Nothing was ever in that much hurry on Mospheira if it didn't have a siren attached. He fairly surely knew what it was and if he was right, it *could* wait, now that it was this late, but he had repeatedly advised security to send official packets directly up.

"Supper will arrive," he said, "and one believes Tom-nadi has finally sent us the Heyden Court blueprints." Tom Lund was an ally, managing University contacts, wringing speed out of University procedures, where it regarded permissions, papers, and contractors. "But we will not let supper go cold. Fried fish, nadiin-ji, has arrived."

"*Ah,*" Tano said, particularly pleased.

Francis House had made a special effort. This evening, a car had run down the hill to Harbor Street, and brought back genuine Port Jackson street food, from an authentic cart vendor.

He'd promised them the real thing this evening, independent of Francis House's chef, who had, yes, done a lovely job. But, he'd explained, he wanted his staff to experience the ordinary of the streets, that the people ate. They'd made a very large order.

And after this much arrangement, and his exercise of diplomacy with the chef, hell if Tillington or the blueprint packet was going to intervene in their native Mospheiran dinner.

4

Off the great hall of Tirnamardi in various directions, amid the gilt and marble, were lower-ceilinged alcoves that constituted rooms of their own, apart from the central space that served as a large assembly room. There was a breakfast room, a reading room, and Uncle's office—and, largest and taking up the whole far side of the space, the lesser dining room, which was being set tonight for Uncle's evening meal.

Cajeiri did not come to dinner alone. He never arrived alone. He had both his sets of bodyguards in attendance, his younger four, and the four gray-haired seniors. As he walked into the lesser dining area, they broke apart, each to an assigned station at various places around the three walls, while he took the eastern end of the table, which was set, this evening, for three. The serving staff poured his tea, and he had time to drink only a few sips before another figure appeared across the grand hall, escorted not by his own bodyguard, but by Uncle's Guild security.

That was Nomari, who had come in from the tents. He had changed to his good clothes and washed up, likely in the same hall where Cajeiri had just washed his hands.

"Nandi," Nomari said politely, taking his seat at the midpoint of the table.

"Cousin," Cajeiri said, equally polite, *assuming*, as seemed likely, that Nomari really was who he said he was. But Great-grandmother would definitely caution him—*if* Nomari was who he said he was, which *was* indeed one of the continuing questions.

Guild security apparently thought it was safe for him to be at table alone with Nomari, despite the table knives. They would forbid it, else, and never let Nomari near him.

Nomari was not a dangerous-looking young man, but he was rough and wiry. Nomari had spent his years doing hard work, holding his own with hard labor and rough people. His hands showed it. His face showed it. The way he walked showed it. He had *not* spent that time learning to be subtle as Shishogi— just wary in the way ordinary people could be wary, uneasy in the echoing spaces of Tirnamardi, aware he was being watched.

Honest? They were still trying to judge that.

But Nomari certainly was not stupid, which was to his credit. And he was respectful of tradition and manners, also a credit. Nomari watched and learned, and he did his best to refine himself. He had been young when he had left Ajuri—and the slightly chancy way he managed lace cuffs and condiment picks in Uncle's elaborate table settings agreed with that.

Servants moved to pour wine—fruit juice, in Cajeiri's case.

"Was it a good day?" Cajeiri asked.

"A productive day," Nomari answered. "You, nandi?"

Not such elegant grammar, either. The Guilds sometimes made up their own rules. But *productive?* That was what mani would call a provocative word, inciting curiosity when manners dictated one could not ask on any sort of business at the dinner table.

"A quiet day," Cajeiri said. "But I have indeed enjoyed it."

After dinner was when they both might get answers, if Nomari could manage to direct the conversation around to it, and if Uncle was ready to allow *productive* talk. Mani would certainly try to get information then, if she were here, but she was not. It was just him. And Uncle.

Uncle was arriving now, not leaving them long together, which was a relief, because he was out of casual topics except

the weather. It *was* clouding up to rain. But what could he say
beyond that? Everything he really wanted to talk about was far
from casual. He would ask—how do you think you can deal
with Great-aunt Geidaro? He would ask—how are you going to
stay alive? And—who do you think you can trust inside Ajuri?
But none of those were appropriate questions at this point.

Nomari stood up as Uncle came to take his seat at the head
of the table. Cajeiri stayed seated—receiving such courtesies as
his father's designated heir was still new, and he felt uneasy in
it, but it was proper, and Uncle above all people was happy
with it.

So he sat, and nodded politely to Uncle. Nomari bowed and
sat down, and a servant moved in to fill Uncle's glass.

"Well," Uncle said, "well, we have a fine dinner tonight, fish
from the coast, caught this morning, arriving on the noon train.
And I have had all the same sent out to our other guests in great
abundance. We shall manage a good breakfast tomorrow, too,
and all subsequent days, the peace of the neighborhood permit-
ting. Supply has arrived!"

They had been feeding the people on the lawn with picnic
food since they arrived, breakfast rolls and sandwiches and
boiled eggs, as much of that fare as the people could wish, but
today the truck had gone out to the train station and come back,
and then gone out again in the other direction, to Diegi, getting
supplies for proper meals. The kitchen, for its part, had been
working since daybreak, baking bread and making soup and
pickle in great quantities.

"Nandi," Nomari said with some feeling. "You are far more
than generous to us. My people, many of them, have not met
such hospitality anywhere."

Uncle nodded, as servants began serving. "Well, well, we are
glad to provide it. We are sending staff out this evening, too, to
be sure of the tent ropes and drainage in the prospect of weather,
so have your people understand that we are concerned for their
comfort, and we are by no means conducting an inspection of

their affairs. Our advisements from Lord Geigi up on the space station inform us there is an uncommonly large system forming out in the great ocean, in anticipation of which we should take some precautions. We expect a strong wind coming in from the southwest, with rain and likely hail. The tents should withstand it with no problems, indeed, but we wish to be sure, in case some of your people should be unfamiliar with such circumstances. My staff will assure the tents can withstand the blow. We may have several days of rain and wind."

"Your concern is greatly appreciated, nandi."

"Be assured these tents have more than once withstood strong weather." The first course was served, quietly, a savory soup. "We use these seasonally for hunts and festivals, and we have taken care that your camp should sit on the highest part of the pasturage, not an apparent hill, but enough of a hill, I think, to keep you snug and dry. The hedges, distant as they are, will likewise take some of the force."

"They are extraordinary," Nomari said, "these hedges. One had heard of them, but never seen them."

"Never?" Uncle was always pleased to talk about Tirnamardi, and it was polite of Nomari to offer a dinner topic himself, after two days at Uncle's table with Uncle providing the discussion. "Well, we are glad to afford shelter within them. Ajuri itself, you may know, had such hedges once. And there was a great hedge to the north, in the old warlike days. It was a great shame to take them down, but they had become neglected, and they do take constant maintenance. They once made a maze, do you know, from Ajuri to Dur, and from Dur up to Sura, which is how the Padi Valley maintained itself unassailable."

"I have heard about the maze," Nomari said. "And I have seen the old line by the north road. But the ones at Tirnamardi were the heart of it."

"True," Uncle said. "And even cannon were not effective against them. Downed, they still obstructed, in the siege of Diegi, among others. Fire was the greatest threat, and so long as they

were green, the defenders still had the advantage. It was a difficult matter there for a rider bearing a fire-pot to get close, and
even so, the result was likely to be put out. So long as the hedges
stood as a maze, the central plains were a difficult place for large
forces to move, which was good for the peace and independence
of the region. But the hunting did suffer immensely as a consequence. The herd tallies go far, far back, and the great herds of the
midlands have prospered mightily since the removals."

"You would never take down the hedges of Tirnamardi,
surely, nandi, for any advantage."

"Never. Never. They are the last of their kind. Atageini
views it as a historic trust. Though, mind, no single section is
original. As the trees age and die and we cut them, we have always kept a section of the heart, and we Atageini have learned
to count the rings to reckon their age and mark events long
before the wise minds in Science thought to do so. We have a
perfect record of their growth, and consequently of the weather,
going back one thousand twelve hundred and thirty-eight years.
We preserve these old pieces to this day, making a continuous
record."

"I had never heard it, Uncle!" Cajeiri exclaimed. "Are they
here?"

"Indeed they are!" Uncle said. "I would show our guest, as
well, should he be disposed to see it."

"I would be honored," Nomari said, "greatly honored, nandi."

"I shall show you after dinner," Uncle said, "where we keep
a great many such things."

It was an excellent supper, more than enough for Cajeiri's
appetite, and a dessert of custard and berries.

Then they had a treat far better than the desserts: they went
down to the basement, where, with his bodyguard attending,
Uncle took them on a tour of his collections. Uncle showed
Nomari the great beast in its case, and they went on to the pot-
tery, and armor and old weapons.

Nomari asked questions, good questions, which pleased Uncle, too. Nomari had read things, and studied things, and knew dates, and Uncle was asking close questions to find out how much Nomari knew—Cajeiri began to suspect that was the case, because Uncle knew history better than anyone. Likely Nomari suspected it, too, and answered everything he could. Nomari knew a lot, clearly, about the history between Ajuri and its neighbors, but that knowledge grew thin in places, and Uncle happily expounded on it, a great flow of things Cajeiri had never heard, and stored up for his own questions someday.

Then, after all the early history of the first rooms, they entered a side room Cajeiri had never seen, in this warren of little halls. They went down a stair to a sub-basement, and Uncle's bodyguard opened a door onto a place quite chill, and turned on the lights.

The walls held rows and rows of varnished slices of wood, with some of their rings marked with little brass buttons, with a legend and date written underneath each piece.

"This is not a cross-section of every planting ever cut," Uncle explained, though it looked as though it might be. "But these are the ones which, taken collectively, show the entire sequence of the history of the hedge system. Fortunately, the early keepers preserved the hearts for superstitious and historic reasons long before anyone ever realized they might be read like a book."

Uncle went on to point out certain pieces of particular significance, showing them a sequence of prosperity and a time of fire, related to a battle at the hedges, where Tirnamardi had stood off forces from the south. That would mean the Taibeni, back in the early wars.

Nomari listened meanwhile and asked more questions, really good questions that Uncle was happy to answer. The evening was all such a success that Cajeiri began to think, which was *stupid* to think, that he really might get that chance to go riding after all, if things with Ajuri really began to sort out.

But it *would* not happen, he told himself. Not this trip. Nothing political ever worked so smoothly or so absolutely trusted as that. Everything had to be sure and slow, because people's lives depended on being sure.

And the matter of being sure continued afterward, upstairs, in the sitting area of the great hall, where Uncle served Nomari brandy. Cajeiri sat with them, with fruit juice. Nomari had received every courtesy due a guest: Nomari was happy, and Uncle was happy. That was, after as many questions as had flown back and forth this evening, a good sign.

With brandy one *could* talk business, and it gave a chance for his question about Nomari's mysteriously productive day . . . but he had no need to ask it, since Uncle himself delved right into it.

It turned out that Uncle already knew what Nomari had been doing: Nomari had been helping Uncle's Guild bodyguards interview his people, with his presence to reassure them.

"Our guest's associates have come from various guilds," Uncle observed. "The Messengers, Transportation, the Treasurers, even, as well as the Merchants and Weavers and such, are all represented, and they have answered freely the names of their houses and villages. Very many tradesmen and skilled workers are among them. And a handful of families once situated at Ajiden." That was the principal Ajuri house. "We are encouraged to know it."

That mattered. It mattered in what man'chi the people out there might hold; and how strong their man'chi might be to Nomari himself. The Guild could tell them more about that, how likely it was these people told the truth and all the truth, and where they had really come from, and how and why they attached to Nomari. That was what Uncle had to know if he was going to break precedent and surprise his political allies by nominating not only a second candidate, but a complete stranger to politics.

"But," Uncle said, "we have missed interviewing a few."

"One is aware," Nomari said, frowning. "And I have, truly, asked them to cooperate, all of them. But for some—my request may not overcome their fear of being written down."

"Do you know these people, personally, nadi, of those who refuse to be written?"

"I know many of them. Indisi of Paita is one. Of the Merchants. I have known him for years, and I personally reassured him the information was proper to give. But he is not a trusting fellow. I put him on the list myself."

"Interesting," Uncle said, "that that name does not appear in Guild records."

The room seemed a little less friendly then. Everything hung still and no servant moved.

"Then I am surprised," Nomari said quietly. "That is the name I have known for ten years. But some of my people have gone under several names, and one has changed guilds. I assure you, nandi, when I find him tonight, I will ask him personally."

"Muri of Sigani," Uncle said. "And Hapeini also called Maigin. And Suri of Ardiyan. They were reported as entering the grounds, but now do not appear among those interviewed, nor does anyone know them."

"I do not know their faces," Nomari said, frowning, "but I will find them and get the information. I asked those who may have given false names to give true ones, but it may confuse the records."

"Fear," Uncle said.

"Fear," Nomari said. "Yes. A great deal of fear. With long years of reason, nandi. One appreciates your understanding, and I am concerned. I shall ask. I will find them."

Three people—not only hiding from Uncle's questions, Cajeiri thought, but possibly maintaining false names even toward Nomari.

Fear of Uncle was reasonable, but if Nomari *was* their lord, and he had asked them all to answer truthfully, it was not only a security problem, it measured Nomari, as well as it measured the people who had ducked the questions. If his influence was not *strong* enough to get the truth from his people, if he could not win their trust and get proper information despite their fears—he was not the man who could walk into Ajuri and take the clan away from Great-aunt Geidaro.

Man'chi did not protect a person from those outside it. But it could make people stand between him and murder. And man'chi went downward, to make lords value their people, and upward, to make people protect their lords with their lives.

Grandfather, as lord of Ajuri, had been afraid. He had shown fear in his situation, and there had been good reason for it— Shishogi, who had sat for years where he was unreachable, commanding the most dangerous people in the world—and Father, not trusting Grandfather—trusting him less the closer he tried to come. But all the same, Grandfather should have been able, if he had been a strong lord, to have gotten enough man'chi, and inspired a band of defenders. If he had had that, he would not have died as he had—alone. If he had gathered real loyalty—he might have made it impossible for Great-aunt Geidaro to take over, even after his death, because people did suspect she was at least complicit in his downfall.

But Grandfather had panicked and lost his people. He knew that now. Grandfather had scared him when he had made such persistent attempts to get close to *him*, because he had not been able to understand the situation—but now he was convinced in his own mind that Grandfather had tried to get close to him not because he was attacking or because he meant to harm him, but because he was afraid, too afraid to go to Father and accuse the people who needed accusing. Probably he had had no proof— Shishogi's misdeeds were locked within a secretive office in a secretive guild.

But he still should have gathered up his courage and done it.

Was Nomari like that? Was Nomari going to lose people and excuse them with long years of 'they have reason?'

That was not enough. Nomari had to say—just—I shall get your answer, nandi.

Or was he more like nand' Bren, who would excuse his worst enemy because nand' Bren *was* strong, and reserved hope of getting their man'chi no matter what? Nand' Bren was scary that way. Nand' Bren scared his more resolute enemies because he was terribly hard to stop once he was on a track.

Great-grandmother, too, could excuse people one would never expect she would excuse. Which made *her* scary, because she was terribly dangerous, and it was not always clear what she was thinking or why she did things.

Was Nomari one of that sort—spooky and having his own ways?

Or was he like Grandfather—scared? Just scared—all his life, and taking Shishogi's orders when he had to?

Even if Uncle decided against Nomari, and chose *not* to nominate him, Nomari would no longer be invisible. He would become a target. If Nomari was right, every Ajuri who opposed Great-aunt Geidaro became a target, and thus far *nobody* had come forward with a personality strong enough to take Ajuri— Father had let Great-aunt Geidaro alone, he suspected, only because a worse thing seemed having Ajuri fall apart entirely. That clan had a history a thousand years old. And it could well go down, after all its losses. It could completely break apart, and that would cause all sorts of trouble in the midlands, at a time when they most needed things to hang together. Ajuri had a lot of tiny subclans, and those would suddenly be in play with every neighbor of Ajuri lands, like a body being picked apart by scavengers.

So Uncle might say nothing further on the matter of missing people and false names, but one could imagine security was concerned. Uncle slid the talk on to other questions, such as the people's willingness to remain camped for any long number of days.

Uncle did not mention that *he* had been making phone calls today. The phone calls were unusual in themselves—Uncle detested phones—and Cajeiri *thought* Uncle might have been calling Great-grandmother, who also detested phones, but his aishid was not sure. Even the seniors said they were not sure. And when *they* were not sure—that could mean they were ordered not to say, or they really *were* not sure, and they were too new with him for *him* to be sure which it was.

But if Uncle *was* calling Great-grandmother by phone, that meant Uncle might be making Nomari's presence here at Tirnamardi just a shade more public than he had done, and cross-checking his information with mani, because the Guild—*the* Guild, the Assassins' Guild—was the one way to get information back and forth quietly. The Messengers' Guild, who handled the phone system, was notoriously corrupt—so that talking about things on the phone was the last thing before announcing it on the evening news.

Uncle's questions leaked to the usual places might also let specific Guilds know what was going on, which was sometimes a good idea, because the Guilds likely already knew pieces of things, and it was sometimes helpful to give them a way to put things together. He had seen Great-grandmother do that, more than once. Father had slipped news out to the Guilds when it came to announcing that Mother was going to have another baby, because all the lords needed to know first, before the people did.

So everybody would act and talk as if they had no idea on one level, but what they did secretly was another. It was always like that.

And letting the news about Nomari loose among the lords could be a good thing, if Uncle was sure he wanted various people to get used to the possibility . . . including the conservative lords that Uncle had just refused to please. *They* might not be happy. *They* might start messaging through the Guild and asking questions and making suggestions—because while custom said Uncle could not follow a rejected nomination with a second one, out of courtesy to Father, there was nothing really stopping him if Father *said* to do it.

But that also meant that fairly soon Uncle really needed to reach a decision that would be really notoriously embarrassing to back down from. So before Uncle took that step, he did need to explain things to Father and get his approval—because, Cajeiri thought, his own senior aishid would have already told the Guild what was going on, and probably have told Father in as much detail as they could.

The true wonder was that Father had not sent anybody of his staff here—which probably meant that Father had not told *Mother* what was going on at her uncle's estate, and maybe Mother thought her son was having a good time, riding his mecheita every day and eating too much.

But Father would surely be watching, and once Uncle had some clear idea what he wanted to do, there needed to be messengers going back and forth, and everybody needed to agree before anything went entirely public.

He had asked his junior aishid if they had heard of any contact from Father—*they* had heard nothing, and he was sure that was the truth. He hesitated even to ask the seniors—the Guild was not inclined to talk about its more political moves. Besides, the seniors, despite their jokes, were just a little too scary, and he did not want to let them know what *he* was thinking, or how much he *could* figure out, in case he needed to slip their notice on something.

Being around grownups was certainly very much more interesting once he knew how things worked. And in this case— Nomari himself might not know half the things he knew.

So he was sure his father would find out fairly quickly whatever his father needed to know, without a nine-year-old son stirring up the highest levels of the Guild to ask too many questions that might, by some mischance, slip into Mother's ears. Father would do something when it was the right time to do it.

Meanwhile, without too much of a stir in the upper levels of the Guild, Father could conveniently pretend not to know anything, until he *needed* to do something.

Cajeiri really hoped Nomari turned out to be somebody they could deal with. He did not, at least, get the impression that Nomari was a bad man. And it would solve so many problems if someday Ajuri could be trusted and be a good neighbor to the Atageini.

There were a lot of terrible secrets in Ajuri, some of which the Guild itself might want to know, and would not want out in public, either. And there were a lot of possible grudges. Nomari had been younger than Jegari and Antaro when his family had been murdered and he had gone into hiding, the only survivor.

But—were those people out on the lawn able to guarantee anything but their votes in the clan? They had no license to protect him, except to fend off attackers if attacked. The Guild had to take over, if Nomari wanted to prosecute anybody still alive.

Nomari was not firmly in charge, clearly, if they had three people missing.

And if there was still Shadow Guild out and about (certainly Ajuri was as good a place to look for them as any) it was definitely not a good time for anybody in Tirnamardi to go too far from the house, or for anybody to take chances, even domestic staff, who were never supposed to be attacked. The Shadow Guild had no hesitation.

That meant he had to think twice even about today's little adventure, slipping out to the pens. Every time he risked himself, he risked his aishid, who had no choice but put themselves between him and an attack. The same was true of Uncle, for anybody on Uncle's staff just going after groceries, for that matter. It was not safe. If three people were supposed to be here and now could not be found, they could have met with trouble, or they could *be* trouble.

So somebody should decide fairly soon whether Nomari should have what he asked for, and whatever they decided, once they decided it, that was going to cause a lot of argument, with good people *and* bad ones, and it *still* would not be safe for a while.

That was inconvenient.

In his wildest imagination, he had hoped until tonight that Great-uncle would do something really extravagant and grand, like gathering up all these people and escorting Nomari to She-jidan himself, putting Great-aunt Geidaro on notice to vacate or be arrested on the spot.

Instead, however, it was Geidaro who had paid them a visit, putting pressure on Uncle. Geidaro was on one level a skinny old woman with a bad temper—but on another, she was really scary. And now, with the greatest threat to her control quite conspicuously being supported on Uncle's lawn?

He bet that Great-aunt Geidaro was trying to figure something to do, and what she did could be crazy and desperate, nothing legal, nothing through the proper Guild.

Great-aunt also had to be wondering where she could go and what she could do if things went wrong. Managing a factory might keep the former lord of the Kadagidi out of trouble, but Great-aunt was too old to change her ways.

Something bad was going to happen to someone before it was all settled. Cajeiri really began to think so. Great-aunt seemed to be doing nothing since her visit, but that likely meant only that she was contacting people the way every lord had to do, to avoid the phone system, and arranging to stop Nomari somehow.

And who would she likeliest be sending messages to, if not Great-uncle Shishogi's people, wherever any of them were left alive?

He'd used to tell himself, when things grew scary, that maybe there were things he missed, things he failed to know, and that grownups were doing smart things a boy might not see. But he was older now, and he had people around him whose actions he knew how to read. So things were, he thought, *exactly* the way he saw them. Everything around him seemed to him to be waiting to explode.

He would have moved to approve Nomari if he were in Uncle's place, he said to himself. *He* would have made a decision and he would have done something before Great-aunt had a chance to think things through. That argued that maybe Uncle was not all that slow, and somewhere people *were* moving, and things *were* getting done.

He just hoped the majority of those things were on *his* side.

5

"One is completely dismayed." Bren tapped the mute as the credits began to roll on Gin's documentary. "It is far worse than I thought." He'd never actually crossed into the Reunioner section, and what he had seen at the time had been primarily through body cams of atevi security, some footage of which Gin had included, likely with Geigi's help. What he had seen just now— "This— How could anyone have justified this? It was cruel and it was *stupid,* nadiin-ji. It was, above all other things, politically *stupid,* even if one had no *moral* consideration."

Because there *had* been choices. While there had been shortages of space as well as supply throughout the human side of the station, the station Mospheirans had lived in luxury, compared to this. Atevi would have shared. They *had* shared, where it came to building materials and water. Yet the Reunioners— station-born as no Mospheiran was, and more aware of the criticality of station integrity than any Mospheiran or atevi yet born—hadn't rioted. Not until *after* Tillington had closed the blast doors. Not until an operation to extract the children, who had scattered after an attempt to hold them hostage.

Had Tillington even believed what he was saying, that the Reunioners were truly a threat to the station? The arrival of the kyo ship hadn't pushed the buttons that closed those section doors. *Tillington* had pushed them, an emergency measure— against helpless people who'd already experienced one kyo

attack, when they, outside of the team that had originally negotiated with the kyo, *might* have been his only source of accurate information on the kyo.

The Reunioners weren't the ones who'd panicked. Or reacted
in baseless hate.

"One might have asked," Banichi said, "how Tillington got
past the examination for participation in the program, but then
one recalls a certain Ajuri who not only infiltrated the most
secret depths of the Guild, but manipulated us for two generations before we found him out. It is difficult, under those circumstances, to cast strong judgment on the human system."

"Unfortunately, Tillington was an appointment, never required to pass an examination. His social affiliations should
have raised alarms. His connection with the corporations
helped corrupt the system so that the corporations themselves
saw cooperation with him as their route to survival. He was
never slow to take credit for things that went well, and to be
sure he was on *Mospheiran* records as the originator of ideas,
the agent of good actions."

Hero? No. Tillington had wanted personal power. The deals
he'd made supported the style in which he'd lived and enabled
the autocratic ways he made decisions. When shuttles had
stopped flying, when the shortages had started—he'd never
shorted himself on anything. When the Reunioners had come
in, people who'd brought with them generations of station
expertise—he'd indeed lost his sense of balance, seeing not an
asset, but a threat to his plans and his dealings, and he'd decided
to invoke ancient history as a logical reason.

His actions against the Reunioners had fouled those waters
for good and all—and created all sorts of reasons for resentment.
At very least they were now obliged to ground the Reunioners
long enough to screen the ones that might to go back up to station life.

"How deep, or how high," Algini asked, "does this corruption reach within the power structure?"

It was Algini's sort of question. It was Algini's work that had helped track the corruption within the Guild. Algini had helped target Shishogi, who had once amused the younger Guild with his resistance to modern methods—methods and procedures which would have exposed his clandestine moves in short order.

"Fortunately," Bren said, "we have Gin, who speaks in ways the industrial officials up there understand. Secrets are currency in their way of thinking. If she preserves theirs, they will preserve hers—and to make that bargain they will trade what they know about Tillington, whose support up there is peeling away by the hour. The officials up there wield a power commensurate with their value to their superiors on Earth—and that value is increasing, in terms of their agreements with the new administrator. Gin gathers up man'chi, and deals fairly, which may be new to the presidentas of these various interests, but they can surely see that man'chi to Tillington has no future up there. He may well be tried for diversion of funds to his own use; and that means people who have dealt with him will hasten to wash the taint off their own hands. He will become inconvenient to his old allies aloft and below. Some in the Heritage Party on Earth may maintain their support for him, but those who support the party financially are the very ones, like Asgard, whose advancement now hangs on Reunioner science, and what it can give them. Gin is mediating agreements between Reunioners with such properties, and those companies who wish to bargain for them. And no one wants to be left out."

"In short," Tano said, "Tillington has become a great embarrassment to many people."

"Unmourned," Bren said. "I cannot pity him." It was hard to translate, not only the words, but the moral and legal problems, to a culture which had no corporations, and where political interests were clan-linked and guild-linked—not to mention, convey it to a species with their emotional links all vested in clan and guild. There were some Mospheiran crimes which were not crimes in atevi thinking. There were some Mospheiran crimes which simply sounded stupid, or insane.

But there were actions which had a perfect congruence, and in which, no, there was no pity due. Malfeasance masquerading as mission? Atevi had just had their own fill of that on the mainland.

"Gin-nandi *has* most respectfully requested, nadiin-ji, that we review those elements involving the aiji-dowager and the heir. She believes they are shown in good contrast to Tillington's bad behavior. They appear as protectors of humans and participants in the negotiations, and to that, I would agree."

The segments involved showed the dowager and the young gentleman in Central, and showed the chess match in the kyo meeting, scenes without sound—the booms and thumps of the kyo might have alarmed the audience. They showed the exchange of courtesies, followed by the kyo ship departing the station—and the piece ended with a dissolve to the treaty document, written in three languages, and sealed with ribbons . . . a very finely detailed shot, for a historic and scientific record.

"It offered no offense," Algini said, "to my eyes."

"None to mine," Banichi said, and Jago and Tano agreed.

"Rani-ji?" Bren asked. Narani and Jeladi had watched, both students of protocol, and Narani's memory was longer than any of them could manage.

"In the old tradition, it would never do," Narani said, "but one would concur in this, nandi. The aiji-dowager's and the young gentleman's importance in these events ought not to be omitted from history. And it would seem the aiji himself has determined his son is ready to appear before the public and give account for himself." A slight bow, and a qualification. "This is an opinion in protocol, nandi. But also that it is the aiji-dowager's personal signature on the documents. That she was directly involved—these things should be made clear to humans and atevi, nandi, so no one can ever claim to the contrary."

"Indeed." The aiji-dowager, more than once aiji-regent over the aishidi'tat, had always been controversial—but she *had* acted, consistently, when things had to be done, often against protocol and against precedent. Create a scandal? The dowager herself generally found television as inappropriate as she found Mospheiran concepts like plebiscites . . . but credit for one of her actions, when so often she had acted in the shadows?

"She deserves great credit for this," Bren said. "People should know—she was the one who made the greatest and first strides with the kyo, and possibly saved us all from a war we could not survive. That should never be forgotten, on either side of the strait."

"One concurs," Banichi said. "The dowager, *and* the young gentleman."

Heads nodded.

"We also have a note from Lord Geigi," Bren added, "that he will remand Braddock and his associates to Gin's authority." Reunion Stationmaster Braddock, his lieutenant, and Inez Williams, the mother of one of those three children about to be brought down, had all been gathered up for scheming to breach Tillington's section doors in advance of the kyo visit, and they remained in custody for threatening public safety. There had been nothing saintly about Braddock's behavior back at Reunion, but Bren personally didn't fault Braddock for making a move to get his people out of the bottle Tillington had put them into, or for his opposition to the ship's officers, who had not prevented the closing of the doors. The fact that Braddock had looked to seize the three children, in whom Tabini had declared personal interest, as bargaining currency in his plan was another matter. But between Braddock's actions and Tillington's— he could not make a great moral distinction.

What blame attached to Braddock in the attack on Reunion Station—was a completely different matter, and much of that evidence was lost. If he can eventually come down to a safe life on Earth—he would not, personally, be upset.

But experience had told him that forgiving history was only safe if one knew what one was forgiving.

"Lord Geigi will be relieved to be rid of them," Banichi said.

"And his other, happier guests, will be packing by now to board the shuttle," Bren said, "so it will be a quieter household for him."

"He has been greatly entertained by the children," Tano said, "but he has a deal of work pending."

Construction of Gin's lander systems, among other matters. Dropping cargo that could drop safely, to free shuttle space. That would be an atevi operation, and Mospheirans would provide and package the cargo.

Things in the heavens were starting to move, pieces shifting position, and *they* had the final preparations to make, the simple matter of housing three children and two families.

On a *world*, with all that came with it.

The weather had come in faster than expected. Outside the big window, Uncle's staff swarmed about the tents, making a second check against wind that was already making the canvas ripple and snap. The camp consisted of three large tents, each enough for at least nine people, and thirteen smaller ones.

But given the greater storm incoming, it was going to be a harder blow come evening, and staff was taking every precaution.

Cajeiri turned away from the great upstairs window while servants prepared tea in the little conservatory nook, and while his bodyguard waited, still on duty. Nomari stood beside a comfortable but modest armchair, and Cajeiri chose his own, with his back to the window, facing Uncle's accustomed place.

They were both waiting for Uncle.

"Did you sleep well?" Uncle had asked Nomari at breakfast this morning, and Nomari, who looked as if, indeed, he had not, had answered—"Not as well as one wished, nandi." But re-

specting the sanctity of the table, "May we speak after breakfast, nandi?"

So Nomari had come back with concern of his own—
understandable, considering Uncle's statements yesterday, regarding irregularities among the people out on the lawn. Cajeiri
had lain awake thinking too, whether Nomari should in fact
have Uncle's backing; and whether events would somehow
straighten things out. He had wondered, heading for breakfast,
whether Nomari would try to gloss over the problems of his
missing followers, or come in with an answer.

And when Nomari had answered as he just had—he had
wanted then and there to know what Nomari had found out.

Breakfast, however, was breakfast, formal and proper . . . and
a person who did not know Uncle might think he had retained
no concern about the missing people at all.

After breakfast, the view of the little cluster of tents from
the window offered no clue, and manners dictated he not ask
now: his father's son he might be, but it was Uncle's place to
have Nomari's report. He felt that keenly.

So they both waited for Uncle to join them.

Uncle arrived at the conservatory nook at his own pace, took
his accustomed chair, next a potted vine. Nomari sat. Servants
provided tea, and Uncle took three sips before he set his cup
down on his little side table. Not just one sip, which would
have indicated disturbance; not most of the cup, which might
warn Nomari he was deeply upset, but a lightly courteous and
leisurely three.

"So," Uncle said. "What troubles our guest this breezy morning, beyond the weather?"

"Nandi." Nomari gave a deep nod. "I personally queried
every person in our group last night, and the three missing,
while seen at first, are indeed not now to be found. Two are
known, but the third, who registered as Hapeini, is known to
one man as Maigin, but unknown by either name to every other

in the camp. One man thought he had seen all three in the camp together on the first day, but no one reports them now. No one admits to them ever sleeping in any tent. I am embarrassed, to say the least, and I apologize. If I can offer any theory, they all three, after registering, left, perhaps at a point when the gates opened for the market truck. They may have felt uneasy when asked for their names."

"Or they are here, but not found," Uncle said, "which is far more troublesome."

"I agree, nandi, and I am troubled by it. I am not done with looking. I have set others to find out what they can."

"Well, well," Uncle said mildly, "you never guaranteed that all these people can face a Guild inquiry."

"No, nandi, I can by no means guarantee it. And they have become expert at evasions. But let me plead, too, that Guild uniforms in such abundance frighten them. I have told them we should trust this is for our protection—that the Guild has changed leadership and to the good—but they are still afraid."

"Is such sentiment widespread in the camp?" Uncle asked.

"Giving their true names is a difficult point for them. But with your staff, your help, the hospitality—they are more hopeful, nandi. They greatly hope for your help."

"Ajuri are our neighbors," Uncle said. "And any petty record with the Guild, during their years of absence, we can forgive. They are our guests. If they are good and respectful guests, they will have the protection and the legal representation of the Atageini, should the Guild raise a question, and one would extend that representation past their stay here, should anything surface later. If the three missing should reappear, and have a good reason for their disappearance, I will hear it."

"It is more than generous," Nomari said fervently. "I shall relay that."

It *was* a lot for Uncle to promise. It was extremely generous toward the people out there, and especially toward the missing. If people scared and running were all it was, Cajeiri thought, they could find their way back to good grace. Maybe some had broken the law to escape Guild notice, or lied on registrations, or even pilfered, all very small things if there was restitution.

But it was troubling, if they were so scared that they were not standing by Nomari under the current circumstances, and the situation reflected badly both on Nomari's leadership and their honesty.

And it seemed very odd that they should not know each other. *Supposedly* they were all Ajuri, and most of them were at least remote cousins, with ties that traced to people *somebody* ought to have in common, but these three people appeared to have nothing more in common than the names they had gone by, which were likely not the right names in the first place.

Nomari had left the taking of names to Uncle, relying on him, since Nomari had come in with no staff, no bodyguard, no lists, nobody but this shapeless lot that had trickled in out of the woods southward, and down the roads from the train station. That had been a mistake never to make, Cajeiri thought, to leave a responsibility at loose ends. One should *know* who these people were. One should ask, and remember names, and understand exactly what problems they had.

There were things about being in charge that he, being just fortunate nine, had learned, and one of them was that going about with no staff and no bodyguard at all would be a very scary prospect. He felt sorry for Nomari in that regard—he truly did not know wholly how to manage; and he thought of what Great-grandmother would say, that if Nomari was going to be lord of a place like Ajuri, he would be another dead lord of Ajuri if he left things like this to chance.

"If you do not become lord of Ajuri, Cousin," he asked, because he thought someone should ask, "what do you think will happen to these people?"

Nomari looked troubled. "Is it your intention to cast us off, nand' Tatiseigi?"

"It is a good question," Uncle said. "Where will they go?"

"Nandi, if your answer to me is no, then I have put these people in danger, and I could only ask you to protect them. Otherwise, they will have no choice but to go back where they were, wherever they were. Either way I shall go somewhere far. Likely somewhere inconvenient."

"Even so, you cannot be safe the way you were before," Cajeiri said, and Nomari looked at him.

"I likely shall not be. But my presence can only draw trouble to them."

"That is your whole plan," Uncle said. "You would not, say, attempt anything against Geidaro-daja—personally."

A small pause. "Nandi, I would trust the aiji someday to resolve the lordship, somehow. I would *hope* there would be someone to set new authority over Ajuri. But one more Ajuri killing will not mend the clan."

"A law-abiding answer," Uncle said, nodding. "Good. Well. But say that I recommend you. How would you survive the year?"

Nomari frowned. "One would hope," he said quietly, "that with such an appointment—the Guild might take an interest in my survival. That they might afford me protection enough to make it possible."

"Would you trust the Guild, since the uniforms seem to alarm your followers?"

"If the aiji can trust the Guild, then I must trust them."

"Could your people?" Uncle asked. "To a specific point— could they *take* their disputes to the Guild, in a lawful way, and could they then abide peaceably by the result?"

"Nandi." A breath, a solemn nod. "A sober and a fair question. Ajuri—has lost so much, so much, for so many years. Would I trust the Guild? If they asked me to go into Ajiden and take power, and not to stay in hiding, I would go in. I would be terrified. But I would go, given their presence with me. I would open records, such as I could lay hands on, and I would certainly

lay them open to the Guild. My interest is in sorting out my
people, the ones whose man'chi is to Ajuri, and the ones whose
man'chi is to something else. I have never *seen* a great house
function well, until this one. I have never met a lord I could
believe was a lord. Now I have met two."

"Counting my great-nephew," Uncle said, and Cajeiri drew
in a breath, not sure he was not being courted, instantly mis-
trustful.

"Counting the young aiji, yes, nandi. I do count him."

"How many follow *you?* Can you answer that?"

"Out there, nandi, sixty-three, less the three; but beyond
that—as to how many, but I would guess two hundred that I
have personally met. I know small groups, five in one place,
three in another, who know other groups. I do not personally
know all the names. No individual of us knows all the names,
or who is living and who is dead. One is at least sure that word
is passing among the exiles . . . that I have approached you and
that you have at least heard our case. In whatever guilds they
may be serving, or in what places, more may come here. One
only hopes they are discreet, and that they offer you no distress."

"Do you think Geidaro-daja the greatest danger you face?"

A pause. "Nandi, the Guild would know that better than I."

The quick answer was, yes, that Great-aunt Geidaro was a
worry. The wiser one was that Nomari might not, at his level,
know who else was a concern. That was a good answer, Cajeiri
thought. Uncle probably thought so, too.

"We are continuing our investigation," Uncle said, "and our
investigation has extended into places the Guild may know and
the aiji in Shejidan may know, but much of it is not ours to ask.
I can only ask your patience with the process, difficult as it may
be. And one other thing."

"Nandi?"

"Accept the hospitality of this house and sleep upstairs tonight. With three persons unaccounted for and not all known to

you—I now insist on that point. You may stand on principle, but you do not serve your people by putting yourself where they may have to die for you."

There was a small silence. Nomari's mouth had instantly shaped *no*, but it stayed unspoken. Then he said, "Nandi, I shall go out and tell my people."

Baji-naji. It had the feeling of things balanced, fortune and chance poised and apt to tip on that point.

"He should go about outside with bodyguards," Cajeiri said. "Uncle. One asks."

"A good idea," Uncle said soberly. "House security will go with you, and stay with you. They may stay in the background. This house will engage the Guild to provide you security—"

"Nandi,—"

"For our *own* reputation, which is in my keeping. You have entered our grounds, you have shared our table. We have reached a determination that at very least, whether or not we take the step of recommending you for office, you should not die on our grounds and that that woman now occupying Ajuri should not have her way."

Nomari drew a deep breath, appeared to abandon what he had intended to say, and gave a nod. "Nandi. One is grateful."

"I do it as well for the young gentleman's sake," Uncle said, "and for the general safety. Do not consider cost. I shall stand for that, until I can reach a decision. Meanwhile my Guild senior will arrange matters."

"I am grateful," Nomari said, there being no choice once Uncle declared what he *would* do. Engaging Guild protection cost a great deal. Money was not a thing that Cajeiri had ever held in his hand, and rarely even seen, but his tutors had taught him what money was worth, and what a typical worker brought to his clan, and what his personal spending might be, and how each and every clan's finances ran, besides the very much larger numbers of the Bujavid, and the branches of government.

And the sort of Guild protection Uncle would engage for

Nomari was, he was sure, senior, the sort that might come out from Guild Headquarters, and probably they would be people his own senior aishid would know on sight.

In the meanwhile they had three people who had either gotten out the iron gate far out of sight of the house, slipping out of the hedges behind the estate truck, or worse, people that had not left at all.

Definitely he should not visit Jeichido in the pens this evening, weather or no weather—not this evening and not the next, and probably not for the rest of his visit here, not supposing that Uncle would even make a decision about Nomari before he left. He understood all of it. He was upset to understand it. He wished that there were *somewhere* he could visit and not have every trouble in the aishidi'tat arrive on the grounds before evening.

But that was the way things were for Father, and for Great-grandmother, and lately for Uncle. They had all sorts of power to do almost anything . . . except to walk outdoors or go riding, or go to the public parks, or to the public plays, or the races, or enjoy anything of the world he saw on television. He would never in his life have that freedom.

He really should not feel sorry for himself for most of it, he thought. But he was deeply, deeply angry about the riding.

Tom's packet contained a hundred fifty-three pages of text, photos, and reduced-size architectural blueprints, all, of course, in Mosphei'. Heyden Court had been built a hundred years ago, probably *without* blueprints of any modern sort. These had been produced after the fact by people doing repairs or alterations. Individual blueprints in the stack were labeled with dates—in effect, showing the various modifications made in the historic house during its life as a residence, as an administrative facility, as a guest house and storage, then as classrooms during the two years of repairs after the Ames Hall fire, and finally as an art museum with upstairs storage.

Along with the house blueprints came diagrams of the on-site garage, the garden with its lighting and water, and a schematic of the grounds in general, right down to the potting shed and sprinkling system—the gardens being, besides the lighting and water, the part of the property least changed since its occupancy by Dr. Heyden and family. Outbuildings were of great concern in any question of security.

Bren and his aishid worked at the dining table, that being the largest work space, amid a collection of half-empty teacups. Bren made a chart of the symbols he knew—a few were mysteries they puzzled out together—for various items such as windows, doors, conduits, and outlets.

"Door?" Tano asked.

"Double door," he translated and Tano scribbled a Ragi symbol.

Did the Assassins' Guild understand architectural diagrams? Absolutely they did, with far more expertise than any graduate of the Department of Linguistics. They knew all about stand-pipes, and he had had an entirely wrong idea.

"One has several recommendations," Banichi said, tapping the front entry, "first of all about the downstairs sitting room. That room should be a security station, and a communications center, with an area set aside for politely receiving guests and callers, but no deliveries to be brought within the residence without examination. Workmen and deliveries, all, all should pass this point."

Security on Mospheira had always been fairly adept at guarding against pilferage and fools. Violent crimes were generally domestic disputes, business partnerships gone wrong, property crimes, and the occasional mental problem. Public security *had* been obsessed with guarding the coasts in certain periods of tension, in fear of an intrusion from the mainland, not to mention an intermittent problem with smuggled goods, but only in the last twenty years had the President of Mospheira even had a security team around him.

Mospheiran security had, however, suffered its episodes of

internal corruption. And the nation had had a brief unpleasant period of Heritage Party rule, in which security had absolutely obsessed on the supposed threat from the mainland. Recruits to the security operation taken in during that period, not so long ago, had to be somewhat suspect in terms of dealing with an atevi-connected program.

But over all, from police to military, one expected an honest professionalism which was willing to deal with a higher threat level—bearing in mind it had never, ever met one, and could not always imagine the possibilities.

The underlying problem was, one feared, precisely the Mospheiran outlook that had delayed the packet downstairs, the pervading notion that orders were subject to their interpretation and that a little later was good enough. Security had never had to deal with truly sophisticated threats—even Heritage's militarization of the coast had been, in continental terms, unsophisticated.

Maybe, Bren thought, he was mistaken in introducing to the island the level of suspicion natural on the mainland. Precaution could go both ways—far too much security might suggest far more industry in breaching it, and he might actually escalate the threat. It might work a sea-change on Mospheiran attitudes and capabilities, even suggesting that children could be a target.

But too little caution could lead worse places, to a scar on Mospheiran history, harm to the children in question, a major problem with the aishidi'tat . . . and turning a young boy's mind to an anger that boy had never remotely felt, a young boy who would, one day, control all the formidable power of the aiji.

They couldn't risk things going wrong.

And that meant that, without the consent or knowledge of the aiji or the Guild, his bodyguard was going to try to instruct a hand-picked set of high-level Mospheiran security in that level of caution, and rearrange the traffic flow of a Mospheiran historic house to more resemble atevi dwelling patterns which were defensible with atevi procedures. While such precautions might look like elegant design, they afforded effective barriers against political radicals and random lunatics of a sort Mospheira had not had to deal with.

"Tom has laid out a schedule for construction, and we shall make suggestions for the modifications," Bren said, "but one is fairly confident that the third floor, which has been a storage space, little altered from its original design, will convert easily to residence—while security modifications are still going on below."

"The first floor should hold no function *but* security," Banichi said. "The doors should be under lower-level guard, with no discretion about their orders; and anything done in construction should be under close watch and supervision, then checked by highest-level security. One would insist the door to the security station should be metal, and resistant to explosives and fire, that the security station in such a place should never be entirely vacated, and that there also be a guarded and monitored security door before the stairs. The lift access should be behind that door, and behind the same arrangement of doors on the lowest level, where it comes to the garage entry, which must be controlled from the upstairs station. There should likewise be a secondary security station and proper secure door on the residency level."

"Giving absolute orders to Mospheiran personnel," he said, "will be a problem. If they have a written protocol, trained personnel will generally follow that—but unfortunately they tend to make exceptions for associates and relatives, and for each other." They *were* his people. Mospheirans had their quirks and their virtues, and his aishid was used to him, so not everything had to be explained. In their view, he was sure, not everything *could* be explained by any logic, but he could at least warn them. "They will be stressed by guilt if they must ignore that. But these will be good people—intelligent people, who will also feel extreme devotion to their service."

"They have enjoyed peace on the island," Algini muttered, "and have been very fortunate."

"One should set down rules," Jago said, "as comprehensive as possible, specifically excluding such associates, giving them a moral basis for doing what is sensible. Likewise it will protect their relations and associates from becoming a pressure point, and perhaps that will be understood."

"Compose it, Jago-ji, and I shall translate." The phone rang, which was not expected at this hour. He turned his chair and reached for it.

"This is Bren Cameron."

"Bren, Tom here. I may have found some tutors."

"The Committee relented?"

"Not exactly." There was understanding humor in Tom's voice, that faded. *"The Committee will not be happy with them, to say the least. If we take them, we have to slip them over into State, with credentials of some kind. Diplomas may not be in their future."*

"Students?"

"Seniors, willing to take the risk. State is my suggestion, not their requirement. They made no conditions, but they're not that worldly-wise. It was my suggestion to pay them—they hadn't gotten that far in their thinking. One of them heard the Committee was balking at cooperating with the Heyden Court setup, and they stopped me on the sidewalk."

"Advance planning."

"None whatsoever."

"On the other hand . . . senior students in Linguistics, with a paidhi in office who shows no signs of leaving—that'll land them in Translation Services if they're lucky, but there's no guarantee. I understand their position, but they're taking a chance. Don't say anything that can get back to the Committee— they definitely won't look kindly on the move. Do you have a way to contact them?"

"They gave me cards."

"Good. Tell them I'll talk to them. I can judge their fluency. I'll need names to clear them past Francis House security."

"I'll take care of that. You've got enough on your hands. Or will have. Gin's documentary is going to land with considerable commotion."

"You've had a look at it?"

"The President's sent out a copy to the Cabinet, to Kate, to Ben, to me, as interested parties—and to various committee heads—including the Heritage caucus. The President's called Moxon in for conference, as a point of courtesy."

Moxon was head of the Heritage senior chamber caucus. That was going to have the phone lines active—and they weren't all that secure on Mospheira, either.

If everything went well, the upper levels of the Heritage Party, which had backed Tillington, would take the warning, back away from Tillington and stay quiet at least for a few months. That would solve a major problem. With the *Phoenix* captains as anxious to get five thousand Reunioners off station decks as Gin Kroger was anxious to comply, it was *going* to happen, starting with the three children about to make that downward voyage. What became of Tillington then was not his personal concern. Tabini-aiji certainly wanted nothing to do with him.

"Well, let's hope Moxon sees what we saw. These kids—the ones from Linguistics—can you get them here this afternoon?"

"I'll let them know. They'll be there. Say at fifteen hundred. I've run background checks, no problems. Clean kids. Good kids, by their manners. They'll be overwhelmed to meet you."

"Well, I hope they'll work. I sincerely do. We have to have somebody, and Committee isn't going to cooperate without a Presidential fiat."

"Agreed," Tom said. *"I'll set up their clearances. And get them a cab. They're students. They'd probably take the bus."*

He would have, in their place. God, his memory strayed back to University streets, and counting change for bus fare. Walking, because he was a few coins short. "Good idea. Thanks, Tom."

"No problem," Tom said, and hung up.

The ultimate resolution of the Mospheiran situation up there was, thank God, *not* his problem. Nor was the arrangement of passage down for the Reunioners or the choice of who would go first. Gin Kroger and Lord Geigi were handling all that, with the help of *Phoenix* security.

He was getting the three children Tabini-aiji was most concerned about, children who had never been to a formal school, and who still would not attend regular classes. They had learned everything they had learned from their surviving parents and from recordings, and occasionally from each other. They had learned to survive on a station shot half to wreckage and faced with a long, nearly impossible reconstruction under enemy watch, with limited food, limited resources, and an intolerable present—with a very good likelihood there would *be* no future.

What in that hellish situation had made them the bright and sensible and practical kids they were, God only knew. Flowers bloomed out of bare rock. Life hung on. And the kids were amazingly hungry to know things, as if any understanding they could get their hands on was food, something to absorb. Something to help them survive. A way to see a tomorrow they could hardly picture to themselves. They just kept trying.

Would they learn as readily in the humdrum of regular instruction? They were already more fluent in Ragi than the last paidhi had been. They had learned it hiding in ship maintenance tunnels, and teaching the aiji's son their ways and *their* language.

They were also too damned clever at finagling their way past security.

They had to understand, here on Earth, with abundant air and food and room, there were still dangers.

They had to know that their getting back to the mainland

and continuing their association with the aiji's son was depen-
dent on obeying the rules.

And they also had to know that five thousand people on the
station were relying on their good behavior to make a good impression.

Tom's news was good news. Students, for God's sake. Brave
souls themselves, running a different set of serious risks. The
full professors had declined to teach the children, scared of the
Committee, which was not all that fond of one Bren Cameron.
The students that Tom had turned up were gambling with their
own futures, on the one chance they might have to *use* the language the way a paidhi would—because there was, by custom
and law, one paidhi, and he was holding that office, with no
intention of dropping dead.

They were even less likely ever to see an appointment as
paidhiin, given the presence of these children, who arrived with
direct ties to the next likely ruler of the continent.

But as teachers of those children, they could find an active
use for their skills. They could get in through a side door, if they
were willing to be content with that, and if they could learn to
handle spoken Ragi—a thing actively discouraged by the Committee. That the current paidhi was colloquially fluent—in
more than one dialect—was not to the Committee's liking. Not
in the least.

"We may have tutors for the young folk," he told his aishid.
"One hopes it may work out, and that the children will be
happy with them and that they will be happy in the work. One
hopes everyone involved with the youngsters will be sensible."

"Kate-nadi," Jago said, "will countenance no bad behavior."

That much was certainly true. Kate Shugart took no prisoners. And Kate was the on-premises guardian of the project. A
veritable dragon, if someone stepped out of line.

"One is very happy to have her," he said. "I am thinking I
shall urge the aiji that the children have at least a short visit to

the mainland once they have settled in—simply to let them relax, understand that we are keeping our word, and understand the terms of their welcome . . . and while they are visiting the mainland, let their parents settle into Heyden Court and learn something of Mospheiran customs—perhaps offer them their own holiday, to see various sights that will be strange to stationers. As for the children, one believes Najida would offer them a limited, quiet visit with the young gentleman."

Eyes flickered with interest. His aishid never asked for time off—nor ever seemed to want it. They were attached to him with a bond that never broke. But a trip to his estate on the coast, and time to relax? Oh, yes. That did catch their interest. Five kilometers off the coast, fishing from the boat, even Guild could relax.

"One wishes," he said wistfully, "that I could show *you* more of Mospheira in this visit. I wish *we* could go up to the mountains and out to the north shore. You have seen very little even of the city."

"We are content," Algini said. "Even this building is interesting."

"Edu-cational," Tano said, and they laughed. That had been young Cajeiri's favorite word, when it came to something he wanted and ought not to have.

"I hope it *has* been," he said, "at least educational."

"The trip to the University," Jago said wryly, "was *very* educational. We were very glad to have seen that. We were glad to have been there."

Would the Committee create all sorts of roadblocks for the students who wanted to do what the Committee had made professors afraid to do?

In a heartbeat.

Would the Committee deliberately create unpleasantness for three absolutely innocent children?

He was sure of it.

Could they? Not so easily. He had brought in a few personal allies, people who could call up the President of Mospheira and say, "We have a problem."

Bet on one thing: Cajeiri's three young associates would never live on a leash, responsible to the Committee on Linguistics, the way he had started his career. They were now and would be henceforth under the oversight of various authorities, including the Department of State *and* the aishidi'tat.

And if at some time they chose not to represent Mospheira, but the aishidi'tat, as he did, that would be their choice to make, too.

"Tom-nadi wishes me to meet these students," he said. "I have indicated they should come here this afternoon. One would not expect them to pose any threat. How they might react in your presence might tell me something about their suitability. But if you think it best, there are ample meeting rooms to use, instead of this apartment."

"I doubt they would threaten us," Jago said dryly.

"I do doubt that. Tom-nadi says they accosted him, with the notion that teachers were needed. They are probably not wealthy young folk. Since I hold the only high post toward which their study leads, their likely employment would have been to sit in a large office reading Ragi trade documents, for very little pay. Still, given the opposition of the administration, if they do this, they cannot go back, even to that option."

"What would move them to this?" Algini asked.

"In their place," Bren said, "at an age close to leaving the educational system, and with a paidhi by no means ready to retire—I think I would have taken the chance, if it offered, no matter the Committee's disapproval. The children will be under the authority of the Department of State, so the University has no direct power over them, and Tom-nadi suggests the same status for their tutors. But if they hope to *have* that job translating trade manifests and such—they will be throwing that stability away, and possibly making lifelong enemies of the

Department of Linguistics, who do have some political impact on translators of all sorts. I shall solicit your opinions on their fitness, wherever we meet them. Shall they come here?"

"One sees no detriment in their coming here," Banichi said. "They *are* young people, are they not? Will they take instruction and stay by it?"

It was a question. "Far better, I suspect, than will older ones who answer to the Linguistics Committee. I am encouraged, Jago-ji. I am actually quite hopeful."

6

Cajeiri, balanced on a ladder, investigating the highest shelves of the library, had all the histories of clans he had never heard of in a long row before him—histories, and drawings. He *liked* drawings. He was fascinated by how a collection of lines could make such dimensional pictures. He particularly loved finding the oldest books, some of which were in a writing style full of hooks and curls that made it very hard to read. One became lost in the printing itself, absorbed in the way a simple character could be so important.

He had found a prize, with both the old text *and* an abundance of drawings that showed towns and places about the Midlands, in a quaint old way of building he had only seen in a few places, ever. "Nadiin-ji!" he said, only in a conversational tone, because the library was such a hushed place, even with only an ornate grill closing it off from the great hall, that every movement seemed to echo. His junior aishid, gathered at a low table, had been looking through books of their own choosing. They looked up as he scrambled down.

And at that moment, with a quick, regular step, a shadow arrived in the doorway of the grillwork. The juniors looked that direction immediately, and stood up. *Rieni* had come. Guild-senior of the seniors.

"Nadi-ji," Cajeiri addressed him, and carefully descended the last two steps, laying the book on the shelf nearest.

"Nandi. Your mother is calling."

In truth, when Rieni began with *your mother* a little chill had struck him, a little fear that something had happened in Shejidan. But—immediately on that thought: "Is my *father* all right?"

"We have no word on that, nandi, other than that your father authorized the call on our equipment."

Well, Father was *able* to authorize a call on Guild equipment, which ordinarily even Great-grandmother would not be able to do, except in direst official need.

"Where?" he asked.

Rieni simply took a little Guild unit from his pocket, adjusted it, and gave it to him on the spot.

"Honored mother?" he asked.

"Where are you, son of mine? Who is there?"

"I—am in Uncle's library, Honored Mother. Rieni is with me, and my younger aishid, no one else."

"No servants."

"No, Honored Mother. Only they."

"What is this about visitors?"

"Honored Mother, do you know a person named Nomari?"

"I once knew someone of that name. I had to look in records to be sure. How did he come there?"

"Honored Mother, he arrived first, and startled everybody; and Great-aunt Geidaro turned up at the gate and stood in Uncle's great hall and demanded Uncle nominate her son Caradi for the lordship. Uncle told her no and sent her away. So then Nomari and Uncle talked, and Uncle put a white flag on the gate to signal Nomari's allies that it was safe to come in, and he asked the Taibeni not to take exception to them coming from the train station. They walked here, mostly. And Uncle took all the big hunting tents out of storage and set them up, which is where they all are now, on the front lawn. And the Guild has been investigating everybody, and we have names." The *we* was impertinent, but it was mostly true, even if he had never seen the list, because he had helped Uncle talk to Nomari. "Uncle had to send out after groceries. There are sixty-three people out there. But we have lost three. So Uncle has asked Nomari to come into the house to sleep until we find them, and asked Guild to guard him. They are being careful."

There was a silence.

"Honored Mother?"

The silence persisted. He was not sure on the one hand whether he had lost the contact, and on the other—it could be one of Mother's silences, which meant Mother was mad.

"What does Uncle suppose is the location of these missing people?"

"Uncle thinks either they slipped out the gate when the truck went in and out, or they could still be somewhere about the grounds, maybe frightened when Uncle started taking names, but there are alarms on everything and there is Guild on the roof and all, so the house is safe. They are being very strict now, and I know I cannot go out to see Jeichido. I am minding what I am told, Honored Mother. I am not going anywhere I should not."

"Your senior aishid was not with you just now."

"They were right down the hall, Honored Mother. I am in the library, there are Uncle's guards downstairs, and the juniors are with me, right across the room. Is there a problem?"

Another small silence.

"You are taking proper precautions."

"Yes, Honored Mother."

"Are you dealing personally with this Nomari? Are you at any time alone with him?"

"If I meet with him, and I *have* talked with him, I am always with both my bodyguards, Honored Mother. I am never alone. Ever."

Silence. But a brief one. *"Is Uncle inclined to trust him?"*

"Uncle has not made up his mind."

"Do you trust him, son of mine?"

He had to hesitate, asking himself the honest answer. "Not yet, Honored Mother."

"Why not?"

"Because—because there are things I want to know, things about Ajuri. And here. That is why I am in the library."

"I am coming to Tirnamardi, son of mine. I am packing, and I am coming, with my guard. Your great-grandmother is in the air this moment, and intends to come there, but this will not happen."

A lower voice intruded—Father's. Cajeiri was sure.

Then Father took the unit, and said: "Son of mine, a moment."

"Absolutely, Honored Father."

Something happened to the unit on the other end. He heard, "How long do you intend to stay? Miri, if you open this nest, we will have no choice but deal with it."

"Uncle Tatiseigi has fairly well opened it already, has he not? It is camped on his lawn."

"Your uncle can feud with Ajuri until the sun turns black, and the fact that he happens to be entertaining his nephew is complete coincidence until you turn up."

"Or until your grandmother moves in, either of which will have the same effect, and she is not coming to Shejidan on an idle whim. This is an Ajuri matter, and a Padi Valley matter, in which your grandmother has no reasonable interest—"

"Except her grandson and her longtime ally."

"My son! My uncle! And my clan! Both my clans, as far as that goes."

"Light of my life, you know once you step into this—"

"It must have a conclusion. I know. It will have a conclusion. I cannot foresee what conclusion, but Ajuri has to be either broken or mended, built up or taken down, and if I have to bring it down myself—I will. It is my clan! Your grandmother has no part in it, and neither does my uncle."

"I have."

"And you appoint lords and you remove them. But this is a matter internal to the Padi Valley Association. My aunt and *this person claiming to be Ajuri both went onto Atageini land and brought this dispute into Lord Tatiseigi's hands. If you set foot in Tirnamardi to take sides before appointing a new lord for Ajuri, you set a precedent that will echo in every associational issue that ever arises."*

"Gods less fortunate, woman! I am somewhat conversant with the law!"

"And you know your grandmother will go there, if I do not. I know that woman. She will have an opinion, she will bring force in, and that will set its own precedent!"

"What my grandmother does sets no precedents. She has no governing authority."

"She has a standing army!"

"Not necessarily with her."

"Oh. That makes all the difference. No. I am Ajuri. And Atageini. I have a right. If you want me to send your son back, that I will do."

A silence.

"I am here!" Cajeiri said sharply, hoping they would realize he was listening, and just stop arguing.

They did not stop. His father said, *"Cajeiri is a guest under that roof. He has reputation at stake, likewise. He should understand that."*

Go home, leave the scene because his mother was taking over? No, he thought. No. He had rather be with his great-grandmother if there was going to be fighting. The thought of his mother in the middle of things such as he had shared with Great-grandmother was just scary.

But Mother was going to do it. She had said why she would. And his father was listening to her.

"You will not put yourself in danger," his father said. *"At no point will you go to Ajuri. I ask that promise. The units with Cajeiri have him as their priority, and your presence must not distract them. I want a double guard on you, from the time you board the train. And listen to them. Do me that favor."*

"You," his mother said, "keep your grandmother at bay. Thank her. And tell her, tell her my reasons."

"I shall—. Gods. Is that channel still open?"

A whisper of drapery, maybe a sleeve. Something bumped the other unit. "Son of mine?"

"Honored Mother."

"Speak to your father."

"Yes," he said, and a moment later, his father's voice, clear and strong:

"Son."

"Yes, Honored Father."

"I trust you understand the risk there. You have a considerable armed force for your protection. Do not separate it, do not attempt to direct it. Listen to it. Rely on your mother's judgment. Do not let her quarrel with your great-uncle. But if she wishes to File on your great-aunt in her own name, back her."

Father might be making a joke. But he was not at all sure at the moment. It was far too serious. "One would understand that, Honored Father." He knew something, something serious his father might not have heard, because he'd said it to his mother. "Three people are missing on the grounds, Honored Father. Possibly they just left. But Uncle is taking it very seriously."

A slight pause. "As he should. But your bodyguard will tell you—it is not always the ones you know to look for who pose the threat. Everyone not of your association is a threat in this situation. We do not know why these people are missing or who they might be afraid of. Stay with your senior aishid. Stay close to them at all times—for the sake of your younger one, among other considerations."

Father was right. He had been thinking about the missing people. But beyond the sixty-three they knew about, three of which they could not find, there was all of Ajuri somewhere beyond the hedge, just over the horizon.

"Trust your great-uncle. He is no fool. Neither is your

mother. Remember who of the great lords survived the Troubles intact. And remember who was with me, while we were sleeping in hedgerows and being hunted by the Shadow Guild."

Lord Tatiseigi. And Mother.

"Remember there is a public perception of this situation, and there is the situation itself. Listen to your bodyguard. And be proper."

"I shall. I *do*, Honored Father. I am doing my best."

"I trust my son. You may tell your great-uncle your mother is coming," Father said. *"I do not want to trust that message to the phones. She will not want to surprise your great-uncle. But she will want, I think, to surprise this person claiming to be her cousin. Do you understand?"*

"Yes," he said.

"I rely on it," Father said, and cut the connection.

There was the call from downstairs security, certainly. Bren picked up the phone, gave a, "Yes, let them through."

And two men from downstairs security escorted the visitors up.

Three collegiates, all male, in—Bren had to be a little impressed—their best coats, if slightly out of fashion, nicely turned out, terribly earnest. That shone through in the moment Tano and Jago let them in. Two pale faces, one dark, registered his presence; three heads ducked in a very nice bow. Hair was pulled back to napes, *not* the fashion on Mospheira.

"Nandi," the dark young man said.

Well. Enterprising lads. "Nadiin," he said, and in Ragi, indicating a sufficiency of chairs: "Welcome. Please sit."

They moved, trying ever so hard not to stare at his bodyguard. They came to the chairs and remained standing until he sat.

Nice.

They stayed absolutely silent, taking in the room, the furnishings—his bodyguard, his staff, who by prior arrangement were quietly making atevi-style tea.

"Your names, nadiin."

"Karl Barnes, nandi." This from the lanky, dark-skinned youth, foremost of the group. "Lyle Fredericks." That was the sunburned fellow with fiery red hair. And from the fairly plump pale lad with thick glasses: "Evan Child."

Appreciation of Ragi manners was not the only thing one noted in these three. *Long* hair, braided, braids tucked under collars. Identical white turtleneck sweaters. Three dress jackets, however out of style. And boots, polished to a high gloss.

Narani and Jeladi quietly served tea. Bren took a cup, waited, as the three young men waited, watching him intently, eyes following his every move, darting now and again to Jeladi and Narani. Bren took a sip. They did.

"So," Bren asked, deciding on small talk, in Ragi, "one understands you are senior students."

"Yes, nandi," Karl said.

"One trusts you are happy in your choice of disciplines."

"Very happy, nandi."

"You live in Port Jackson?"

"My family home is on the North Shore," Karl said, and then said, "Lyle, Evan? You can talk."

"Bretano," Lyle said. "I come from Bretano."

"Carswell," Evan said. "A very small place."

"I know Carswell," Bren said. "Up in the mountains, is it not?"

"Yes, nandi."

Lyle had blushed a brilliant red, and mostly gazed at his tea. Evan's hands shook and he clutched his cup between his palms, while Karl tried to maintain a casual demeanor.

"You are all three in the foreign service track?" Foreign service meant only one thing, that they were on track to replace *him* should he meet some untoward accident. They knew something about custom. They had grown the braids. *He* hadn't had time, when the appointment as paidhi had unexpectedly come his way. Perhaps, he thought, they had decided to be ready, should he suddenly demise. Lately that had been quite possible.

"Documents, nandi," Karl said. "All three of us are in Documents."

Translators of invoices and occasionally of broadcasts. Librarians and accountants—*not* in his track.

"Your accent is really quite good." Bren took another sip of tea.

"One is profoundly grateful," Karl said, studying his teacup. "Grateful, nandi." With an improved, courtly pronunciation.

"We are very honored to meet you," Evan said. "Most sincerely." And Lyle nodded, adding, "We are honored, nandi."

It was an absolute conundrum. "They teach a much better accent in Documents these days," Bren said. "One is impressed. Is everyone in Documents this fluent?"

Again, blushes, intense study of the cups in hand, and Lyle said, very quietly. "One is flattered, nandi. No. We study."

"Who is your instructor?" he asked.

"Murdock, nandi. Murdock-nadi."

A little correction of protocol, respect for a scholar. An impeccable courtly accent that came and went with a little hint of Mosphei' in the vowels. And a deference he was not used to.

Beyond that, he had never heard of Murdock.

He set his cup down. Immediately, with no extra sip, three other cups went onto side tables.

"We are an infelicitous number," Bren said. "With what presence would you improve it, with my major domo Narani, or with my Guild-senior, Banichi?"

Karl said, "With the Guild-senior, nandi."

Correct in protocol. "Banichi-ji," Bren said, and Banichi silently took the empty chair, while the others stood about, listening, and a hundred thoughts sailed past—not least among them, that the atmosphere and the program had changed massively in Documents, or these three *might* be part of a very different kind of study program, one aimed at information-gathering. It might be a program initiated during the Troubles, when the Mospheiran military and no few plain citizens and volunteer groups had helped the Guild holdouts on the continent, and *needed* some dealing in the spoken language. Likewise the Mospheiran President had had to find ways to communicate with Lord Geigi up on the station. So maybe there *were* changes afoot, even in the halls of Linguistics.

"What *is* your course of study?" Bren asked sharply, on business, now that the teacups were set down. "Are you part of an official program?"

"Documents, nandi." Karl maintained his story. "We are all in Documents. Nothing official. We did help—we were volunteers during the—during the bad period. We translated. Everybody translated who could."

"You learned court Ragi from that?"

Downcast eyes and a furious blush. The manners. The shyness. The hair, particularly Karl's, which, tending to very tight curls, had been fought to a smooth braid.

Any normal collegiate would have shown up even for an important interview in a team jacket and canvas runners, not a years-old dress jacket.

"Why do you want to work with the Reunioner children?"

A long pause. Then Evan said, "Nandi, it is so much better than Documents."

That was understandable.

"Do you *like* children?"

"I have three brothers," Lyle said.

"Sister," Karl said. Evan ducked his head and said nothing.

"Has any other person engaged you to approach the paidhi-aiji?" Banichi asked, in that deep voice that made its own silence.

"No. No, nandi." From Karl. Emphatically and with the correct honorific.

"Why, then, were you moved to accost Lund-nandi on the public walk? Could you not have sent a letter?"

Silence answered that question. But the obvious answer was . . .

"You have no official standing," Bren said. "Is that correct?"

More silence, and much less happiness.

"I remain curious," Bren said, "as to *how* you perfected your accent."

"Machimi, nandi. We study the machimi."

"Is that a course?"

"No," Evan said. "No, nandi. An association. A *club.*" Evan used the Mosphei' word. "We study them."

The machimi plays were not in Documents. They were in Literature, an excruciatingly badly translated collection, as he knew them. Nobody accessed atevi drama, except Atevi Studies, which was a branch of Anthropology, and entirely divorced from the Department of Linguistics.

"A *club.*" He used the Mospheiran word himself. "Tell me more about this *club*, nadiin. One is intrigued."

"We have copies," Kurt said. "We *made* copies."

"We translated them," Evan said.

"We show them," Lyle said, and lapsed into Mosphei'. "With subtitles."

Subtitles. On a form of Ragi the University deemed untranslatable, with a web of double meanings and subtleties of gesture and manner on which Anthropology wrote papers, plays which atevi themselves regarded as classics, immortal, capable of speaking to generation after generation in a psychology buried deep in atevi instincts. One did not understand machimi without understanding something of what went on in atevi minds.

"Which is your favorite?" Bren asked.

That provoked a little stir, one looking at the other. "Athami he Anati," Karl said, naming one of the north coast classics. "Likewise," Evan said. But Lyle said, "Notija Andoi."

One depended on man'chi, the other on a truly arcane sense of obligation conveyed by a mysterious artifact. Neither was transparent.

"Subtitles," he said in Mosphei'.

"Yes, sir," Kurt said. They looked, despite their age, like three kids apprehensive of a chastisement.

The long hair—he'd had to hide his during his visits home, or expect stares on the bus. A knowledge of court Ragi, the language of the classics. A *club*, for God's sake.

"Your work?"

"We had a sponsor. Professor Short, over in—"

"Anthropology."

"Yes, sir."

"Is he still your sponsor?"

"He died three years ago. We're sorry."

"I'm sorry, too." Short had been a rebel spirit himself, wildly eccentric: he remembered a plump old man with outlandish wisps of white hair, an affinity for plaids, and sandals no matter the weather. "God. Dr. Short. I'm amazed the Linguistics Department approved."

"They knew," Karl said in Mosphei', "and they didn't approve us meeting after Dr. Short died. But we're just in Documents. There's a few over in the Foreign Service track, but they keep it quiet, don't attend the meetings."

"How many are you, do you know?"

"Fifty-two. Maybe." Lyle looked uneasy.

"Fifty-three if you count Thea," Evan followed up quickly, and Karl shot him a warning glance.

"She's four."

"But she never misses a machimi," Evan persisted. "She's Lyle's sister. She watches when we're at Lyle's house, she sits and doesn't even fidget."

"She speaks a little," Lyle said, "but I can't say my mother approves."

"Fifty-three is, however, a more felicitous number," Bren said solemnly, but amused, and the young men all relaxed a degree. "It is not a bad thing. What, exactly, does this *club* do when you meet?"

"We hold meetings. We translate the machimi. We have parties. Dinners. We show the plays."

"And speak Ragi to each other."

"As much as we can, nandi."

"One hesitates to ask. Do you also maintain the jahaji?" That was the predecessor to the Assassins' Guild, enshrined in the machimi.

"A few of us." Evan's voice was very quiet.

Banichi gave a soft laugh. From the Guild on business, that was an officially amused reaction.

"Where do you meet?"

"In apartments, nandi," Kurt said.

"And how does the University regard this activity?"

There was a solemn, down-hearted silence. Then, in Mosphei', "They've never really said anything," Kurt said.

"Yet," Lyle said glumly.

"How *will* they regard your seeking out Lund-nadi?"

The look the three exchanged said it all.

"You could greatly damage your future prospects. You know that."

"Yes, nandi."

"I will tell you," Bren said, in Mosphei', to be sure they understood, "if you go into this on a trial basis, and you commit any indiscretion that brings a problem to these children or their parents—who do accompany them—there will be no mercy. No second chance. Their lives will be difficult enough, with inevitable public attention, and considering their connection with the aiji's court, there must never be anything to bring the program into disrepute. I cannot quarrel with the braids. But no outright demonstration of your particular passion, nothing else that makes you look different than any corporate employee or attracts the notice of the news—who *will* be watching you. Business style and discreet communication—no speaking Ragi in any public venue, in the hearing of anyone but the children and their parents. Tell me why I say this."

"We can't be weird," Evan said. "We can't have it reflect on the kids."

"That's pretty well it," Bren said. "You have to look like

University people. You can't do or say anything that makes people think you're in any wise different."

Hope dawned on three faces. "Do we get a trial?" Kurt asked.

"You will get a trial," Bren said. "And I have to warn you, you'll be mothered by the woman I still hope will agree to be in direct charge of the children, and you'll walk in mortal fear of the woman who will be overseeing the project. Dr. Kate Shugart has a sense of humor, but you have to earn admission to it."

"Sir," Kurt said, "we will be so much on good behavior."

"You'll also make close acquaintance with the State Department. And you will not expose the children to this club of yours without direct clearance from me. *Understood?* The children's doings will be secret, their lives will be classified, and everything we let the public see or hear about them has to fit how children ought to act in nice little ordinary neighborhoods. Do you understand why? I'd think, with the braids tucked under collars, that you might understand."

A pause. "Yes, sir. I think we do."

"You'll have one other complication: these children can speak kyo."

"Kyo. The *aliens?*"

"The aliens, yes. They speak it, never mind how, though likely they'll tell you in time, but wherein they do speak it, *you* should speak it. I won't give you my notes at this point, but what they know, you should record, and learn—if you don't, I'm quite sure they'll be speaking in it to get something past you. They *are* kids. Understood?"

"Yes, sir."

"You'll be their teachers for math, history, geography, science—all that. You'll live on site, *in* Heyden Court, and you won't leave it without notifying Dr. Shugart. You can go where you like and meet with friends and family, you can have your club and you can socialize as you please—but no negative attention, no scandal can result from it. I take it you may have an interest in girls . . ."

Nervous laughter, glances aside.

"No scandal. Absolutely none. Manage that aspect of your lives carefully, conscious that it can impact your futures and affect the children in your care. And understand that in the political climate that may develop once five thousand more Reunioners land on Mospheira, there may be people looking for any fault they can find . . . even in three young kids, or their associations. There is a stirring of political opposition, and it may touch off unstable people. There may be some politically motivated individuals who will use any means whatsoever to get to *you*. Including getting to your social contacts. Politics. Serious, dangerous politics that may turn *your* lives in ways you can't predict. That's what I've met. It's what *you* could meet. You will have to live under security the rest of your lives. It can affect your relationships, it can upset your life, it can affect everything. Nobody warned me. I'm warning you. Either you're committed to this—or not. You *can* back out of this. You *should* back out if you want to take any different track."

"Committed," Kurt said.

Evan nodded. "Committed."

"Yes," Lyle said.

"I'll recommend you," Bren said. "My consent may seem remarkable—given your unorthodox approach. But I will recommend you. I daresay the braids *wouldn't* get by in the offices of the Department."

"No, sir. But they don't pay attention to us down in Documents."

He nodded. Shoes were optional, down in the depths of Documents. "Skip the classes. For good. You're going into the employ of the State Department, under Dr. Shugart's direct supervision. For pay."

"We have transcripts—" Lyle said. "We brought them."

"I've got them," he said. "I'm estimating, among the three of you, someone can come up with grammar, math, science and history equal to a ten year old's needs. I'm estimating you can keep ahead of the kids, academically, though they may actually outpace you in physics. What they tell you about Reunion will be classified until further notice, and let Dr. Shugart do any official communication with the State Department in that regard. She'll see it gets where it needs to be and no further. I'm very serious about that. Nothing gets out. You are not to be a source for *any* news item. Understood?"

"Yes, sir. Nandi." They made little bows. "We are so excited," Evan said.

"Fifty-three people. Devotees of the machimi plays."

"Yes, sir." A faint, faint murmur.

He nodded. "That's not a bad thing. That's not at all a bad thing. Do many understand them?"

"Most . . . most need the subtitles. But not always."

"Good. That's good." He truly thought it might be, though it led in scary directions. "One additional matter: no matter your excitement, you must not gossip about this assignment, your careers, or the children—including within your club. You may not talk about it in others' hearing. Discretion." He said it in Ragi, in which it was a much stronger word, and embraced a lot that he had said about their social lives. Then he said, in Mosphei', "And on the matter of girls."

"There's one," Lyle said in Mosphei', blushing. "Sort of."

"I know that," Bren said. "From the time you talked to Mr. Lund, there has already been a background check, stiffer than you passed to get into Linguistics. There will be monitoring of your contacts' contacts, for security reasons. You're allowed a private life. But it cannot intrude into your responsibilities to the project. No pleading can alter any of your obligations, no stranger can come onto the grounds of the project without approval, and the project will take precedence over your personal lives until the children are grown, possibly after. Does that condition upset you?"

A little uncertainty. "No, nandi." Shakes of heads. A belated one from Lyle. "I understand," Lyle said. "I do understand, nandi."

"If you have policy questions or personal problems, you will ask Dr. Shugart. Remember these young people are under the aiji's protection. He will know what happens to them. He will know *your* names. Do you understand that?"

"Yes," the answer was.

Taking on three students with families and attachments meant setting Shawn's security more deeply on the matter of their backgrounds—finding out their connections, arranging it so no problems assailed their families and friends. It was what happened when one worked for State. Or held office. Or worked security.

But they didn't know. They couldn't know how scary it could get. They got up when he did, they bowed, they went through the courtesies, they expressed how very happy they were—and they were sincere and overwhelmed. He read that. He was a little worried at the imitation of atevi style, at the fervent thanks and the good wishes they paid him personally.

He stood there after they left, staring at the shut door and asking himself if he was at all smart to take their assurances and their good intentions and most of all taking people who were *too* enthusiastic about their crazy project—*subtitling* the machimi plays, for God's sake, popularizing a near-sacred atevi art form on this side of the straits. With a club of like-minded souls. And long hair. Young men—who likely still thought they might manage a normal life on the side. They were in for more than they possibly understood.

But—he said to himself—their fluency, give or take some quaint expressions a couple of centuries out of date, even in the aiji's court—gave him better than anything he expected. Their fluency, their awareness of manners, was transcript enough. There were years to work things out. There were years that would lead everyone places these kids—including the three kids he'd just met, about the age he'd been when he'd first crossed the strait to a whole different world—couldn't imagine or predict.

Sometimes one just took a deep breath and rolled the dice.

"You have accepted their statements," Banichi observed.

He drew a breath. "I could find no better candidates in the halls of the University, nadiin-ji, and of that I am reasonably certain. I know my choices over there, and there are far worse."

He wanted copies of those subtitled plays. Wanted to know how accurate they were, whether interpretation went off the rails on any points.

Wanted to know something about those fifty-three club members—just to be sure he understood what influences might go back and forth.

And he was just—professionally—curious.

"They are quite in awe of you," Jago said. "You say humans do not feel man'chi. But it did seem so."

"Many things look more impressive when one is young."

"Ah," Jago said, sounding entirely unconvinced. "Is *that* what it is?"

7

Boji felt the weather coming, no question. He bounded from perch to perch in his filigree cage, pried at the cage door with his small fingers, spilled his water dish, and, more uncommon, ignored the offer of an egg.

"Hush, hush," Cajeiri said, laying a hand on the cage. He and his bodyguard and his two servants occupied the largest guest suite, and his servants, Eisi and Liedi, had done their best with Boji, offering him everything they had to quiet him. Boji kept bouncing and screaming, and Cajeiri hoped that Nomari, lodged down the hall, could not hear it—it sounded as if they were murdering the little wretch, who, if ever he escaped his cage, had a suite full of precious, fragile things to bound onto and away from.

It had been a mistake to bring Boji, who could not be let out of his cage, and who was unhappy about it. He had not settled, and now the weather, threatening storm, had him entirely overwrought. It was only going to get worse.

"Move his cage back to the servant passage," he suggested to Eisi and Liedi, since they had put Boji's massive cage right next to one of the tall windows—for Boji's pleasure, as they had thought at the time. Thunder and lightning would not make Boji happier, that was becoming clear, and with Mother coming—

With Mother coming, it was going to be even worse. He had offered to Uncle to vacate the grand suite, which was usually Great-grandmother's when she was visiting. This suite was

right across the hall from Uncle, who would not appreciate Boji's screeches either, and his own usual, more modest suite was
down the hall, where he would be perfectly content to be.

Except Nomari was in that one right now, because they could
not guarantee his safety otherwise, and besides—that suite
could not accommodate his double bodyguard, as this one could.

Besides all *that*, Uncle said that in strict protocol he should
stay put, because he was his father's heir, now, and *outranked*
Mother.

That disturbed him. That deeply disturbed him, as something unbalanced in the world. He and his mother had not gotten along so well as they ought, but she was his mother, and she
should have respect, especially since—the thought even more
disturbed him—she probably had been born in this very suite,
when her mother had been the highest-ranking person in the
house, excepting only Lord Tatiseigi.

He had never thought of that before, and the thought made
the rooms seem haunted with the past, a stolen baby, a marriage that had gone wrong and led to everything else.

Uncle was having the servants open up the upstairs floor,
which was repaired since nand' Bren's aishid had blown up the
floor. There, too, an important person had died—but not a person he was sorry about.

If one began to total up people who had been born here and
people who had died in Tirnamardi, naturally and otherwise, it
was a lot of people, and the whole place was full of ghosts.
Grandfather had lived here. Grandmother had died here, well,
on the lawn, near the gates.

It thundered and Boji screeched, just as Eisi and Liedi began
to move his cage. Boji went on screeching as the massive cage,
as tall as they were, and twice as long, rolled over the ancient
tiles, the brass wheels doing, he fervently hoped, no damage to
the floor. Cajeiri stayed as he was, by the window, but back a
little, close enough to see the sky, which still was cloudless on
this side of the house.

But that was not what was piling up to the southwest. He had seen that dark gray line from the windows in the great hall, before he came up to change for dinner.

He was such a fool to have brought Boji on this trip. A fool to have him here, a problem in the heart of important problems.

He was a fool to think he could go anywhere, ever, without just his arriving tipping over some small situation into big problems. He wished he could be like Great-grandmother, or Father, and have the means to solve them himself. Right now—

Right now it was comforting that he had the senior aishid. Father had said—for your sake and for the juniors, both, it was a good idea, and now, since talking to Father, he kept hearing that warning over and over again, thinking that, yes, his young aishid would do their best, but it was true they could also get killed trying to protect him.

They had been, at times, his accomplices in doing things he knew were slightly forbidden—but now he was thinking not only that he had been selfish and stupid to bring Boji and keep his staff busy with a spoiled and unhappy parid'ja, but that if he did something else stupid on this visit he could get his bodyguards killed, especially the juniors. It was not just that they were responsible for him. He was responsible for *them,* and when things became this serious, they could only hope he used his good sense.

So he waited patiently, not standing any closer to the window than his senior bodyguard said was acceptable, and let his valets move Boji back where at least the lightning and thunder would be less scary for him. He waited to let his valets also see to a dress shirt and coat for dinner.

Mother was coming. He was worried for her safety just in getting from the train station tomorrow. He *hoped* Mother and Great-grandmother would not have a towering fight when Great-grandmother arrived in Shejidan, which would set both of them into a bad mood.

He was trying so hard not to be angry with the whole situation, and to keep a pleasant expression on his face. His young bodyguard took the initiative to bring him his vest and coat, since time was short and his valets were still trying to settle Boji in what had been the quiet of the service hall.

His staff was clearly doing the best they could. He had brought Boji here because he had not wanted Boji upsetting his mother while he was gone, and he had not wanted to leave his valets again in Shejidan with the sole and lowly duty of caring for a spoiled fool's spoiled pet. Everything he saw going wrong on this trip was a chain of his small personal decisions—*because* he had not been willing to accept all the responsibility his father had settled on him. Because he had wanted one piece of his foolish childhood to stay with him on this trip and he had wanted to enjoy the part of his birthday celebration he had not gotten before the whole Shishogi affair had happened. He had been thinking only of his own affairs, and not thinking through, entirely, that from the time Father sent him on his own, Father had expected him to think ahead and not backward.

Well, between his bringing Boji and his going out to see Jeichido, he had certainly failed in that.

Father had said—listen to his senior aishid, to protect the junior one. Father had never expected Great-aunt Geidaro to show up. Father had never expected Ajuri to make a scene, or refugees to be camped on the lawn. And he supposed that it was a certain degree of trust—or a concern for making things worse—that Father had not sent a swarm of Guild here to bring him home.

Father had not. And things were not going to settle soon, he feared. They were likely to get worse, as early as tomorrow.

He and Mother did not get along that well. And worse, there were times when Mother and Uncle did not get along that well.

And there was the question what would happen when Mother did meet Nomari, and what truth might come out, much as he wanted to know it.

There were questions he wanted to ask Nomari before Mother

took over and barred him from asking or hearing. And he could hope to show up early at table, and hope that Nomari did.

Or he could, if he and his aishid could turn him out ready for dinner a little early, catch Nomari in private, with no question of dinner-table propriety.

Maybe it was stupid and even a mistake that could hurt the situation. Maybe it was smarter to let Mother, who knew things, do all the asking. But if he never asked, given Mother's tendency to keep her secrets to herself—he might never know, and he *needed* to. If he was supposed to rank higher than Mother, if he had someday to make decisions, he *needed* to, did he not?

Eisi and Liedi came back at least to be sure his coat and cuffs and collar were proper, and that he was turned out in a professional way.

"One is grateful, nadiin-ji," he said to them. "One so appreciates your patience on this visit."

They protested it was not patience. But it was. Everybody was patient. Everybody all his life had discounted his stupid mistakes because he was not the one allowed to decide the important things. Uncle handled things. And at least by noon tomorrow, Mother would take over, and Mother had her opinions, and she would very certainly say he was too young, and it was not for him to know.

But if he *never* knew, how could he ever make smart choices?

Mother had been born here. Grandmother had died here.

All the scary answers might be right down the hall.

He said, quietly, "I think I am ready. Nadiin-ji, I am going down the hall. I wish to talk to our guest."

"Yes," Antaro said, his junior bodyguard completely agreeing. The senior bodyguard was not all present—only Onami was. Onami simply gave a little bow and left to the rear of the suite, to report, doubtless, what he was up to.

He waited for Veijico and Lucasi to join them. And as they

arrived from their quarters, Onami came back with all his unit, Rieni still fastening his jacket.

Eight bodyguards. All just to go talk to his cousin, who, because of three missing people and an oncoming storm, was staying just two doors down from his.

But at least his senior bodyguard had offered no word of protest to the venture. He wondered—he could not help but wonder—what they were thinking about him, whether they were sending reports to the Guild—and he kept imagining what those reports might be. *The young fool went out and risked us all while he fed his mecheita. His spoiled parid'ja wakes the entire suite at night. He travels with the creature and imposes it on his uncle, who may be able to hear it. Now he ventures to disturb serious matters with unplanned questions . . .*

The question he had in mind was far from unplanned. He had worried about it, slept with it, dealt with his great-aunt over and over in his mind, and now he wanted to ask it.

He arrived at Nomari's door, where Uncle's guards stood.

"He is here, nadiin?" Cajeiri asked.

"Yes, nandi," the answer was.

"Advise my cousin I am forbidden to set aside any of my guard." That was a convenient excuse. If he was asking questions, all of them needed to hear the answer and judge it. "I wish to speak to him."

"Nandi." One of the men rapped on the door and opened it, and briefly passed the word inside, with the door standing ajar.

"Yes," he heard his cousin say, and when the door opened wider he walked in, finding Nomari with the servants Uncle had appointed for him, and evidently in the last stages of dressing for dinner. Nomari's coat was on. He looked composed enough.

"You are dismissed, nadiin," Cajeiri said to the servants. "I take responsibility. Thank you."

The two bowed and left quietly, amid, now, ten bodyguards, with the door still open.

"Is there news, nandi?" Nomari asked.

"Of the three missing?" Cajeiri asked. "No. One wishes there were." He thought of saying that his mother was coming. But he was not to do that. That was his mother's business. "I have a question, nadi. May we talk before dinner, very quickly? May we sit?"

"Nandi." Nomari indicated the little seating group, and offered a chair. Cajeiri sat, settled back, drew a deep breath.

"There are points of curiosity," he began, "and one thing I want to know. *Who* killed my grandfather? And why?"

Nomari's glance was direct, quick, wary, before he lowered his eyes in a slight bow. "In all respect," he said, "I—have no way to know that."

"But you might make a guess, might you not?"

Nomari hesitated, gave what might almost have been a laugh, but was not. "Shishogi," he said. "Shishogi. Shishogi. That is my understanding, nandi, at least—that is my guess for whatever went on."

It was his own guess, too. It had been ever since he had known Shishogi existed. It was so simple and likely an answer. But he distrusted it. He distrusted every quick answer that lacked detail. "But why would Shishogi be upset with him? Did my grandfather tell him no on something?"

"I would not know, nandi."

"I cannot know, either," he said. "So I cannot be sure that it *was* his order. Why would he? My grandfather had quarreled with my father, and he had become unwelcome in our apartment, and in the Bujavid, but was a quarrel like that enough? Everybody quarrels. And quarrels end. Was that the reason? I do not think so."

"One simply, nandi, guesses. That is all we ever can do."

"I am nine. I am *not* stupid. Neither are you. You can say it so *I* will understand."

Nomari gave a deep nod. "Then I most earnestly beg your pardon, young aiji. I was about three when your grandfather brought your mother to Ajuri, and I was not supposed to ask about that. There were always a lot of things no one was supposed to ask. I grew up with those rules. I was never supposed to talk about certain people. I was never supposed to ask questions about anybody except inside, with the doors shut, and then my parents would say I would know when I was older. By the time I was your age, I began to think not every clan was like ours and I began to think my parents were afraid of something. I had no idea what they feared, but I was shut out of discussions, and when I asked my brother, he said I should not ask questions, that if I ever needed to know something, our parents would tell me. My brother said everything was safe unless I brought trouble down on us with too many questions, or if I went listening at locked doors."

That was scary, Cajeiri thought. He well understood listening at closed doors—or having his bodyguard or staff do it—and hearing far too many worrisome things.

"Until I came here," Nomari said, "Shishogi was a name no one mentioned—ever—in the family. Ajuri were in the Guild. In many guilds. And still are. And people said we had a powerful man somewhere in the Guild. But I never heard that name mentioned. People would say, 'there is a whisper' that this should happen, or that 'there is a whisper' that something should not. People would say, 'we have eyes high in the Guild,' and people would say that if Ajuri wanted something done it could be done, that though we were a small clan in size, we could dictate to other clans who would be lord, who would marry and not, but we should never say who had done it. I thought—at a certain time I thought myself wise and cynical. I thought it was just our small clan trying to be important. But when my father heard me saying that, he said I was a fool, that I should be quiet and do what others did and not draw attention to our household, that we had troubles enough, and people who were too independent disappeared. That scared me, but I asked my father why we put up with such things, and he said that I was not old enough or wise enough to know what I was saying. That was one thing. I found out later—" A little breath. "I found out later that my father had tried to support Lord Benedi, and when Lord Benedi went down—so did my house. And I ran, and became one of the clanless, and tried to be wiser."

"Where was my mother, then?"

"She also left. That winter."

"What did you know about her?"

"From the first, that she came with secrets around her, things I should not ask, and I was supposed to avoid association with her."

"But you knew her."

"I did. She was younger. I watched out for her as we got older. I was afraid she would get hurt. Your grandfather kept her very close, but she was good at getting out past the precautions."

That was interesting. He thought he might have gotten that talent from Father. But no, then. From *Mother.*

"How did my grandmother die?"

Nomari went very still for a moment, wary. "I do not know, nandi. In all truth I do not know. She had just given birth. *Why* she was out riding, what prompted that decision—is a question to which I have never heard the answer. It is my understanding she fell. How—I have never heard either."

Cajeiri let the question lie there a moment more, and Nomari said:

"Nandi, your grandfather was a cipher to everybody. He was difficult. He came back with his newborn daughter in his keeping and with Lord Tatiseigi angry at all Ajuri. First there was an alliance. Then there was a lasting feud. Your grandmother was dead, Lord Tatiseigi was an enemy, and your mother was brought up Ajuri."

"Explain it. Explain everything, Cousin. This is important."

Nomari went expressionless for a moment, then let his face show worry. "I am no judge. I was a boy myself, too young to understand. Understand, I am only three years older than your mother, so my memory around the events is very slight."

"Explain to me what you know. Or what you have heard."

"This, then, nandi. Komaji-nandi was never expected to be lord. He was sent to marry out, for an alliance, a contract marriage with your uncle's sister. The agreement was to produce, first, an Atageini child—an heir, your uncle having had no luck in that way; and a second child, an heir for Ajuri clan, a tie that would firm up the associational ties. But you know what happened. . . ."

"I do *not!* That is the difficulty. My *uncle* does not! Do you?"

"Whisper is," Nomari said, "that that name in the Guild—Shishogi—sent orders. That the match was his plan. That your uncle had no children, likely *would* have no children, and that the Atageini bloodline would fail, excepting Lord Tatiseigi's sister. The politics of the time—Atageini always dominated Padi Valley politics . . . being a larger clan, being constantly involved with Kadagidi and even Dur, and feuding with Taiben, while Ajuri, being small, simply got along as best we could. Ajuri—the plan was, as Ajuri in general knew it, to assure that a future lord of the Atageini would have Ajuri blood, and conversely that there would be an Ajuri with Atageini blood, to tie us more closely to Atageini, in the heart of the Association. By what Ajuri has ever said about the affair, that was the intent. And it might have been a good idea. But—what I have heard, what I hesitate to say—is that the marriage was a deception from the start. That it was never Shishogi's intent to supply your uncle an heir. That he ordered Komaji to bring your grandmother and the child to Ajuri. And that Komaji, unable to persuade her, killed her, and took the child, your mother."

He had hoped for better. "So Grandfather killed her."

"One is not certain of that, nandi. It is well possible that he did *not* kill her, even possible that there really *was* an accident, but more likely Shishogi had those in place who *would* kill her. At that point, Komaji, your grandfather, was suspected of the act. He had no place of refuge *but* Ajuri, and no way of escape but to take the child while the house was in turmoil and run for Ajuri, rather than face your uncle. How he passed the gate, how he managed to escape—it is possible there were indeed persons other than your grandfather involved and that he had help. It would have been difficult, however it was done, but he did arrive in Ajuri. Lord Tatiseigi at that point might have had less enthusiasm to recover a half-Ajuri child and acknowledge a legal tie that your grandmother's death had already broken. Your uncle hated Ajuri from that time. There was no peace— until your mother found her own way back. She ran away from Ajuri in Shejidan, at the Winter Festival. She went to your uncle's tent, and forswore Ajuri."

"For a few years." He knew that part. "Then she ran away and went back to Ajuri, but she did not stay. She left again. Why?"

"Perhaps," Nomari said, "it was man'chi for her father that brought her."

"She had none." He was relatively sure of that. "But she had also quarreled with Uncle. One has no idea over what, except Uncle's rules."

"Perhaps it was confusion. Perhaps there were too many stories about what had happened. I would not venture to guess, nandi, I would not, in that matter. And all that I have said—all this is what I heard inside my family, not in the clan at large. One never said these things aloud. Only in bits and pieces and whispers."

"My grandfather," Cajeiri said, "was assassinated. That is a fact."

"Yes," Nomari said. "I have no doubt."

"He was coming in this direction. Uncle thinks he might have been coming here. But he could also have been trying to reach the Kadagidi."

"I would not think it was the Kadagidi."

"Why not?"

"Shishogi's chief ally was in charge there."

It fit. Everything fit with what he remembered.

"Do you think," Cajeiri asked, "that there are still Shishogi's people operating inside Ajuri?"

"I think they recently came to call, nandi."

Great-aunt Geidaro. And, regrettably, Meisi, Dejaja, Caradi, all the house, families deeply entangled with Kadagidi, in all senses.

One last question. "If Uncle were to back you, and Father *were* to name you lord—how would you take the lordship?"

"I would not walk into the hall and expect Geidaro's welcome," Nomari said. "I would hope to have Guild help . . . honest Guild help. I would take their advice. I would establish safety for well-meaning people within the house. I would ask Guild help to extend that over villages and towns, but that is much slower coming."

It was not bad. It was what he would do. But he was nine. He was almost moved to say, "I think you should talk to my great-grandmother," but *that* would not be a good idea. Mani could keep him alive and shake Ajuri to its foundations.

But *Mother* was the one with an interest in the Ajuri lordship, and by what he had heard on the phone, Mother would never forgive mani if she did interfere.

About Mother's safety—or her ability to deal with Ajuri and stay safe—he was far from certain.

He was far from certain he had even yet gotten all the truth in Nomari's answers. But they were out of time.

His whole bodyguard had heard . . . including Guild so senior they could call right to the Guild Council and check out any story as fast as people could possibly move. He already knew there were holes in the account about his grandfather, but then—so many people had died, and left everybody to figure out what had really happened. Even Uncle had not been in the house when Grandfather had doubled back and stolen Mother from her crib. None of the servants had questioned. They had thought Grandmother was dying out by the gate and had asked for her baby.

Grandfather had been such a man—who could have murdered Grandmother. Grandfather, at very least had breached the contract of the marriage and stolen Mother from the clan that should have brought her up.

It sounded like Shishogi's doing, to be sure that the only heir Uncle had was brought up Ajuri, so that they could play politics twenty years on, and little Ajuri clan could gain a voice of influence in Atageini, the largest clan and the oldest in the midlands. He believed that part. He frankly did not think Grandfather ever thought more than three moves ahead. Greatgrandmother would have slaughtered him at chess. He wished it all *had* been done on a chessboard, and wished he could have met his grandmother, and wished that Mother had not had so much unpleasantness to find out about her father.

"Do you think," he asked Nomari, "that my mother was happy with her father?"

"I think," Nomari said, "nandi, that she was less happy as she grew older. Komaji protected her. I know that. He was very particular who came near her, but she—hated being confined. She excelled at finding ways to slip out. We did talk, now and again. She always asked me things about goings-on in the house—cross-checking what she was told, I always thought, and she would never argue with what I said. She just listened, and sometimes she frowned. I never called her father a liar. But I was afraid for my own house if I told her some things. She thought Lord Tatiseigi had not wanted her. That he had blamed Komaji for her mother's death, and that he had been so bitter he had threatened Komaji's life and sworn he would give your mother to the Assassins."

"To the Guild, you mean. To *be* Guild."

"To be Guild and not to know what her clan was."

It was a way that unwanted children could be handed off, and the Assassins were a refuge of the clanless. So was Transportation, the other oldest Guild besides the Merchants. It was an outrage to do that to someone, to make them wonder all their lives.

It was a lie, what Komaji had said about Uncle, but what could Komaji say? That she was *stolen* from Atageini? She would have set out walking. Mother hated secrets—when other people had them.

It rang true. It truly made sense.

He stood up. He had a moment ago gotten a slight signal from Antaro, who was keeping track of the time.

"We should go down to dinner," he said to Nomari. There was, as there had been often in the last few moments, a muttering of thunder in the west.

8

"Their fluency is greater than most of the professors," Bren said to Tom Lund, regarding his three young visitors. Jeladi poured the after-dinner brandy. Tom Lund, portly, immaculate, and every inch the corporate power, had come to an on-premises dinner with Ben Feldman, whose slight untidiness, slight nearsightedness, and tweed coat looked to be anything but corporate power. Technicals, computers, plots: that was Ben, and no sane corporation would try to fit him in a suit. The two of them had been key to everything that had gone on in the early station restoration. They'd been partners with Gin and Kate, and were among the very first people he'd called on in the recent emergency.

So they'd walked away from corporate money and gone to work—again—for the President. For Mospheira. For the planet.

And right off, Tom had sent him—well, an *interesting* set of translators.

"I'm glad," Tom said. "I thought—they're either faking it, or not, and you'd know. There's apparently quite the little underground group going on, not happy with the Linguistics Department. As the Linguistics Department is not happy with them. They have meetings. Atevi dress, what I hear, is the option at meetings and events. And they haven't confined their membership to Linguistics students. They take all comers."

Including a baby sister. That was just a little scary, for a linguist who'd come up through the system. There was another time in history in which humans, newly arrived on the planet, had become enamored of all things atevi—had tried to *be* atevi. That had indeed led to massive miscommunication, and the Linguistics Department had long preached the doctrine that attempts to communicate to an alien biology had led to a war that had nearly wiped humans off the map.

But it was *other* attitudes, he was now convinced, that had done the deed, the presence of humans who, last down, had brought weapons into the equation, and worse, believed that they could take over and administer a situation that the first-arrived had been managing inexpertly, to their way of thinking. In so doing, they had unknowingly voided all agreements the first-arrived had made with the atevi lords.

Theirs had been a way of thinking not unrelated, in the modern Mospheiran mind, to the Reunioners who'd bollixed up alien contact and wanted a share of their station, their own having been taken over.

In some measure it was true: Reunioners were responsible for much of what had happened in alien contact. But it was not an attitude unique to Reunioners. He was surer of that than he was of sunrise.

And he was equally sure not all the early mistakes had happened on the human side of the map, just as humans hadn't made the only mistakes in the Reunioners' dealings with the kyo. By no means.

A war *because* of trying to communicate?

Not in essence. A war because of a lot of things that would have been worse had they not been able to talk. And it had taken two hundred years of foot-dragging on both sides of the strait before they'd decided to communicate, really communicate.

But there *were* indeed some words humans shouldn't take lightly or use carelessly with atevi, and vice versa.

"I did caution them against involving the Reunioner kids anywhere near their organization," he said, "and I hope that caution holds. Even against the kids' own wishes. The *object* of having them here is to make the children Mospheiran."

"Then being Mospheiran has to be equally attractive," Ben said. "Granted Mospheira has a lot to offer, in terms of tweaking the right instincts. But honestly, Bren, aren't they another step over the line? Won't they be? Someday *they'll* be making the decisions. They'll hop over any barriers we set."

"Just let's not have the three students throw the gate open prematurely. The group scares me a little. I could wish we did understand each other better. But in a crisis, in a fit of emotion, we still do things for different, gut-deep reasons than atevi do— it's not the thinking part of the brain that makes the decisions. And on both sides of the strait, there are people who just don't see that there's another way to react . . . some that can't accept that there's not one true way for everybody that's a proper being. And there're always some that just don't spend that much time thinking."

"Type A predominates in Linguistics," Ben said wryly. "There's going to be a lot of resistance, a lot of upset experts. God, they do hate change over there."

"I've noticed that," Bren said wryly.

"Ultimately, however," Tom said, "change will happen."

"Best in space," Bren said. "That's the place where, if ever the lines come down, they will come down safest, the way they're coming down in Central, where people have to work together doing the same job, for the same reasons, even if they don't meet. But atevi don't want it to happen down here, and that's their right. And regarding the dress, the more humans look *like* atevi, the more atevi expect reactions humans don't have, and vice versa. That part we always have to be aware of, and allow for, in people who have *their* right to their own feelings."

"That man'chi business," Ben said.

"That man'chi business. That friendship business. That romantic love business. Parental love. With atevi, man'chi seems to cover most everything and clan covers the rest. I understand man'chi. I just don't feel the directionality of it, though Jago informs me if I attempt to shield my aishid from gunfire again she will personally shoot me, which does make sense. Intellectually."

Mild amusement.

"I did ask my aishid—" At the moment Banichi and the rest were in their own bedroom, likely enjoying a rare relaxation of their own, in this doubly secure place, with trusted allies behind closed doors. The conversation was all Mosphei', and they had satisfied courtesies at a shared dinner. "I asked their opinion about the three lads from Linguistics. They're like me, amused, a little worried, a little touched. If there's to be change, I think—let it come from the station. Leave the cultural hearts of the island and the continent untouched. We need to be what we are, at home. And there needs to *be* a home, to satisfy our instincts. I think that wisdom will win out."

"I'll caution them," Ben Feldman said. "But the background check—I started running that when Tom told me about them— they're clean. One's an honor student; one—Lyle—is on academic probation, a downturn in marks after a series of perfect scores. Evan's hopped from bio to languages. Family background's ordinary, not affluent, no criminal records in any generation. Parental occupations are grocer, small-business bookkeeper, child care, farmer, fireman, and artist. Varied. But nothing stands out as a problem."

Ben never dropped a stitch. No matter what the job of the moment. At the moment he had Presidential security on tap, and he'd clearly used it.

"Have you talked to Kate?"

"Mmm, yes," Tom said. "Kate's running her own background checks—on the construction crew at Heyden Court. She's had a little problem, a little graffiti, and she's spitting fire."

"That isn't good." Graffiti under the circumstances might betoken something far more serious. "I take it this had implications."

"A hand imprint," Tom said. "The hand is something that turned up during the coup on the mainland. It's been connected to the Heritage Party, but they insist it's not theirs, that it's a different group. When you preach opposition to working with the aishidi'tat, odd thing, all sorts of creatures get into bed with you. It is disturbing. They haven't found any sabotage. Possibly it's someone opposed to the Reunioners, with no disposition to actually do anything, but it's certainly no joke and Kate's not amused."

"I'm not terribly surprised," Bren said, "but it's sad it turned up so early."

"Sad isn't Kate's word for it," Ben said.

"I'm sure I'll hear about it. She was supposed to be here for dinner. Called to beg off until late. Now I know the reason."

"I'm not surprised."

"So when did this graffiti happen? Why didn't she say?"

"Turned up this morning. I think she's figuring you've got enough on your list and it needs Mospheiran resources. She's called the President, had his people on it, the same ones that'll be running security once the project's on the ground. They're interviewing everybody that was on site, and they're making it clear that licenses are at stake. Information is tentative, but they know what shift was where. They're developing a timeline to confirm it, and, odd thing that bit these characters in the rear back during the Troubles, *hands* are pretty uniquely identifiable. I'm sure they'll get the one responsible and follow leads under whatever door it takes."

Opposition hadn't wasted time. "I hadn't heard of these people. Shows how long I've been away from the island. Why a hand?"

"It started out as a labor protest," Tom said, "when we were using non-union workers on the docks, dealing with shipments during the coup. It spread to opposition to us aiding the Guild on the mainland at all. It doesn't even seem to represent a specific group—more like upset individuals, random acts of dissatisfaction with atevi contact."

"Possibly the same sentiment," Ben said. "Possibly expanded now to mean opposition to the Reunioner landing. It's at least not friendly to the project at Heyden Court, and the workmen do know the guts of that building, so it's a security issue, even if it's just some sort of labor discontent. It could be just that. But considering the project—"

"To say the least," Bren said. "It's worrisome."

"The project's bound to be a magnet for troubles," Tom said. "But we'll handle it. I understand you're going to be talking to the security team, setting up a system. Something about new equipment."

"My bodyguard will talk to them. I'll translate. The Guild doesn't usually discuss its methods. But there is going to be at least this small exception. They're handing security a plan and a set of principles for perimeter control that I think they'll understand fairly readily. And thank you, incidentally, for the blueprints."

"Easy to do. We'll be receptive to any advice."

"There will be some," he said. "We're moving fast. We're moving blindingly fast. That alone is going to put Heritage on edge. It's my sincere hope to have the publicity around the kids die back quickly, as nothing happens. But I'm sure there are those who are working in other directions."

"We can be very sure of that," Ben said. "The hate messages have started. Ironically, the head of *Linguistics* seems to be getting them, as, in the beliefs of some who haven't listened well for years, the person in *charge* of your actions. Some are just irate. A few include threats of harm."

He actually felt sorry for the unpleasant chairman of Linguistics, who would not be used to such things. It was also, considering the personalities involved, complete irony. "He should hand them all to the new security team," he said.

"Preferably unopened." It was a matter of evidence on the envelopes, tracing problems, determining their severity. "Tell him that—and don't say the suggestion came from me, or he'll never listen. He should definitely let security handle it."

Cajeiri had very carefully not told Nomari that Mother was coming.

Neither did Uncle mention it at dinner, or after, when they took brandy by, this evening, a small fire in the hearth, given the slight damp chill. It was warm and cheerful in the great room. But the storm that had threatened was coming in, and the wind was driving rain against the windows so hard one might fear for the glass.

"That may be hail," Nomari remarked.

"I should not be surprised," Uncle said. "But then you do know the local weather."

"I remember storms, yes, nandi. One when I was six, I think, that took a number of the tiles off Ajiden's roof."

"Ah, yes, that one. We lost tiles as well." Uncle's humor improved with the shared recollection. He had been a little preoccupied, perhaps, Cajeiri thought, worrying about the other sort of storm to come, when *Mother* arrived in the morning. Uncle nodded, remembering, and began to say something when the lights went out, putting them into total blackness except for the candles.

Everything was suddenly antique, gilt, and carved lilies atop the pillars, lit solely by the two candelabras in the sitting area.

"Oh, pish," Uncle said. "The transformer has just gone. Staff should start the generator in a moment. Country living has its inconveniences."

"It is such a magnificent hall," Nomari said, "from this vantage."

"One is gratified," Uncle began to say, but then a distant mecheita squalling sounded, and all about the space, black-uniformed Guild reacted subtly, hearing that, reading signals on the bracelets Guild wore, small sparks of light in the flickering shadows. Thunder rumbled and cracked.

And Guild shifted suddenly, entirely on guard, some headed for the stairs.

Cajeiri's bodyguard moved up and simultaneously Rieni touched Cajeiri's arm, a signal to get up, quickly. Cajeiri did that, seeing bodyguards similarly moving about Uncle, and others around Nomari.

"We are quite peaceful here," Uncle said sharply. "Forget us! What is going on with the stable?"

"The stable gate, nandi," someone said, and Cajeiri caught his breath, seeing all the possibilities of disaster unrolling in the peals of thunder. "The grooms have retained three. They are trying to saddle."

"Gods unfortunate!" Uncle swore as Cajeiri had never heard the old man swear. "Fetch my riding crop! Why is that cursed generator not going? Boy! *Nephew!*"

"Nandi!" Cajeiri said.

"Stay here."

"My people," Nomari said.

"Stay here, stay safe, nadi, and do not trouble my staff!" Uncle headed out into the dark, Guild attending, going toward the broad stairs.

"Are they loose?" Cajeiri asked his own bodyguard what seemed obvious, but the information was scant. "Are they loose on the grounds?"

"Yes," the answer came from Antaro.

"Go, you and Jegari. I have enough protection. Go! Help my uncle!"

"Yes," Antaro said, and she and her brother separated themselves into the dark, joining the shadows that were Uncle with his bodyguard going down the central stairs by flashlight.

Three mecheiti retained. The rest of the mecheiti had escaped the gate onto the grounds, and one dreaded to hear any worse disaster. The stables were at the rear of the house—the

Ajuri tents were in front, and there was no barrier, none, but a small modern hedge and a flimsy gate that let onto a garden path beside the house. The greater grounds had no fence but the massive ancient hedges.

"I am going to the windows," Nomari said, getting up, and Cajeiri did likewise, but Guild bodies separated them at that broad expanse. There was nothing to see. The beveled panes reflected candlelight, and outside was a rain-spattered sparkle of lighted canvas, with the whiter flash of lightning.

"I have to go out there," Nomari said.

"No," Cajeiri said, shivering in the urge to go with Uncle, to do everything he could—which was to do *nothing.* "No, we should stay here."

"Cousin, . . ."

"Cousin, *I* would be out there, too. My mecheita is surely with the herd. But I do not ride the herd-leader. We cannot help. Two of my aishid are Taibeni. I have sent them, and that is all I can do. We can do nothing running out there in the dark but attract the mecheiti's notice and lead them to the tents."

"Or lead them in another direction," Nomari said, and turned from the window, headed away.

"No," Cajeiri said. "Nadiin, stop him!"

Guild moved, not with firearms, but moved. Nomari dodged and made it nine steps into the great hall, toward the stairs, but Veijico and Lucasi, among the foremost, were equally quick. Uncle's guards, who were assigned to Nomari were there, too, and seized on Nomari, who fought to get free.

Cajeiri drew a deep breath, afraid, afraid things were going to go terribly wrong, but they would not be helped if Nomari tried to draw off the mecheiti—it was something the grooms might try. Those out there would be bending every effort to keep the mecheiti from reaching the tents in front of the house, but mounted, it was risky enough to do. He was scared for Uncle, who stood the best chance of getting the herd-leader in hand, but there were few places anybody afoot could climb up out of reach, and one slip on muddy ground out there could be the end. It was a terrible way to die.

Thunder crashed, time—time dragged by, and now there were voices in the lower hall, distinctly voices, he was sure of it. A gust of wind flattened the candle flames. Doors had opened.

"Staff has run out to warn the people," one of Uncle's guard said from near the windows. "Nandi, one cannot see, but there is a light—they may be at the tents."

"Gods," Nomari said.

Moments passed, terrible moments. There was no repetition of the gust. There was only the occasional coded communication. And they were still in the dark. In the chaos, nobody was attending the generator.

It seemed quiet, however. It was still quiet, when a splintering crash sounded from the side of the house, far and faint, but that was, Cajeiri thought, the garden gate.

"They are not holding them," Nomari said in distress.

"Nadi," one of the Guild said, "our lord is in charge out there. He has mounted up, he has ridden out with the grooms. The herd has broken through. Our lord is attempting to get to the fore of it."

Likely riding one of the habitual hindmost, Cajeiri thought distressedly, trying to make a lower rank mecheita run between the herd-leader and the vulnerable tents, trying with voice and quirt to get the herd-leader to turn. The leader would have been the *first* out an open gate, and Jeichido and the other leaders right with him.

"He is risking everything," Cajeiri said, trying to satisfy Nomari. "He knows the mecheiti. They know his voice. He will try to distract the herd-leader and turn him back. Staff will have the stable gate open." He could see in his head everything that would be going on out there. He knew how Uncle had to get a lesser mecheita to cross the herd-leader's path and, if possible, physically turn him. He had read how it was done. He had never seen it done, and it was a wild chance. Uncle was too old to take a fall. And he was risking it, risking the tusks—even peace-capped, dangerous. "He is good, Cousin. He is a very good rider. And Antaro and Jegari are out there—if anything can be done on the ground, they can do it."

"Gods," Nomari said, hands clenched together.

Lightning flash overwhelmed the candles, casting darting shadows. Thunder shook the ancient window, assaulted the ears. The glass was awash with water.

Uncle, Cajeiri thought, Uncle, be safe! Be careful!

Just then the lights came on full in the area, and in the great hall beyond. It was no relief. It reflected back off the windows, making it impossible to see out.

"Let me go down," Nomari said, "only as far as the main doors."

"It is not safe, nadi," Uncle's guard said. All about were grim faces, Veijico and Lucasi with their two companions at risk, Uncle's guard desperately concerned and on edge.

A downstairs door opened, a gust of wind that stirred draperies and extinguished candles. There came shouts from outside, muffled by storm and stone, more than one voice.

Cajeiri looked to the man by the windows, who had turned to try to see. That man exchanged words with someone on Guild communications, then turned to them. Veijico and Lucasi stayed close by, never leaving him. Rieni and his unit were there, communicating with someone, but not saying what they heard.

"They have turned them, nandi, nadi, they are moving across to the north side. Our lord has turned them. They are going around to the orchard, and through that to the stable. The gate is open, the staff has put up a barrier to close off the way beyond. There are two tents down, but others stand. They did not go through the camp."

Nomari folded his arms and bowed his head, never having budged from where he stood.

It was too soon to ask who was hurt. It was very likely, with two tents down, that someone was.

It was also too soon to ask how the mecheiti had gotten out

a gate that was built to frustrate mecheita cleverness and mecheita strength. It was a heavy latch, a deep and solid socket, and the latch was on the outside with no way out of the pen except to climb the rails once that gate was shut. Mecheiti were not built to climb rails, but they could reach high.

"Is Uncle's physician prepared, nadiin?" Cajeiri asked the guards. "One thinks he should be. Someone should bring the Ajuri into the lower hall in case the herd goes *around* the stable."

The guard hesitated, looking at him, estimating, doubtless, his nine-year-old self and whether anyone ought to listen to him.

"One asks," Nomari said. "One asks that."

"We do not know the nature of what happened, young gentleman, or who may be out there."

"Nevertheless," Rieni said. "The young gentleman is right. Bring them into the foyer. Establish the inside doors as a perimeter."

There was still hesitation, a glance exchanged, but seniority won. Uncle's guard, including those with Nomari, moved then, with some speed.

That left himself, his senior and half his younger aishid, alone with Nomari.

"One is grateful, nandi," Nomari said. "One is beyond grateful. Let me go down there."

"No, nadi," Rieni said. "We are spread too thin for the circumstances. We do not know that this was an accident." Thunder cracked, and lightning whitened the window. Cajeiri flinched, nerves on edge. "We are in a compromised condition as the main doors open, and as we have people scattered outside. Our concern is the young aiji's safety. That is paramount, nadi. Let us do what we can do."

"Nadi," Nomari said on an exhaled breath, and with a slight bow. He sank into a chair, and Cajeiri settled into his own— across from Nomari, if nothing else, to free his bodyguard of worrying about him *or* Nomari. Rieni set to making calls and giving orders.

The front doors opened: one could hear them. The secondary doors, at the landing below, remained closed. There would be people, likely Guild, running out to the tents to advise people to come to the steps, which themselves would afford protection. The foyer below, with the beautiful porcelain lilies, would hold everybody. He hoped they all made it. He hoped the haste down there would all be in vain, as Uncle and the grooms got the mecheiti back into their pen, and had the gate latched.

Worst of all would be if the herd went all the way around the stables and came full around the house again, escaping back toward the tents, with people out running for safety. He found himself shivering, knowing he had given the order, knowing Guild had backed it. It had been smart to do: that was Great-grandmother's question, always—figure it, what could go wrong, what could go right; and what could go wrong was the herd coming around again and seeing unprotected people running . . . that was the most terrible thing, and the herd could cross the back of the house so fast . . .

It seemed forever. But he heard voices down below, heard people there, frightened voices, no word distinct.

Nomari was listening to it, lips pressed tight, hands working, his eyes focused on nothing in particular. He was there in that place, at least in mind, maybe listening for voices he knew.

"Nandi," Veijico said, at Cajeiri's elbow. "We are hearing— there are injured. They are bringing them in. Guild are injured as well. We do not know who."

"Yes," he said.

And a moment later: "Nandi, the mecheiti are in. The gate is shut and latched."

He let go a breath, found his hands clenched. Great-grandmother would not approve. He relaxed his hands and his shoulders, relaxing his frown. "Did you hear?" he asked Nomari.

"Yes," Nomari said quietly, as voices continued in the foyer. "Thank you, nandi."

"I think Uncle would offer a brandy, if you wish."

"I shall wait," Nomari said. "I shall wait until I can drink it with Lord Tatiseigi."

That was politely said. Cajeiri nodded. "One hopes Uncle will be here soon," he said.

They waited. They had the number of the Ajuri, Rieni said, and their names, and they were identifying people in the foyer as rapidly as they could.

But still they had not had word about Uncle Tatiseigi.

Then Jegari came up from the stairs, alone, soaked and dripping. "All is well," he said. "The pen is shut."

"Uncle is all right." He said it from hope.

"He seems to be," Jegari said. "He took a battering." He had a grayness about his face, and looked, at the moment, shaken. "Taro has a minor break, we think, her lower arm. She will come up as soon as she can."

"She should go up to the suite," he said, dismayed. "Eisi and Liedi should attend her. She should not try to be on duty."

"She will argue, nandi," Jegari said. He was bloodied, soaked, his cheek scraped. Drops of water that fell on the marble floor were tinged with mud and blood, and Jegari was still breathing hard. "Nobody was killed, that we know. I should like to sit, nandi."

"Do! Please!" he said, Veijico and Lucasi both hastened to move a carved bench forward, and to urge Jegari to sit down, wet as he was. One of the house quietly came with a single cup of tea, and Jegari took it in his hands, sipped it, visibly shaking.

"Cold out there," he said, breath hissing. "One regrets, nandi. I am quite in order, just winded. Thank you."

"What happened?" Cajeiri asked, and Jegari drew in a deep breath, everybody listening, himself, Nomari, Veijico and Lucasi, the seniors, the servant standing close.

"We intercepted on foot," Jegari said, "from the garden supply—we thought there would be rope. There was. We met them coming round—we could not stop the foremost. I managed to get a loop on one, managed to get him aside and haul myself up while he was backing like a fool. Taro's shied into the garden gate, and next turnabout of my own, I saw she was up, and I thought she was all right. How she stayed on one-handed, I do not know, but there was not much choice. We chased after the herd. I had no quirt. I just used the rope end and tried to get up to the fore before they reached the tents. Lord Tatiseigi—he had ridden from the pen. He brought that little hindmost up with the leader. He outrode the grooms, and he shouldered the herd-leader—he stuck to him with heads swinging and dealing blows one could hear above the storm. I swear if he were a younger man he would have been on the leader, to cap all. As it was, credit to the grooms, he had a saddle under him and a quirt, they were behind him, and he drove that poor youngster, pushing the herd leader around and around. The youngster fought, gods, she had no choice, poor creature. I was afraid she would go down with him, and I know she will need stitches. A few Ajuri came out with flapping cloth—shirts, whatever, trying to keep the herd out of the tent row—but one mecheita ran afoul of a tent, which took down the tent and snagged the damned—excuse me—the rope." Jegari drew in a large breath. "The tent was dragging behind that fool, confusing everything, cutting right into the herd. The herd-leader turned to run across the front drive, and we had them going. We chased them around the corner to the orchard, and we feared they might go on beyond the stable to come round again, but they took the shorter path past the stable pens, and we had them. The house staff had opened out the gate and set carts and kitchen tables, I know not what more in the gap, all the way to the house. The herd turned into the pen and we had them. Staff swung that gate shut, and we slid down and let our mecheiti go in, excepting Lord Tatiseigi—he is with the physician, nandi. He fell, getting off. He swears he is all right, and he ordered the grooms to tend that little youngster, but we carried him in. Taro walked in on her own—it was the first I knew she was hurt. One of the grooms also took a battering, thank the gods for the peace-caps, and thank the gods we did not have to go around the house again."

"Nadi," Nomari said, "thank you. *Thank* you."

"It was a ride," Jegari said, and looked up as the servant quietly handed him another cup of hot tea. "Thank you, nadi. Can you find a towel? I should not be sitting anywhere."

"Stay seated," Cajeiri said. Jegari was wet as if he had swum a river, and there were small puddles gathering under his feet and beside him on the bench. "The people from the camp are all inside, safe. It was well done. It was very brave." He wanted Uncle to be all right, he wanted Antaro to be all right. He felt a chill himself, thinking that it had been a situation out there he could not possibly have helped—that he had not the strength or knowledge to have helped. Jeichido had surely been right at the head of it all, and he could not have done what others had done. "I should go see Uncle."

"No," Rieni said. "We can inquire from here. This is an established perimeter. Everything is in order. You are not to budge from here, young aiji."

"One understands," he said quietly. "Those people in the foyer. They probably need something warm. Tea. Blankets." He knew they could not open the doors and admit all those people upstairs, throwing Guild precautions into chaos. Thunder was still rolling, though it seemed farther now. One question occurred to him above all others, a question at the center of everything. He did not believe Uncle's grooms would have left that gate half-latched, with all the preparations they had made for the storm. "Three people missing, nadiin."

"We are calling roll right now," Rieni said, "of staff and guests. And checking surveillance. We are spread thin, given the situation. We have established zones and no one is permitted to move out of areas without notice. Light is not on throughout the house, and we understand it will not be on so long as we are on the generator, and the storm has some to run. We have no light in the upper floors or in the basement, none in the south halls."

"Eisi and Liedi."

"One is certain they are safe. There is a guard on that floor. We have advised Headquarters and we trust they will advise your Father that we are standing fast in a tenable position, and we will be much better once the power comes back on. Until information develops, we assume there was unlicensed intent in this, possibly aimed at disrupting your uncle's Ajuri guests, possibly intended to create confusion in which they could do targeted murder. We are in contact with Shejidan and we know that whatever this is, it is not a licensed operation. This is the situation, young aiji. They have handed us chaos, but this was a very risky operation for the perpetrators, if fear is all they planned to generate. If there is something yet to come, it has yet to manifest."

"Search the basement and storage," Cajeiri said, recalling the last time Tirnamardi had seen a crisis.

"We are doing that," Rieni said, "very particularly. Well-advised, young gentleman."

Onami said something in verbal code, and Rieni looked interested. "Where?" Rieni asked, and Onami said, "Near the orchard."

Then Rieni said, "We may be down to two unaccounted for. There is a body."

9

"I've met the boys," Kate Shugart said, over a late-hours brandy. They were alone in the sitting room, Banichi and the others being off in their bedroom with the thick lot of blueprints, making notes for their meeting with Mospheiran security. Kate had her casted leg propped on a footstool, and sat in the depths of an armchair Banichi found comfortable. She was graying blond at the moment, wore a turtleneck and, uncharacteristically, a skirt, which one assumed was easier with the cast.

Mountain-climbing. Kate hated boredom.

And hadn't hesitated at the job offer to oversee the entire Reunioner project.

"Your opinion of them?" Bren asked, in a chair opposite.

"Earnest lads. Whimsical. I've done a little inquiry of my own. They're on notice from the University not to instruct outsiders in Ragi . . . threatened with expulsion and legal action, in fact. The contraband vids—with subtitles—have proliferated out of library control. And they're really not happy about that."

There *were* laws restricting communication in Ragi to licensed translators. Old laws, broken routinely on docksides where trade went on, at airports where atevi pilots landed and refueled.

"The University isn't happy with them."

"Not with the dress, not with the hair, not with the open meetings. Outraged about the stolen vids, but they can't pinpoint a responsible party. Since their sponsor died, they're officially no longer a club. They're forbidden to put up posters. They're forbidden to pass out flyers, but they're still on the books as a University club, bound by University rules on pain of expulsion, and required to present member lists. Even if they're no longer a club."

"The University is going a bit over the edge."

"Mostly about the vids. They're requested those be turned in. It hasn't happened." A smile quirked Kate's mouth. "Oh, come, Bren, you've noticed the hair, the manners. You have ardent admirers. *Fans.*"

He so hoped the heat in his face didn't show. "They're attracted to the atevi style. The art—"

"The organized teas and the dress," Kate said with an arched brow. "They used to meet on University premises, in the library. Now they meet on their own, usually at private homes, and what's the Port Jackson police to do? Raid a tea party? We have absolutely no official word that *anybody* from the original University club has ever been caught in such an indiscretion, and the police *have* visited, but all they see is people in fancy dress, and the organizers, or those alleged to be organizers, certainly not hanging about to talk to the police. They grow their hair long, they have their private dinners, they occasionally carry weapons, which the police does take note of . . . but no one has ever been caught with ammunition, so again—" A shrug. A smile. "The club sprang up during your absence. The Linguistics Department has, for some odd reason, set a hair standard for admission to higher studies. And disbanded the club officially, while requiring they go on providing their membership lists, which I'm sure aren't inclusive of people not in Linguistics."

"I suppose I'll have created a controversy, taking on these three."

"Has that *ever* bothered you?"

"I've tried to minimize my disagreements with the

Department—well, generally. But in this case—better these three than somebody Wilson sends us."

"I'd agree."

"They're *not* to host teas in Heyden Court. I made that clear. And for God's sake don't go to one."

Kate grinned. "You *know* me."

"I do."

"Well, I'll be busy. I'm pretty sure I'll be too busy for that. Trust me."

"I do that, too."

"Have you heard from Sandra Johnson yet?" Kate asked.

"No."

"I have. We've been in contact, this evening for a long call. She's agreed. Says she's calling you tomorrow."

"That's very good news. She's had a concern about her family. About their future. Sensible fears. I have to put their welfare on your desk right along with those kids."

"We talked about that. She says her husband's a bit worried. But they're excited. Big opportunity for the kids. And actually *more* security. They've had brushes with problems from your past before—a little scary for them at times, and they're definitely a soft target."

"I'm sorry to hear that. She's never told me."

"Well, you weren't at hand when the major problem really came up. And they got through it. Two ways to react to that. Try for obscurity, or take an official position, with actual power. Ms. Johnson's not that much on power-wielding. But I've assured her I'm not at all shy of it."

He let go a long breath. "She's not shy when it comes to getting to responsible people. She's smoothed my path—gotten the unreachable out of the University and the State Department more than once. On the other hand, she is uprooting her family; and her husband and kids can't suffer for it."

"I know what she wants. She'll be *inside* the shell of normalcy. She'll create it. She'll be well ahead of kids' pranks *or* outside nastiness from outside the perimeter. She's dealt with *your* situation long enough to have very good antennae for what's not right, and *she's* not shy of acting on a suspicion. Her husband's no fool, either. Good choice, Bren."

"I hoped so. I very much hoped so."

"The remaining question is that trio of University rejects who'll be inside her security bubble."

He grinned at her. "I told her if they get out of line, turn them over to you."

"It's going to be a—"

The phone rang.

"Hold that thought," Bren said, stood up and picked up the phone.

"Bren," Toby said, an entirely unexpected voice out of the night. *"Bren, we're coming into dock, number 20. Can you send a car?"*

Toby. On *Brighter Days.* Coming in to dock. It was not planned. It was *nowhere* in the plans.

God, was the instant thought, with a cold chill. Something untoward had happened on the mainland. There had been weather out there—damage was possible—but he thought it had stayed to the south . . .

"Absolutely," he said, asking no questions over the phone. Toby broke the contact and he simply cleared the call from his end and called the desk. "A car, immediately to berth 20 on the dock. Number of passengers uncertain. Armed security, for their safety."

"When, sir?"

"Now," he said. "Also send a team to remain with that boat until it leaves, no one to board without the owner's clearance. And a third unit to escort the car."

"Fifteen minutes, sir."

Fifteen minutes, for Mospheira? His complaints had not gone unheeded. He might be gossiped about as an unreasonable and self-important autocrat, but they were moving on it.

Late, well into dark. Toby *might* have wanted the secrecy. But coming at all was a change in plans. And there was no way to ask what was going on until Toby came through the door.

"Advise the President that my brother's boat is coming in. It is not expected to be here. I'll talk to him. I'll call the President myself once I know the reason."

He hung up, and turned to see Kate limping her way to the exit.

"You know where to find me," she said, opened the door and closed it behind her.

"That woman," Uncle said, having settled in his chair, and his voice shook with rage. "*That woman* is behind this. I have no doubt. We are Filing Intent. We are Filing Intent against that disgraceful woman. See it done!"

Great-aunt Geidaro, Cajeiri thought. He had never heard anyone declare those terrible words, not seriously. They made a little knot in his gut and nested there, chilling as the thunder and the storm outside.

Uncle had arrived in an dreadful state: he had no coat, only a shirt cut up the sleeve, because his right arm was bandaged and in a sling, with blood seeping through the wrapping. His hair was wet and hanging in strings, the ribbon all draggled. The knee of his trousers was torn and likewise bloody, the side of his trousers stained with mud. Uncle was clearly in pain, the lines of his face gone deeper and in no pleasant set.

"Nandi," Nomari said—he had risen while Uncle's bodyguards saw Uncle seated and comfortable. "I offer most profound regret for the situation. Let me go to the foyer. My people—"

"Sit, *sit*, nadi. I insist you sit! Trust us to care for them. The less moving about the halls, the safer for everyone. The Guild has divided the house, and people moving between their zones on any authority *might* distract from things we should be watching. Guild is still searching the grounds, despite the weather. We are providing blankets, warm water, food, and drink, hot tea and brandy, all the comfort we can muster for your people. We will not turn anyone back out into the camp tonight. We are clearing the lower hall: staff are giving up rooms and beds for them tonight. Be content with that."

"Nandi." Nomari had already sunk into the nearest chair. "One is extremely grateful."

"We are obliged for our guests' understanding." Uncle was clearly in pain. The servant provided brandy, and Uncle took a left-handed sip and exhaled a long breath. "We have a dead man by the stable fence and two tents trampled into the mud, with their contents. We do not know the dead man's name, but we *believe* it was one of our three missing. How the herd got him, we may never know, but that latch can be stubborn at first encounter. They would have pressed that gate if they found a stranger working at it. His misfortune, to be sure."

The latch was shielded above to prevent clever mecheiti from working at it through the rails, and if the herd had detected someone out there, anybody working with it had better make the right moves fast. If that gate gave way, if one did not jump to the right, and get up the rails to the ladder that led up the stable wall, the only refuge else was the house entry, which was of course locked. The rails were not high enough, and the orchard was too far if he had not gotten a head start with a specific tree in mind.

If he had been knocked down at the gate—there was no chance.

Nobody who knew mecheiti would have risked it. Surely not.

"I am supposing we are one problem less, unmourned at least in this house." Uncle shrugged, and winced. "If the two other missing persons were anywhere near, the herd would have taken them down. It is a broad meadow, the rain is coming hard, and I do not want to send riders out until this lightning abates. There *are* gaps in our hedge. It is *not* as secure as we would wish, though we have patched the gaps with electronics, which go off for all sorts of reasons, usually four-footed. Guild is searching afoot. I hope we shall have answers by morning." With that, Uncle cast a meaningful glance toward Cajeiri.

Mother, Cajeiri thought uneasily.

She might not come. Guild had likely been reporting all of this, and Father and Guild Headquarters would know by now what was going on here. Rieni's unit was standing there, likely informing the Guild moment by moment, and Rieni might already have gotten an order to pack up, to get him back to Shejidan with or without Boji, storm or not. He did not want that. *He* could do nothing for Uncle, but his aishid already had helped, tonight, and his senior aishid was likely the best mode of communication Uncle had, not to mention their contact with the high levels of the Guild. And Father.

But Mother—was not going to be happy when she arrived. If she arrived. It might not be safe for her to come. It surely was not.

She would know that. Her bodyguard would know.

"As to your situation, nadi," Uncle said to Nomari, "I am considering it in a new light. I am still gathering information. But that woman will *not* continue in Ajuri, come what may."

"She is *my* enemy, nandi. I have never doubted that. She— and all her brood.'

What of my grandfather? Cajeiri wondered. He had never thought to ask that directly.

Grandfather had been Uncle's enemy. There was *no* question of that.

So many secrets. So many sides. So many people dead. Another one had died, tonight, even if it was just. And nobody was willing to say things in the open.

Someone should.

"My grandfather," Cajeiri said. "Was *he* ever your enemy, Cousin?"

"No," Nomari said at once. "No, nandi. He was not."

"It *is* a pertinent question," Uncle said. "A good question. What *was* your man'chi with Komaji?"

"I never knew him as a lord, nandi. I had left. I thought, when I knew he had taken the lordship, and the Troubles were ending—I thought—I hoped—he might truly be Ajuri's answer, but I admit I was surprised to hear he had stepped forward when Kadiyi died. I was *not* surprised to hear he was staying in Shejidan, and I thought he might manage to stay alive. But then I heard that Geidaro had come to Shejidan. I was not that surprised to hear it—but I began then to think that things had not changed and would not change in Ajuri. I thought—something will happen. Komaji has no power. He cannot get power. Geidaro is calling all the moves. I thought it then, and I—I thought maybe I should go to my guild and warn them, that maybe their leadership could tell others. But so many of the guilds had troubles. I thought—if there is anything to be known, they know. They surely know. Surely the aiji knows. And what do I know, in my own guild? And how do I interfere in the doings of lords? I might cross the aiji's plans. He might be gathering evidence. Or arranging to do something. And then Komaji was dismissed from court. All Ajuri were dismissed. It hardly seemed the time for another Ajuri to step into the light and say there was something wrong—everybody knew that, already. But I thought, when I heard he had gone back to Ajiden—Komaji will be dead within the year. And who else can they find to put up?"

We did not trust *Grandfather*, Cajeiri thought with a little chill. Grandfather was getting much too close to Mother. So was Geidaro—*much* too close. And all Mother's maids were sent away. Did *we* kill Grandfather, by sending them all home from court? Did *I* kill him, because I told Father he scared me?

"So you would manage Ajuri from the safety of Shejidan," Uncle said. "Is that your plan, nadi, should you gain the lordship?"

"I would hope for Guild protection in doing it, nandi," Nomari answered. "And I would *listen* to them. I am not trained to the lordship. I know it. I know that the Troubles extended inside the guilds, into the Assassins' Guild itself, but I hear—"

Nomari paused, and perhaps rethought something. Or decided to say it anyway. "I hear things are better. I know Ajuri has lost its chief voice in the Guild. I hear that there is a massive change in the Assassins' Guild—who, and why, and all that—I know no more than most people, I suppose, except that Ajuri's voice within the Guild is supposed to be dead. You likely know a lot more than I do, nandi, but I measure the change in the Guild by knowing that Shishogi is dead and that the Guild is now supporting the aiji. I know that the Kadagidi are out and no longer a threat. I know that people in general are not as scared as people were. People talk now in a way they never would when Murini was in power. The people who used to watch the train stations and take notes in the ticketing office are all gone—that, almost from the day the aiji came back. They ran, those scavengers. People travel now. People go on vacations, and visit relatives. That is *my* gauge, nandiin. That is what I want to happen in Ajuri. I have no family left to promote. All I have is those people out there. *They* are my concern. I am sure now, personally, that once I leave your house, the Guild is all that can keep me alive. I know I need help. And advice. The thought of going to the legislature and voting on laws scares me witless and I know I would feel like a fool. What do I know? But Ajuri cannot go on murdering its lords and killing people. Ajuri has had the wrong allies. I want better for us. I want us to *be* better."

Uncle nodded. "Well answered, that."

"I would join in you in Filing against Geidaro, if it would be of any use."

"No, nadi. I would counsel against complicating your claim to Ajuri with a legal action, which the Guild might deem had to be dealt with ahead of the other. We cannot do better than the Guild witnesses we already have to the woman's actions in this hall. Let us see what tomorrow brings."

"I bow to your expertise, nandi."

"My own aishid will transmit the Filing of Intent—to have it clear whence it comes. I shall sit here a time. I am not a placid man. But it is a momentous step, and an unpleasant one. Tomorrow—tomorrow, we shall see what the day brings. Young gentleman, will you wish to retire to your suite?"

"No, Uncle. I had rather stay where I am."

"So, well, be advised your great-grandmother's plane has arrived safely. We have that news. She is in Shejidan. I have every indication she will be hearing the business we have had this evening. She will be asking about your welfare. One suggests a message from you tonight, nephew, would ease her concern."

Cajeiri read between the lines of that one. Mani had landed with every intent of taking the train tomorrow, and Mother was packing to take the same train. It was possible security was so tight that Father had not told mani that she could not go.

It was possible that the situation had become so dangerous that Father would tell Mother to stay in Shejidan and let mani and her bodyguard come out to Tirnamardi after all. He could only imagine how his mother would react to that.

Worst of all would be if Father ordered *him* home. He did not think Father would have them bring Nomari in, not with questions unanswered, and with a downstairs full of innocent people attached. That would be dragging a lure right past the news services, and that would not be good for Nomari's situation. It would drop the untidy mess into Father's lap. And that was not good for anybody.

"I shall call her," he said, "before I go up to my rooms."

"Very well. You may retire, young gentleman. Escort our guest up, if you will. Nadi, there will be a guard in the hall all night, for your protection. By the misfortune of the scoundrel who loosed the mecheiti, we judge they are not highly skilled scoundrels, but we dare not make that generalization. Sleep in confidence that if there is trouble, it will not find us unaware."

"Nandi," Nomari said, and Cajeiri stood up, thinking that perhaps a phone call from him would not be the thing, after all, but his bodyguard could reach Cenedi, mani's Guild-senior, who would tell her he was perfectly fine.

"Come, nadi," he said to Nomari. And: "Uncle, please take care and come to bed soon." He had no doubt Uncle had an agenda as well, part of which was to File, on this stormy and infelicitous night, and not to start the day with it.

Send messages to Father? Very likely. Possibly to Great-grandmother, both through the Guild.

Second-hand communication would cool the response a little. But the situation would be the same: Mother and mani both demanding the Red Train to go to Tirnamardi in the morning.

He did not envy Father tonight, not in the least.

10

It was a fair wait, but the phone finally rang to advise that Toby Cameron and a Barbara Letterman were at the desk, with a parcel. Could Mr. Cameron confirm re the lady, and the parcel?

God, was she going under *that* name lately? "Absolutely," Bren said. "To both. Yes." Being inside Francis House was probably high on Barb's list of personal goals, just to know she'd been there—but it was a more practical matter: if Toby was coming ashore, he *didn't* want to leave Barb alone down at the harbor, just in case trouble happened to notice his brother was in port. The question was, had Shawn gotten his after-hours message, and was Mospheiran security guarding *Brighter Days* at dock the way he had asked?

He waited. Narani and Jeladi added a chair to the little sitting arrangement and added a few stones, for numerical balance, to the little arrangement on the table. Barb wouldn't notice. Probably Toby wouldn't. But it was polite, and it made atevi feel better.

A knock came at the door, and Jeladi let the two in, welcome faces, welcome smiles—at least it didn't seem a crisis. There were bows all round, atevi courtesy. The mysterious parcel, about the size of a loaf of bread or a few jars of pickle, went into Narani's hands. Banichi and Jago took their accustomed places, standing, at least for the moment, in the informality they maintained with Toby; Tano and Algini went to their quarters, where they maintained certain equipment that might hear anybody in their hallway.

There was tea, inevitably, no matter how Bren yearned to have the news that brought *Erighter Days* into port.

"Has it been calm cut there?" he asked. "There was quite a system blowing up."

"It went just south of us," Toby said, "and headed fairly well northeast. The midlands are catching it tonight. But we've been fine."

"Good." Three sips, the minimum, and Bren set his cup aside. "I take it there's a problem."

"It's more than a storm that's hit the midlands," Toby said. "And the weather can't help. I understand that much. The navy ship sent a small chase boat over with a verbal explanation and a sealed letter. The aiji's not yet calling you in, that was my information from the other captain, that I should not expect to carry you out, but there's some trouble of some nature, and it involves Ajuri."

A narrowing circle of problems, not least among them Ajuri's lack of a lord, Tatiseigi's recent nomination, the young gentleman visiting his uncle, and a Conservative firestorm about the impending legislative session: he could think of all those things on one intake of breath as he took up the cylinder, one of the aiji's own, which meant the letter had been hand-carried all the way . . . with consequent delay.

He broke the seal—likewise Tabini's own—and extracted the letter. One of the larger cylinders, and rather a longer letter than most of Tabini's communications.

He read it as he sat.

Bren Lord of the Heavens, Lord of Najida, paidhi-aiji.

A problem has arisen.

You will likely be aware that my son is paying a visit to Lord Tatiseigi at Tirnamarai, on the occasion of Lord Tatiseigi having made a white recommendation to the lordship of Ajuri . . .

A white recommendation. One that was meant to fail, and

thus make it awkward for the Conservatives besieging Tatisei-gi's door to demand another of him: he understood that at a stroke. Tatiseigi had done it and retreated to the country, while Tabini, clearly signaling no disfavor at all toward Tatiseigi, had then sent Cajeiri visiting—ostensibly simply to ride his new mecheita and have a holiday, but in practicality, did the boy visiting alone and escorted by a new security unit have any political significance?

Did the sea hold water and fishes?

One naturally did connect Cajeiri's visit to the Ajuri nomi-nation, and pointedly to the aiji's annoyance with the people trying to make Tatiseigi take the heat of the Ajuri question, and *try* to transfer it to the aiji's office.

But . . . it seemed there was another problem.

A young man has now shown up at Tirnamardi claiming to be Ajuri, the son of Senari, half-brother to Benedi . . .

Benedi. Lord of Ajuri before Kadiyi, before Komaji. Dead, all those lords. Assassinated, in a chain of events mysterious until one understood the power behind it, a self-serving old man em-bedded deep in Guild chambers, who'd made and unmade lords one after another purely to protect his own power, and to pro-tect his power structure inside Ajuri—a power structure which had yet to be wholly dismantled.

The direct-line claimant for the vacant lordship would be the aiji-consort, Damiri. Or Cajeiri himself. There was absolutely no chance in hell Tabini would approve either. There was the baby, Seimiro, Damiri's daughter. No chance of that, either.

But there was apparently another claimant coming forward, actually wanting that deadly office.

And *why* would he want it? Who was backing him? That was the question.

"Trouble?" Toby asked.

"Potential for it, certainly," he said. In present company, he hadn't controlled his expression. "The Ajuri lordship," he said, "has an entirely new claimant." He began to read, silently.

This person, calling himself Nomari, claiming to be the son of Senari, which would give him a natural claim on the lordship, arrived at Tirnamardi asking to be recognized. Geidarodaja also arrived uninvited and, being admitted, advanced to Lord Tatiseigi their own recommendation, Caradi, of Geidaro's house, also present with them. Heated words were exchanged, Geidaro disrespecting my son's presence, and Lord Tatiseigi accordingly bade Geidaro and her associates leave the premises.

Nomari's arrival seemed to set Geidaro in a state of high agitation, which fact alone would recommend him to Tatiseigi, and indeed, it seems to have had that effect. Tatiseigi reports Nomari as well-spoken though lacking some graces, a sensible and earnest fellow with considerable toughness of mind and body.

I have checked my recall and indeed, Senari and his wife and elder son were assassinated the same week as Benedi, but a check with the Guild confirms that Nomari was not among the dead. Nomari, who would have been fifteen years at the time, could have escaped the event and fled the house. The person claiming to be Nomari appears now as a member of the Transportation Guild, but representing a scattered association of Ajuri fugitives of various guilds, both trade and service, who have begun assembling at Tirnamardi in support of his claims. Sixty-three of them have been admitted to the grounds and sheltered in tents.

Tents. With weather coming down. It would be no luxury camp, for certain.

Considering there is still some question of this person's identity, Damiri-daja has determined she should go to Tirnamardi and settle the question, since she was acquainted with Nomari as a young child.

It was certainly not what Tabini would want, Bren thought, drawing another breath.

My grandmother has the intent to fly to Sheidan with every likely intention of taking the train to Tirnamardi herself and participating in the solution.

God. Ilisidi and Damiri under one roof—with the Ajuri succession at issue? How old was the letter?

Old enough, definitely for Ilisidi to be there.

And with the issue of political balance in the aishidi'tat, the Western Association, strongly affected by the outcome, dared they contemplate the aiji-dowager, head of the Eastern Association, throwing her considerable power into the question of the political destiny of the oldest and most central association in the aishidi'tat?

It was politically explosive, on every front. No wonder Tabini wrote to warn him. He *might* have to go back to the mainland before the shuttle landed.

Would Ilisidi really persist in her intent, given that Damiri was going out there? Ilisidi well might, unless Tabini flung himself bodily between his grandmother and the train station.

Under the circumstances, and himself apprehensive of further upheavals in Ajuri, Lord Tatiseigi has asked the Guild for any and all information it may have on this Ajuri claimant, with a view to issuing a second, true nomination, either personally or through a person other than the aiji-consort—I have made that condition clear. I have requested Guild investigation at a higher level and with extreme urgency.

Along with Lord Tatiseigi, I had hopes that the investigation might show this young man, however uneducated to a lordship, as having told the truth about his whereabouts during the last nine years, and having a good record in his guild.

So the first reports indicated, and I leaned toward appointing him despite his lack of experience, the moment I received a nomination. But now the Guild Council has broken its silence and declared that the young man has been for some time the subject of an ongoing and high-level Guild investigation.

Shadow Guild? That was the immediate and unsettling thought, any time the character of Ajuri came in question.

The young man has indeed done intermittent work in the places he claims, and he is a member in good standing in his guild. These claims are true. What he has not mentioned, however, is his intermittent relationship with Lord Machigi.

Machigi. Lord of the Taisigin Marid, a strong holdout against the Shadow Guild—a charismatic young leader in the south, who had resisted the Shadow Guild as doggedly as he had resisted the rules and laws of the aishidi'tat.

As paidhi-aiji, Bren had personally negotiated an alliance between Machigi and the aiji-dowager. A human set of senses couldn't take in all that Machigi was, but intimidating, yes— one of those scary personalities that didn't so much pay out man'chi as draw it to him. He'd felt that force, in a human way, in his first meeting with Tabini. He'd felt it from Ilisidi.

And if there was a lord in the aishidi'tat that might, by sheer force of personality, challenge Tabini for power . . . Machigi was a man to watch. Machigi *wouldn't*, sensibly, make a move against Tabini. Machigi's aims were all directed at the southern coast, the Marid, at doing something about the constant ferment of rebellion, plot, and counterplot that had divided the region for centuries. Machigi's enemies were the two northern districts of the Marid. His principle ally, of recent date, was the aiji-dowager, who was canny enough to keep him at arm's length—

But for the future? If Tabini ever stumbled, before Cajeiri himself had his majority—and if Ilisidi herself was by then out of the picture, there was *that* young autocrat sitting down there in the south—a man the northern provinces would never call lord.

And, God, if this Ajuri claimant was under *Machigi's* influence, appointing him to a lordship in the Padi Valley Association could mean a key member of the centralmost, oldest association of the aishidi'tat holding man'chi to a southern power rather than to Tabini's line.

That was beyond worrisome. He and Ilisidi were trying to

draw Machigi closer to the central government right now, and any problem arising from this Nomari as lord of a small clan would likely be far in the future—but would appointing this young man to Ajuri now create a major problem for Cajeiri once *he* took the government? Ajuri was a tiny clan—but rehabilitated, it would have kinship to both the aiji-consort *and* the next aiji. It would *not* be a minor voice in the foreseeable future.

The Guild suspects that this person has acted as a spy for Machigi in the rail center in the Senjin Marid. Details of its operation and cargoes would have been of great interest to Machigi during the Troubles, certainly. The Transportation Guild cover would have been a great asset to a spy, providing a means of mobility during a time when travel was watched and reported. Detail and proof of Nomari's involvement in Machigi's informational network, as yet, is lacking. Nor is that connection, if true, a wholly damning fact: Machigi was a point of resistance and held the entire southern Marid safe from Shadow Guild control. It is, however, a worrisome entanglement for the future.

Machigi and his predecessors had also held out against guild centralization, notably refusing the Assassins' Guild: Machigi, like the aiji-dowager, maintained his own local units, and they had their own training. There was a Transportation Guild in the Taisigin Marid, but it was also not affiliated with the central guild: it was seafaring, involving ships, very little involvement with the roads, which had been notoriously ill-maintained, and nothing at all with the rails, which were still non-existent in Machigi's district.

It was a very interesting place for an Ajuri in the Shejidan-based central Transportation Guild to have spent the troubled years of Tabini's overthrow.

I am requesting my grandmother, since she is en route to Shejidan at this hour, to change her plans and use her good offices urgently to investigate this Ajuri claimant's ties to the South, bearing in mind her great-grandson's current where-

abouts, the need for secrecy, and the risk to him should we fail to detect any worrisome collusion.

We are, to put it succinctly, concerned, and have far too few firm answers, considering the double-sided potential of this claimant, and the changes such an association might work in the political balance.

Dur and Gan in the north, with the North Coastal Association, not favorable to Machigi, abutted the Padi Valley Association, which was directly at issue, with Ajuri a member.

But equally to the point, the South Coastal Association—Lord Geigi, his own holdings at Najida, and the Maschi holdings, as well as the several townships of the southern coast—bordered the Taisigin Marid; and if *those* all linked up in a cozy unified interest, a string of associations—it could actually be a good thing, for the stability of the aishidi'tat.

But if Machigi reiterated his old demand for control of the west coast and made a grab for the South Coastal Association, a link to Ajuri could become a very serious problem. Machigi had surrendered his ancient claim in favor of a current trade agreement with the dowager. Gifts had been exchanged. Documents had been signed.

Warm assurances had preceded disasters as well as successes in the aishidi'tat.

We do not say hasten your business on the island. But once that business is complete, do not plan any delay at Najida. Let nand' Toby convey you across the strait with seemly leisure, bearing in mind that during that passage you will have a naval escort which can place you in direct contact with Shejidan, at all levels.

Should there develop an urgency in this matter before your departure from Mospheira, you will receive a phone call from your staff in the Bujavid with the words 'the aiji suggests.' If that should happen, at that point, engage a plane without delay, fly to Shejidan, and report to me in all haste.

Until then, assume your highest immediate priority still to be the safe arrival and settlement of my son's young associates.

You may give an abbreviated explanation of this message to the Presidenta. Tell him we have a political matter under review in which you may be needed, but we hope that it will not be necessary to recall you to the mainland early, and assure him that your sudden departure would be unrelated to his government. Destroy this message without fail. It is not information we wish to share.

"Not good news?" Toby asked.

"Yes and no," he said, and rapidly, in Ragi, for his staff, "Nadiin-ji, an Ajuri claimant has arrived at Tirnamardi asking Lord Tatiseigi's help, but Guild Council now informs Tabini-aiji that, during Murini's time, the man has some association with Lord Machigi, a matter regarding which he has not been forthcoming. Damiri-daja is going to Tirnamardi. The dowager is arriving in Shejidan also with that intention, but the aiji is asking her instead to apply her energies to Machigi and learn what he knows."

Toby could follow a little of that, Barb maybe could pick up the proper nouns, but his staff allowed their concern to show.

"Toby, excuse me. I have to answer this, and much as I would wish to host you overnight, you need to get my answer back to that ship out there, and I need to compose it while I have it all in my mind. Rani-ji, will you kindly serve refreshments, possibly a sandwich to take with them? They have had rather a hasty trip in. I do not know whether they may have managed meals."

"We would be grateful," Toby said, in his perfectly passable Ragi. "Bren-ji, write. We shall take it."

Bren pulled out a chair and sat down at the end of the table he used for a desk. He reached for paper and a fountain pen, not the usual flattened steel quill he preferred for Ragi, but Tabini had deciphered his thready emergency notes before.

Aiji-ma, I shall do as you say. In preparation, I have brought in able associates to deal with the day-to-day issues of the children's security and instruction, and the Presidenta is mustering allies to deal with whatever disturbance may spill from the station down to the island in political support for Tillington-nadi, so much of my work here is done. I have made your position very clear on matters of population balance aloft and the Presidenta both welcomes your statement and intends to use that declaration to reinforce his own position, that Tillington's removal was more than justified.

Lord Geigi will have informed you that the kyo departure has proceeded according to agreement and that he is working closely with Gin-aiji and Jase-aiji to bring the Reunioners to Earth. This will in itself ease food shortages, which will remove a major cause of tension on the station.

Regarding Machigi, aiji-ma, I have only my last encounter with him to guide me, and I cannot answer your concerns, except to say that he has longstanding problems in his region that cannot be bettered by involving himself in the contentious north. Whether he is wise enough to see this I cannot say with authority, but my impression of him is that the time is not right to make any move that would breach agreements with the aiji-dowager. If he has any contrary notions, I hope the dowager can indeed remind him of the advantages of his cooperation with her.

I am extremely concerned for the welfare of everyone at Tirnamardi, and if at any point my return can serve a good purpose, I will respond immediately.

I shall consult with the Presidenta without revealing the nature of your concern and I shall destroy your letter completely.

Nand' Toby will convey this letter to his navy escort at all speed, and will stand ready to carry any further message.

He finished. He capped the pen, folded the paper and sealed it in an envelope. Narani had lit the waxjack—that spidery, delicate piece of equipment had come with them in its own wooden case—and he put his own seal on the envelope.

Toby would courier it out to sea, that being the route Tabini had chosen—not even trusting an air courier. This message had stayed firmly in known hands all the way to him and it would follow the same route back again—likely there was a chase boat waiting with the naval escort to get his reply back to Najida, by bus to the airport, and by a single courier, all the way to the Bujavid, with no pauses, no other change of hands. He had the verbal code now that would mean take a plane at Port Jackson and come: and he knew the nature of the problem that had arisen in Tirnamardi, the sort that might simmer for months, or not. It wasn't the fastest mode of communication Tabini had chosen to establish, but, barring bringing the Guild Council into the question, to extend their network onto the island, with all those security risks and diplomatic problems, it was the most contained, with the least public notice attached.

No publicity about the situation on the mainland, no order to return, and not the utmost haste—just a *be ready* and an advisement what the signal would be that he had to get there.

Damn, however. Damn.

He was still shaken. Toby and Barb were certainly relieved, having likely broken speed records getting to port, but having no idea what they carried, whether it was war, treason, assassination or imminent death in the aiji's immediate family. There was no extreme urgency in Toby's getting out of port and getting the reply to this back, but there *was* a risk of public attention to Toby's boat being in port, all sorts of possible rumors that might disrupt matters in progress, at least with speculation, on *this* side of the straits. Best *Brighter Days* slip quietly back out to sea before too long.

"I think there's time for a proper dinner here," he said in Ragi, for Narani and Jeladi and his aishid. "No great rush on the reply," he said in Mosphei'. "We're handling the details, now, and the aiji says take my time coming back even if called—at least to go by boat, avoiding any appearance of haste on the other side of the strait. It's a delicate situation, that probably doesn't need a special flight landing in Shejidan, with consequent attention. So you'll eventually be taking me back to Najida: that plan hasn't changed. But I can't stay at Najida. When I do get home, it's a good bet I'll be headed straight from the dock to the airport."

"Do we want to know what *is* going on?" Barb asked.

"Not particularly. It's not war and peace. Just Padi Valley politics—two unfilled appointments and a candidate that's turned up with a somewhat troublesome affiliation. At least an affiliation that requires some careful analysis. Sit there, at the table, have some teacakes. Or wine. I have to contact Shawn and advise him the world's safe. I'll just send a note over to him, considering the hour. Are you going to need fuel, going out?"

"*That's* going to be a problem at this hour."

"It won't. I'll see how inventive Shawn's security can be on their own. They'll get it over there quietly."

Narani poured wine, and Bren sat down and wrote a note. *All fine. Toby's come into port with a message from the Bujavid, time sensitive, regarding a nomination very important to the aishidi'tat, but by no means affecting my current mission here. Tabini-aiji just wants me brought up to speed. Toby will be out again not long after midnight, with no public notice. we hope. I'll explain at your convenience. I'm requesting Toby's boat refueled: I'm requesting your security see to that.*

He sealed the envelope, wrote on it, *President Shawn Tyers, his eyes only. Not an emergency. But it needs the President's attention within the hour.*

He'd lay odds Shawn had gotten word something was going on, that the appearance of *Brighter Days* in the port had not gone unnoticed by security, and that Shawn was *not* sleeping. Shawn had every right to expect an advisement what was going on . . . but had not asked. Yet.

Ilisidi and Damiri face to face under Tatiseigi's roof, trying to sort out the Ajuri succession? Shawn would have no concept. Neither would Toby.

His aishid certainly would. He had passed the letter to his aishid for disposal, and yes, they did read such things.

Not an emergency, true. But capable of becoming one that might need the paidhi's personal connection to the aiji-dowager to help sort out.

And within ten minutes of sending the envelope to Shawn, and while Toby and Barb were having supper and he was having a second dessert . . . the phone rang.

He knew who before he picked it up.

"Bren?"

"Shawn. No big problem. I asked security to keep an eye on the boat."

"They're doing that."

"Can they arrange that refueling? Hate to ask, but—"

"Done. Is it a crisis?"

"No emergency at all. A troublesome situation I've dealt with before. The aiji wants me to keep up to date in the event it gets active."

"Happy to hear it's not a disaster. Tomorrow? Nine?"

"Make it eight," he said. "Security's coming for the initial briefing at 10."

"How about breakfast on the balcony at six?"

"Six it is."

11

"**N**andi," someone whispered—Lucasi, Cajeiri thought, muzzy with a hard-won sleep. "Nandi. Jeri-ji."

The room was utter dark except a light from a side door slightly ajar, making a partial silhouette—Lucasi, definitely, he thought. And the storm was still thumping and spattering away at the windows, behind the drawn drapes. "Antaro," he said, an inquiry. Antaro had come up to the suite, battered and bruised.

"Antaro is sleeping. Your *mother*, nandi. Your mother is at the train station."

"Is it morning?"

"Far from it, nandi. The seniors have gone downstairs to the security station to find out the situation. We only have the advisement."

"Has the car gone out? Is Uncle aware, Luca-ji?"

"Lord Tatiseigi is asleep. The physician gave him a painkiller and he is not to be waked. Nandi, your mother has brought the Najida bus."

"*Nand' Bren's* bus?" He could hardly believe it. But the big bus *could* travel by rail, on its own car. And it was bulletproof, mostly. It was good news. But they had to get the bus off the rail car, and that was a complicated operation. "Wake Jegari. Tell him—tell him contact his uncle's aishid and get riders to the station." Taiben moved to protect its own interests, and in response to very few outsiders. "Wake Eisi and Liedi. I have to dress." It came to him that, if Uncle was asleep with painkillers—who *was* in charge? Who was ordering the house staff, and who was advising security, and who was going to open the gate to let Mother in?

He was the person of rank. He was not being stupid. Here he was in the dark in his nightshirt and there was nobody but Guild to order the things that needed to be done, and Guild was not supposed to be in charge. When Guild *had* to be in charge, things were really out of order, and he did not want Uncle's house to meet Mother like that.

Lucasi was off on his errands. "Light, nadi!" Cajeiri called out, and Lucasi flung the lighted door wide, calling on Jegari to assist. Cajeiri hurled himself to the edge of the huge bed and slid off, already shedding his nightshirt, thinking first that anything he could find would do—and then that he did not want to meet Mother looking haphazard at all.

"Nandi?" Lights came on in the room. Eisi and Liedi arrived from their quarters, and now, distantly, Boji made himself heard, screeching and rattling his cage.

"Breakfast dress," he said, and what explained everything: "Mother is coming early. Quickly, nadiin-ji. Uncle is asleep and someone has to order the house."

"Yes," Liedi said, and the two of them hastened to the closet and the upright, in hurried conference.

There was no time for a bath. Veijico arrived. Cajeiri was putting on his underclothes, but he was far from embarrassment. Antaro came out, too, cradling her broken arm, a robe over one shoulder, and with her hair unbraided. "Taro-ji," Cajeiri said, "go back to bed."

"It is not that bad, nandi. I can deal with communications."

"Then sit, sit, soon, please!" He had no desire to have Antaro collapse amid all the other confusion. "I need the seniors to know I am awake, and dressing. I shall be in the great hall as quickly as I can. Find out what they know."

He had no idea what he ought to do first, except to get dressed as quickly as he could, and to find out what people did know. He had heard mani and nand' Bren and Uncle deal with staff emergencies, and he had the sketch of it all in mind—information, orders where orders needed to go, and things thought of before they became a problem. Mani had told him more than once, Trust your staff. Do not oversee *their* work. Think! Think of the things they will *not* think of!

Think faster than the seniors? That was not likely. But it was *proper* order the Guild wanted—someone to be in charge, to just hear what was going on and speak to the other side, if there *was* another side. And in the case of Mother coming into Uncle's house with Uncle abed and all the Ajuri here in the house, there really was *another side.* There was what Uncle would want done, and *he* was the one on the premises, able to authorize doors opened, that otherwise really should not open, with just staff in charge. It was an important thing. A principle, even if Mother was more Atageini than he was. He outranked her. So it was for himself as well as Uncle that he had to stand in the great room and hold the place. Mother might be in a bad mood. Mother might come in angry with everything and start giving orders.

But she could *not* order the staff or the house Guild if he was standing there. Everything had to wait for Uncle.

Shirt and coat went on together, shirt tucked in, lace settled in proper fashion. Liedi braided his hair. "Which ribbon, nandi?" Eisi asked, and he had no hesitation.

"Ragi." Which of all clans, Mother was not. Father was. And he was.

He let it be tied, he had a look in the mirror, seeing Jegari arrive behind him.

"Have you reached them?" he asked.

"Seniors say your father ordered the bus, ordered a Taibeni escort—there are thirty-three persons in your mother's party. She is bringing domestic staff, her own aishid, and two senior Guild units."

"Senior to mine?" That could upend everything.

"No," Jegari said with satisfaction. "Not in the field, and not, for that matter, attached to *you*, nandi."

He had not thought that through. Not quite. *Father* had assigned the seniors, that thought flashed through like a lightning stroke of understanding, lighting up a whole landscape of precautions Father had set in place. Nobody, effectively, could countermand his senior aishid. That was both comforting—and scary.

Deep breath. "Advise Rieni what we intend to do," he said. "We are going to open the gate only when the bus arrives, the Taibeni escort should stay with the bus as they come onto the grounds and get Mother to the front doors, and once they are inside, then the Taibeni may ride out again and let Uncle's guard take over." Internal things began to occur to him. "Mother is supposed to have the apartment I have *usually* had. But she has a senior escort. And domestic staff. And Ajuri have the lower hall, at least tonight. We have a lot of people moving about. Ask the Taibeni if they could camp outside the grounds for a day to watch the gate." It was wet, it was still stormy, and it was asking a lot, but the logistics of it were clear: they came with their mecheiti, and bringing foreign mecheiti to camp on the grounds was begging disaster. It was going to be risky enough just for them to ride in and out again.

"Uncle's staff can solve it," Jegari said. "Antaro and Veijico will go to the security station to bridge communications to us. We shall arrange everything with our clan. You should go down to the hall, nandi, and order things from there."

It was good advice, a good plan. He took a deep breath, straightened his shoulders back and went toward the door.

His aishid was with him. The seniors had already gone downstairs. Night watch had sent up the message, he was sure; Lucasi had waked him, and now they headed down the hall quietly and quickly, all still by lamplight.

Downstairs, a few lights were on—the generator was still running, and a few servants might have been sitting about, night staff, entitled to that informality, but word had spread, and staff came to them as they came down the stairs.

"My mother is coming," he began. "With thirty-three staff and Guild combined. Uncle is asleep with medicines and I shall meet her. She has transportation and escort. She will need the suite next to mine and her additional bodyguard and servants will need places."

"Shall we turn out day staff, nandi?"

One could only wish Saidin-daja were here, instead of managing Uncle's affairs in the Bujavid. But the old man running Tirnamardi was next-best. "Anido first." That was the head of night staff. "He will manage. My mother is arriving by bus. Once they are on the road, they will make good speed." He was relieved to see Rieni coming up the central stairs, and looked to him. "Rieni-nadi. Uncle should rest. I can at least do this. Thirty-three persons. With my mother. And the bus."

"Indeed. We are aware, nandi, and things are on track. The bus is offloaded at the rail station, they are boarding, and Taibeni will be meeting it halfway, to be near when it reaches the gate. Staff is stirring. We shall manage."

"You are not to take orders from my mother, Rieni-nadi, if they go against mine."

The expression was absolutely proper, but was that a little reaction? "We assuredly shall not, nandi, except in matters of courtesy and comfort."

"In courtesy and comfort, yes." Mother would arrive tired and probably cross. "I am going over to the conservatory to sit and wait." Mani always said, *Never dither. Sit. Be where staff can find you and do not pester them with questions.*

Tea for himself and his aishid might be trivial, but thinking of that, it had to be ready for Mother, too, if she wanted it. "Tea and cakes," he said to Lucasi. "In the conservatory—enough tea, when they come. I shall sit." He had Lucasi and Jegari, and now Rieni and Haniri, who were guard enough to satisfy Mother's sense of safety.

"I shall ask," Lucasi said. "Gari-ji, go and sit."

They went to that far side of the great hall and sat, himself and Jegari. Rieni and Haniri, disposed to formality, shed it and quietly sat with them, resting while it was sensible to rest. There had not been a great deal of sleep for anyone. At some point the seniors must have gotten warning that Mother was on her way—and possibly gotten it late, if she was moving under extreme security. He decided to think so, at least, that they had been abed like the rest of them when word had come, and Lucasi had advised him of it while they were still finding out the first available details.

Mani was in Shejidan. And Mother had taken the train—it must have been midnight—and *somehow* gotten nand' Bren's bus up from Najida. Could one even do that, through Shejidan, in that short a time?

Father might have sent for it, because of its protections.

"How *did* Mother get the bus?" he asked, while they were having tea, and while the great hall was having its lights come on, one set and the other.

"We are wondering the same," Rieni said. "Not to mention the Taibeni escort. It may have taken the northern route to get there."

Father could move the Taibeni. It was not sure that Mother would even try.

So his parents were working together, with Great-grandmother arriving, and the bus on its way and the Red Train likely loading and under Father's orders before Great-grandmother stepped in to take it over.

He saw the politics stacked up, towering stacks of arguments one way and the other. But politics and potential arguments had gotten Mother here, launching out in the middle of the night. Great-grandmother was not *quite* stranded, once the Red Train rolled, but the politics of going ahead with her plans became extremely awkward.

Mani would not come. He was fairly sure of that. Mani would not fight with Mother in Uncle's house. But later . . .

"The bus is apparently well on its way," Haniri said, having picked up a message. "One does not believe we were brought current until the bus was well away from the train station. In the interests of security, young aiji."

"One worries," he said, "regarding the two Ajuri missing still—and the gate—"

"A unit is in place, young aiji."

He nodded, imitation of Father, he realized when he had done it. "Good," he added, and sipped a fresh cup of tea.

Five servants in a string came up the stairs with stacks of fresh linen, headed to the second floor at great speed. It was the fastest, not the most discreet route for staff, and they were being as quiet as five people could. The laundry below probably had no power, so long as they were on generator, and he had no idea how long it might take someone, somewhere, to repair the lines. Mother was coming up to a very strange Tirnamardi, with only the main floor brightly lit, probably not even the outside lights, and the rain still coming down.

Rieni said, at last, "They are at the gate, young aiji, and it is opening."

"Well," he said, "it is a short drive now."

He imagined he could even hear the bus now. He set down his teacup and strained his ears, and after a few moments, indeed, it was, probably just topping the rise after the gate. He knew that engine. He gathered himself up, and his aishid did, and they went to the central steps, where important guests would come.

He took deep breaths, listening to the bus pull up outside, and catching the slight draft from the outer door. He almost told Rieni and Janachi to go down to meet Mother, but he realized then that Mother's own guard would be coming in advance. She certainly had escort.

The lower doors opened, in the hands of Uncle's staff, carrying hand torches in the dim first foyer below the landing. Guild came in first, and then Mother entered, in a warm wrap, and with the other team of her aishid. Behind them came Mother's maids, two in number, and more uniformed Guild, while Mother climbed the stairs.

There was one question he had not asked his aishid: do they know what has happened here?

He was not sure Mother did know, and likely he was not the person, alone, that Mother expected to be standing atop the stairs.

"Honored Mother," he said, and she did look puzzled, and a little worried as she came up the last steps.

"Son of mine. One takes it we have lost the electrics to the storm. *Where* is Uncle Tatiseigi?"

"Asleep, Honored Mother. He hurt his arm. So when we knew you were coming—"

A baby cried, a bundle in a servant's arms, and he recognized Beha, Seimei's nurse, attending on Mother.

His sister.

With everything that was going on.

"Sister is here," he said, appalled.

"You are distressed."

"Honored Mother, we have all the Ajuri in the lower hall, we have a dead person out by the stables, we have no light or power, and Uncle is Filing on Great-aunt Geidaro." It was a completely disorganized account. He finished it, desperately, with, "Will you have tea, while staff finishes with the rooms?"

"Son of mine, *what* has happened?"

So Guild had *not* talked to Guild in specifics while Mother was in transit, only advising them at the very last. Mother had spent the night on the train. And there might be a great deal Mother did not know.

"Mother, we have hot tea in the conservatory. As yet my sister has no bed . . . staff can arrange one. Please sit a moment. Staff is moving as fast as they can."

He had confidence his aishid was passing those orders, to make them true. Seimei was fussing—likely at the lights and movement, at an hour when any reasonable baby was asleep. Mother took the steps toward the great hall and the conservatory, and Beha came with her, along with Mother's aishid, her aishid from the Bujavid, so at least one knew the level of confidence immediately around them, while the rest might be strangers.

They no more than sat down in the conservatory before Uncle's staff was moving in, to offer tea, even sandwiches should the aiji-consort wish . . .

"Tea," Mother said, the bare requirement of hospitality, and leaned aside a little to look at Seimei, who was burrowing in Beha's arms, shutting out the light. "We shall have a bed in a little while, daughter, just a little while."

Tea was ready. It was a three-sip question, and *Cajeiri* took the three, almost without pause, then set the cup down, waiting for the others.

"Mother. Someone loosed the mecheiti a few hours ago, in the storm. Uncle gashed his arm and Antaro's arm is broken, but they are all back in."

"We were signaled there was trouble," Mother said solemnly. "But half an hour later we had advisement it was safe enough to proceed as planned."

Guild would have made that judgment, but Rieni had not known at that hour that the Red Train was already moving, Cajeiri thought, and that Mother had brought Seimiro. That all had been secret.

But would Mother have turned back, and would Mother *not* have brought Seimiro with her where she went? He had not been thinking from Mother's side of things . . . coming here as Atageini *and* Ajuri, into the middle of a mess that had upset her life from before she was born—and in which Father had forbidden her to intervene. Until now.

"You are here," Cajeiri said, "and it *is* safer now, with all the Guild arriving. Uncle will be up in the morning, one is sure."

"But you were not involved in the incident."

"I was not, Honored Mother. I sent Antaro and Jegari outside to help Uncle and the grooms, but I stayed right in this chair and Rieni and the rest were right beside me the whole time. I could by no means do what Antaro and Jegari could do. Or Uncle."

"You were very sensible," Mother said. "And you wake to meet us in your great-uncle's stead, at our unreasonably early arrival." Mother nodded. And nodded again to her own thoughts. "Well done, well turned out, son of mine. Your father will be proud."

Are *you?* he wondered, wishing, once, to hear her say that. Seimei was hers, only hers. He . . . was his father's. That had been the agreement. And of course she brought Seimei where *she* went, with no way his father could legally object. That was the way it was. She was Atageini, Great-uncle's niece, born in Tirnamardi. Keep her away? Father could not have. If the advisement had been that Tirnamardi was overrun, she would have come—he had that feeling. She was *from* here, and he was not.

Well, he thought—seeing a trio of upstairs servants coming down the stairs toward them, likely to say that rooms were ready—he could not mend that.

"You likely know that Nomari is lodged upstairs," he said. "There are guards in the hall, and he is not to leave his room. Late as it is—"

"We are too tired to deal with his situation," Mother said.

"One understands. But likely he will come down to breakfast, if Uncle does. And likely Uncle will come down, if he possibly can."

"Is he badly hurt?"

"He fell," Cajeiri said, "and what he did was very hard, terribly hard. He will be upset to have slept through your arrival, Honored Mother. I know he will."

"It continues," Mother said, frowning. "From my birth, it goes on. So he has Filed on Geidaro. I cannot say I regret the need. I tried peace. But I did not know what I now know. Does the Filing encompass Meisi?"

"I do not think so, Honored Mother. Great-uncle did not mention Meisi or Caradi or Dejaja."

"That probably is apt and fair," Mother said quietly. The servants were standing by, and she acknowledged them with a nod. "Are we ready?"

"We are," the oldest said. "We have found a crib, daja-ma, and made it clean and soft and free of dust. It has been a long time since there was a baby in *this* house."

"Well," Mother said without comment, "then we shall go up. We all shall go up." She and Beha rose, and they and their guard went toward the stairs. Cajeiri walked with her as far as the bottom step.

She turned, at that point, looked at him critically, up and down. Then she said: "Well done, son of mine. *Very* well done."

12

"The gist of the message was a little stir about a replacement for the lordship of Ajuri," Bren said to Shawn. It was a break of dawn breakfast on a balcony. Beyond the stone railing was a vista of hills and the tops of tall trees, this side of Francis House being devoted to formal gardens, and those gardens well-guarded.

They were utterly on their own, the servers dismissed entirely. It was help-oneself service, informal as it came, with a portable work table and stools in the adjacent room for Banichi and the rest: Shawn's staff was trying to improvise. A light breeze, nothing like the bracing wind off the mountains of the continent, ruffled the tablecloth.

"The central association," Shawn said. "Padi Valley Association. Kadagidi's still out, too, isn't it?"

"Exactly." He was talking to a man who'd spent his early career in the State Department. Shawn had a fair knowledge of which clan was where, how closely certain ones were tied to Shejidan, and which ones were traditionally trouble. But the map had shifted radically in a few areas, nearly overnight.

"The aiji's son is in Tirnamardi with his great-uncle, and Ajuri's upset, which is a little concerning, but nothing unusual. Kadagidi's not yet in play, but in the background of it all. Practically speaking, there's no way in hell Tabini's going to let Ajuri go on indefinitely the way it is. It's being run right now by a woman who's part of the same pattern of plot and counterplot that's made Ajuri a problem to the region. Kadagidi's in a more stable state: their governing line is deposed, and Tabini has to find some reasonable successor, but thus far they're still under audit, trying to reconcile the books and find out who did what. Whoever does succeed to the lordship has to have a mandate from the clan as well. It's that whole mess. But Kadagidi is far from a stage of seeking a nominee. Ajuri, however, is heating up. Tabini wants me informed on the mess in the notion that, when I do get back, I may need to step in. I'm *not* anxious to walk into Ajuri. But I will, if that's what it takes."

Shawn nodded and took a piece of toast. "Glad to know what's going on. Our navy tracked your brother out, sure now he's under the eyes of the aiji's navy, all safe and well."

"Thanks for that."

"We want him safe, too. And I had every confidence if it *was* something urgent, you'd have told us at least the gist of it last night."

"I would. Surprises don't make for good relations. Bottom line, my mission stands for now, but I *could* be called back to the mainland if things heat up."

"Speaking of heat," Shawn said, and Bren paused in a sip of tea, waiting.

"I reviewed Dr. Kroger's documentary. I also understand Gin's sent it to Asgard Space, who sent it to earthbound Asgard."

Scary but logical. So Gin had chosen to warn them.

"And?" he asked.

"Asgard aloft messaged Gin last night that she had their full support and that they were settling the Andressen case and not going to trial, giving Andressen everything he asked. Earthbound Asgard sent *me* a message that they're changing their stance on her appointment, that they now approve it."

"They were the chief opposition."

"The most moneyed opposition. Asgard's read the wind and

they're changing course. The tech coming in with the Reunioners is worth getting into bed with us radicals, and the Heritage
Party, I forecast, is going to feel the pinch in their pocketbook."

"Major."

"Very."

There was Asgard Materials, Space Division, and, on Earth,
the original Asgard Corporation, a major mining and industrial
force on Mospheira from the earliest days of Port Jackson. The
Space Division had found itself approached, unofficially, by a
Reunion refugee with research papers salvaged from Reunion,
and, in the administration of the former stationmaster, Tillington, Asgard had made a private deal for the papers—involving
an exception for a security clearance for one Andressen, Ketil,
and a special tutoring program for one Andressen, Bjorn.

Illegal, under the rules—both arrangements. But Stationmaster Tillington had bent rules—for *considerations*, one of
many under-the-table arrangements Tillington had made.

This particular case had had repercussions. Asgard, afraid to
buck Tillington's power, had broken a dozen station regulations
about screening for employees and no few terrestrial statutes
involving intellectual property, corruption, bribery, and falsifi-
cation of tax records.

"Central to the issue, Asgard Corp doesn't want a prosecu-
tion, they don't want a senate investigation, they don't want an
audit, and they don't want Simon Aslund arrested."

"That's the Asgard Space administrator."

"Chief administrator, yes. Gin calls him a good administrator, in point of fact, whose point of view is that, knowing those
records existed, he bent the rules to get them, fearing they
would be lost, the way things were going; and he's defiantly
willing to take full responsibility. Gin asked him if he would
give a deposition in the Tillington case and have it on record
that *he* didn't initiate the deal, and the Asgard lawyers said yes,
he would, contingent on an amnesty for the Andressen matter,
up and down."

"That part had been underway before I left."

"Well, he's just given the deposition. And Mikas Tillington is being officially arraigned up there for charges ranging from corruption, bribery and intimidation to crimes against human- ity, though the ship is demanding the latter charge be dropped. It may *be* dropped, on grounds that the precise act, sealing the section doors, was arguably necessary. The fact it had *become* necessary due to his actions—would only complicate the case and possibly weaken the other charges. Unfortunately. But we *have* him on corruption. We have enough to keep him out of any political appointment hereafter. *And* to keep him out of the legislature. He'll be legally ineligible, with that on the record. Now, the Heritage Party has been gearing up to make capital on him as a hero. But—" Shawn said cheerfully, "the Aslunds who run Asgard on Earth urgently want the case against Asgard Space settled. They want Simon Aslund cleared, and they want to retain rights to the materials Andressen sold them. To get those, one of their own is going to have to testify against the Heritage Party's newest hero. Asgard being one of the chief con- tributors to the Heritage Party's election campaigns, the situa- tion could flare off in a number of untidy directions."

"Tillington won't be quiet," Bren said.

"The question is whether the elder Aslunds are willing to drop their opposition to all things space-connected. Simon is their rebellious teenager. So to speak. The elder Aslunds didn't want involvement in space in the first place. Now Simon stands to make them another fortune."

Simon Aslund, running Asgard Space, was over sixty. The Aslund twins, Karl and Holman, running Asgard Corporation on the ground, were fifteen years Simon's senior. At least.

"The elder Aslunds are going to *have* to think about their policy. That's sure. One end of Asgard funding the faction apt to ruin the other, which has become the *real* moneymaker, is not going to sit well with the next generation of Aslunds."

"And the grandkids, down here on Earth, have been the

primary activists in the effort to get Simon out of his troubles. Word is, the elders, Earth and Space are still squabbling, that there's bad blood between the twins and Simon. They'd like to see him fail, at any cost. I doubt we'll ever know the whole of it, but the grandkids see the writing on the wall. Elisabeth Aslund is sensible—she's the one who's been in contact with us. The one we sent the file to. Her brother Maarten is a bit harder to deal with. He's the one who's insisting on sending their lawyer up to the station to broker the agreement with Gin. Simon's elder son, Lucien, is up there with him, his second in command, and contracts man. He's trying to calm them all down, first telling Maarten and the board that their Earth-based lawyer can't get a shuttle seat, no, not during the current supply crisis; and no, Simon doesn't want their lawyer up there, since the situation *is* settled. Simon is *not* happy with Tillington. He hasn't been happy with Tillington since the Reunioners arrived, and honestly and off the record, I *do* believe his decision saved the Reunioner scientific files, because *he* realized their value. If he did nothing else, he alerted Gin's administration to the situation and son Lucien Aslund has helped us arrange a sane legal process that protects everybody but Tillington. So now there's a framework and legal status which allows the Reunioners who have such records to sell them without being cheated. And the companies can now deal with sure knowledge of where title to the files actually rests. All that at the stroke of Simon Aslund's signature on the agreement with Gin Kroger. In some cases of competing claims and diverse files, Gin's uniting the possessors of certain files into bargaining groups with legal standing. The feeling is there are some valuable processes at issue, but nobody knows what. Some scientific advances we don't yet know the value of. There's a scaling clause in the residuals package."

"Two hundred years of independent research, if nothing else," Bren said, "has to produce something." In his mind was a kyo ship proceeding far, far faster than their own ship could manage. He took a sip of tea. "Asgard Corporate. In your opinion, how are they going to react to Gin's vid?"

"The grandkids, at least, right along with Simon and his sons, are already viewing Tillington as an ongoing liability. Trouble is—the Heritage Party. The senior twins, Elisabeth and Maarten, helped fund the party in the first place. The Heritage Party, during the Troubles on the mainland, praised Tillington to the moon and back for keeping the station going. They backed him as protecting the station in his actions against the Reunioners, and made a major case of it. Now—the party has to go on backing Tillington or pretend they never said anything of the sort. And I'm not going to phone them and warn them the case is settled, and Tillington is toxic. My party won't let them forget it, unless *they* back off the Reunioner issue and quit agitating against them. One truly great stroke of luck—and likely the source of the escalating tension within the Aslund family—Simon Aslund recorded his sessions with Tillington. Every last one of them. The Heritage Party *can't* claim we're fabricating evidence."

"Excellent," Bren said. "I only wish they'd be so sensible."

"The party leadership," Shawn said, "the ones that just oppose *me*, we can deal with. I have periodic contact from the Aslund twins. And they believe I *should* be opposed and checked. Not a bad thing, if Heritage were not the avenue they've used. They're thorough conservatives on questions of cooperation with the mainland, but even the twins aren't blind ideologues. They were upset with our involvement trying to get Tabini's government back, because they didn't think it would work. But they weren't complaining when you showed up safe and Tabini did end up back in charge. So the Aslunds and I do get along at arm's length. The kyo scared hell out of them, atevi have always scared hell out of them, and the clear evidence that the atevi's high-level delegation was what sent the kyo away from us peacefully may have stirred up the Heritage faction to a fine froth, but the Aslunds have possibly begun a reassessment of their position. They're not stupid, downright brilliant in their own arena, and the word that the kyo have technology we don't, that the Reunioners have observed it, and that Tillington almost mismanaged the affair into global disaster—has shaken them."

"Good."

"We have to meet behind the bushes, so to speak, while we're continuing our usual politics. And we hope to get intelligence on a section of their party that they may now find highly embarrassing to own. My party won't hit them on it—so long as we get their cooperation, and what Simon has on Tillington apparently involves threats of more than business nature. Not that I *like* the Aslunds as bedfellows, but it's practicality. They've now got to reposition themselves and shed some old allies. What I foresee is that Heritage is likely to split, right down the division of ideological opposition to my party's policies, which I can respect, if not like—and the fringe who can't get over the Abandonment."

The Abandonment—the psychological wound on the Mospheiran consciousness, which some cultivated to their own advantage. Heritage took it as the origin-point of national identity.

"I suspect brother Simon in particular is acquiring the long view: he sees the writing on the wall and he's using the situation to push the twins into action with the help of his son Lucien. Gin says encouragement for the inclusion of Tillington's behavior . . . the meltdown in the command center, and the situation on the station—actually came out of Simon Aslund's office. Official stance, regardless who thought of it."

It was convoluted enough. The Aslunds had a reputation.

"Heritage won't believe it," Bren said. "They'll claim it was all taken out of context."

"My bet is," Shawn said, "that once Heritage loses their chief contributors, the bulk of the party will peel away to take a more moderate position, with new voices, and that the

Heritage Party as we know it will splinter into those that are willing to take a new tack—and those that are going to take Tillington for their martyred saint."

"Without the funding."

"Without the Aslund millions, at least. But if it goes the way I see, I don't think they'll be a political party. I think they'll be a problem, and problems pushed by fanatics tend to fund themselves in small, nasty ways."

It *was* a rational scenario. He could very well see it, given Asgard cutting off the money flow. Those still obsessed with a fiction two hundred years old were not going to change their minds. What really *had* happened was *not* what was still taught to kids. And replacing that treasured mythology with the *Reunioners'* version of history was going to stir up its own storm.

Not to mention that the ship had its own two versions of the truth.

Not to mention the War of the Landing as seen through some atevi chronicles, not widely publicized, even on the mainland. For two hundred years, atevi had mostly heard the human version, the human excuse for it all—for the same reason.

In terms of keeping the two sides apart—that version worked.

But the two sides *weren't* keeping apart any longer. And old truths might meet and recognize each other as scary—at some unpredictable moment, with unforeseeable consequences.

"Shawn, I think it might be well to take a serious assessment of *your* protection. That's what my mainland-attuned mind thinks of. When things go unstable—the unstable start moving."

There was a moment of silence. Shawn looked sober, not scared.

"There's nothing that different," Shawn said. "They've always been there, a certain portion of unhappy people who just can't figure why they don't have what they planned in life. When we landed, it was the ship's fault. Yesterday it was the atevi's fault. Now it's the Reunioners' fault. I'm sure it will somehow become the atevi's fault again. I don't know how the radicals will get there, logically, but they'll work at it. It's their calling in life, I suppose, until the heavens open and deliver a dozen human ships ready to transport us all back to the human Earth."

That thought hit the pit of Bren's stomach. He didn't comment. Couldn't comment.

"I just urge," he said, "that you take more precautions than you're used to. I know it's tradition. I know the President has to be close to the people. But we can't lose you. The world can't lose you."

"I take it seriously. I do. I just can't armor up like an atevi lord. Tradition."

Bren laid a hand on his midsection. "Let me tell you. My bodyguard insists. Tabini-aiji insists. And yes, I hate the damned thing. But it makes them happy. And I have a spare, Shawn. We're about the same size."

"Oh, good God, Bren."

"It's not a hundred percent, but it's something, and you don't have to advertise it, just wear it for public events."

Shawn stared at him, stared a moment into blank space. "What do I do? Keep the coat buttoned?"

"Effectively, yes. Two choices, beige or green. Take your pick. You can have either. Take it as a gift."

"Beige, then. I take your point."

"Ship tech, the material."

"Damn it, Bren, it's the opposite of the world we want to create."

"It's insurance you'll be there to see it." A moment of silence, and a contemplation beyond the balcony. "We've got this barrier to get over. But it's five thousand people. Not a flood."

"The ideas will be."

"They're here to learn to be Mospheiran. Their world is already changed. Gone."

"It has to leave traces."

"And will, but they've lived in wreckage, Shawn. Nothing's whole. Not families, not habits, not jobs, nothing. The kids coming down—they never saw their station whole. Their whole conscious lives have been wreckage, ruin, the ship, and the station—and not the best side of the station, either."

"I had in mind a program," Shawn said. "It seems almost naive, but—a national day. A new emphasis on what we are. Not a commemoration of the Landing or the War—we've got that. But a day for what's traditional to us. Trips to the beach, or the mountains, a family holiday, just—enjoying life. Neighborhood festivals. The graces we've developed. Create holidays that don't refer back to the War of the Landing and blood and riot. Things like—oh, national tree plantings. Hiking trails. Nature. Family. Picnics. That sort of thing. I've thought of it."

"It's not a bad idea. You're dealing with five thousand people who've never seen dirt. Or trees."

"I think we should do it. Maybe if the Aslunds do fund a new party, it's one thing we can agree on."

"I wish you luck with that," Bren said. "I truly do."

The Heritage Party—about to fragment over the Tillington affair, and possibly to do it catastrophically, on Gin Kroger's broadcast and the Aslunds' desire for what the Reunioners brought . . . and do it a handful of days before the first Reunioners landed.

The fracture just about assured Shawn would win the next election.

But it was the rational opposition in the upper echelons of the party that had kept a lid on the irrational fringe over the last chaotic years.

Absent that—

"Lord Geigi's going to send down some gear that will make Francis House more secure," Bren said. "Understand, my bodyguard, on their own, is making a decision in the field to secure that residence, and to show your people some things that the Guild doesn't, as a rule, share. It's not without precedent, but it's a decision Tabini-aiji and the Guild Council will review. And they will eventually, very likely, demand concessions from Mospheira in return, likely during shared responsibility for Reunioners landing on atevi shuttles."

"We can work that out. And we'll keep that gear secure."

"The aiji will expect to share all tech and all processes, regardless of patent on this side of the straits."

"Our policy is leaning toward patenting the processes and sharing the science. A win for the companies and a win for the public. But we understand the aiji's position."

"Regardless of patent. I say this, in the capacity of my office *as* paidhi-aiji in the Mospheiran sense—I hope this won't agitate anyone. Just to have it straight. Regardless of patent, nothing held back. Atevi industry will take the identical information, including the patents, and share it across the board, and the aiji will license production in geographic areas that make sense for the aishidi'tat. If Mospheiran companies, with their patents, want to operate on this side of the strait, that's Mospheira's economy. Atevi companies won't compete. But they likewise won't share their developments except under trade agreement . . . regardless of starting from the same initial operation."

Shawn gave him a level look, having paused in his delivery of an egg to his plate. It persisted a moment, consideration of every bit of commercial information due to slide across the board, its effects on mining, materials science, transport, and societal well-being, Bren was quite sure. Shawn had all the experience, all the detailed complexity in mind. Bren returned the stare just as frankly, just as obdurate, and with two hundred years of the Treaty behind him.

"It would not be in either side's interest to seek changes in the Treaty over this," Shawn said.

"The aiji will undertake to share his own discoveries with Mospheira in due course," Bren said. "How Mospheira allots the patents therefrom will be Mospheira's problem. We expect that same openness to come from your side."

A slight smile touched Shawn's mouth. "We'll take the security advances you're handing over as an earnest of that."

"You can. Honestly. But in your own interest, don't disseminate them at this point. We'd only have to bring up other systems you really, culturally, don't want on this side of the water."

Ironic amusement reached the eyes. "Trust. I'd never have predicted we'd have Guild security inside our perimeter."

"We *can* do this because we're *at* parity. We've chased it for two hundred years. We're there. Two different economies. One technology. We won't give up all our secrets. Nor should you."

"We. Being the atevi."

Point. Definite point. "I *am* that, where it counts. I've no hesitation to say so."

"There's a certain comfort knowing I can contact the atevi mind that easily. You. Lord Geigi, who did his best during the bad years. It *is* different, dealing with you these days. It's a good difference. You seem at peace."

"I am. Linguistics is not going to be happy in the least as things change, starting with those three kids. But a direct contact is a good thing. You're always a phone call away from Geigi. Or Jase. He'll help you as quickly as I will."

"We haven't tended to rely on the ship."

"You can rely on *him*. If ever I'm not in reach. Seriously. Trust him. You can tell him anything."

"I take that as a solid fact. But—I continue to rely on you. I won't cut you free of us. Understand that. Linguistics can have its fits. But I get my advisements from you. I depend on it."

"I'll do my best," Bren said.

"Gin's documentary is forceful, beyond forceful; but if you're predisposed to believe it's all a lie, that's the only color some will see. And once Heritage splits—we've got the spillage, and we'll have to expect problems."

"I take it *your* security has names. And expectations."

"Plenty of them," Shawn said. "But it's the quiet ones from out of nowhere that cause the worst trouble."

That, in Mospheira's history, had tended to be the truth. It wasn't the ones that vented their anger that acted out irrationally. The ones to watch were the disconnected, the ones atevi called the clanless, who didn't join much of anything.

"I'll send that gift," he said. "Use it."

13

Everybody was late, everybody except the servants, most of whom had had their sleep, and except security, who decidedly had not. "Wake me when Mother or Uncle wakes," had been Cajeiri's last instruction, which had routed itself from bodyguard to bodyguard, and turned out to be later than he thought. He had no problem but lack of sleep, but Antaro was very sore and Jegari was nursing sore muscles. They were a sad little household, none of them looking cheerful, with Boji now starting to fret about his second breakfast, and Eisi and Liedi trying to see to everybody's wardrobe concerns while pacifying a spoiled parid'ja.

"Lord Tatiseigi is awake," Rieni said. Rieni's team and Mother's senior aishid—which was actually from Great-grandmother—had taken turns in the security station all night, but at least it was turns, and not long watches.

"How is Uncle?" he asked. "We might advise his physician."

"The physician is indeed on his way down," Rieni said, "but your great-uncle is insisting to dress and inquiring about breakfast. How he may descend the stairs, however, is a question."

"Please keep me aware. And Mother?"

"The aiji-consort is just waking," Rieni said, "by all we know."

"Then I should hurry," he said.

He washed, and dressed in his other good coat—likely Uncle's staff would do their best but cleaned and pressed wardrobe every morning was no longer a certainty. They would have to do as they could best do, and he did not expect even Mother to be critical.

Nomari most probably was awake as well, with staff stirring about, but the guards on his door would not permit him to go walking about.

He had *no* idea what to do about Nomari and Uncle's admission of him as a guest in the house.

But Uncle was up, and one was very glad to believe that Uncle was back in charge of his own house, at least in the important points. Uncle had the natural advantage in the courtesies balancing Nomari and Mother, and he truly thought it would be better to go to Uncle personally and explain how things stood, even if staff talked to staff with the details.

"I shall call on Uncle," he said, and his bodyguard, all eight, set themselves in order and moved with him, even Antaro, who was a little unsteady on her feet, and wearing her jacket over the injured arm.

Given Uncle's injuries and it being Uncle's house, it seemed excessive, however, to come in with all his bodyguard. "Wait here," he said, and, there being no response to a quiet knock, opened the door himself and slipped in, reckoning that Uncle's staff was likely all busy with Uncle, or just exhausted.

He had never seen the inside of Uncle's rooms before. They were less elaborate than he would have thought—there was, conspicuous on one wall, a helmet, a lance, and a shield that he had no doubt at all was something very special. It all looked old, and the Atageini lily figured on the metalwork. On one table was a figured pot with a seasonal arrangement, and a tapestry on the other wall, faded though it was, was a beautiful scene of ancient Tirnamardi, flying its banners on the outside.

The *age* of Tirnamardi decorated this room, a deliberate sparseness and aged functionality. These were real weapons, the swords above the door. They were not decor. The drapes were tapestry, and the floor was wooden and unpolished—the wooden section of floor in his room was polished till it shone.

"Well, Nephew. Welcome." Uncle had appeared in the inner door without his seeing, and he turned in half-guilty surprise.

"Staff informs me," Uncle said, "how you managed. How very well and sensibly you managed."

He felt his face quite warm. "One only hesitated to disturb you, Uncle, and Mother, well, one is sure she felt the same. Staff did everything."

"The Ajuri are settled, your mother and sister are safe, and we have lived to see the sunrise. Searchers have found only the one dead man, who can only have been up to no good at all, and we are secure. Well done. Well done, all of it." Uncle walked in, using a cane this morning, which was no wonder at all. "How are your two young bodyguards?"

"Both well, both moving gingerly, and greatly in awe of what you did, Uncle, getting control of the herd. I wish I might have seen it."

"I am very glad you did not. That poor two-year-old. —Heisi."

"Nandi?"

"How is the youngster doing? Ask the grooms."

"Nandi."

"It was a night," Uncle said, again to Cajeiri, and walking slowly, with thumps of the cane on the flooring. "It was a night, indeed. Have you spoken to your mother this morning?"

"Not yet, Uncle. I wished to know whether you will go down this morning."

"Ah, well, I have not lain abed a day in twenty years. I shall go down after a while. Though I think I shall ask staff to arrange breakfast. The question remains how staff shall compose a table, with your mother and our other guest. Shall you ask your mother, young gentleman?"

"Yes," he said. "I shall go advise her."

"Staff may serve breakfast to our other guest. One trusts breakfast for the lower stairs must soon be underway."

"Nandi," the major domo said, "it is."

Uncle had a habit of waving his hand when dismissing a topic. Between sling and cane, he could manage no more than a flick of the fingers. "Kindly go, nephew. Invite your mother. We are, we understand, saying *nothing* to Nomari-nadi. He must simply wait. —We may tell him, Heisi-ji, that we are still taking account of the damage last night, that his associates are safe, warm, and breakfasted, and that with injuries to myself and others, we are moving just a little slowly and out of order this morning. Tell him . . . well, mention *nothing* about the great *bus* sitting in the driveway, or about the arrival last night."

Nomari had been shut in his small suite, with Guild at the door, since midnight. He surely was pacing the floor by now, Cajeiri thought, and looking out the window—which would tell him nothing: the north windows overlooked the hedge and the closer part of the orchard, neither of which might inform him what was going on.

"I think," Uncle said, "that we shall unfold the table and have breakfast here, in this room, in half an hour. Advise your mother we are keeping no great state this morning. We do not wish to be outdone."

Mother was indeed awake, dressed in pale green and paler lace, with Beha and her other staff, and her bodyguard. A crib stood in the corner, and standing by it, Beha held Seimei in a fringed blanket. "We have been inquiring about Uncle," Mother said, "and we are very glad to hear he is up and about. Half an hour, you say. And will this Nomari attend?"

"Nomari is next door," Cajeiri said. "And one believes Uncle will leave it to you how and when you will meet him. He has not been invited."

"Well, well, and what is *your* estimation how this meeting should be, my wise son? You have dealt with him."

Perhaps it was an attack, for his presumption. A challenge to the fact, embarrassing to him, that rank *did* put her here and not in mani's habitual rooms?

The first sounded one way and the second sounded the other, and he found nothing to do but to say politely, "He does not know you are here, if staff has done as they should. One might wait. But the secret might not last."

"Indeed," Mother said. Seimei fussed a little. "Walk with her, Beha. And not near the window. She frets at too much light."

Beha turned away from the window and Seimei was quiet, then.

"I do not think we shall take your sister to such a meeting," Mother said, "but come, let us call on this person and see what he has to say for himself. I am beyond curious."

"Yes," he said, and walked with Mother to the door, with her guard, his guard, and the whole entourage except Beha and Seimiro. They went outside, they went to the left, where Uncle's guard sat watch at Nomari's door, and that guard rose to hasty propriety.

"Advise the gentleman he has visitors," Mother said, and one of the pair opened the door and went in to deliver that message.

"Nandi," the same guard said, exiting and holding the door open. Mother walked inside, Cajeiri did, with all their bodyguards—there was no preventing that under the circumstances.

Nomari was standing by the little table, in quite a modest suite. He looked at them in shock, surely, then gave a little bow and looked up.

"Nandiin," he said quietly.

"You know me," Mother said.

"Not for years," he said. "Not since we both left."

"I do not recognize you," Mother said.

"I would not know you, Damiri-daja, except I have seen pictures."

"Time," she said. "I have no doubt who I am. There is some doubt as to who you are."

"There was a statue," he said. "And you were bound to sit on it."

"Someone else might know that."

"There was a fence, too, and you were bound to climb it. I would think you still have a scar on your elbow."

"That, someone might know. It was a fair scene I made."

"There was a day," he said, "that we ate orangelles, that you stole."

Mother ducked her head and folded her arms, then looked up. "That I did. I bribed you to silence. And you were the one cook blamed."

"My father knew the truth," Nomari said, "so there was no consequence of it. I told him. But *your* father said I was a bad influence."

Mother nodded, and nodded again. "You indeed are that Nomari."

"Daja-ma." Nomari gave a little bow. "I am glad for your good fortune. I am glad, baji-naji, that you are where you are, and well. I hope you can find it possible—to take up the welfare of Ajuri. It is not resting in a good place right now."

"*You* are claiming the lordship, do I understand correctly?"

"In the absence of any other, daja-ma, who could claim a trace of the right. I would step back in an instant if you took it, with the aiji's support. I have never wanted it, I have never thought of it, except when my family died, but I was a boy, and I was a fool. Now I know who ordered my family killed, I know the name in the Guild that moved things, and he is gone, and revenge went with him. Whoever takes up the lordship now—" Nomari paused, seemed to rethink whatever he had been about to say, and gave a shake of his head. "Now the clan is in difficulty and the leadership it has is not what will bring it out again. *Someone* has to take it out of the disgrace and the trouble. Someone not a caretaker. The whole clan leadership is wrong.

Too many have scattered, too many that would die in a fortnight if they came home. There are too many inside who are trying simply to preserve their farms, their shops, their children, and they cannot not speak out where they are. They are *not* the ones to make a move, with so much at risk. But myself, I have no one. I have nothing to lose but my life, and I am willing to take that risk—not to throw my life away, not to throw away the ones who have come here to support me and appeal to Lord Tatiseigi. Geidaro has been here, daja-ma. Your son can tell you. She has made threats in this house, under this roof, and last night—last night—you have surely heard what happened."

"I have heard," Mother said quietly. "And Lord Tatiseigi has Filed Intent on my great-aunt in consequence. But—she might say in her turn—perhaps it was one of *your* people who loosed the mecheiti last night, to persuade Lord Tatiseigi to a move which *could* advantage you, nadi."

There was stark, dreadful silence. Cajeiri held his breath, and saw shock on Nomari's face. Shock and dismay. Mother had cut deep.

"Can you think that, daja-ma?"

"The Bujavid has a proverb. Who gains most?"

"If I have lost your good opinion," Nomari said, "then I have lost my oldest ally, and I am likely dead. But I do not admit that possibility. And I swear to you I had no hand in it. Nor would shelter anyone who did."

There was a terrible silence. Cajeiri thought of saying, *He has not seemed like that.* All he knew, all he had felt around Nomari for all the time here, said that he was in absolute earnest. But Mother stood there, looking at Nomari, waiting for some answer.

"It has been years," Mother said. "People change."

"They do change. You have changed, daja-ma. You are not that little girl."

"And you are not that boy. What are you? A workman? A *spy?*"

Nomari's brow knit.

"What have you to do with Lord Machigi?" Mother asked sharply.

An intake of breath. Then a nod. "I have dealt with him, daja-ma. Somewhat. For a while. It was a place to be."

"Indeed, the district of a lord who held off Murini's people would offer some safety—a refuge for someone trying to escape the notice of the rebels. But you were not in the Taisigin Marid. You spent *your* time up in Senjin."

"Spying, yes, for him. To warn him if Senjin moved against his border. To watch the rail up there, what moved, what cargoes. I watched the watchers on the railroad. I informed him. I also informed my people. I told many of those people gathered downstairs where to move, where safety was, because Murini's moves and Ajuri's whisper from the Guild were the same thing, bent on finding us and killing us singly, if they could. I spied for Lord Machigi. And I spied for every Ajuri trying to stay out of the reach of the Guild. No few of us were down in the Marid, those that were not sheltered in the guilds and trades. We informed each other, we gathered information, we moved people about and we warned people where we knew the hunters might be getting close. Open that gate last night, with *my* people in the way? No, nandi, that I did not! Nor can I believe my people did it."

Machigi, Cajeiri thought. A spy for Machigi? Machigi was their ally now, or said he was, so it was not so bad, but it was still the other side—of the three sides there had been. Machigi had always been at odds with Father, from before Murini's time. Shishogi had been backing Murini; and Father and Mother had spent two years dodging people trying to kill them, sleeping in hedges, trying not to bring the hunters down on the allies they had.

"Have you *continued* to work for him?" Mother asked, relentless.

"On occasion I have," Nomari said. "And done it with a much better will, daja-ma, once he made peace with the aishidi'tat."

There was a silence then. "Come to breakfast," Mother said. "Lord Tatiseigi is suffering from his fall. He will have breakfast in his quarters. You will be welcome."

Welcome, Cajeiri thought. After *that!* He was not sure he wanted breakfast himself.

Should he say, Nomari has been very proper, when Mother had just attacked him for the purpose of getting at the truth? Should he say anything?

Yes. He should.

"Honored Mother, he has answered questions for *me.*"

Then he thought, too late, of the things he *had* asked Nomari before everything had happened, and how reluctant Mother was to talk about herself, or Ajuri, or any of the unpleasantness around her goings and comings in Ajuri.

"Indeed?" Mother said. "What is your opinion, son of mine, of what he says here and now?"

There was nothing for it. "That it sounds like the truth."

"There are shades and degrees of that," Mother said. "But the boy I knew has apparently walked in the borderlands of it as long as either of us can remember. Nomari."

"Daja-ma."

"You may not call me Damiri. I left that territory when I married, understand. But I am *disposed* to remember that we are cousins. I am *disposed* to find out what you intend. We cannot draw on what was. I accept who you were. I want to find out who you *are.*"

"Daja-ma, I have *no* fear of the truth."

"Then let us go to my uncle's rooms," she said, in that light tone only Mother could manage, "and let us have a pleasant breakfast."

Breakfast was a casual, pleasant affair in Uncle's rooms, with everyone on their best behavior despite the surprise of Nomari's arrival. But Uncle was still very sore and tired easily, and Mother wanted time alone with Nomari, and so there was very little after breakfast talk, and nothing of substance said, other than Mother's assurance to Uncle that she truly believed Nomari to be her cousin.

And then, on their return to the room she had, and Nomari's place, next door, she asked . . . *asked* . . . Cajeiri to give her time alone with her cousin, in the same words and tone she might have used to his father.

That had never happened before. If she wanted him out of the room, he was dismissed.

It was respect she offered. Respect to the aiji's heir . . . and, dared he hope, respect for his own handling of the situation? Was he, then, behaving as his father's heir should?

Certainly he was trying.

Or was it just because Nomari was there and she was keeping to the proper forms to keep a family quarrel out of Nomari's sight? Either way, as much as he wanted to be in there, as much as he wanted to hear what Nomari had to say, Father was depending on Mother's evaluation of Nomari, and his being in there might keep her from asking the very questions she most wanted answers to.

So he left.

But with Uncle in bed, Mother and Nomari in Nomari's sitting room, with security still tight everywhere both on the grounds and in the house, Cajeiri found himself at a loss for occupation. He could play with Boji, but somehow he found himself just staring at the cage, without an inclination to do anything else. He could remember his younger self and his associates playing with Boji, but it seemed faint and distant, like a memory of watching someone else. He could take Boji out on his leash, could toss things for him to catch . . . could go through all the motions that other Cajeiri had made, but it just . . . no longer appealed. Things had grown much too serious. His senior aishid was downstairs, conferring with security. Antaro was with nand' Pari, Uncle's physician, who wanted to see her arm. Jegari was with her—*he* was limping this morning. Veijico and

Lucasi were left, but they had no particular cheer in the situation.

Staff appeared at the door, delivering a message with no cylinder, just a folded paper with no seal. That was uncommon. Maybe it was just kitchen asking where he wanted lunch.

But the address on the folded paper, *Cajeiri,* was entirely informal, and it was *Mother's* handwriting.

Perhaps, he thought, Mother was inviting him to come into the meeting. He unfolded it in anticipation.

Son of mine,

Be patient.

I know you wish to hear your cousin's answers, and I wish you to hear him. But answers flow more freely considering memories we separately have of Ajiden. Be patient. I have yet to find him in a lie and I am learning things to which you would have no key.

Soon.

That was not what he hoped. But it was extraordinary on its own. He read it several times, trying to find a barb in it, but he failed to find one. It was blunt, to the point, but considerate, just in the fact she *had* written it and sent it—almost the first time she had ever addressed him so nicely all the way through any exchange, when it was something that could not be overheard.

He thought maybe he should burn it. Letters containing politics often needed to be burned, and burned fairly quickly: in the absence of a fireplace, a small dish would serve. But he was inclined to keep the letter. He read it yet one more time, then decided he could just keep it secret awhile, and folded it, and tucked it into his inner coat pocket, a little treasure—of a peculiar kind. It was certainly to be removed before he surrendered the coat to Eisi and Liedi—little there was that they had not witnessed, in his ongoing difficulties with his mother, but all the same, this was committed to paper, and involved Nomari, and was chancy to keep.

Silly, he thought himself. Mother had been particularly polite. He should be more so.

He sought paper and pen to answer. *Honored Mother*, he wrote.

Thank you. One understands. I shall be in the library reading this afternoon, or in my rooms. Please send for me if I can be of any help. I shall have my bodyguard with me constantly.

He finished his lunch, and went down to the vast library only with Veijico and Lucasi, but the library was actually closer to Rieni and the seniors.

He read. But it seemed that every book he pulled out was a history of the valley or the memoirs of some important person, which only made him think about Mother and Nomari and what was being said behind that closed door, and wishing he might be called in.

Finally, he chose a book of historic engravings at complete random and headed back upstairs to his room, with Lucasi and Veijico in attendance—Antaro and Jegari had gone back to the suite to rest, so Lucasi said, and would meet them there.

As they passed Mother's suite, however, a sharp, angry howl erupted from the room, almost the match for Boji when he was upset.

Seimei.

Seimiro.

His sister. The protest was over as quickly as it began, but he stopped, listening for a second outcry, and quite sure that her nurse, Beha, was with her.

Still . . .

He went to that door and rapped softly, for himself, with Veijico and Lucasi behind him.

They were taking no chances. Guild asked, through the door, who he was.

"Cajeiri, aiji-meni, nadiin. Open the door."

The door opened without hesitation. He walked in with his

book, with Veijico and Lucasi, gave a little nod to Beha, who was bending over Seimei, trying to cajole her to better humor.

He gave the book to Veijico.

Seimei was in her crib, waving a fist at a sparkling trinket Beha had just hung above, and just beyond her reach. It was *not* a reach. It was an attack. Seimei had an opinion of being carried off from her nursery with the beautiful tall windows in the middle of the night and taken on a train, and then a bus, and then put into a strange bed and a strange room. Seimei was having the second adventure of her very young life, the first having happened the very night she was born.

Father probably had not approved her being brought here, all things considered, but Mother had the right. It was in the marriage contract.

Nobody, however, had asked Seimei what she thought.

Nobody had shown her any choices, either. And now, Mother was absent. There was her nurse Beha. Four domestic staff. And, he was sure, a double handful of Guild in the back rooms, watching over the place—but Seimei was not appeased.

Beha bowed to him and quietly retreated to a needlework stand beside the window, settling where she could be available, watching, ready to intervene, but not intruding while Seimei was quiet.

"Hello, Seimei," he said. "Do you recognize me in this place?" He reached a reasonably clean hand into the crib, intercepting a flailing hand with a fingertip. Tiny fingers curled around his finger and pulled it to a waiting mouth. Everything, according to Antaro, ended up in babies' mouths, which was why, he supposed, that trinket had been hung out of reach. But it seemed a rather mean trick. And had not satisfied her at all.

She was so very tiny. It was hard to believe he had been this small and unaware himself, nine years ago, having not a clue even for the simplest words, unable to ask for what he wanted, unable to walk or run or remotely understand the twists and turns of ambition and politics.

But last night and this morning, he had been in charge of . . . everything. So many people had been depending on him for stability and reassurance, when—what did he know, more than others?

Some things. Some things he knew. He had done things others could hardly imagine. Been to deep space and back. Talked to the kyo.

And last night, he realized now, was only the start of his life. For the rest of his years he would have an increasing number of lives depending on his good sense—more than just his aishid, who knew on their own what to do, and whose job was to protect him. He would have innocent people on his hands, people who needed help, and protection, and who knew nothing of the political shots that sailed past them. He was his father's heir, and nothing would change that course of things. Ever.

Which eventuality he would very much like to avoid for many years to come.

There was so much to learn, yet. There were so many things he could not understand.

And his sister would follow, baby steps at first, right down his track. She could hardly help it. He could hardly warn her at this stage. She would not have all of it. But she would *be* in the heart of it.

Golden eyes peered in his direction. The color was beginning to clear: it had been an odd dusky brown not too many days ago. Now they looked as if they might go pale gold, more like Father's than Mother's.

He might be jealous of that, one day. People said Father's eyes were an advantage, that they made his opposition uneasy, because they seemed to pierce right through to the truth. His own eyes were more like his mother's, definite gold with bright strands that caught the light, up very, very close.

Pretty was what everyone said about Mother's eyes. He didn't want to be pretty: he had much rather be fierce like Father, and have his enemies at a distance.

But looks did not make the man, he had heard that often enough, too. And he was becoming more like Father, or so people said. Which was not surprising. Mani had reared Father, and Mani had had him more often than his parents had, growing up. Mani and even nand' Bren had been his teachers, far more than Mother ever had.

Will you be more like Father? he asked his sister in his head. *Or like Mother? You have them both to draw from. I would really advise you listen to Father first.*

Mother would have the rearing of her, but Mother's own childhood had been very uncertain. Mother had been reared around . . . there was no other way to say it . . . very nasty, insane people. Her father must have been afraid every day. But Seimei would have Father and all the Guild to keep her safe.

And she would have him. He would not let her grow up scared.

But his sister could not grow up too protected, either. He wondered if Mother would have brought her into this mess, had she known everything that was going on. He *hoped* she would have. He hoped she wouldn't protect Seimei too much. Seimei had to grow up strong and able to make decisions.

Not *his* sort of decisions. Not Father's—unless something happened to her big brother. But—Seimei had the same inheritance—the very same—that he did. Except what he already held.

Things suddenly came clear to him, *why* Mother had come, *why* Mother had brought Seimei to Tirnamardi, to lie in this crib, this very crib that had been gathering dust in a storeroom until last night.

He ran fingers along the carved, polished vines that were the rail, noted the headboard, that was a carving of lilies—Atageini lilies.

No baby had lain in this crib, he thought, since Mother had. Not since Mother had been stolen from it, and the whole history had begun. Mother had come back to Atageini lands once, running from Ajuri and all that was going on there—maybe running from her father, or running because her father had told her to. She had lived here—and gone back again. And left Ajuri on her own. She had not brought Ajuri into the marriage with Father. There had been no agreement with any clan—just—Father had wanted her, married her, and stayed with her, when he knew his grandfather and great-grandfather had had a lot of marriages and all sorts of tangles from them.

Mother had survived, with Father, at the edge of Uncle's estate, during the Troubles, hiding in hedgerows, possibly even in the great hedge of Tirnamardi from time to time. She had surely known Uncle would welcome them and try to protect them, that soft beds could be had—just that close—when they were sleeping in some leaky shed. But she had not left Father, no matter how hard it got.

Now with Seimei so very tiny, Mother came back yet again, and laid Seimei in the bed she had had once, before Grandmother had been murdered, before Grandfather had fled with her and started the whole awful chain of events.

Mother had brought Seimei to a place under siege, for one thing, because Seimei was *hers*, as he was not, and that was her right, in her marriage with Father. A child for Father, and a child for her, in her own right.

Not a child for Ajuri. No, not for Ajuri. That was not the place Mother intended for Seimei. This cradle was what the staff had brought, perhaps hopefully, and if Mother had not wanted it, she could have told them to take it away.

She had not said that. She had surely guessed whose it had been and what it was. And she had laid Seimei in it, in a nest of Atageini lilies.

Uncle has no heir, he said to Seimei in his mind, her tiny hand in his. *That is where this whole thing began. He has no one. When he lost his sister he became alone, and he has lived that way ever since, except when Mother or Great-grandmother was here.*

Mother brought you here, he said in his mind, gazing into eyes only beginning to take on awareness. *Mother brought you here, because you are hers, and you are Great-uncle's heir.*

Uncle is old, and he is hurt, and Great-grandmother may be his ally, but an ally is not what Uncle needs most now. He needs to know, in dealing with a lordship in Ajuri, that the lordship of Atageini will not fall vacant after him.

It will not be now. I hope it is not for a long time But to bring you here, now, in the middle of all this—I think Mother would have waded through an army.

Seimei's eyes drifted shut. Opened again. She freed her hand and patted his, if a series of blows from a tiny fist could be a fond gesture. He smiled at her. She stared at him. And hit his hand again.

There are people, sister, that you will have to know. Mani, and nand' Bren. Father, of course. And Uncle. Uncle can seem fierce, but he will never be that toward you.

You already have enemies. You were born with them. So was I. Mother and Father, Uncle and Great-grandmother will stand them off for now. But you have to be smart. Smarter than your enemies are.

And you have to see things and learn things and meet different people. Mother will try to keep you safe, but you cannot learn the things you need, just being safe. You have to do reckless things, and take chances. You just have to be smart enough to survive them. I can help. I will help.

Uncle could have died last night. That was a scary thought. A really scary thought. And without Seimei, the Atageini at that point would be in the same state as Ajuri and Kadagidi, with the whole Padi Valley Association, excepting only the sub-clans and Taiben, which was a new member, sitting lordless. That was the whole ancient heart of the aishidi'tat, with the Shadow Guild possibly lurking in the corners of Ajiden.

If Seimei was lord too soon, would Mother take over—at least until Seimei was old enough? Mother would. It would upset all their lives, and Father would be more than upset, but Mother would step in.

That had to be what Mother was thinking, next door, asking Nomari questions.

But choosing an heir . . . how could Uncle know how Seimei would grow up? Who could tell whether or not she could draw man'chi to her the way a lord must? Mother could not. That had always been the trouble. Mother on her own could not do what Uncle did.

I will not let you grow up weak, Seimei. That much I can see to. I will see you grow up strong. I am not sure I can teach you to be wise. But I shall teach you books. And maps. And mecheiti. I shall teach you to ride. You have to learn. You will manage one of the oldest stables in the aishidi'tat, and mine will be the newest.

And if Mother can make good sense of Nomari . . .

If we can possibly rely on him . . .

Nomari had said he had never met a real lord before, and now he had met two, meaning, so he said at the time, Uncle and himself. And he had been a little suspicious Nomari was trying to flatter him.

But was that the case? Had he been truthful? Nomari had met Machigi. He had *spied* for Machigi. Was that the lord Nomari had meant, and not him at all?

Or was Machigi *different* from a clan lord? Machigi had ruled like an aiji in the South. He had the ability to draw the man'chi of the southernmost clans, and he had evaded Father's invitations to come to court—that was nothing unusual for a Marid lord. He had survived the Troubles and the actions of the Shadow Guild in the South, who had wanted to kill him as much as they had wanted to kill Father. After Father had come back to power, Machigi had negotiated an association with Great-grandmother, through nand' Bren, but he had sent a trade representative to Shejidan instead of coming to the capital himself to deal with Father, and he had not taken his seat in the legislature. The whole Marid went unrepresented there. But Machigi had kept himself surrounded by his own Marid-born bodyguards and safe in his own hall. Machigi dealt with Great-grandmother, and *promised* to give up his claim on the west coast. But Father never quite trusted him. Nor did anybody else, even Great-grandmother.

Was *that* who Nomari admired? Machigi was dealing with Great-grandmother, and Great-grandmother might be able to distract him to ambitions in the East, but the whole Marid was still like a bubbling pot, apt to boil over, situations never resolved, and able to bring war to the whole south coast. With ties to the center of the aishidi'tat—he could become a problem to the north. Machigi was a problem, and mani intended to turn him to her own projects in the East, far, far in the other direction. But in the future—mani had no heir, either. Or she did, but it was Father, and him, but they could not rule in the East.

Machigi had no heir. And without him, there was the Senjin Marid and the Dojisigin Marid ready to start trouble again.

All this—time would do. And someday—he would be sitting where his father sat. With all of this.

He wished desperately that he were in that room with Mother and Nomari. He wished he knew what they were saying, what memories they did share, and whether Nomari himself had what it might take to survive longer than Grandfather had.

He wished he had some sense whether Mother *could* get the truth out of Nomari—whether he *felt* she was someone he had to answer. She was aiji-consort, and *Father* respected her. People were polite to her, and she stood toe to toe with mani and traded words, which very few people would ever do.

But could she impress somebody like Nomari, who was like a puzzle-knot, a different problem on every surface? Had she the force Father saw in her? She had attack: he knew that. But was it all? Only Ajuri had ever been keen on attaching to her— but they had had ulterior motives; and a lot of the lords had no confidence in Mother, repeatedly asking why Father chose a permanent attachment to someone of no personal advantage.

That was what most people thought of Mother. She thought too much. She felt too angry. Could she manage to stir something in Nomari that would make him—*make* him be loyal to Father?

And to him?

Mother can be a problem, Seimei, he thought, brushing a black fuzz of hair on his sister's head. *I hope you can deal with her. Mother lost me, even though I try very hard, but then she remembers she is angry at Great-grandmother, and me, and I do not know if that will ever change. Do not let her separate us. We are going to have problems. And if you can be as powerful as Uncle is, it would help so much.*

I so hope you get to know mani. I am not sure Mother can ever be what mani is, and if you are to be lord of Atageini, you must become more like mani than Mother.

Even without mani, you will have me and I shall teach you how to pick a lock. And I shall show you the back passages in the Bujavid. I think those are good things to know.

I wish you could be older overnight, so that I could begin to show you these things right now.

You come to me, Seimei, whenever you need to. No matter who I am someday.

He was Father's heir and that meant taking the aishidi'tat into the future. He had been to space and met the kyo. Seimei would never do that. He would have to show her the importance of technology and tell her where it was taking them.

But Seimei was going to take Uncle's place and that meant something just as important. She would inherit that library, and the bedroom with real weapons on the wall, and the room of tree rings in the basement and all the other wonderful things down there.

Seimei would have to preserve all those traditions Uncle protected. Because they mattered. He saw just the edges of the ways they mattered. So he had to ask Uncle about all those things, to be sure, absolutely sure, no matter what happened, that Seimei knew.

He looked down at that small sleeping lump, and thought of the work ahead of him, feeling just a little overwhelmed.

You had better *grow up smart, younger sister.*

14

Breakfast and impending lunch, with four of Shawn's best security units, severely taxed available space and seating in the Francis House apartment, but Narani and Jeladi kept tea and sandwiches coming, a hospitality apparently unexpected in Presidential security sessions—

A break came welcome, to judge by the relaxation of tensions and apprehensions. By mid-morning, the new had worn off and the mood had been all business.

Diplomacy was definitely called for. These agents were veterans, experienced, fiercely proud of their own service, and Bren began it all with a reference to trust, cooperation, and atevi confidence that they were the very best protection for a household in which Tabini-aiji had a deep personal interest, and trusted for a special cooperation. These sixteen men and women would be the keystone to the security surrounding the Reunioners.

"What I am about to say, what my staff is about to say, is mostly unprecedented—but not entirely so. The Guild, indeed, the whole aishidi'tat is grateful for the assistance of Mospheirans in maintaining communication and a flow of supply during the crisis on the mainland. The new Guild leadership views those efforts very favorably." One did *not* say that the same people who had once fought human influence, the same ones who had worked most closely with Mospheirans during the crisis, now *were* the Guild leadership. The identity of the Council leadership was not given out, ever, least of all to Mospheirans.

"Tabini-aiji is deeply concerned for the welfare of these three children, who are uniquely attached to his son and heir, specifically because he foresees that attachment may make them a target. He could create a home for them on the mainland, and surround them with protection, but he also knows that is not the human environment these children need for their growing up.

"So he is grateful to the President for providing a safe place and the security they will need. They're ordinary children in an extraordinary situation: but they have had extraordinary experiences. They are relatively fluent in Ragi, they were companions to the aiji's son on the voyage out from Reunion, and they will be the first Reunioners to live here, ahead of all their community—which unfortunately focuses attention on them, both good and bad, and necessarily places them at risk. You know that better than I do. They will intermittently be guests of the aiji's son. Someday they may hold my job.

"But their maturing in the human sense has to take place in a human setting, for their own mental health, and they need have a sense of security in their residence as well as the ability to travel about safely and learn what it is to live on Mospheira, so it will not all be within the walls of Heyden Court. The President picked you for a responsibility somewhere between parental and protective—because you will be in personal contact with them. These kids will look up to you, take your advice—try your patience, maybe, in the way of normal children. They're good kids, in all senses. They come with parents who've been through the destruction of their whole world, and who've lived under desperate circumstances, but the parents are also good people—a little lost in the enormity of the events they've endured, but trying their best. You'll deal with them, too, and with the staff who'll be in charge of Heyden Court—who, I can assure you, are absolutely top administrators, people who will operate with a direct link to the President, and who will listen to you. They're the best. As you are—hand-picked by the President, to be in charge of a situation that links directly to the stability of human and atevi cooperation. *That's* the importance of this post. It's a pilot project, in one sense, and two governments are looking to you to make it work and keep these kids safe.

"In that light, it's useful for both atevi and human security to understand each other's operations.

"And through my bodyguard, the Guild is offering a cooperation which would have been impossible even a few short years ago. They are willing to open their operations manual, so to speak. They have suggested easy modifications to the premises, which are well in progress, that enable a relatively small force to deal with everything from minor incidents to well-organized attacks on the building. They are very interested, themselves, to hear what you know: they believe that your insight, given your experience protecting the President, gives you a unique perspective on the problems that can come up. They're going to be sharing some of their classified operations with you in the process. This was their decision, a Guild decision in which I had no part, and is an indication of just how much the aiji is ready to trust you."

That drew interest. The Assassins' Guild was notoriously secretive.

"We also have recommendations for equipment the station is providing—ship tech. Monitoring equipment. I am no expert in any of this. My bodyguard has given *me* standing orders to keep my head down and stay there." That drew mild amusement, a little lowering of guard. "And in that spirit, I'll ask them to take over and I'll simply translate from now on. They'll explain the physical changes they've suggested in the Heyden Court site, what they are, and how it can translate to better security."

Not starting with procedural changes, but changes in the building. Blueprints. Accesses. The methodology explanation slipped right into the simple changes. They were putting an atevi-style control in place, creating an environment with numerous checkpoints, with protected communication and restriction on doors and hallways, so that nobody from the outside stood a chance of reaching anything critical at the heart of the arrangement.

The approach to this first meeting had been Banichi's suggestion, aimed at protecting the pride of these men and women, outlining how the design worked, and with that, offering new tech to sweeten the deal . . . a case in which the paidhi-aiji performed his original function, arbiter of technology, for the first time in years . . . only, this time, coming from the atevi side to Mospheira.

With Shawn's specific orders in their hands, and assured of issues like rank and pay, the several teams had arrived with an understanding that the kids' problems were going to range from Reunioners having adjustment problems, to domestic political heat, and curiosity—high on the list, the attraction the place might pose to both the curious and the violent, not to mention the kind of craziness that could come *from* the Reunioner hard cases, given time and opportunity and a workshop.

"So how would *you* set up, in specific?" was the opening question from Mospheiran security, one which never, *ever* in the history of the Guild had Mospheirans been able to ask. *Banichi will not answer that*, Bren thought, ready to deflect a problem. "He asks specifics of how the Guild would set up," he gave the translation. "I shall refuse."

"No, nandi," Banichi said. "We shall answer."

Banichi then began to answer, point by point, giving reasons and information that one was sure might cause consternation in the Guild Council, with as well-disposed a Council as had ever sat in charge of Guild operations. Guild *never* provided such information, even in theory, let alone discussed the rationale behind it.

But Banichi did, and sitting by was Algini, whose rank in the inner workings of the Guild Algini never admitted, not even to him . . . listening, Tano and Jago as well, as something truly unprecedented went on. Station security could *observe* Geigi's security in action, could know *what* they did and *where* they were, but *why*, the soft tissue of it all, was not something Guild even told their employer, unless it was need-to-know.

Mospheiran security liked a set of standing orders that covered contingencies, and that they surely had in this: they looked at the set of barriers to intrusion, they asked questions, and then Banichi used his own bracelet to demonstrate the hierarchy of flash codes that provided a fairly uncrackable communication. The only thing an opponent might know was that it was going on, but what was being communicated—no. The code changed. Often. And this—nobody but the unit knew, though Bren had the notion that there were some master codes that could mean one thing reliably, and Banichi said nothing about that.

The Mospheiran team listened—they more than listened: they drank it in, asked intelligent questions, to Bren's estimation, and then Banichi asked, "What would *you* do, nadiin? What would you change?"

"Considering the set-up," Ing said, senior in the group, "we're happy. The sensor system would be more than welcome."

That was going to come down from the station on the same shuttle as the kids.

A fair cordiality had set in. They already had Shawn's order swearing that they would have his support, that they would wield a very high level of authority, with direct access to Shawn's office, and to the paidhi's office, at need. They would be in the executive, but shielded by State, with broad powers to deny access to premises and to protect their charges.

Maintain confidence without arrogance, Shawn had written in the authorization that had gone out to each member of this hand-picked group. *Your mission is to protect three children and their parents, who may have to be protected from their own innocence, but never treated as ill-meaning. You will be representing our government, in response to a request from the* head of state of the aishidi'tat, and it is not impossible that you may at some point be in direct communication with atevi authority. Conduct any such interaction in consultation with my office, but you may respond directly, even in Ragi, if that becomes possible.

You will also be dealing with our own citizenry who may or may not be operating in innocence. The program may stir controversy and attract problems. You will also become a resource for law enforcement and courts, in the lengthy process of acculturating other Reunioners. You will be their advocates, occasionally called on to instruct and protect, occasionally to advise and intervene in dealing with problem individuals.

In the execution of treaty obligations, you will not be operating within civil law. You will operate under the military code, responsible directly to the President and the State Department, so long as the aiji requests you to remain. You are empowered to detain and restrain, physically if necessary. You have the power to arrest, to search and seize, and to use lethal force in the protection of premises and persons.

It was high rank they were offered. It was executive responsibility. It was dealing directly with a foreign power and with foreign professionals. He had handed them his own list of cautions.

A University official demanded entry? No. The University was no longer in charge of Heyden Court. It was under long lease to the government.

Someone urgently needed an exception to a security rule? Surround it, search it, neutralize any threat, isolate the principals from any risk and consider the situation.

There was a fire on the premises. Distrust fire services and strangers alike, protect the principals, and call it an incident, not an accident, until one had determined a cause.

There were people to deal with as authority within the building, with an absolute security clearance and a direct Presidential access equaling theirs: Kate Shugart, principally, who would be there or be reachable. Tom Lund and Ben Feldman as backup. They were clear on that.

"These people are quick," Banichi remarked during a break, "and they are good. We are reassured." Bren translated it for them, and these dour, wary people took that in with guarded pleasure. Mospheirans had held a notion of the Guild as passionless and approaching supernatural abilities, which the Guild had never taken pains to deny. But the two services had managed to enjoy tea and cakes and agree on specifics. Mospheiran security seemed to take to heart Banichi's points about the third floor arrangement, and communication—the promise of advanced, secure tech that could give them an edge. No bracelets: the Guild did not pass those around. But a sort of mutating code they could use with their own audio system. Cordiality absolutely blossomed.

"So will you still be here," one asked, speaking directly to Banichi as they had begun to do, with Bren translating, "—will you be here to set up this new tech?"

"There will be an expert coming down from the station, to set up and instruct, with manuals. A Mospheiran expert."

Bren translated that, which pleased them. "And," Bren said then, the preset agenda having reached an end. It was his job to explain this final element—the human part. "The Reunioners themselves—not the children or their parents, but the ones to follow. By the time they come down, you may be advising other units on what they have to expect. We've found the children's parents to be good people, good parents, cooperative if occasionally confused. That won't be directly your problem: but that's the most of the Reunioners, completely helpless with daily life down here. In this case—the children know, but the parents don't.

"As time goes on, however, there'll be more of them: that's the idea. Five thousand of them, and other units may be asking you for your expertise. They're far more of a mixed bag of the good and not-so-good. The last-down may not be willing participants in the program. And while they'll look just like Mospheirans, in some ways atevi thinking and atevi solutions might make more sense to you than their approach to a situation. By that time, you'll know a lot more what they came from. They've never been on a planet, they've never seen rain, or a sunset, they've never experienced natural ground or walked on a surface that doesn't, in some small degree, curve upward. They don't know how to use a kitchen: that's all been done by professionals. There's hardly any aspect of earthly life they're prepared to understand. And they've lived all their lives inside a structure. Corridors, not roads, are their native pathways. If one of the last-down goes rogue or goes missing—look to the underground: ventilation shafts. Even sewers. Open sky can be upsetting to them. Think of a bus, if someone slams the brakes on. That's been their world: if there's a threat, open spaces can kill you. They'll seek confined areas. These are people who've survived two devastating attacks on their station. They've lived in the wreckage, nursing a living out of barely functioning machinery, never knowing when the next attack might come to take them out.

"That's what they came from. What they came to, here, was in some ways worse, because they were promised everything would be better. Aboard our space station, they've lived jammed together in conditions we wouldn't ask an animal to endure—not even decent water access. One assumes there's the usual proportion of problem cases and good citizens you'd find right here in Port Jackson, but bear in mind, these are the survivors. The resourceful ones. Unfortunately, the experience didn't instill virtue in all of them. Station's trying to identify the problems before they come down, but there are no records, no identification, and no available witnesses in many cases. They'll be landing down here with a brand new ID and in most cases, no record at all, not of their education, their prior jobs, or their skills, or past activity. It's all to determine. And there'll be some that won't adjust.

"These hard cases won't be *your* problem, unless their

behavior impacts the safety of the children, but you *will* be dealing with public perception and public assumptions. The landings are bound to generate controversy, more so as it gets to the not-so-virtuous, and how you speak about your charges and the Reunioners in general to the news will matter. *You* will have good people to deal with. And I can assure you they *want* to be here. They look forward to it. But they may have small moments when the strangeness is more than they can handle. Be patient.

"You'll also be dealing with three University students, who'll come and go. They're not to bring in outsiders, and they know that. They're kids. Language students, who'll be the kids' teachers. They're not professionals. If there's a problem with them, talk to Dr. Shugart. She'll bring them right.

"Questions?"

An exchange of looks, slight shakes of heads, then Ing said, "We've seen the documentary from the station, Mr. Cameron. Nothing you've said surprises us. We understand it's to air this evening. Should we expect trouble? Should we be proactive?"

"Always," was Banichi's response when Bren translated that, and: "Place yourselves in areas of gathering this evening. Take note of reactions."

To which Bren added: "Pubs. Bars. Judiciously, of course."

It was, Bren thought, seeing them out the door, a success, a long session, but a good one. They were due a second, more technical session tomorrow.

"They will do," Banichi said. "One believes they will do well."

15

It had been a long day. The Ajuri had gone out to recover their camp in the morning, and staff had gone out to help set up the collapsed tents and secure the rest, taking in muddied bedding to wash and restore as much as they could, first in tubs filled from the pump—wet work, with rain still sifting down, before bringing it into the lower halls. There were few comforts out there, but staff provided chairs and benches, and a table with an endless supply of tea and small sandwiches.

And the shiny red and black bus had loaded up amid it all, to make a run to Diegi. Uncle, despite nand' Pari's pleas, had flatly refused to go, and as the next best thing, nand' Pari had sent along his notes for the hospital in Diegi to review. Antaro had also resisted going, protesting that it was only a green break, that the wrap and splint had been done by Uncle's own physician, but it was swelling, her fingers showed it, she was reluctant to take painkillers, and Veijico and Lucasi added their opinions to Jegari's that she should go. Cajeiri firmly finished the argument without even asking the seniors to step in.

"One day, Taro-ji. Just a day. If I am not safe for one day with your teammates and the seniors, and Uncle's guard and Mother's, then I shall never be safe enough. Go. Have it seen to. Please. As a favor to me. The bus is going anyway, and you will be as comfortable sitting on the bus as sitting with us."

Antaro had boarded, though not happily, and Jegari with her. Domestic staff boarded, and then four of Uncle's guard in full kit. Who had ordered them along as protection, Cajeiri was not sure, since Uncle had slept most of the day, but he suspected his own seniors might have, with two of the missing still at large, and especially with Uncle just having Filed on Great-aunt Geidaro. It was a comfort. Antaro and Jegari had brought their own communications and weapons with them, but it was a comfort all the same.

So the bus at long last trundled off down the long drive toward the gate and vanished behind the roll of the land. It would be a little more than two hours to Diegi, an hour there, and two coming back. There was no question of the Taibeni camped outside the gate accompanying it, at the speed it could make all the way to Diegi. It would be off, on a well-maintained road, so Uncle's people said. They were sure the bus, large though it was, would have no problem with the bridge, which was steel, so staff said, and wide enough.

"One hopes they are right about that," he said, and Veijico said quietly, "Staff has checked the load limit. They are well within it."

So, so many things to think of, doing the simplest thing. He could not get completely ahead of the seniors, he saw that. But then, as mani said, he should not get in the way of his staff.

The bus would come back loaded with supplies. They had more people to house and feed, counting the Taibeni camp now as well as Mother's guard, and Mother's staff, and, which he again had not thought of—there was no knowing when troubles might cut them off from supply. He was used to thinking of Shejidan, where everything always was easy—but Tirnamardi sat separate, and the roads were few, and not completely safe, considering the neighbors.

He had been getting a little prideful in his handling of things. But staff seemed to know exactly what was needed, and would have taken the estate truck if the bus had not been at Mother's disposal, and Mother had offered it first to Uncle, for *his* trip to hospital, so it had just grown from there. There were groceries needed, and blankets and pillows, clothing since the disaster that had taken the tents down; portable showers, hose, and water dispensers, laundry soap, flour and vegetables and eggs and all sorts of things. One tent had to be repaired, but by afternoon it was up along with the others, and everybody was back under canvas—Cajeiri could observe that, at least, from the windows.

Mother was still talking to Nomari, and Uncle was still drowsy with painkillers.

So Cajeiri knew. Cajeiri had the report, direct from Rieni.

Uncle's men on the roof had taken shelter during the lightning—*they* had not been overseeing the pen when the gate had opened, but equipment had been, and Rieni said that there were images, however shadowy, of what had gone on—but since Uncle's Filing, they were a Guild matter under investigation, and by law, not for him to see. Their surmise was right: one man had gone to open the gate and the herd, sensing a stranger, had pressed against it and pushed it open prematurely. One man had fallen, two had bolted toward the orchard, and on a second search they had found yet one more set of remains, scarcely recognizable as what they were, mixed with the mud and a pile of brush.

So now they were down to *one* missing visitor.

There were other indications, too, that the three individuals had indeed been in hiding near the stables, in the granary, which pointed up a security gap, but not one easy to exploit, so Lucasi said later. The juniors were forbidden to say yet what senior Guild thought, but indications were that one man had survived, and likely gotten through the hedge outbound, north, where there was a gap from earlier in the year. Amid the chaos of the storm and the mecheiti being loose, there had been multiple alarms from the sensors along the hedges, as small creatures fled, so that well might have included one man running for his life.

"Or running for Ajuri," Lucasi said.

It was at least a relief to know—which he was *not* supposed to say to anybody—that they *had* had alarms, and they *did* know things that were going to matter. Lucasi called it *evidence.*

That was the cold little word. Uncle having Filed on Great-aunt Geidaro, now there was *evidence* that Great-aunt Geidaro had set people in among Nomari's people who had done damage and injury to persons who were not Guild. *That* was against the law.

He had no doubt she had put them there. But the Guild in its consideration would want evidence like names, and connections.

And once they got that, if the evidence indeed piled up to back Uncle's charges, Great-aunt Geidaro was going to get a letter from the Guild advising her to appear and answer with a Filing of her own, or to reach a settlement with Uncle—which was not highly likely. Great-aunt probably was not the *only* one living in Ajiden right now who had murdered people, and if there was one place the Assassins' Guild Council likely really wanted to go into and search for evidence—it was Ajuri—that being Shishogi's clan. Shishogi had set a device to go off in his own office in Guild Headquarters, and he had taken a lot of Guild records with him, by what Cajeiri had overheard and gathered. But that was not saying that there might not be evidence in Great-aunt Geidaro's rooms. Or elsewhere in Ajuri.

Guild had already gotten into Kadagidi and gone over whatever they could find. They were still holding that under guard, and looking for certain people.

But what they could find at Ajiden, combined with the Kadagidi records, might answer so many questions—

Even about Grandmother.

Mother and her bodyguard had spent *hours* today in her suite talking to Nomari alone, and the promised invitation to join them had never come. It was secrets again, things that Mother could ask Nomari and that Nomari probably had to answer. Likely she had gotten involved in it all and never found a moment to call him in.

He had been frustrated all day, trying not to act frustrated— spending his time in the library, and talking, twice, at some

length, with Uncle's major domo, Heisi, about things Uncle
was not well enough right now to see to, questions that really
Heisi wished not to be left to his own discretion, when it came
to the renewed camp on the lawn.

The good news of the day was that the little two-year-old
that Uncle had ridden had gotten onto her feet and drunk water
and eaten right at the edge of dark. She had a name now. Uncle
called her Kasuo, which was an old word for brave, and said he
wanted that youngster given everything special.

"They have taken her out into the pen," Onami said, when
he brought the news.

"I should like very much to see her," Cajeiri said, and before
his aishid could object. "Only from the window."

"Yes, nandi," Onami said and Cajeiri headed for the door.
Three steps down the hallway, his aishid—which was Onami
and Janachi while Antaro and Jegari were gone, filling out the
four, with Veijico and Lucasi—stopped him, waiting, while they
stood utterly still—receiving something from the downstairs
office, likely.

"Nandi," Onami said, "a moment. Stay."

And without a word, Janachi headed downstairs at speed.

"What is it?" Cajeiri asked, seeing frowns.

"Janachi is going to ask, nandi," Onami said. Bracelets
burned a steady red. "We should stand here, but perhaps back
from the window."

"Mother is with Nomari," he said, alarmed.

"Her aishid is receiving the same alert, nandi," Onami said.
"Likewise those with Lord Tatiseigi, and those watching the
camp. This is an active alert. *Something* is in progress."

They stood a moment. Then Janachi came hurrying up the
stairs from below, out of breath. "The bus has come under fire,"
Janachi said.

One wanted to swear. He knew the words. But he kept them
inside. "The bus is bulletproof, is it not?"

"To an extent," Janachi said. "But we believe they are safe, and we have word that the bus is still moving. We are moving a force to the gate and alerting the Taibeni camp so that when they arrive, we shall have no additional problem."

"Geidaro," Cajeiri said. "Nadiin, *where* is the bus?"

"We are not at present sure," Onami said. "We cannot use Guild communications, nandi. They may be compromised."

"Is it Shadow Guild?"

"We cannot discount it, given who is involved."

"Uncle has to know. Mother has to know." If it was Shadow Guild, there was a whole range of weapons they *might* have, everything to match the Guild protecting them, with means to understand signals. "Nadiin-ji, *Father* has to know."

"We have advised Headquarters, and they will contact your father. Right now, we are listening, and all of us are on full alert."

"*Is* my great-aunt doing this?"

"That, young aiji, is a very central question. That bus is well-known. They *may* believe nand' Bren has come back from Mospheira to take a hand in this. They may know your mother is here. They certainly know that you are. And if their intelligence has somewhat penetrated the house, they may even know that Lord Tatiseigi was supposed to be on that bus. But most of all, they know that bus *will* gain access to the estate when it comes back, and one hopes that the staff has not talked imprudently in gathering supplies, and told them more than we would estimate they do know."

"Given the targets available at Tirnamardi," Onami said, "and with Lord Tatiseigi Filing on Geidaro-daja—the remnant of Shishogi's organization may have decided to take a massive risk. They have lost every time they choose to fight in the open. Headquarters has not reckoned any northern remnant capable of mounting a large action, but with Lord Tatiseigi Filing on your great-aunt, and Headquarters having a request that will bring Guild action into Ajuri, what remains of Shishogi's organization may be willing to cast everything they have on this one throw."

He was here: that was no secret. Uncle was. And Nomari. Now Mother was, with Seimei. If the Shadow Guild could get in, if it could kill even one of them, it would more than throw the whole Padi Valley into chaos. It would encourage every enemy Father had. They could *still* bring down the aishidi'tat, and do it right here.

But moving people across the southern mountains—meant rail.

"How fast can they get the *southern* people up here?"

"Not fast enough, young aiji. *That* is why your great-grandmother will be asking Lord Machigi to make a strong move at the Dojisigi and Senjin."

The two northern districts of the Marid were the strongholds of what Shadow Guild remained. He understood that. The seniors were giving him the truth, as much of it as they would give Father, he strongly believed it, but they were not going to need advice from a nine-year-old boy. He drew in a deep breath and promised the only thing they could want from him. "I shall not do anything stupid, nadiin-ji. Please advise my mother. And Uncle."

"We will be doing that," Janachi said.

Great-aunt Geidaro had done stupid, extravagant things before now, and Great-aunt, if she had a remnant of Shishogi's power in that organization—might be determined to go down with everything she could muster. And the Shadow Guild might come in determined to take everything away from her—like the records the Guild wanted to get from Ajuri.

The Shadow Guild would be smart to do that and vanish—without attacking Tirnamardi.

"If the Guild does not act on the Filing soon," he said, "Great-aunt Geidaro will destroy any records. She is spiteful."

His aishid looked shocked. And Janachi gave a little nod. "Very possibly, young aiji. Hers or Shishogi's, or maybe both."

He had felt responsibility one way—and the other—responsibility for Great-aunt's life; responsibility for everybody's safety. Now he just felt angry. He knew the enemy. They were the *same* enemy as they had ever been in his life, they were somewhere behind the reason Father had sent him and mani up to space, and now they were back again, coming into Uncle's own hall, threatening Uncle, and now attacking the bus where Antaro and Jegari were, and threatening Mother, and Seimei and everything he had. He ran up the steps, remembered halfway that he was not supposed to run, and stopped, facing his combined aishid, who were right behind him. "I shall go to Mother's room, with her Guild. Onami, Janachi, I swear I shall not be stupid. Go be with Rieni. I shall not leave the upstairs, no matter what. Go!"

The seniors had more important things to do than stand about in his vicinity. He had Veijico and Lucasi. He headed down the upstairs hall, full of dark thoughts, and heard Onami and Janachi going down, doing what he ordered.

It was not *fair*, he thought. Which was the way Boji thought. Boji was much on *fairness* and whether he got an egg when he was good.

Fair was not the way people fought for power. He had learned that a long time ago. Uncle had Filed Intent, the way things were supposed to work, the way the Guild was supposed to operate: they considered the petition, they investigated the incident, and sometimes they launched an extreme action, with Guild on both sides. But the Shadow Guild had ignored those rules. They just murdered people, *any* people, people who had done nothing against the law in their lives.

Great-aunt Geidaro had attended Mother when she was expecting Seimei.

That was the most perfectly awful thought he had ever had drop into his mind.

He reached Mother's door, where two of Mother's bodyguard were on watch, and hardly bothered to knock.

Beha was at her needlework. She looked up, stood up in alarm, gave a little bow.

"Young aiji," she said. "What is the trouble?"

"Someone has attacked the bus," he said, and went to Seimei's crib, where his sister stirred and grimaced, disturbed in her sleep. "Hush, hush, little sister. Nothing bad will come."

But there were pictures in his mind, Grandmother dying, and Grandfather stealing the baby from this crib.

Who was Beha? She was Macanti, a subclan of Abeiri, over on the west coast. But who was she, but somebody Father had found? Father had thought Beha was loyal. Great-grandmother's people were Mother's guards. Surely if there was anything in the least suspicious in Mother's staff, now, they would find it.

The door opened. Mother came in, and by her expression, the news had gotten to her.

"The bus is under attack," Mother said without preamble, in a hushed voice. "We do not yet know the outcome." She came to the crib, and looked at Seimei, and touched her, then looked at him. "You must not leave this floor. You must not be in the hall right now."

"I know," he said. "My two seniormost are downstairs in the security office. They are trying to find out about the bus."

"Antaro is on it."

"With Jegari. And Uncle's staff." He felt as if the blood were draining out of him. "I am worried, Honored Mother. I want to do something."

"We are not defenseless here," Mother said. "Nor are they."

"I know. I am remembering—I am remembering Great-aunt Geidaro. When Father sent her away from the Bujavid. She was angry then. She did not show that face to everyone. But I saw it. It was scary. Lady Adsi was upset." That had been Mother's chief of staff. Adsi *would* have been where Beha was, if Father had not thrown all Mother's Ajuri guards and her staff out of the Bujavid, right along with Grandfather and all his people. "Honored Mother, I am thinking—Ajuri stealing you away from here

was one thing—but stealing *another* baby, out of the Bujavid . . .
I am *glad* Father sent Lady Adsi away. I am *glad* Lady Adsi was
not with you when my sister was born. I would not trust *any* of
them with Seimei."

Mother took on a strange, bewildered expression, and for a
moment Cajeiri tensed, thinking she would say something
hurtful, and throw *him* out. But she walked over and sat down,
looking as if someone had struck her.

"I am sorry," he said.

"No," Mother said. "No, son of mine. You are no fool. Adsi
was close as a sister to me, from far back. Would Ajuri clan dare
steal another child? And your father's child, at that? And would
Adsi do such a thing, with me? When Murini went down, with
his regime in ruins—Ajuri rose on *my* favor as high as they possibly could. They had gotten to the Bujavid. They were asking
for a permanent apartment there. What more could it gain by
stealing my daughter? *Nothing.*"

"Very bad things, honored Mother."

Mother gazed at him, eye to eye. And they were back there,
then. In the time just after they had gotten the Bujavid back,
when they were still hunting Murini down.

Ajuri had been invited into the Bujavid in those days. Had
come in, as allies.

"I think back now," Mother said, "and I was so upset when
you claimed my father frightened you. I was more than upset
when your father banished him and sent all my staff away. Furious when your great-grandmother installed her own people.
But you know things, son of mine. At times you do know
things."

"I cannot claim I understood anything then. But I came in
from outside. From years with mani. And I had a bad feeling. I
think, honored Mother—I think it was not so much that *Grandfather* frightened me—personally—well, he did. But it was more
than him. *Fear* went all around him. All the time. *All* the time.
Even when he was laughing."

He struggled to make sense. But Mother gazed at him as if she had gotten something of what he meant.

"Your father," she said, "felt *exactly* that. Did he say so?"

"Not to me, honored Mother, but I felt—I felt it in a lot of them and I felt it most in Grandfather, even while he was scaring me. I think—I felt sorry for him. And scared of him at the same time. Terribly scared."

"You are *different*, son of mine." She lifted her hand, held it out to him. He walked close and took it. Her hand closed gently, warmly, on his. "I felt so deep a connection to you before you were born. I was scared, too, sometimes. I had dreams. But I knew—I have read—there really *was* something in you that never let me rest, or really sleep, the whole while. I felt I fought for my sanity and my life, bringing you into the world; and after I had you, I was so protective of you. I was so upset with you. I was so *proud* of you. And of being alive and sane. And all the matter of my father killing my mother, and what I was, or was not, was tangled in it."

It was scary to hear. His hand was trapped. He wanted to pull away and not hear more of it. But her hold grew stronger.

"When your father took you away from me and sent you up to space, to be with your great-grandmother, I was so angry. When she took you away even from there, and things went so wrong—"

When he and Great-grandmother were off at the far side of space, rescuing the Reunioners, and Mother and Father were hiding in sheds and hedgerows, with people hunting them . . .

"—then something of that feeling of anger and fighting for breath did come back to me. And it was not just in my head, but I knew what it was. I knew that there would be a baby. But with Seimei, it never became what I felt with you. Your father and I laid plans, and we sat in the cold rain and we plotted against the plotters. We stung them, from time to time, when we could. We held our anger and we did not attack head-on— for each other's sake. And we won. Ultimately, we won, and I saw you named your father's heir, aiji-apparent, the night your sister was born."

He would never forget that night. Ever.

"Your sister is not like you, son of mine. Take care of her."

"Honored Mother, I will."

"She may take after me."

"That would be all right."

Mother gave a faint smile. And let go of his hand.

"We will never lose to Great-aunt Geidaro," he said. He believed that, even if he was worried for Antaro and Jegari and everybody on the bus. "We just will not lose. We are smarter than that."

"I know we are."

"What do you think of Nomari-nadi?" he asked.

"Nomari-abi." That was to say, *cousin.*

"He *is*, then. I am glad."

"Are you? He was my ally, a long time ago. What he is now— I am less sure."

A question occurred to him. "Why did he go to Machigi?"

"He said it was because Machigi *was* holding out against the Troubles. I asked him whether Machigi knew who he was. He said he gave his clan and said his family was gone, but whether Machigi investigated beyond that, or ever intended to use that connection—he claims not to know. He says he would not betray Ajuri's traditional associations. Which may be the truth. I asked him where his man'chi resided. He said he would give it to you."

"To *me*." That was a surprise. "Why?"

"Is there ever absolute reason? It was an odd thing to say. Not quite political. So it may be honest. A way of deflecting current questions. Or right now you have offered a fixed point in his world. An anchor, while other things are in motion. And so, son of mine, who holds this man's man'chi. What shall we do with Nomari?"

He drew in a breath, thinking it a test. "He is certainly better than Great-aunt Geidaro."

"With southern connections," Mother said somberly. "But then—"

"Nandiin," Onami said. "We have information arriving."

"Is Uncle awake?" Mother asked. "Advise him. Go. Find out."

"Nandi?" Onami looked at him, and he nodded, quietly.

Onami went . . . but no further than the door. Haniri arrived, with, "We are bringing the Ajuri back into the lower hall. The Taibeni are aware and taking position. The bus is in difficulty."

"Advise Uncle," Mother said, and Cajeiri quickly said, "Yes."

People moved. Cajeiri stood still. So did Mother. Seimei fretted at the activity and Beha moved to take her up.

"There is trouble with the bus," Haniri said. "We are receiving word from the driver that they have again come under fire, and they are considering fording the Riesa stream rather than take the bridge, which they distrust. The driver is Najidi. Staff knows the area and they are advising to use the ford, but the bank is steep and that is a long bus."

Bogged helplessly in mud would be a bad situation, Cajeiri thought, wishing there were something he could do.

"Taibeni are moving out to escort, and to take control of the bridge," Haniri said.

"This is a main public road," Mother said.

"Indeed," Haniri said. It was illegal to interfere with any public road, and it was *Mother's* bus, temporarily, if it came to that, which was even worse. Cajeiri did not know that crossing. He knew the maps. He had known the maps for years. But he could not call up the appearance of the bridge, or its situation.

Geidaro had not had warning enough to stop the bus on its way to Diegi. But she had had ample time to arrange most anything for the bus coming back.

He wanted to pace. To move. To do something. But all he could do was draw a deep breath and wait.

And wait. Beha took Seimei back to the servants hall to tend her needs, since she was continuing to fret.

The guarded door opened. It was Onami. "Lord Tatiseigi invites your presence, nandiin. He is holding to his own suite. He has contacted Shejidan."

"We shall go there," Mother said, and looked at Cajeiri. "Shall we not?"

He was unprepared to be asked his opinion, now that things were going wrong. But Mother was signaling him to observe protocols, and he gave a little nod. "Yes. *Yes,* honored Mother."

"Stay," she ordered her own guard. "Watch here. Guard my daughter."

So only with his patched-together guard, senior and junior, they went out into the hall together, and down to Uncle's room.

16

They found Uncle sitting by the tall windows, in his dressing-gown with the injured arm in a sling. In front of him was a moveable writing-desk, and a small glass of brandy despite the hour. Most uncommon, there was a telephone on the desk.

"Do not get up, Uncle," Mother said, and Cajeiri added: "Please."

"You have informed yourselves," Uncle said, "of the attack."

"Yes, Uncle," Cajeiri said.

"The bus has stopped short of the bridge, for fear of a mine. Some fool shot at it, apparently thinking to hit the driver, but the glass held. There is a ford, but it is chancy with that size vehicle, and there is some thought they hope to panic the bus to attempt that instead of the bridge. I am in contact with Shejidan."

Meaning Father, one hoped. Or Guild Headquarters. Cajeiri pictured the place, or tried to. The bus was a fortress. But if there were a lot of attackers moving in . . .

"So. Do sit. This Nomari. I am informed, Niece, you met cordially."

Uncle was completely changing the subject. Why? Cajeiri wondered. Why were they talking about Nomari, when the bus was under attack?

"We did," Mother said, taking a chair. "Cordially, and at length."

"He did not deny his ties to the Marid."

"He did not," Mother said.

Cajeiri found a chair. He sat down on the edge of it, to have his feet on the floor, and leaned on the arm, to have something his hand could clench.

"We have delayed dinner tonight, for ourselves. For the camp—we are pulling the camp inside again and feeding them an early supper to keep them busy and allay their anxiety. Out again this morning and in again this evening. If this goes on, we may have to declare these people regular guests, one and all."

"Uncle," Cajeiri said. "Forgive me. The *bus.*"

"The question of our guest's associations is indeed germane, Nephew. We have a Filing in play. And we have your mother's cousin and a large number of that clan under this roof, with an active attack on our personnel and with the Taibeni lord's niece and nephew on that bus."

Antaro and Jegari *were* that. *Three* clans involved in what could become a second Filing. The pattern spread out like tiles on a gameboard. The whole Padi Valley association in upheaval, because the Taibeni were the one clan that traditionally settled its own quarrels, never asking in outside Guild, though no few of them, like Antaro and Jegari, and many of Father's body-guard, *were* Guild. *Father* was Taibeni, at least on his mother's side.

War, he thought, with unease at the pit of his stomach. To involve the whole Padi Valley Association, it only wanted Kada-gidi, who could not bring any force to bear, whose house was occupied by Guild at the moment, the claimants all barred—or dead.

Kadagidi was not organized. But if elements of it wanted to cause trouble . . .

If they *were* causing trouble and if it was not even Great-aunt Geidaro at all . . .

"Kadagidi might try us," he said aloud. "But that would be stupid."

"That is, however," Uncle said, "one reason we cannot assume who has moved against us. Nor can we call on the Guild occupying Kadagidi: there is a public trust there, of art and history, and they cannot leave it unprotected, particularly since their leaving it would upset the Kadagidi townships. This is why I have called on Headquarters, and on your father."

"Dur," Cajeiri said, thinking of the yellow plane that had more than once flown over their troubles. "They are at least borderland associates. And they would come. Nand' Reijiri would bring the airplane."

"That," Uncle said, "would give us eyes on the bus. And on the whole situation."

"He always said he could be in the air in minutes, if ever I needed him. And he could tell the Taibeni where the attack is coming from. If the bus can just hold on. I can call nand' Reijiri."

"They have more than an airplane," Mother said. "They have tributary clans bordering the subclans of Ajuri. Calls to them could warn the subclans it would be very unwise to contribute to whatever Geidaro may be doing."

It was getting scarily large, the situation of a bus and a bridge. Father had to know. He was sure Father knew. He had been in scary spots, a lot of them, but he had always had mani and her young men, and nand' Bren, and Banichi and all—not Mother and Uncle and his little sister. He wanted today over with. He wanted to be having tea and cakes with all his aishid and everybody all right. Right now it was spreading to five clans and the whole midlands, and clear over to the coast.

There was absolutely nothing on the news feed from the continent. The atevi feed from the mainland was occupied with the usual nature documentaries and occasional reports on agriculture and exports. Which was not necessarily, in Bren's experience, good news. The silence from his major domo in the Bujavid could be reassuring that nothing disastrous had happened; but knowing the situation regarding Lord Tatiseigi and the nomination, it was worrisome, especially given the Machigi connection, and Tabini's couriered message to be ready to move. He had obligations here. And *something* was definitely going on over there.

Concentrate, he told himself, on the job at hand. A few more days. That was what Tabini wanted from him right now.

Easier said than done. Gin's documentary on the station crisis was going to air.

There *was* considerable advance publicity on the Mospheiran news about it, with advisements the program would contain images of the kyo, which as yet had been limited to images of the ship and discussion of its unprecedented speed. There was a lot of public interest in that.

There was advisement too, that it would include the dowager and the boy who had, also unprecedented, been the first atevi of rank to touch down on Mospheiran soil, however briefly—when they had come back from their long voyage. Mospheirans tended to feel proprietary about their own famous events. There was no other way to put it. However peripheral it was to far larger things, they had seen something extraordinary happen in their lifetimes, in their neighborhood, so to speak, and forever after that topic could fire up their interest to a passionate degree.

Well, the boy Mospheira had caught one glimpse of had grown half a foot since then, was maturing, was carrying himself with a different bearing—Mospheira would see that. Mospheira would react to that. The boy—*their* boy—was taller, older, becoming somebody important on his own. They, residents on a world they didn't at all control, had seen history happen. All but touched it. And owned it.

He understood it. To that degree, he was *still* Mospheiran. What sped through their lives and their public notice had made an indelible impression, something that touched that was *in* that documentary, and would be talked about tomorrow—one hoped—favorably. And the boy—might well overshadow any messy details about Tillington's tangled dealing and all the legal questions that stemmed from it. Gin had her own good sense of how the public mind worked. Tillington would be safely yesterday's news, if the Heritage lot, funded by the Aslunds, was about to take a new tack.

One could only hope. Best if Tillington could just retire and cease to be a problem.

Bren worked on his own notes for Heyden Court. His aishid played a round of chess—watching Algini and Banichi was interesting, even with their long pauses. There were flurries of moves. Then a pause. Algini won.

Banichi demanded a rematch.

Uncle sent word down to the Ajuri folk, and to Nomari, what was happening, and what they were doing. Uncle let the Ajuri have access to a storeroom, where there were places to sit, and they were able to bring in chairs, and a samovar, and a very limited supply of brandy. Haniri went down to speak to Nomari and to tell him, in front of everyone, what was going on, and to assure them that they were not blaming Ajuri, and that they were getting help from Dur and Taiben and support from the Guild in Shejidan.

That was all true. There was shooting, and the bus had occasionally fired back; they were not reporting their condition either good or bad, and in Uncle's sitting room, Guild wore frowns, wishing, Lucasi said, that they were out there. There *was* a Guild presence on the bus, besides Antaro and Jegari, but they had *their* duty to everybody on the bus, and though they had armament, they were not going to leave the bus, which was what needed to be done to get at the attackers. It was late. At dark, the situation might get worse. The driver *needed* to know whether the bridge was safe, or whether their enemies, who had already done enough to be charged, would have gone the final step to outlawry and put explosives under the bridge.

And the Guild that supported Great-aunt Geidaro was not that strong on law and honor.

"We *want* them," Veijico muttered. "And we are sure Onami and Janachi also want them beyond words, not to mention what those on the bus feel. This is an affront against you, against your mother, against Lord Tatiseigi, and against the Guild."

Uncle's Filing had set things up. Great-aunt's own actions were setting things in motion.

Why? he asked himself. She was very old. She might still be able to beg off and retire, if Uncle allowed, in a place remote enough. But maybe she was going to throw her people at the Guild and do damage, just because she could.

She could *not* think she could win.

If she called on her Guild to negotiate a way out, even now, there was a chance, a small one, true, but some chance, especially for the people who belonged to her.

But that was not Great-aunt Geidaro's choice, evidently.

The phone jangled quietly. Uncle's Guild-senior picked it up.

"The aiji," the Guild-senior said, and handed the phone to Uncle.

"Aiji-ma," Uncle began, and there followed a conversation in which Uncle's side was, "Yes," and "We have," and "Yes."

Phones were not safe for secrets, but they could bring bad news. Uncle listened for a space, and then nodded grimly.

Cajeiri waited, his heart beating fast.

"The Guild Council has ruled," Uncle said, handing back the phone. "The Guild will be in communication with Dur as well as Taiben and with us. The Filing is accepted."

It was happening, then. Shishogi had ruled the lords of Ajuri for all his life, for all Mother's life, and whoever was lord of Ajuri had done what the old man demanded. And Great-aunt Geidaro might think she could go on as she always had, making people afraid, threatening them—killing people, maybe with what was left of the Shadow Guild trying to support her as the last connection with their old power. The Shadow Guild might have its nests down in the Marid, but with Kadagidi under

Guild watch, maybe Great-aunt Geidaro, in the heart of the aishidi'tat, was what they had.

But she was not, after all, Shishogi. Shishogi had been so quiet nobody had ever thought he was in charge of anything. He never would have come into Uncle's hall making threats.

Maybe that was why nobody had ever taken Great-aunt Geidaro seriously—except people inside Ajuri who knew she was in touch with power that killed people. To everybody else she was just a fussy old woman who wanted to be important. And she was *both*. And cared nothing for what it cost others.

Now she and the Shadow Guild or whatever was left of them were trying to settle in Ajuri, and threatening *his* mother, *his* father, *his* sister, *his* great-uncle, *his* household; and he looked at the oncoming twilight with mixed dread and hope. Guild on both sides might use the gathering dark to start moving on whatever they intended to do, and Cajeiri sat quietly, thinking about that big black block of a building in Shejidan, and people meeting inside it who had agreed they should set Great-uncle's Filing in motion and do something. He sat *willing* the Guild Council to speed their response, stop sending messages back and forth and do something, *finally*, to stop Geidaro. The mess had been going on in Ajuri all his life and mother's. And it was the Guild's own internal problem that had let it all happen.

Now—they just had to stop it, here, around a bus and a bridge. The Guild Council should see that.

But he had been around politics every waking moment of his life, too, and somebody was bound to argue they could not have *two* clans in the Padi Valley sitting leaderless, while they sifted through records for more cases.

Well, they had that situation now. Great-aunt Geidaro was not even a lord. She had just taken over, a caretaker who had been caretaking every time a lord of Ajuri died, never anything official. Geidaro had been running things for years and years, behind Grandfather, behind all the lords that had died. They had lived so long as they did what they were told, and they died when they failed, as simple as that.

And she was just old, and bad-tempered, and people gave way to her and tried to satisfy her. She had complained, complained, complained while she had been in the Bujavid, about *little* things. It was too hot. It was too cold. Her mattress was uncomfortable. Her servants were clumsy. Everyone should just go on and not worry about her. She was used to discomfort.

It was all, one could suspect, a way of making people pay attention to the stupid things she was complaining about, and not pay attention to what she was up to. Everybody who met her agreed she was a pain and a trouble, but nobody in the Bujavid had ever suspected her of murder . . . until Father threw Grandfather out, and Great-aunt Geidaro and every other Ajuri with her.

So they had not had to listen to her, or meet her, until she had shown up at Tirnamardi, with that awful sharp voice that just cut to the nerves. It was easy to hate dealing with her.

And was she *really* behind all the bad things? It could not be the nephew she was asking Uncle to nominate—unless they both were good at hiding how smart they were. It could not be Aunt Meisi, whose interests ran to pretty clothes and jewelry; and it could not be Dejaja, who was young, and nicer than all the rest.

No, the one *old* enough to be the center of it was Geidaro: Uncle was as old, and he was sure Uncle was not mistaken.

Could Nomari turn out worse? Or as bad? *That*, he saw in terms of the map he kept, with all the pins. His connection with Machigi could tie very old troubles to the heart of the aishidi'tat—or it could be a way to keep Machigi quiet, content to have an ally with relatives in the Bujavid.

If Nomari turned on them, then *he* would File, he swore he would. He was years from having the legal standing—but he could move those that had. He had moved one of them, with that phone call to Dur, with a little yellow plane that was winging its way toward the trouble on the road.

And mani might say he was wrong to ask Dur to involve itself. He saw her across the chessboard saying, "When you bring your hand near a piece, Great-grandson, you betray your thinking. Keep your hands in your lap. Unless you wish to deceive."

Deception had nothing to do with this. He had people of *his* man'chi on that bus, and he wanted them safe.

Whatever it took.

Supper was light, from Francis House kitchens, simple sandwiches. They had ordered it that way, on what had been a long day, a second session with Mospheiran security—leading up to a stressful, perhaps a long, evening. The television had been on at low volume all evening to catch any change in broadcast plans. But none came. And toward the end of supper, there came an advisement that they were airing the promised documentary in fifteen minutes. That was as scheduled, no surprises.

Silently they took places within view of the television and turned up the sound. Banichi and the others, having seen it before, with Bren translating, settled to view it again, with occasional hushed comments or questions on subsequent thoughts.

There were no alterations in what they had seen. It ran in its entirety, nothing added, nothing edited out. It finished.

And immediately, Mospheiran to the hilt, the network provided a panel of people to talk about it.

"Who are these people?" was Jago's logical and suspicious question.

"Heads of guilds?" was Tano's guess.

One could wish it were so easily explained. "Political leaders. A teacher of science. A person to ask the questions. An advocate at law. And the head of a citizen association."

"Have they legal standing?" Tano asked.

"No," Bren said. "They simply discuss. There is no legal standing of the group. The television directors have assembled them."

"Then they do not vote."

"They do not vote," Bren said. "But they may influence opinion."

His aishid was doubtful. But the discussion opened. There were remarks considering the kyo—images flashed up, so his aishid had no difficulty understanding the topic. The matter of the Reunioners came up, and, God help them, the network's rehash of the petal sail landing of two hundred years ago, with questions about the return of the ship . . .

Which could get into difficult and emotional territory. The citizen association seemed bent on taking it there, talking about expense, and privilege . . .

But the breaking news flasher came up, along with the Mospheiran Space emblem, and then the image of the station in orbit—fading to Gin, at her desk, with that emblem on the wall behind her.

"This is a live broadcast," a male voice said, "from the office of the Mospheiran stationmaster, Dr. Virginia Kroger."

Suddenly the brief interlude with the network analysts made a certain, calculating sense. Time for the pollsters to take the temperature of public opinion after the documentary. Time for Shawn's office, and Gin's, to assemble the pieces of their own response, virtually on the fly.

"Good evening, Earth," Gin began. "Grim as it's been up here, we're making progress. Rapid progress. We have, first of all, improved water access and sanitation, we're delivering health care, and people are getting fed. This is drawing on emergency supplies from both sides of the station, but we have undertakings from the atevi stationmaster that they will devote one flight out of four to foodstuffs and critical supplies, as we work to improve conditions.

"There is, over all, optimism up here. Having met the neighbors, we can say they are different, very advanced, and not easy to understand. Let me talk about that.

"First, they don't want close neighbors. They indicate they

want us to stay out of their space and not try to visit them, though we now have the ability to communicate with them.

"This suits us very well. They don't want profound changes in their way of doing things any more than we do . . there's certainly no way we can live together, or share an environment with them. They can't be comfortable in our environment, and we can't be comfortable in theirs. We can stand it for short periods, but certainly not long-term.

"So never think they plan to move in—Which is a good thing, because we simply cannot match their ships. We can see what they do. The science by which they do it indicates to us that we have a lot left to discover in the realm of physics, and that we can be very glad they don't want war or territory. On the other hand, they do not regard us as backward savages: they are very pleased with the notion that here are two species sharing a world and being reasonable toward each other. That seems to give them a good impression of our character, which gives us a good impression of theirs. And there is the remote possibility, eventually, of a limited trade, likely at the site of what was Reunion Station, which we have agreed upon as a boundary point between our territories.

"We have been further into their territory than they were willing to tolerate, and thanks to skills we have, and they clearly admire—we were able to communicate with them, talk with them, and reassure each other, and arrange an agreement by which we assure each other's safety, now and for the future.

"But what they did not see, and what we were very anxious they not see—when the kyo ship appeared inbound toward the station, at the very critical hour that we needed to organize a mode of contact with a foreign power which, in a misunderstanding, could attack and destroy us—we were presented a crisis in leadership on the human side of the station that set us all on the brink of disaster.

"Fortunately the atevi stationmaster very quickly contacted

both President Tyers and the aiji in Shejidan, to assemble the same team that had dealt with the kyo and achieved peaceful contact at Reunion. Paidhi Bren Cameron, under dual authority of President Tyers and Tabini-aiji, along with the aiji-dowager and the aiji's young son, representing the aishidi'tat, commandeered the next shuttle to launch and arrived on the station to take over contact. When they arrived, the human-side administration resisted and obstructed—to such an extent that conditions on the human side of the station headed for an environmental breakdown—and created a situation which threatened to meet the kyo with a station half in collapse.

"Considering that the key to successful negotiations with the kyo was the demonstrated cooperation of our two species, this could not be tolerated.

"Mr. Cameron and the atevi delegation took temporary command of station communications in order to open dialog with the kyo. They likewise cooperated with ship command in stabilizing the antiquated area of the station that Station-master Tillington had opened to house the Reunion refugees, an area he had sealed at the kyo approach, compounding the strain on already chancy systems, which resulted in break-downs in water and air, putting life support systems for the refugees, including families and children, on the brink of failure. This had to be addressed as an emergency while Mr. Cameron and the atevi delegation were actually dealing with the kyo visitors, and while they were trying to present the status of our world as a peaceful and civilized place.

"The visitors have departed peaceably. We are now engaged in a program designed to increase supply and lessen demand of life-critical materials for all station residents, in all areas. Unfortunately, the area of the station where the refugees are housed is the oldest part of the station, scheduled for renovation even before the arrival of the refugees, and constantly plagued with mechanical emergencies. The station was not designed to support its current human population, and the faster we can bring down the number of Reunion refugees—their number includes children as young as two months—and eliminate the strain on station resources, the sooner we can repair broken systems, shut down the hazards pending repair, and restore everybody up here to reasonable and safe living conditions.

"The emergency aloft is over, but critical operations remain, and we remain seriously overcrowded. I am grateful to President Tyers, the Committee on Science, the Justice Department, and the State Department for unwavering support. I am also grateful to my opposite number, Stationmaster Geigi, who has worked out a schedule involving the atevi shuttle fleet that will get vital supplies to both sides of the station, while reserving downbound shuttle space for special cargo and passengers. Right now the overcrowding is stressing systems, and we have an urgent need to bring the population level down to what is safe and useful. The refugees, only five thousand in number, are a drop in the bucket on the island, but more than we can support up here. So we will be sending them down in small groups, whenever we can find shuttle space, and we are working on that. We will be landing some of the refugees on the mainland and ferrying them to the island, courtesy of the aiji, at his expense, since our shuttle space is less than the mainland's. We will be parachuting other cargo and materials down to mainland wilderness drop zones, because there is some imprecision in such landings and we have no wish to drop a cargo on a town. The aiji will ship Mospheiran freight over to Port Jackson, also at his expense. For all this, we thank Lord Geigi, the aiji-dowager, and the aiji in Shejidan. Our atevi neighbors share the station and share its risks, and in this case, they are contributing to its relief for everybody's benefit.

"In short, we are back in business up here. Production is getting underway, shuttles will be lifting foodstuff and other essentials for life, and station-based companies will be sending our goods down. The station is safe, and restoration of normal operations will be a top priority.

"As for the refugees, there are five thousand to come, no more than a large village, to live their lives, and lend their skills and knowledge to their new home. They have yet to discover what a sunrise is like. The world will get the benefit of their science, their energy, and their knowledge of a region of space bordering our new allies.

"We look forward to resuming ordinary operations in every respect. We look forward to an era of cooperation with our neighbors the aishidi'tat.

"Thank you and good evening."

It had all been too fast a flow to translate as it went, but they all had *been* there. His aishid understood more Mosphei' than they spoke. They had to know the topics, at least.

But now the Presidential seal flashed up, the five-pointed star in a triple ring.

"Shawn-aiji," Bren said, and the seal gave way to Shawn's office, and Shawn at his desk, with that symbol on the wall behind him. The screen split to Gin in her office, then to a white-haired, prosperous looking old man Bren did not immediately recognize, in a book-lined office that was clearly not the space station.

"Thank you, Dr. Kroger," Shawn said, *"for a difficult and dangerous job well-done. And you have the support of the Mospheiran people for the job that follows.*

"I'm pleased now to introduce Mr. Maarten Aslund, Senior Chairman of Asgard Corporation, who also has a statement."

God. Maarten Aslund. *Publicly* with Shawn on this one? Bren drew in a deep breath and hoped for the best.

"Mr. President," Maarten Aslund said. *"My brother Simon, my sister Elisabeth and I are in full support of the administration's quick action, and in equally full support of Dr. Kroger's initiative to stabilize the station operations. We are proud of the role Asgard Space has played in support of Dr. Kroger, and notably in the rescue of valuable documents and knowledge—"*

God, Shawn, I *so* hope you haven't gotten in bed with the devil on this one . . .

"—*which might have been lost with Reunion, a wealth of industrial and scientific material developed over two centuries of independent space-based research . . .*"

Never mind Asgard and Asgard Space had had a corporate war over Asgard Space's refusal to run major decisions past Asgard's board.

"*We commend Asgard Space for its efforts in this regard, and we are pleased to say that Asgard Space has helped create a legal framework within which this material can be used, creating jobs, and offering new processes and materials for the betterment of lives on Earth, while safeguarding the interests of those who rescued this science from the disaster at Reunion and brought it safely to us.*

"*We are pleased to announce a grant for the handling of such documents which may be in fragmentary condition, and for interviews to preserve the memory of Reunion survivors whose experience in these areas of manufacture may be helpful, before their memories dim.*

"*We also applaud the President, the station administration and ship command for steps taken to recover and preserve information on our recent visitors. We enthusiastically support the treaty terms and the legal settlement of the Andressen papers and we hail Dr. Kroger's legal initiative as a just and fair solution. Mr. President, thank you.*"

Shawn nodded benignly.

"*Mr. Aslund, we welcome your support. My fellow citizens, if you have questions, there will be a televised open-line forum tomorrow at noon, with various experts accessible.*

"*I trust you will join me in thanking our allies across the straits, who will be providing free transport for much of the effort, and who were likewise engaged at highest official levels in arranging the kyo treaty. Special gratitude to the sitting paidhi, Mr. Bren Cameron, and to various entities who have cooperated to make this good outcome possible. I particularly thank Mr. Aslund for appearing personally on short notice and I profoundly thank him for his patriotic support. Good night and a peaceful rest."*

Well, *that* was a fancy bit of political footwork. Asgard Corporation had closed ranks, on world and above, and the whole Aslund family was now officially aboard, setting a stamp of approval on Gin's actions, with the legal cases settled. The Heritage people right now had to be in a state of shock. The upper echelons of the party were, in a one-minute address, given no choice but fall in or fall out. The rank and file had the same choice: follow the leadership to a rational acceptance of things lately denounced as a conspiracy—or try to reorganize an opposition without the party names that were familiar to everyone, because one could bet the politicians would follow the Aslund money.

The fringe—well, the fringe would stay the course. There was no persuading them. Everything was all a lie and aliens were secretly running the government by mind-control.

"*That* was interesting," he said to his aishid. "The elderly man was one of the two heads of Asgard, siding with the Presidenta, calling Gin-aiji a commendable and wise official, and promising prosperity to all, with support of the landing of the refugees and an implied condemnation of Tillington."

"The Heritage folk will be startled," Banichi said.

"To say the very least."

"Startled people," Jago said, "can do very stupid things."

17

It was almost full dark, and time for supper. They had come down to the great hall, to the sitting area, not for supper, but to be closer to the security station in the lower hall. Mother had come down with her guard, and Beha had brought Seimei, who looked about her at the lights, and wrinkled her nose disapprovingly at the echoes. Great-uncle had come down, too, insisting to put on an evening coat, but he had his wounded arm tucked inside it.

And Uncle had walked down the huge stairs. Staff had tried to get him to ride the servants' lift, which was a slow and chancy-feeling thing back in the servants' hall. It had a very old motor, it was noisy: staff used it to get laundry and furniture and such things up and down. No, Uncle would have none of that. He came down the steps with his aishid and two servants hovering about him for fear he would fall, and occasionally taking his one useful hand off the rail to wave off his major domo.

"Do not notice," Mother said, with her back to the situation. "He will not wish to be seen in difficulty."

That was probably true. But it was scary. Cajeiri was glad when Uncle reached bottom safely and his staff, attending him across the broad central floor, saw him seated with them in the sitting area without incident.

Cajeiri's stomach had been upset even before he watched Uncle come down the steps. He had thought Uncle might be ordering supper for all of them, but there was no sign of that, and the table over in the dining area was unlit, with no sign of activity. The kitchen had provided an early supper for the Ajuri waiting down in the servants' hall and storage areas, and surely there could be some sort of food at this hour if anyone had wanted it.

Cajeiri thought he should want something, but he found even sugared tea was too much for his system. He asked for unsweetened tea and could not even summon interest in the wafer that came with it. He sipped the cup, staring often at the reflection of the lights on the darkening windows, no help for his stomach at all.

"Perhaps," Uncle suggested, "we should ask Guild to be at ease."

That was a kindness, but one he could not order regarding Uncle's guard, under Uncle's roof: he felt that, at least, and he was glad to agree, so that his bodyguard, and Mother's, and Uncle's, could sit down for what was going to be a long wait. Guild arranged their own knot of chairs over by the second pillar of the area, a quiet collection of Guild staying in touch with security downstairs. Veijico and Lucasi wore uncommonly grim expressions—no question where their thoughts were.

There was no word from that gathering. Uncle talked quietly with Mother, discussing the road from here to Diegi, how it was now, how Mother remembered it, none of which helped anything.

Reijiri had taken off in his plane hours ago. They knew that. One of the big planes could cross that space very fast and fly at night with no difficulty. The little yellow plane was much slower, and he was not sure it was at all safe for Reijiri to be up there in the dark. He had asked, and Reijiri would try . . . but he worried now that he had asked something too hard, and that Reijiri would put himself in danger.

There was no question that the hedges, and the Guild, and the stout walls that had withstood cannon would keep them all safe, whatever was happening out on the road.

Guild could come from Shejidan. They might be on the way right now. They might have started hours ago. He *hoped* so. He wished most of all that they had reassurance from the bus.

Lucasi left the congregation of Guild over by the pillar, came to him and dropped down beside his chair. "Nandi. We have deserted you. We are not finding out anything of note. There *are* Guild units moving in. They have gone up to Diegi by rail, to get transport."

"Is there *any* word from the bus?"

"A signal, at regular intervals, that they are all right."

"Could not our enemies send it?"

"They could, nandi, but if the wearers felt they were about to be overwhelmed, they would send a code to that effect. We believe they are still aboard the bus, still safe."

He dropped his voice to a near-whisper. "*Why* did the enemy give a warning shot?" That had bothered him since he had heard it. "Were they *stupid?* Or *are* there explosives?"

"We suspect there are not." Lucasi said quietly. "We suspect they organized this in haste. We do not believe they were con-strained by the law of the aishidi'tat or the rules of the Guild, but they may not have found the means. The shot alarmed the bus and stopped it, in fear for the bridge. They *may* have hoped the driver would attempt the ford, and in that situation, the bus could become stranded. The driver *could* turn around and go back to Diegi, but to retreat from such a flimsy attack, under the circumstances? Lord Tatiseigi is not in favor. I tell you, nandi, so that—"

"It would be bad to retreat," he said. "Antaro and Jegari and another entire unit are on that bus. What would they advise us?"

"They can hold that bus unless the opposition brings in heavier armament, Jeri-ji, which is why we are moving first to interdict all intersecting roads from the west." That was to say, Ajuri. "And we should—"

Antaro paused, eyes fixed on infinity for a moment. "Some-thing has happened."

"What?"

"One is not sure. Something has changed."

"Favorable?"

"One believes . . ."

There were running steps on the lower stairs, and one of Uncle's servants arrived, breathless. "They are moving, nandi. The Guild is moving. The plane—the plane has dropped flares to light the positions. The Guild-senior says—" Pause for breath. "We shall have them."

"Go," Cajeiri said to Lucasi. "Find out. Ask. I am perfectly safe here. Go!"

Lucasi gave a handsign to Veijico, who came closer, while Lucasi ran for the stairs. They were *not* using uncoded communications, not even within the house, not trusting anything when they had other means to rely on—like code that would be disseminating with the units sent into the field.

One hoped. One desperately hoped.

"Lucasi will find out," he told Mother and Uncle quietly, but Seimei stirred and began to fret, and Mother took her onto her lap for a while, seeming to pay no attention.

"Flares," Uncle said.

"Fireworks, Uncle, to light up the grounds."

"We are aware," Uncle said, frowning.

"Ajuri has skirted the rules for years," Mother said.

The rules of engagement. The rules against explosives in places where the public might meet them, or attacks that might harm bystanders, or specifically shooting from airplanes, of which there were only four left, of nand' Reijiri's type, in all the world. There had been seven, briefly. But an open cockpit of the first planes had invited things the Guild disapproved, intensely.

Reijiri would not be shooting at them, however. Fireworks hedged the prohibition against explosives. But it was not, quite.

They waited, anxiously so. Seimei grew quiet against Mother's shoulder, and stayed that way.

Then Lucasi came back up the stairs, at a run.

"The way is clear," he said. "The bridge is clear. More Guild are coming down from Diegi, and Taibeni riders are standing guard on both sides of the bridge. The enemy has withdrawn, but Guild-senior advises us be ready and do not let our guard down."

"By no means," Uncle said.

"Are they safe?" Cajeiri asked.

"Those on the bus are perfectly safe," Lucasi said. "The bus is somewhat damaged, but they can move. Guild will inspect the bridge. Everything is all right."

One could breathe, then. Almost.

"What of Reijiri?" Cajeiri asked. "Is there word?"

Lucasi nodded. "Yes, nandi. He is heading for Diegi. Guild there is ready to receive him. He drew fire: one is uncertain whether the plane was damaged, but it is on its way, and Guild will meet him."

One had no idea where Reijiri was going to land—he was not even sure there was an airstrip at Diegi. But Reijiri had used pasturage and roads, before this, and Guild meeting him was good news.

"Nandi," Lucasi added, with a small bow to Uncle, "one believes Guild will move on the matter of your Filing. One has no idea at the moment whether that is the Guild Council or whether there is an operation in the field. That is what they know downstairs."

"The woman will have received a letter, if that is the case," Uncle said grimly. "*That* may indeed be behind this. Folly. But it would be nothing different than I have known of this woman for decades."

So there were units moving that were not part of Uncle's guard or his. The attack had not drawn off anybody from Tirnamardi or the guard over Kadagidi, Cajeiri was relatively sure. It had brought in Guild from Shejidan, maybe from Diegi, or even northward.

It was all scary. Cajeiri had not thought of people shooting at the plane. Or about landing anywhere but here. But there were tents on the lawn, which he had not even thought to say. He was so glad they were taking care of nand' Reijiri.

Now—whatever was going on—they had to sit and wait for the bus to come, and wait for reports to be far more specific.

"Well," Uncle said, "we shall get things moving now. I hesitate to enter the formality of dinner amid such disturbance. Under the circumstances, will service here suffice?"

There was a two-breath silence, and then Cajeiri realized that in this matter, too, Mother waited for him to say. His own stomach was in knots. He was all but shivering in pent-up desire to do something. "One would agree," he said calmly, since that was what he had to say, and Mother said to Beha, "I think it safe to take her up to the suite, Be-ji. There may yet be commotion tonight, but it will not pass the doors. See she gets her sleep."

Beha left, taking Seimei, one of the two servants departing with her. Uncle gazed after her as she went, concern furrowed into his expression. The pain and the disturbance that had had Uncle frowning all evening changed for an instant and became— wanting something, wanting it, very much on this chancy night.

Then Uncle glanced back, and down, and the expression was gone. He seemed only very tired and a little worried. A servant poured him tea, and listened to instruction.

Mother had not watched Uncle, but Beha, going away. Mother always fussed with Uncle, had run away from him once, to public comment, a great embarrassment to Uncle. But relations had gradually gotten better—over time.

Cajeiri looked at his own hands—well-manicured hands: his valets saw to that. He held a very precious ancient cup. It had a painting in the bottom, which was a djossi flower, pink-edged. One had to drain the cup to see it. When he had been very young, he had been so amazed by such a set in mani's suite aboard the ship. Hers had had white flowers. They might have been from the same artist.

There was so much of Great-uncle's life that extended back and back to years he could not reach. Years when mani had been regent, years before that.

So many, many secrets. So many years of Ajuri and Kadagidi wanting power over Atageini, and Atageini holding power over them and never, ever being beaten, not even in the worst days, when Father had been overthrown and the conspirators had raised Kadagidi and Ajuri as high as they had ever been—they had not dared touch Uncle. Maybe they had accounted him old, and heirless, a shadow power that would just go away without effort.

But that all seemed apt to change tonight, the whole long history of Uncle's feud with Ajuri, fighting them for years, without even knowing what a dangerous thing he was fighting. Now they were about to be overthrown, and Uncle would have the most potent vote besides Mother's, as to who should be lord of either Ajuri or Kadagidi.

Father would listen to Uncle. Even the Liberal legislators listened to him, because Uncle survived everything and knew so much.

Mani knew that much. But who else? *Father* had learned from mani, and *he* had learned from her and from Uncle.

But how could a boy learn everything?

One had to drink the cup to see the secret at the bottom. Magical, when he had been a child.

He could not drink them all, could he? It was never a matter of drinking them all. It was a matter of connections who, together, could do that for every clan, every village. He had his map, and his pins. Dur had come to help tonight, not only because Uncle had asked, but, he was convinced, had come more gladly because *he* had asked.

Taiben, who had been technically at war with Uncle, now was helping them, because of Father, but also because of him, and because of Antaro and Jegari, and Father's Taibeni guard.

They were not alone in whatever was about to come.

They had to protect all that was fragile inside Ajuri, too, and get it out of Great-aunt Geidaro's hands, and put it safely somewhere, in the hands of somebody who would not break it more than it was broken.

That was how the aishidi'tat stayed alive. One put the fragile things into good hands.

He set the cup aside. A servant filled it, and another set down a plate with three little sandwiches. He was not inspired to eat. His stomach was still too queasy for that. He just sat, and listened for news.

"Two of the enemy unit are down," Onami said at one point, all the Guild up here listening to the flow of information from Rieni and Haniri and Uncle's guard downstairs. "The rest are running."

That was good news. Then:

"The bridge is clear. The units from Diegi are arriving with trucks. The bus is starting to move."

It was good. It was all good news. He reached quietly and took one of the little sandwiches, which tasted good. Uncle, he noted, finally ate one of his. So did Mother.

"They are safely across the bridge," Janachi reported. "They have two tires damaged, but they are not impaired from moving."

"We shall replace those at our expense," Uncle said quietly to his major domo. "See to it. Advise Najida."

"Perhaps," Mother said, "we can also send word to Nomari downstairs, that the situation is on its way to being resolved. They should bed down and spend the night, if they have not already."

"That would be good," Uncle said. "Yes. Small gain in everyone waking through the night."

Cajeiri took another little sandwich, hopeful, now. It was past midnight. Well past midnight.

Long day. And sleep was spotty. Bren waked, aware of Jago sleeping beside him—longtime arrangement, that—and tried to stay still. Jago tended to wake at any movement, a noise as soft as a sigh. He truly wanted a drink of water. But he wanted more to let Jago sleep.

There was too much on his mind—too much changed.

"You are thinking," Jago said out of the dark.

He swore she could detect a change in his breathing, between waking and sleep. And wake to it herself.

"Nothing dire, Jago-ji. Nothing to disturb anyone's sleep."

"But the changes afoot are considerable."

"Beyond any doubt."

"Others will be thinking tonight. And wondering."

"I do not doubt that, either."

"Are you confident, Bren-ji?"

"A fool would be confident. But we have done what we can do."

"The children will be launching," Jago said.

"If they have not already. We will know in reasonable time, but they will not announce it to the world at large until they have actually begun descent. Time enough to assemble a herd of dignitaries. Time enough to arrange security.'

"How many dignitaries?" Jago asked.

"Dignitaries, about a hundred. News services, half that."

There was a moment of silence.

"You will speak?" Jago asked.

"I had rather not. I had far rather leave it to Shawn. Unless he insists. We shall welcome the children. That. But no more than that."

"After that, we shall be going home."

"Yes. Are you anxious?"

A small silence. Then: "I shall be far less anxious, Bren-ji, once we leave Port Jackson."

"Nandi." A touch came at Cajeiri's shoulder, and he waked, *not* that he had been fully asleep—he hoped not—but his young aishid protected him from embarrassment: he had, he feared, drowsed just a little. Uncle had had a brandy, and so had Mother, and nobody had said anything, surely. Gods, he hoped he had not been noticed. Guild and staff were awake. Well, except one young servant, who sat on a bench in the alcove, his head against the wall.

"The bus," he said.

"Nearly here," Veijico said quietly. "Janachi and Onami have just gone down to check, but house Guild is already out at the gate, and Taibeni and the two trucks with the Diegi Guild are moving with the bus. About a quarter of an hour. Our team-mates' parents are traveling on the bus. That is what we know."

So Antaro and Jegari's parents *were* here, among the Taibeni, and they *had* ridden out to assist. He had suggested before that Antaro and Jegari introduce them personally to Uncle, but the Taibeni, though they had ended the state of war with Atageini and repeatedly assisted Uncle, kept their distance, officially; and being kin of the Taibeni lord, everything they did was political.

He still hoped they would come in to be introduced to Uncle this time. There was so much going on in the region. But he was glad enough that he could look forward to getting his aishid back together again and the lot of them upstairs—to sleep late: he hoped so, granted only Uncle declared a late breakfast.

It was all good news now . . .

Except—

Guild reacted, all about the area.

"Find out," he said, and Lucasi, against protocols, ran for the stairs, nobody senior protesting.

"The gates will be opening," Uncle said. "If our neighbors dare that, they will have an unpleasant surprise."

No information. The Guild changed the codes. But there was too much in Shadow Guild hands, and with the infiltration, they took nothing for granted but faces they knew, and judgment they trusted. He understood that. But it was maddening, the cautions, the need for them, the utter stupidity of rebel

Guild fighting for a handful of dead people . . . Or maybe not
dead people.

Great-aunt Geidaro? She was not pretending stupidity. Her
whole course of action was stupid.

But she scared people. She scared them with threats.

But what she had that could scare the Shadow Guild, that
the regular Guild wanted to get their hands on—

Was records. Just pieces of paper.

"The gates are opening," one of Uncle's guards said. "There
is gunfire in the Taibeni camp, but they are opening the gates
to get the bus in, nandi."

Lucasi came flying back up the stairs, and Janachi and Onami
were behind him, bringing rifles in hand.

Something blew up in the distance. Cajeiri sprang from his
chair, remembered he was forbidden to run, but he crossed the
sitting area to the diamond-paned windows at a run all the
same—it was impossible to see the gates, but he could see an
orange-tinted cloud. "There was an explosion," he said. "There
is a cloud where the Taibeni camp is."

"The bus is moving," Janachi said. "There has been a separate assault on the Taibeni camp. Those in camp indicate they
are safe. The bus convoy is holding back until this resolves itself. Those *inside* the grounds are observing, ready to defend
should the gates have difficulty closing."

"Those gates," Uncle said angrily, "are a thousand years old,
and we are not anxious to see them damaged by that damnable
woman!"

The fire-stained smoke was diminishing. There was a glow
that might be headlights.

"We have them," Onami said.

"Well!" Uncle said. "And do we have the bus?"

"We do, nandi, and those inside will open the gate. The attackers on the camp have fled, leaving a number of them in our
hands."

"Is it over?" Mother asked.

"It may be, daja-ma," Onami said. "The gates are opening. The convoy will come in. The Taibeni escort will come in with them. The Taibeni camp is reporting—" A strange amusement came over Onami's face. "They say the attack did not expect the camp to be occupied. The explosion was to take out the gates. As it was—it did not get there."

"Mecheiti with war-caps," Janachi said, "were very persuasive. The intruders into the camp surrendered on the spot when they saw themselves surrounded by riders, and begged to be let go. *That* has not happened."

A servant arrived in haste, quietly, but urgent—with a phone in hand, with a large coil of cord. "Nandi. Nandiin. Geidaro-daja asks to speak to you. She begs to speak to you. She is under attack."

Mother's face was grim. Uncle's was set in stone. The servant waited. Then: "I shall hear her," Uncle said. "But what she says had better be quick and to the point." He reached out his hand for the phone, and servants hastened to plug it in and convey the receiver to Uncle.

"Turn up the volume," Uncle said. "There are two more who should hear this outrageous woman. This time, we shall have witnesses."

Staff complied, turning up the dial on the phone body.

"Geidaro-nandi," Uncle said, fully polite, and beside him it was quite clear that Rusani, his Guild-senior, was recording the conversation.

"Tatiseigi! Call them off!"

Uncle looked at Rusani, who dropped his official face to give a little *no* signal.

"Have you a problem, neighbor? We seem to have a commotion on the road, which involves the bus which transported the aiji-consort, which *happens* to belong to the paidhi-aiji. Shots have been fired."

"*There are Guild in the house!*" Geidaro shouted, interrupting. "*Call them off, call them off now!*"

"You have your own aishid," Uncle said. "They can perfectly properly enter dialogue—"

"*I cannot reach them! Tatiseigi, call these people! Call them back! I am willing to negotiate!*"

Rusani said, quietly, "Guild has not yet moved in that area, nandi."

Uncle said, bringing the handset again somewhat nearer. "Geidaro, are you certain they are in the house? My aishid has no word of an action."

"*Oh, gods!*" Great-aunt said. There was a loud thump and wood splintering, like a door giving way. "*Get out! You have no right! You have no right—*"

Gunfire then. And a shriek. And glass breaking.

Uncle looked taken aback. "Geidaro?" he asked.

There was no answer. But the connection stopped. Dead.

Uncle said, "Well, that was highly unpleasant." And handed the phone back to Rusani.

Cajeiri looked at his mother's stunned face, and at Uncle's somber one, and needed to know for certain what he had just heard. "Do you think she is dead, Uncle?"

"If she is not, she is in worse case. Someone she took for Guild, but *not* taking orders from Guild Headquarters? We should move regular Guild over to Ajiden as soon as possible, Rusi-ji, or we shall lose those records."

"*Surely,*" Mother said, "she had the sense not to keep them in her desk."

"Probably they are too extensive for her desk or her office. This has involved decades. Ajiden has understructure as extensive as Tirnamardi's. Finding everything may take the intruders time."

"The ones attacking us tonight," Cajeiri said. "Are *they* Shadow Guild?"

"My guess is *not*," Uncle said. "I doubt the Shadow Guild will commit numbers to the field, particularly in the north. They maintain their little cell in the south, in the Dojisigin Marid, but that remnant is not ready to take the field, even in the Marid. Geidaro has watched Shishogi go down: her own power is slipping, and the next lord of Ajuri is on the horizon, at which point her power ends and the real Guild enters the house with a great interest in records that may be in all those cellars. I suspect the Shadow Guild has moved in to preclude that event. They may have urged Geidaro to throw everything she can at us, promising her their support, simply to keep us at bay—and if Geidaro is *not* dead, at this point, they will be asking her where those records are. This is my guess. Attractive as it may have been to them to strike at the heir or the aiji-consort, or even my lesser-ranking but provocative self—their greatest vulnerability is those records in the hands of a woman losing power with every tick of the clock. Will they rescue her along with those records? I do not think they will want the notoriety. She is *not* a faceless presence. I think we shall find her dead. We shall be *lucky* if we do not find Ajiden in flames. Baji-naji.— Rusi-ji, I trust we are now moving aggressively on the situation."

Rusani nodded once and solemnly. Cajeiri's own aishid said nothing; and there was a solemn chill in the air. "Go," Uncle said, and Rusani headed off, with one of that aishid, down the stairs.

"So—these people who attacked us?" Mother asked.

"Geidaro's," Uncle said. "Very likely Geidaro's, whatever force Ajiden and the townships can muster. *Her* ambitions have been consistently against us. I think the Shadow Guild will count itself lucky to get in and get out. But *that* operation is not in our hands."

"The gate is open, nandiin," Janachi said. "The bus is coming in. With the trucks from Diegi and a number of the Taibeni."

Uncle did not react for a moment. Then he nodded.

"What is the situation with the convoy?" he asked. "Where do we stand? Do we have information flow back?"

"There are prisoners, nandi," Janachi said, "taken at the bridge."

"With the trucks?"

"Yes," Janachi said. "They are following the bus."

"Let us get our own back into the house," Uncle said. "Then deal with our problems. Rusani will be contacting operations in the field. Things out there will move, but they will refer to Shejidan, and we shall not advise our Ajuri guests until there is some outcome. They have enough distress in their laps. Our people, meanwhile, are our concern. We *have* contact again, and I am encouraged we have not heard anything about injuries to our people."

Antaro and Jegari. Cajeiri thought.

If Taibeni were escorting the bus, not only their mother and father were among them, but uncles, aunts, and cousins. Cajeiri wanted so badly to rush downstairs and meet the bus at the front steps, but that was not going to happen, given the situation.

"We shall go down," Mother said, as if she could read his mind, "at least as far as the foyer. We shall meet them there. Uncle, stay here. Let us in your stead. Please."

Uncle's will to go down was strong. But Mother had offered a great courtesy, and Uncle gave a grudging sigh. "One will be in your debt for it. *Thank* you, niece."

We, Mother said, which truly, in Mother's case, meant more than one person. She said it for *him*. "I shall go," he said quietly to his aishid, including Veijico and Lucasi. "We shall go. Probably our people are all right. But we will not be content until we know." He rose from his chair, gave a considerate little half-bow to Uncle, and joined Mother on the way, listening hard for the bus, and he thought he heard it, or the trucks, in the far distance. It might be imagination: he wanted it that much. But it grew stronger, after pausing for a moment, on such a still night.

They were indeed inside, on the grounds.

They went down the steps to the foyer, with Mother's guard and his. Onami made a quick run down to the security station in the lower hall, advising Rieni of their presence and intentions, and came back up at a run, with the sound of engines now definite in the distance.

"Antaro and Jegari are all right," Onami said. "So are all the people on the bus. They are traveling with Guild as well as their escort. The trucks have something over thirty prisoners taken at the bridge and in the camp, but the trucks will hold back while the bus unloads. Stay on this level, nandiin, please. Your security asks, to prevent distraction in the situation, or delay in getting everyone inside."

"Definitely," Mother said, and in a few moments, probably as the convoy topped the little rise to the level of the house, the sound of the bus and the trucks became much clearer.

Cajeiri found himself shivering a little, which he told himself was the hour and scant supper, and not fear at all.

The bus braked, sighed, at the steps beyond, where Guild waited. There was a little delay. Then the doors of Tirnamardi opened to let the passengers all come in. First of all was Antaro, with Jegari, with Uncle's servants behind them.

"Taro-ji!" Cajeiri called out. Antaro looked up brightly, and walked up the steps on her own, though with Jegari at her elbow. She gave two little bows, one to Mother, and in Mother's presence adopted a reserve she would not have had.

"We are so glad," Cajeiri said. "We were worried!"

"We were not suffering. We had plenty of fruit juice, plenty of pillows and blankets," Jegari said cheerfully, "and Taro slept through half of it."

"I did not," Antaro said. Two other Taibeni had come in by then, tall, older, in the brown and green of their clan, Antaro and Jegari's parents, both, who stood there a moment, took in their presence, nodded a little courtesy, then slipped back out the door.

"Nandiin," Cajeiri exclaimed. "Honored Mother,—"

"They have mecheiti on the grounds, nandi," Antaro said. "They need to get back as quickly as possible."

"Geidaro may be dead," Cajeiri said. "We are not telling everyone. Has any word gotten to the bus?"

"Not to us," Jegari said. "We had several Shejidani Guild come aboard, but we were officially told stay seated and stay quiet, and they were up to something. There was code flashing at one point, so I think something is on the move. —Dead. How?"

"It was not Shejidani Guild," Onami said. "But yes, units *are* moving in that direction."

"They are about to offload the supplies," Janachi said. "With the trucks and the prisoners to follow."

"We should move everybody upstairs," Mother said, "and get these two young people a place to sit down, at very least."

"Nandi." Antaro made a little bow, casted arm tucked close.

"No one in the whole house is sleeping tonight, except, perhaps, my daughter. Come. Son of mine."

"Bring in only the perishables," Heisi was calling down to inbound staff. "Leave the rest until daylight. Tea and sandwiches in the kitchen, nadiin!"

It was considerable commotion inbound, with Uncle's staff and packages. Janachi quietly barred ascent for a moment, holding back the tide to let them and their aishid come up to the main floor and back to Uncle, who was talking to someone on the phone, with a servant standing by. Father, perhaps, had called to find out the state of things; and indeed, when Mother came near, Tatiseigi offered the phone to her.

"Yes," she said, and, "Absolutely." And, "It may be a good idea."

Oh, please, Cajeiri thought. He did not want an order to go home. It was dangerous getting to the train, for one thing, even on the bus, dangerous for any escort Uncle might send to bring the bus back, and for another—he had *begun* this problem. He wanted to see it through. He wanted to be sure both Uncle and Tirnamardi would be all right, and that was still in doubt, tonight.

Mother handed the phone back to the servant, and looked toward Antaro, who was settling carefully into a chair, with Jegari close by.

"They will likely not go upstairs and rest," Mother said.

"They probably will not, Honored Mother. What did Father say?"

"It was not your father, son of mine. It was your great-grandmother."

"Mani! At *this* hour! Is everything all right?"

"She wishes you well. She is in Najida. She says that Lord Machigi—we take it that he is meant—is in good health and wishes you well."

"I am very well, Honored Mother!" He was astonished that mani and Mother had even had an agreeable conversation. "We are all well! Has he anything to say about Nomari-nadi?"

"That he is pleased to know he is well. We are all so very well, son of mine, that the very fact your great-grandmother has called at this hour *from* Najida, where she is meeting with Lord Machigi, fills us with delight. She knows what is going on up here, she is tracking it as closely as she can, and, greater wonder, she is thus far satisfied."

Lord Machigi out of place—he almost never left his residence in Tanaja; and he and mani were meeting in Najida, which was *very* out of the way for Lord Machigi, but one of the safest and quietest places they could both reach—indicated *Father* was talking to Lord Machigi, through mani, and that very large things were shifting.

At this hour.

"You do not think, Honored Mother, that it was *Lord Machigi's* people who—"

"It would not be legal, and it would stir the Guild to enter the dispute at a time when Lord Machigi is in negotiations to have the Guild recognize his bodyguard. No, son of mine, I think our first surmise is the true one. The Shadow Guild is closing up shop in the north and would like to lay hands on whatever records reside in Ajiden—elsewhere, if they could cart them off, but we have not made that easy, one trusts. With luck, we have made it highly inconvenient."

He had always thought Mother was smart about *some* things, but he had never thought she was smart in figuring out enemies and allies. She certainly had spent her life upsetting both clans she had ties to.

But then—she had been hardly older than he was when she had made her choice to leave her father and try to live with Uncle. And maybe she had just been too young then to know who was lying.

"I hope we *have*," he said dryly, "made it inconvenient."

"Did she call you?" Mother asked Uncle. "Surely she must have. At this hour. And from Najida."

"She did call," Uncle said, "which makes me think your husband is not sleeping tonight, either. One suspects I was second on 'Sidi-ji's list of calls tonight. One takes it for a signal she has reached some specific understanding with Lord Machigi—which is a good thing. We also have Dur coming in, early tomorrow. Breakfast. We should abandon the notion of sleep tonight, I think."

"He will understand," Cajeiri said, "if we were to pass word to him to come later, he would well understand."

"He has done us a great favor," Uncle said. "At personal risk. One hears there were two shots that struck the plane."

"One hopes he is uninjured," Mother said.

"Fervently we hope it," Uncle said. "But Guild in Diegi is taking good care of him. Meanwhile we have our own difficulties: another inundation of Ajuri, these less trusted but in our keeping. Ruheso informs me we have an infelicity of forty-four in custody, sixteen in uniform, the rest in civilian clothes, twelve taken at the bridge, thirty-two taken in the assault on the Taibeni camp, evidently with the intent to reach the gates with explosives. One hesitates even to mention the inclusion of armed civilians *with* Guild leadership, on which I am sure Guild Council will have a word. These folk are arriving by truck. To keep them from escaping and returning to Ajiden at this juncture, we may now have to put *them* under canvas *and* keep the other Ajuri in our lower hall, or have the two groups come to blows. I have sent word down to our guest that we have such a difficulty, and I am officially, in the name of the At-ageini, curious to hear his response—your pardon."

Someone had come running up from the stairs, one of the house guard, a woman who presented herself at Uncle's signal, and gave a little bow. "Nandi. He wishes to see you. He wishes to see these people. He wishes to meet them and speak to them."

"That might be useful. Bring them up. Bring them *all* up, as many as wish to come, his followers as well." Uncle looked at the two of them. "It might be well for you to go upstairs. At least for the young aiji to go upstairs."

"Respected Uncle," Cajeiri said. "No. I wish to hear this."

Mother darted a worried glance at him.

"I have my aishid."

"Two of them disabled."

"Two able, and a very senior unit, Mother, who will protect me, above all else. And *I* shall stand next to Uncle and you, so we shall all protect each other. *You* are safer with me and my guard here."

There was a moment of silence.

"We shall bring up more kit," Janachi said. "Daja-ma, and no one in custody from events tonight may come up here unrestrained. This is a requirement."

"So," Cajeiri said. "Uncle?"

"With that restriction," Uncle said. "These are historic premises. We shall have no gunfire, nadiin, none."

"We shall have that understood," Janachi said.

So they waited.

Adrenalin had somewhat ebbed. It was surely past midnight, and events and decisions had begun to pass in a kind of charged fog. Cajeiri sat still, beside Mother, beside Uncle. He had a little doubt of his own good sense—of everyone's good sense, inviting a confrontation up here, in so much space. And it began to occur to him that Mother, being Ajuri, could become entangled in what happened, as much as Nomari. Uncle surely knew it. Mother surely was thinking it.

"Antaro-nadi." This from Uncle, in the long silence. Unprecedented, that a lord addressed a member of an outsider aishid by name. But Uncle did.

"Nandi."

"The two-year-old is moving about and eating."

"One is very glad, nandi."

"She has even picked a quarrel with her agemates."

"One is not entirely surprised, nandi. She will not forget what she did when you asked it."

"Your arm, nadi. What did the hospital say?"

"That you have an excellent physician, nandi. They were entirely complimentary."

"Indeed." Uncle nodded, pleased. "I shall tell him."

There was a quiet commotion, an orderly ascent of the side stairs below, by a number of people. The Ajuri belowstairs were coming up, more than sixty of them, with Nomari and Uncle's guard, with a few more Guild, who brought up the rear.

"Well," Uncle said, " now we shall see, shall we not, what this young man has at his core. What *will* he do, do you think?"

Bringing in Nomari's supporters—and Great-aunt Geidaro's, at once—with such a question . . .

Cajeiri drew in a long, slow breath, assembling the thought that, at the moment, he understood why Uncle partnered with mani. It was the same intent, curious expression, that put

Nomari in front of his enemies—enemies Geidaro had sent to attack Uncle, or Mother; and who might have attacked Nomari, if the situation had brought them face to face.

Now—*what will he do?* Uncle asked.

What, Cajeiri wondered, would *he* do? And what stirred in him said—*take* them. Lay hold of them. Say what needed to be said and do what needed to be done, and if any of them stood up against him—

Take that person, for the sake of everything that depended on him—because he was *responsible.*

Nomari came up the stairs first, worried-looking and distracted, and the commotion of sixty and more people followed him. Uncle's bodyguard spoke to him, indicated where the people should arrange themselves, and they clustered together, looking about, some of them.

"Assistance," Uncle said, setting the cane he was using, and began to get up. Cajeiri moved to assist, ahead of old Heisi, who assisted from the other side. Uncle moved under his own power once he was on his feet, and his bodyguard was around him. It was clear where Uncle meant to go, to deal with Nomari, and Cajeiri watched anxiously, standing back out of the way, aware that a much more dangerous crowd was to come.

"Nandi," Nomari met Uncle with a bow.

"I have no decision yet," Uncle began. "Geidaro not long ago called this house in the belief people who had entered Ajiden were ours. They were not, nor to our knowledge were they sent from Shejidan. This leaves ominous possibilities, and we have passed that word to Shejidan, in respect of the law. In any case, we do not expect Ajuri will continue under that leadership for much longer. What we are prepared to deal with, as having invaded *Atageini* territory, is a mingled force of civilians *and* Guild—the latter of whom may be Ajuri. Or may not. In any case—they are not Atageini. The question is—what do *you* want done with them?"

"You are saying, nandi, that Geidaro may be dead."

"I am saying that, whatever falls out of this, we have questions as to why these people have attacked the paidhi-aiji's bus on a public road, and whose orders set this plan in motion. They are yours. Discover answers. And tell me."

If *he* were the recipient of that tone and that frown, Cajeiri thought, *he* would understand Uncle was giving him a chance, and one chance, to settle matters. He wished Nomari to understand that. He watched Nomari's expression go from worried to resolute, and he hoped—hoped that Nomari would realize—that Uncle was handing him a test. Do this, and gain something—or fail, and lose trust, and lose Ajuri.

He could not signal Nomari. He *should* not signal him. There was no time for a gentle introduction to a peaceful household. Either Nomari was able to take hold of the situation—or he was not. If he failed, he had a small hope of going back to what he had been—

But it was little likely Ajuri would let him. Or that the remnant of the Shadow Guild would leave him alone, or let those near him have any peace.

It was all here. Now.

"It is in your hands," Uncle said, "how you will handle this."

And Uncle turned and walked back to his place. Cajeiri likewise drew back. Uncle told staff to turn his chair. So they turned it to let Uncle observe. And Uncle sat down, cane across his knee, in the hand he could use, and waited and watched.

The foyer doors had shut a few moments ago. Now they opened, opened on the lower stairs, too, all the way to the night air, with a chill, rainy draft and a commotion on the stairs below, nothing distinct, but the tread of feet and a voice giving directions to "Go up, keep in line and be respectful of the premises."

Guild came first, taking station about the area with rifles at carry. Then a sad gathering of people trailed up after them, dirty, many muddy from head to foot, and every three tied elbow to elbow, the middle person with neither arm at liberty.

Downhearted, distressed, resentful. . . . they were all that, only a few managing to hide all expression.

Nomari and his people outnumbered them—sixty-some clean, quiet, apprehensive people, maybe recognizing the newcomers, or maybe not. It was not certain that all the prisoners were Ajuri. Guild among them had not been specially restrained, just bound to civilians, not their teammates; and without their jackets. They were especially grim-faced; and deeply embarrassed, one could be sure.

How could anybody make something of these people? Cajeiri wondered. They had just attacked a bus and a Taibeni camp on Atageini land and Uncle had Filed Intent on the woman who had given them their orders. They were no longer a threat in the night, injuring Uncle and others. They were prisoners, clustered together in a strange place, facing justice with the Guild and with Father.

"Listen to me," Nomari said. "You have arrived in a very difficult place tonight, lordless, lordless since Komaji went down, cut off from Shejidan, voiceless in the legislature. Is it all your choice? No. But tonight it is. My name is Nomari, of the line of *Nichono*, last of her line. Shishogi murdered my family. I escaped. It is no unique story. Many of those with me can say the same. We stand opposed to Shishogi and all his works. We stand opposed to Geidaro, who followed Shishogi until he died. And hearing there were proposals afoot to name a lord—I take it as a responsibility, a man'chi to my father, a son of Nichono, to my mother, a daughter of Lord Benedi, to my brother, who *would* be standing here if he had survived. I have spent recent years in Transportation, finding ways to move Ajuri that Shishogi was targeting to other places, to safety. Do I know something about Shishogi's operations? Yes. From the targeted end of them. I know what he did. I have a long list of those he killed—Ajuri and other clans as well, including the aiji-consort's mother, Lord Tatiseigi's sister. We have been deadly neighbors to all around us, except Kadagidi, who may yet pay a heavy price for its crimes. But there is innocence left in Ajuri. I know where that is, too. I set my own name into nomination for the lordship, and if I last no longer than Kadiyi or Komaji, so be it. I have come too far not to try. I am the last eligible of the line. Have me, or have chaos, and I promise you, if I come into Ajiden there will be changes. I will *not* seek revenge, I will not pursue old grudges unless they rear up alive again. I will not have whispers and threats and names no one dares pronounce. Clan council will have its doors open, not guarded. And Ajuri will *have* an advocate in Shejidan. The aiji-consort, her son the heir apparent, our one-time ally Tatiseigi of the Atageini and the Taibeni as well have said it: we *have* the connections to regain our good name and make a real peace with our neighbors of the Padi Valley. We can regain our respect in the aishidi'tat, with powerful allies on every hand, or we can go down the dark path Shishogi set. Make your choice. Make it tonight. The Guild that Shishogi corrupted has restored itself. *We* have a chance to recover ourselves, settle our differences through the Guild, *under* the aiji in Shejidan, and expect a future for us."

"Hear him," somebody shouted from among Nomari's people. "This is our lord. This is the man who kept us alive. This is the man who risked his life time and again to bring people out of Ajuri. This is the *other* name no one would speak— because he protected us, he moved us to safety, he gave us warnings, and on one occasion—he killed a man to save us, much against his nature. He did that for us."

Nomari ducked his head. Lifted it again. "I cannot regret it. I cannot be proud of it. But I never want to face that again. Ajuri has to change. Ajuri cannot go on killing its lords *or* its children. There is a long, long list of wrongs, and no profit to keeping them endlessly repeating themselves, generation after generation. I call an end to it. I call for an absolute *end* to it. I do not know you people. I fled Ajuri when I was fifteen, and I know *these* faces, but not yours—but whoever you are, if you are clanless, if you are Ajuri, if you have a grievance, say it. But if you want an end to the killing—join us."

A man sank down, pulling his neighbor, and three of them went down together, to their knees. Others did. Even one and another of the Guild.

"Speak for us," one man said.

"Nandi!" another said. Others said it, and others, "Nichono!"

The air had all of a sudden changed. The room seemed charged with something—not electricity, nothing so sharp; but a power that could be inside or in the air itself, Cajeiri was not sure, a situation on the edge of scary . . . too many people, too much distress, but all of it cycled around one man standing out there, his followers swarming around him and others, some of them, overcome together, meeting some of the exiled, some trying to talk to Nomari, all at once. It was disorderly. It was the sort of thing that made Guild nervous. But, Cajeiri thought, it had to be. It had to be let happen.

Names were exchanged, questions asked, promises made. The whole great hall had started two opposing groups and become one large knot, as so much of anxiety poured out, all about. "I shall tell him," Nomari said to one person and to another, "I will try to find out, if our neighbor will back me. If Tabini-aiji approves." And, "Shejidani Guild is moving on Ajiden. We cannot help, even if we could get there, nadi-ji. We cannot. They are trying to protect the staff, the house and grounds. That is what I know."

And then, "I shall do my best, nadi. I shall ask the Guild."

Uncle tapped his cane on the floor, a ringing, repeated sound that brought, fairly quickly, silence.

"Nomari-nadi," Uncle said. "Neighbor. You say you are willing to take the lordship." A hush fell, everyone listening. "I am willing to support you, should your name be mentioned to the aiji, and that will happen, perhaps tomorrow morning."

There was a rising murmur. Uncle thumped the cane—Great-grandmother's style.

"At that point you will *have* representation again, and I shall have no problem sitting down with your lord to regularize relations, which I trust will wipe out old grievances, and make people of all clans safe in their homes and free from threat—from anyone. Nomari-nadi, orders to your people are your orders, but your host requests that those with assignment below go rest; and those without it, you will be let free. Go out to the tents, which will be guarded against *any* disturbance of the peace. And do not seek to leave the grounds. Your chances are better with my forgiveness than Guild tolerance, not to mention the Taibeni beyond the gates. We shall not see anyone arrested or held to blame tonight: make your confessions to the grandson of Nichono and let him sort it out. But do it all downstairs, nadiin. We have very little of the night left, and I am an old man who needs his sleep."

"Nandi." Nomari gave a deep bow to Uncle. "Aijiin-ma." To him and to Mother. And to his people. "Come, nadiin. Let us go down. Let us talk for a moment, all of us, before some of us go outside."

Was that it? Cajeiri asked himself. Was Uncle forgiving them, and was Mother?

They had to. If they went on, the quarrel never stopped, did it, even if Grandfather and Grandmother were dead, and Nomari's family was, and Geidaro and Meisi might be dead. Even Dejaja. He would be very sad about Dejaja. He hoped—hoped the real Guild moved fast, and that nobody innocent was caught in the situation.

He looked at Mother. saw her frowning and solemn, and likely thinking—thinking about years and people and things Nomari might know, but none of them did. If anybody could stop what Uncle was proposing, Mother could.

Nomari turned back from the crowd of people that was

moving down the stairs—where Guild was quietly freeing everybody but Guild in uniform. Nomari came and bowed to him and Mother, and said just, "Thank you. Thank you, aijiin-ma."

Mother just nodded. Then she said, "Stay alive, Noma-ji. Do not forgive them all. Just stay alive."

18

Morning. And Jago was not in bed.

That was not uncommon.

But arising, finding the gathering of the whole aishid, in uniform, about the little table in the main room, with the samovar and writing materials—at this hour, with the sun not yet up—

That was *not* usual.

"Is there a problem?" Bren asked, fearing anything from disaster on the mainland to an imminent assault on Francis House.

"Everything seems quiet now," Algini said.

"Tea?" Tano asked.

When his aishid offered tea, it was not necessarily without questions or solemn consideration instead of the traditional calm and reflection, but it was, at this hour, a start on whatever problem was up.

He pulled out one of the two remaining chairs, the one next to Banichi, and sat down. Jago offered a teacup and Banichi poured from a teapot that ran a little short.

"It may be bitter, Bren-ji," Banichi said. "Let us make another."

"Bitter tea I can drink. Bitter news—one hopes not, nadiin."

"No. We received a general alert, called down from Lord Geigi. The code *was* a contingency, with a device that nand' Toby left with us. We hoped not to receive any such."

Communications. *That* had been the package.

"A contingency, nadiin-ji." Bitter tea was an understatement. They had made it strong. "Guild equipment?" He might have to explain that to Shawn. He needed at least a sketchy knowledge.

"Military," Banichi said. "So the aiji *can* contact the navy at any inconvenient remove without the involvement of *any* Guild. The navy will not be happy to have it with us, and we are asked, in a note from Tabini-aiji, to keep its existence confidential, even from the Guild. It links to Lord Geigi. Who links to the aiji. It activated itself last night with an extensive report more current than nand' Toby's. We as yet had no reason for you to intervene, and we decided you *might* be called to travel today, with need for sleep and a clear head. So it was our judgment. We reconsidered it hour by hour, until your regular waking."

"I joined them two hours ago," Jago muttered. "And by then it seemed settled."

"What?" Bren asked. "What is settled, nadiin-ji?"

"Geidaro attacked Lord Tatiseigi," Banichi said. "Apparently the Najida bus was involved. The aiji had it transported up to Lord Tatiseigi's estate, for the protection of the aiji-consort, her daughter, and the young gentleman, but none of them were aboard at the time."

"Her *daughter*. Surely she was aware of the danger . . ."

"Absolutely she was. And she took the train, thus preventing the dowager taking it—and the bus. Seimiro is, among other things, a child of the Atageini governing line, extinct except for—"

"Except for Tatiseigi," Bren concluded. Damiri was playing power politics with everything she had. Ajuri was at issue.

But Damiri surely had no intention of putting an infant forward as lord of Ajuri.

No. No infant claimant could hold that deadly office through all the vulnerabilities and mistakes of growing up. Absolutely not. It was Atageini itself Damiri intended—

holding out her daughter not only as an heir for a nearly-extinct and critically valuable line, but offering Tatiseigi a successor with a very close tie to both the present and future power of the aijinate.

And offering it now, as Tatiseigi was in a position of shaping the future of the region.

God, when the woman finally rolled the dice, she set out her pieces in full battle order, no backing away, no mistaking her reasoning in this.

"She is challenging Geidaro," Bren said. "And Tatiseigi both. But this claimant for Ajuri and his followers—and our bus. I understand the aiji bringing up the bus, but—none of them aboard. So why attack the bus? Am *I* somehow at issue?"

"The bus was making a supply run," Algini said. "The Ajuri may have mistaken its mission."

"There had been prior trouble," Tano said. "Lord Tatiseigi was injured in what may have been an Ajuri move the night before. And several clans are now involved. Taiben was there as added protection for the young gentleman. Ajuri following this Nomari are camped on Tatiseigi's grounds. And Dur has now flown in, likewise to offer support."

"Lord Tatiseigi Filed on Geidaro," Jago said, "after the incident in which he was injured, and before the bus incident. Taiben is there. Dur. And local Guild. Guild Council meanwhile shelved all debate on the Filing and moved units toward Ajiden on an emergency basis. Meanwhile someone, apparently in Guild uniform, killed Geidaro and a number of the staff, then started a fire in the lower hall. Staff managed to put it out. Guild is now on the premises, and they are attempting to trace the murderers. The belief is that they arrived from the Marid."

There were *two* sources in the south who might wear Guild uniform. One was the Shadow Guild. The other—

Could be Machigi, who had an association with Nomari.

"The fire-setting argues someone wanting to destroy what the Guild wants its hands on," he said. "And knowing they had no time. Machigi would be only too happy to have Shadow Guild records carted to Shejidan in their entirety."

"That would be true," Algini said somberly. "And it would certainly be a question in Guild Council, but indeed, it is not likely Machigi who would be incriminated by records in Ajiden."

"Which leaves us without Geidaro—no loss; and with a still-viable claimant." He sat still a moment, absorbing it, trying to make some sort of reasonable sequence out of it. "Is it possible Shadow Guild caused whatever problem injured Lord Tatiseigi?"

"Possible, yes," Algini said. "Ironic, if their move led Lord Tatiseigi to File on Geidaro. Ironic if they then had to finish *her*, in hopes of destroying those records before a new lord might take Ajuri. Shishogi's records, if they exist there, would be of immense interest. I do not doubt there will be a rapid assignment of Guild units to Nomari—I would suspect the assignment is tentative, but that somewhere in that movement of Guild in the region, there are two units ready to introduce themselves to this young man."

"Meanwhile," Banichi said, "the young lord of Dur is repairing his plane in Diegi, but he is moving Guild in by rail. Likewise the lord of Taiben has personally entered the camp outside Tirnamardi's grounds, to be sure there is no further mischief there. The situation does seem to be well covered."

"God." That, in Mosphei'. He sat there, stunned, as Tano replaced the cup of tea with a fresh one. "I leave the mainland for a few days and the world changes."

"In a certain sense," Jago said, "one may be grateful to Damiri-daja. Lord Tatiseigi has rarely moved at extravagant risk to himself. People in general have accused him of timidity. Some even say he survived the Troubles by being too timid to take personal risk—"

"While he was sheltering the aiji on his land."

"Yet he has this reputation," Jago said, "that he *will* not run a risk."

"Damiri-daja has brought her daughter to Tirnamardi," Banichi said. "That, and the young gentleman's presence, make a difference. I would not be surprised if Damiri-daja has not, privately, before anything of this happened, informed Lord Tatiseigi that she *would* visit, would bring the child—and with Ajuri suddenly in contention, and considering that Geidaro's visit had tipped the balance—she made the move."

"Damiri-daja attempted to rehabilitate Ajuri," Algini said, "during her father's lordship. She was upset when Tabini-aiji ejected all that house from the capital. But when her father was assassinated, that was a serious blow. When Shishogi went down, the very night Seimiro came into the world, she both acquired an asset independent of her husband, and, from the new Council, began to get undeniable information about Ajuri's involvement in the coup."

"Geidaro's intrusion into Tirnamardi may have seemed more ominous to her than it did to Lord Tatiseigi," Banichi said, "on that account. Ominous, indeed. And she was not about to cede this situation to the aiji-dowager. She was going to go, she was going to bring her daughter *into* Tirnamardi, she was going to meet this candidate for Ajuri and pass judgment on his fitness. And though she likely had not expected the situation to take the turn it has—she brought more high-level reinforcements, not to mention what Tabini-aiji had already sent with his son."

"Most of all," Algini said, "she brought with her an heir for Atageini, a child of the ancient line, which is the very point on which the whole Ajuri-Atageini feud began. So quite suddenly— Lord Tatiseigi is no longer made of glass, apt to leave chaos if he falls."

"And Geidaro," Banichi said, "who sat perched atop records the Guild feared would be destroyed if she were threatened, may now be dead, and those records—are in play. That is an outcome more deadly to the Shadow Guild than any physical attack."

"Whether or not they are found," Algini said, "the Shadow Guild now cannot trust they have not been, and the names of every resource they have may be exposed. Only the Guild Council will know. And the Shadow Guild's resources may start disappearing." Algini rarely smiled. He smiled now, with a particular satisfaction.

God, the window onto the sky showed only a suggestion of daylight arriving. They sat here in the last of the night, with the sea between them and massive changes on the mainland, with the sky about to deliver them another change in the world. Things seemed out of control, speeding toward some different destination than a day ago.

"Frightening," he said. Change tended to be that.

"One force is shoved aside," Banichi said, "and another comes into play. At this point we do not know what, but there will be reactions, definitely, from those who will not like what results."

"No one is ever satisfied," Tano said.

"Machigi," Jago said, "is sitting in the southern Marid with a teen-aged fool entertaining the Shadow Guild in the Marid's northern provinces. He has concerns far closer to his border."

The fool in question was Tiajo, Lord of the Dojisigin Marid, who had leapt beyond the control of her father, convinced she was invulnerable. And Machigi was building strength, but not to join Tiajo. To take her down, likely, but the aishidi'tat had rather, at the moment, have a weak Shadow Guild flattering a fool in one province than a full-blown war destabilizing the whole south.

Ilisidi was dealing with Machigi. And might learn interesting things. Or convey them. *She* could assure Machigi of something he wanted even more than he wanted the north—use of the southern ports for something other than fishing boats.

"I ask myself," he said, "whether my absence may have

helped bring this situation to a crisis. Certainly the aiji-consort would not have welcomed my mediation, under the circumstances—it being a deeply personal matter. And I am doubly glad the dowager is keeping Machigi's attention at the moment."

"That," Algini said, "is potentially the most dangerous man in the aishidi'tat. One has to wonder what this Ajuri may have learned about *him* during the Troubles."

"The shuttle is on its way," Bren mused, "and I shall wrap up affairs and make a quiet return. Landing at Najida will indeed be the best entry—quiet, with the Red Train accessible to get me back to the Bujavid with no notice at all. There are indeed questions to ask. One is beginning to feel the whole continent has shifted."

Having Antaro and Jegari upstairs, shed of their weapons and gear, and sitting for a bit in comfortable chairs—was a wonderful gift. Knowing Uncle and Mother were likewise upstairs, and that Sister was peacefully sleeping down the hall, put a cap on a night that, now that dawn was creeping into the window, had them all exhausted.

It was just a little sweetmeats and tea, in lieu of the meals they had missed—though Antaro and Jegari confessed they had all eaten quite well on the bus, which had brought in all manner of supplies: staff and Guild alike had indulged, while the bus was pinned down and the world was in crisis.

And they faced a real breakfast in a few hours—a very late breakfast, since it was to include Reijiri, who had been up all night with repairs to his plane. Uncle decreed that morning would come four hours late, since there had been no real sleep for anyone except, perhaps, Sister, who had been sheltered from it all. Staff and guests and refugees and all, they were to go to bed and have a few hours, one hoped, without alarms.

Rieni and Haniri came up upstairs, finally; they had spent the night in the security office, which had been dealing with defenses and communications both. They reported that Nomari was indeed doing just as Uncle asked, and that everything downstairs was quiet, with operations turned over to Uncle's people and two of Mother's guard.

And they both collapsed wearily into comfortable chairs, while Eisi and Liedi provided hot tea and a plate of spicy sweets, which they declined. "We have drunk far too much tea," Haniri said, "and eaten to stay awake and alert. But good people are in charge there. We could rest—if we had not drunk so much black tea. I doubt we shall sleep for three days."

"Is there any word from Ajiden?" Cajeiri asked.

"Not yet, except to say the fire is out and the search is on-going."

"Some of the people with Nomari," Rieni said, "we suspect are the risen dead, the same as the senior officers of the Guild who managed to survive the Troubles. Families inside Ajuri will have unexpected reunions that may or may not go well, inheritances that may soon be in question. And that will be Nomari's problem to solve, granted his confirmation. But that is another day's problem. It is all on the strength of man'chi, whether he can hold the troubles in check, and whether he can compel settlements of differences. He has been rather too gentle and too agreeable. Until an hour ago."

"You heard that," Cajeiri asked.

"One rather thinks, nandi, that *that* is the face he has shown to those in the tents. To those he has persuaded to follow him. Did he wish to deceive us? We have asked that question. We have asked your mother's aishid how he was when he spoke to her in private. And the answer is—he wears more than one manner. Speaking to your mother, he began to be yet another person, honest, her aishid believes, showing his grief for his family and his intent to overthrow Geidaro, but reserved in address. With you, with your great-uncle, respectful and cautious. With some of his followers, intimate and affectionate.

With his followers in general, one suspects, much more what appeared in the hall."

"He helped Machigi," Cajeiri said. Mani had said that Machigi was safe to deal with only when he had something to gain. But he did not spread mani's advice about to everybody, and Rieni and the rest were still new. "And now he may become Machigi's equal."

"That might be true in more than one sense," Rieni said, and that was certainly worth thinking about.

No more troubling word had come through the military connection Toby had brought. There was quiet word from Geigi, by phone, that the young gentleman's great-uncle was extremely regretful that the bus had suffered a little damage, but that it remained serviceable, and that any future damage would be repaired before it was freighted back to the coast.

"That does not sound, nadiin-ji, as if they are quite through the problem," Bren said.

"No," Banichi agreed. "It does not. My personal guess is that the bus is being reserved to move the aiji's family, possibly Lord Tatiseigi, *and* this candidate for Ajuri wherever they need to go."

"How long may we expect the Guild to be searching the Ajiden understructure?"

A little silence, then, from Banichi: "Say that they have the means to do it without undue disturbance of the structure. There will be no hidden compartments, not even a space as large as a tea-tray, but what they can find it. I would say within a few days."

"Of course *what* they find might require more attention."

"Explosives?" He was appalled.

"Say they are proceeding cautiously," Tano said. That was Tano's field; and if they had been anywhere in reach, Tano would have been involved, one was quite sure.

But they were not in reach.

And his aishid, as he did, simply had to wait and take the little information they could get.

What did arrive, however, after breakfast, was Kate, and a pleasant surprise, Sandra Johnson—Kate on her crutches, in a businesslike summer shirt, with a horrid brown print skirt that had not come from any house of fashion; and Sandra in modest blue, looking as if she worked for a bank, and porting a box of donuts—to the interest of them all.

"Welcome in," Bren said, not having had a chance to say so in person.

"We're so excited," Sandra said.

"I'm so glad to have you," Bren said. "Anything you need. Soon as you need it. Sit down. Cup of tea. Donuts all round. We're on Mospheiran manners here, understanding you have a lot on your schedule. Finance all working? You're going to be in?"

"No problems," Kate said. "Tom's established a house account, put us on the list: money's no difficulty. Last delivery was last night, excepting the household goods. Those arrive today. We'll be moved in. Sandra's kitchen arrived last night."

"Beautiful things," Sandra said. "Wonderful things. The range has eight burners!"

"State of the art," Kate said. "And a refrigerator that could supply a small shop. We're not going to starve. The van's coming in today. John and the boys are seeing to that."

The arrangement had Sandra and her family and Kate all living in the outer security bubble, involving second-floor space, complete with kitchens and private living space, and a specially fortified van for excursions. Sandra's husband was going to have a computer link to his job. The two sons, a shade too old to socialize with the Reunioner kids and a shade too young for the lads from Documents, were enrolled in the University school, John and the boys having their own security somewhat loosely attached when they did step outside the bubble, but definitely present. It was *not* going to be an easy adjustment for the boys in particular.

But Kate had said it: Sandra's past association with him meant there already *were* dangers in a heated political climate, and there was no getting around it. It was an island. People knew things. People knew connections. And having Sandra's family drawn into a secure environment while Heritage outrage would focus on an increasing number of Reunioner arrivals— was better than hoping the packages that arrived at a modest house in Bretano contained no surprises.

Get through this, get the Reunioners down here over the next several years, and various lives could reach some sort of normalcy.

It was his hope, at least, that Heyden Court would revert to a museum, or office space, or whatever it needed to be, in a world that had found the Reunioners not that difficult to assimilate.

One hoped it, on so many grounds.

"The boiler is going," Kate said, "and modern air conditioning is going in. Today, or I'll be having a private conversation with the workmen. The old central vent is dismantled, and there will be two independent systems. The new vents are too small for passage. The dumbwaiter system is going, plastered over and with no cable. And there is a modern security link phone in Sandra's residence, in the kids' residences, each, in my residence, and in my office. Security will blind-order groceries and supplies, so that anything ordered in is going to be safe."

"And meanwhile," Bren said, "you have to give these families some notion how Mospheirans live. Cooking. Handling money, for one thing. They've only had cards and rations."

"Sandra's job," Kate said. "Sandra. Sandra's family. Even the kids."

"They know to be careful," Sandra said. "They know the problems. But they want to help."

"They're your kids," Bren said. "I trust you, and John. They'll be an asset."

"Security says we can do excursions," Sandra said. "John and the boys already have a list of things the kids have to see."

"And school," Kate said, "will begin for them on the 23rd. Time enough to settle in. They'll have two hours in gym and art, then some academic tests to figure out where they are in various subjects."

"Knowledge of Mospheira," Bren said to Sandra, "zero, knowledge of the universe at large, probably greater than ours. Definitely the instructors will have to figure all that out. But the kids will learn—faster than we expect, likely."

"Sandra and John will be on premises at their arrival to get them settled in, show them how to deal with household knobs and buttons, and maybe walk them around the premises, which *you* might like to do."

Bren shook his head. "I'm going to need to get back to the mainland pretty quickly."

Sharp, quick look. "Trouble?"

It was Kate. And Sandra. He had no need to conceal anything.

"It's not impossible I should have to go back to the mainland early. Don't take it for alarming if I do. Not for public knowledge, there's a little activity in the central clans that's apparently come to a crisis, and I hope it will settle quickly with no further damage. Or turn out with a situation better than it was. Which is apparently a possibility. So is worse, unfortunately. If worse—I *will* have to go. Sandra, Kate will fill you in, but the phones between here and the mainland are an absolute sieve for information. The Messengers' Guild has been a problem for as long as electricity has figured in it, and probably before that. The system doesn't get fixed because all sorts of sides know how to operate with it as it is, and nobody trusts it would *really* change, only that their side would be disadvantaged if reform came through, so it's been going on for years. It's getting inconvenient, but everybody's made so many accommodations to get around it, it's almost an industry in itself. Communication to and from the space station is where it gets really inconvenient, and Lord Geigi and the head of the Messengers are always back and forth in territorial issues—he *does* ignore them, at need. He tries to do it as infrequently as possible: Tabini used a courier on the first message, but things must be changing rapidly, so Geigi's been brought in on it, and protests from the Messengers' Guild may probably be flying even as we speak."

"But it's safer over there now," Sandra said hopefully. A question. "You're not getting shot at."

"Not too recently," he said, not quite a joke. "Honestly, the situation is overdue to settle—the patch on it has been wearing thin over the last entire year—so it coming to a head is not a bad thing, granted they really have found a viable a solution. Keeping the peace in the central region has been . . . difficult, to say the least, for years."

"Are we need to know?" Kate asked bluntly.

"Both of you are. Keep it close, even from the kids, Sandra, though I wouldn't exclude John. Kate does know specifics of the history. She'll fill you in."

"Understood," Kate said. "What about the tutors?"

"I want those three," he said, "close to the kids. Right from the start. I'm thinking of taking them with me, at the landing. I'm being called to the mainland. I can't stay any longer than that, and I'd only be an atevi presence in the event that really should be Mospheiran. The kids' and parents' first impressions shouldn't be of being deserted to a crowd of dignitaries and a row of cameras, either. I think having the people who *will* be dealing with them part of the first scene is important. You two could be there, if you like."

"I'm not for that sort of thing," Sandra said. "I just don't feel comfortable being pointed out. My family—my boys—I don't want them on television."

"I quite well understand that."

"I'll be happier behind the scenes, myself," Kate said. "I'll meet them at the house. The young folk, however, are a very good idea—for one thing, they'll need to get used to that publicity. It'll follow them whenever they take the kids out."

It *was* a good idea. And formal dress to match the dignitaries— that wasn't who the University lads were. Best everybody who did notice them saw ordinary students, typical University dress; best the kids saw them as what they were, just friendly, enthusiastic, and young.

He did need to tell them—street clothes, please, just plain Mospheiran street clothes.

19

The yellow plane took one noisy pass over the house by way of announcing its arrival, and made a pass over its landing strip in the south pasture, a strip designated by one of the house staff with a small bag of flour.

Cajeiri was able to watch from the stairwell window. It was beyond frustrating not to be out there when Reijiri landed. But he was not a fool. Things were still unstable in the region, and he stayed by the window as he saw Reijiri come around again and line up on the mark.

Uncle's guards were out there. Reijiri's own were due in on the train in a few hours and the bus, with two new tires from its own storage, was going to pick them up. He had Antaro and Jegari back, and Rieni and all his unit, so if anything came of what was going on at Ajiden, or out of the Ajuri camped on the lawn, it was not going to reach them here. Still—

He had had a look out the front door this morning. The bus was a truly sad sight, by daylight. The right side windows and the windshield were a mess, hit multiple times, but not broken; while the body was going to have to have panels replaced, so he could fairly well guess where the guns had been relative to the bus.

And here he stood, watching a little plane coming down, under power, but riding the wind, too, light as a leaf. He had been too worried to think too much about Bren and the island, and the landing there, which was a little scarier, but now it flashed up like a vision. That great heavy machine, bearing *his* people down to the world to stay. He had spent so much worry on Uncle, and Mother, and his sister, and Nomari, he had just trusted the other end of nand' Bren's trip to nand' Bren—to be there when his associates landed, and to set up things so they would be happy, and safe. Of course they would get down safely. The shuttles had never failed. Of course nand' Bren would take care of them and have everything set up for them.

But now—seeing the plane land—he thought of that, and he wanted to be there.

He could be no help at all. And Father would never approve his going to Mospheira. That association had to stay as it was, and his associates had to learn to live there, which he could not help, either. But his chest tightened when all that flashed into his mind, and he knew—he knew how out of touch he was, and how unsettled everything was.

Nand' Bren had promised he would try to set up phone calls, so that he could talk to his associates—not too often; but now and again, to know how they were. They could certainly write letters.

And if it were not all working out over there, he was sure word would get back to the Guild that there was trouble, and that Rieni would hear about it at *his* level, even if Antaro could not. And surely Rieni, if he was all that he seemed to be, *would* advise him, no matter how things were going here in the midlands. There was nothing they could do, but he trusted Rieni would tell him.

The plane touched delicately down on the grass and rolled out of sight behind the stable, to that place where people would be waiting to meet it.

"You have not heard anything," he said quietly, still gazing out the window, "about nand' Bren, how he is doing? When my associates are landing?"

"We have heard nothing, nandi," Antaro said, and Rieni said, "We have heard that the paidhi-aiji is safe and well and making progress, but nothing about the landing. They likely will not announce it until the last moment, nandi-ma."

"Tell me, good or bad, the moment you know something."

"We know no reason to worry," Rieni said. "No hint of trouble has gone through the system. But we would not know specifics while we are in the field."

"You can ask that we track a situation," Haniri added.

"Do," he said. "Where you can."

"Yes," Rieni said.

What else can you do, he wondered, that my younger guard cannot?

No more, certainly, than my father lets me know.

He will know how nand' Bren is, and how things are.

"Anything involving my family or my associates. Anything that can touch them, nadiin. Uncle. Nomari. Lord Geigi. And Machigi."

"Machigi, nandi." Rieni sounded a little surprised.

"He is associated with my great-grandmother and with Nomari. I want to know."

"Yes," Rieni said, with peculiar emphasis. He meant it, Cajeiri thought. Rieni was not sorry at all about that order.

"You should also tell Antaro," he said. "They always need to know—all the situation."

"Yes," Rieni said again. "This is entirely acceptable."

He could not hear, at this remove, whether the plane's engine had stopped. He thought it would have.

"I was thinking," he said, "that Gene and Artur and Irene must be landing soon, and nand' Bren will see they are settled. When he gets back, one hopes we have his bus fixed."

"Right now," Rieni said, "it is useful. It will be useful in getting you and your mother and sister back to the train station, if nothing else. Your aishid would value that level of protection, all things considered."

"Mother is not talking about leaving, is she? I do not think she would, right now."

"It is our opinion she will stay to see Ajuri resolved."

"Uncle has phoned Father."

"Yes," Rieni said. "It is at that stage of things. And Guild teams have been searching Ajiden the last several hours. Even if they find a cache of records, they will not assume that is the *only* such. They will search until they have searched everywhere."

"What is this thing they have, that lets them see through walls?"

A pause. "There are some things we know that are not need-to-know, young aiji. You are better-served if the Guild retains *some* secrets."

"I am better-served if I know what my resources are!"

A second pause. "*We* are your resources, nandi. We hope to be adequate."

Frustrating. But the question had tested the boundaries, and found them.

Fortunately, Antaro's team *would* tell him, if *they* knew. So he would know things.

The plane had indeed landed. Lucasi and Veijico were out there, a matter of courtesy, since *he* had asked Reijiri to come. "Tell him," he had instructed Lucasi and Veijico, "that I would have come, but security will not let me."

"Yes," had been the economical answer, so he was sure that message would pass. And there would be a guard on that plane so long as it sat out there, Uncle had promised that.

They no longer had Great-aunt Geidaro to worry about. The Shadow Guild posed a much more serious threat. But the Shadow Guild itself had to be really worried now, with Guild investigators searching every nook of the understructure at Ajiden with, as he had learned from the seniors, that mysterious equipment that could find even hidden compartments. Nobody was going to be allowed down below until the Guild had finished, partly, the seniors had said, as a safety measure, to be sure there was nothing planted on the premises.

That was a scary thought. But the enemy had already tried to burn Ajiden, which the servants had prevented, so maybe they had been moving too fast to set up anything more thoughtful.

All that was going on, and Uncle had sent an advisement to Father. So, probably, had Mother. Probably Guild communications were flying all over the place, messages from Taiben and the officials at Diegi and Dur and places he had not thought of. Not to mention advisements from the Guild in the field.

Now he saw Reijiri and all the escort Uncle had sent—including three of Uncle's servants, who were bringing Reijiri's baggage—emerge from behind the corner of the stable. They angled toward the back door, not as elegant a reception, but certainly safer and more convenient than having to walk all the way around to the front where the tents were, housing individuals whose man'chi was still, as mani would say it, not quite baked yet.

It was time to run—well, to walk sedately, because his senior aishid was with him, and Antaro and Jegari were still not in the best form—up the servant stairs and down the hall to reach the grand stairs and the great hall before Reijiri did. Mother, he was sure, had already headed downstairs. Uncle had. Back in their suite, Eisi and Liedi had already had their breakfast brought up, Boji was back beside his window, fussing, though he had already had *his* breakfast, too, and he had sunlight and a blue sky outside.

They reached the head of the great stairs that led directly down to the great hall, and he was so tempted to slide them on his heels, but he walked quite properly, and just as he reached the landing, a noise on the central stairs of the foyer below advised him that Reijiri was coming up from the lower passage, having passed through the hall where Nomari's people were.

Cajeiri reached the main floor and immediately diverted himself to the central doors, where, indeed, Reijiri was, and Uncle's escort. Reijiri let an expression of delight touch his face. So did he.

"Aiji-meni," Reijiri called him as he reached the main floor.

"Nandi!" he said, in an exchange of bows. "Come to breakfast. Everybody is here, well, probably except my sister. She sleeps in the morning."

"The little one is here! I hope to see her!"

"You shall. Come! Come!" He waved Reijiri toward the dining area—staff having, he found, set up breakfast in the formal area, not the breakfast nook, where Uncle and Mother and Nomari stood waiting for them.

"We present our other guest," Uncle said after initial formalities, with a nod toward Nomari. "Nomari grandson of Nichono, cousin to the aiji-consort and her line, and soon to be a neighbor to us if Tabini-aiji approves."

"Honored, nandi," Reijiri said.

"Sit, everyone," Uncle said. "Let us have our breakfast in proper order."

"And a splendid one, nandi," Reijiri said. "Laboring at first light to assure myself that the fuel pump was sound—and it was and is—I kept myself going with the thought of midlands pickle and sweet jam."

"Well, if you have cargo space you shall take a case of each," Uncle said. "Calling you was the young gentleman's notion—he has utmost confidence in you; and well-placed, I may say. That is a splendid machine. I approve of small craft with clear purpose, more than these lumbering great sky-freighters. We should paint them in colors, for every capital they visit. Bring some distinction to them. One will never mistake that brilliant little machine of yours, Lord Dur."

"One is greatly flattered, Lord Atageini. And indeed, I do make a distinctive target."

"Were you hit?" Mother asked.

"Four times," Reijiri said, and the fact that he made breakfast conversation of it showed how lightly he took the matter. "One enterprising fellow *might* have nicked the fuel pump, except that after the little affair down by Najida, I took Lord

Geigi's recommendation—and gift—and put several quite resistant panels in place on the underside."

"I think we must all thank him," Mother said.

"Profoundly," Uncle said. "And how is your father, nandi?"

"Oh, well," Reijiri said. "I am remiss, nandi. He extends his sincere good wishes."

"You have called him, I hope, to assure him of your safety."

"I notified staff as soon as I landed at Diegi. I am quite sure he was not sleeping, but he would never confess it."

"Of course not," Uncle said.

It was a cordial breakfast—Reijiri and Uncle, and Mother, and himself besides Nomari. Everybody knew each other, everybody owed Reijiri and his father the old lord a very great deal, over past years. And Uncle's kitchens had spared no effort to put on a massive breakfast, the extent of which Reijiri, who was a thin, wiry sort, nor very tall, could not near absorb. There was tea, there were eggs, pickle, toast, berry jam, sweet pickle, and four sorts of salt fish, salt game, and some fresh, from the market, besides the breads and pastries. It cast Uncle in a very good light, and anything left over would go to Security, to staff, and back to stores.

At the end of it, when they were about to adjourn to a quiet seating in the conservatory, Nomari came to Uncle with a request to go below and out to the tents.

"It will give you a time with your guest," Nomari said, "and me a time to report below. I would like to bring both groups together, at least as many as wish to, and see what we can find out."

"Useful as that might be," Uncle said, also quietly, "it will be more useful to them if you stay here right now. You may find it much to their benefit."

Nomari paused, as anybody would, having been handed a puzzling promise. Cajeiri heard it and thought, Uncle expects something even before the sitting is done. A message from Father, maybe.

"Come," he said, when Uncle walked away, leaving Nomari

confused. "Uncle is up to something. One is not sure what he is up to, but he would not lie about it. Come sit by me. I shall introduce you specially to Lord Reijiri."

"Yes," Nomari said, like Guild, like the trades. And they settled together near one of the large potted plants, an orangelle that was trying to produce fruit, but it was still green.

Uncle spoke with staff, quietly, then said to all of them, "Lord Keimi is riding in to join us, with a small company. He has passed the gates."

They were coming in with Taibeni mecheiti, and the road came between the house and the small cluster of tents.

Small wonder Uncle would not want a crowd of people out there, with strange mecheiti arriving. Staff would be there, to be sure that the people in tents stayed out of the way. Grooms would be alert at the stables behind the house to be sure the herd stayed quiet. The wind direction mattered, and he had no idea, confined inside, what problem that might present.

More—Antaro and Jegari had every reason to believe their parents *might* come in. They had only touched the foyer last night—high-ranking Taibeni were not given to visiting strange manor houses, or *any* house but their own lodge in the heart of the forests. The lords of Taiben, in all of time, had never come visiting anyone in the association, and Lord Keimi was coming at least as far as the steps to speak to Uncle. That was something, in itself.

The shuttle is now under ground control, word came, hand-couriered from Shawn's office. *Station handed off control to Port Jackson, as of 10:48 local, landing at 11:30 tomorrow. They're entering low orbit and they'll be waiting out a little weather to our west. Weather tomorrow morning looks good and a morning landing is optimum—politically speaking. I told them just for God's sake be safe. The airport landing makes me nervous as hell, but I guess they've got all this down to routine by now.*

Well, *that* certainly changed the plans for the day. "Kate," Bren said in a brief phone call. "That wall color we argued over? How about gray?"

"Gray," was Kate's response. "Goes with everything." Deep and audible breath. "I think we can do that."

God knew what mountains Kate was going to have to move between now and tomorrow morning.

Red would have been just too damned obvious.

That ductwork revision had to be finished, that was all—unless the kids were going to be Shawn's guests in Francis House until it was, and that was just far too political. Crews might work all night, but it was going to be finished.

"The shuttle is confirmed for tomorrow shortly before noon. They will land at the airport. The spaceport runway is still under construction. The runway there would serve in an emergency, the freight handling apparatus is fully functional, but the public facilities are not, as one understands."

His aishid was all attention. It meant—going home, and novel as the experience had been, they were glad of that.

But it also meant what his aishid dreaded most: public appearance. It meant watching the kids arrive, and turning them over to Shawn's security, hoping that nothing would go wrong. It was not a situation the Guild was used to dealing with, but it was what they had to do.

"I intend to be as minor a presence in the event as I can manage," Bren said. "We shall be there as faces the youngsters and their parents know and trust. We shall meet them, assure ourselves they are well—then we shall introduce them to Shawn, and stand back and stand aside to let it be a Mospheiran affair. Their arrival at their new home—I do not think we should be at Heyden Court at all. They should not be seen as passing into *our* hands. The three young students will be there. The children will meet Kate-nandi. And Sandra-daja."

"Cake," Tano said. He had mentioned that cake more than once.

"I have no doubt there will be cake," Bren said, amused. "I suspect, however, that she cannot manage midlands pickle, which the children have come to enjoy. I suspect Narani might greatly please her with that recipe."

"Perhaps," Narani said gravely, "Sandra-daja will reciprocate with the secret of icing."

"One does not doubt," he said, making a mental note to ask that, among the diminishing list of things they had yet to do.

He hoped—hoped Irene was not sick, coming down. She had been, the first landing. And she was coming solo. Irene had escaped her mother. Renounced her mother, however tangled those feelings might be.

Irene had stood on her own, on the station. She'd gained the dowager's approval. But administratively, she'd had to have some parent, so administratively, and he hoped, practically, she'd been handed off to Gene's mother, a quiet, humble-mannered woman with a son who'd also grown up much too soon, trying to take care of a mother who was coming apart. Anna Parker survived something terrible, maybe more terrible than the others, maybe less; but once she'd escaped the horror of the refugee section of the station, she'd begun to change. She'd been far more at ease among the atevi than Artur's family had been. And when told she was to stand in as Irene's parent, she'd positively blossomed. Being given responsibility for Irene had seemed to work a change in Anna Parker, a spark of . . . self-confidence, perhaps. Self-respect, at least. Whatever it was, he had hopes for it. Irene seemed to touch a basic kindness in Anna Parker, a lot like Gene, and that—that might be what Irene most needed.

In point of fact, between the two possible options, Artur's father had seemed a little strict, and Anna Parker had seemed permissive enough to get along with Irene's independence, that was all. But maybe, just maybe, it would work out better than all right. He hoped so. He hoped everything for those kids, on whom so many hopes rested.

Not least among them Cajeiri's. The three kids were a friendship made in hellish circumstances. Cajeiri's wiring was as different from them as his aishid's was from his own—Cajeiri collected associates, collected them with a set of standards and a complete passion for their collective welfare, because—well, that was his nature. He was not only atevi, he had an aiji's drive to take power and run things his way.

And thanks to Ilisidi, a strong sense of responsibility came with it, a need to figure out what was right and what worked. His emotional makeup and the kids' was not key and lock, but it was a good set of interlocked branches, young trees grown together. Cajeiri would understand atevi, the others would understand Mospheirans and Reunioners, and the world was going to change, with those kids well-grown and in charge someday.

He'd cast one leaf onto the waters when he'd set one Guy Cullen into a relationship with the kyo.

He'd cast another when he'd supported Cajeiri in his insistence on maintaining an association with humans, a situation that likewise had yet to prove itself.

He'd been a risk-taker in years past. With nothing to lose, he'd cast himself down mountain slopes and let himself fly in a set of decisions that had no delay and no second try. He'd found skiing cleared his head for his regular problems. It had kept him from expressing his opinions in the Linguistics Department, it had kept him and Toby in touch, no matter his mother's favoritism, it had prepared him to deal with Tabini, God help him.

There were just some times he had stopped and looked back and thought—God, was I there? Did I just go down that hill? I'm an absolute fool.

Here he was in charge of three children's lives and safety, working them into the Mospheiran *government*, making them virtually Shawn's kids, dragging every resource he could command into the setup. He was bending time and lives, shaping how the Reunioners were going to fit in, how the whole sequence of events that had separated the colony into two antagonistic packets, one bound to land, one headed off with the ship—was finally going to resolve itself.

Or not.

He had the sudden view from the snowy mountaintop, the dizzying perspective of the downhill skier, the whole lower course beginning to be obscured with fog. Mist covered everything. He had been in that situation. It still recurred in dreams.

No choice, no way down from here but to launch and go. It was a lifetime too late for anything else.

Information arrived in the conservatory in bits and pieces, through Guild communications, mostly, though there was a phone call that Uncle took personally, and listened, and nodded as if the person on the other end could see him. "Uncle," Cajeiri wanted to say, "you have to say something." But whatever it was seemed to satisfy Uncle . . . one thought it might involve Lord Keimi coming in, maybe permissions at the gates. "Not at the train station?" Uncle asked then, and frustratingly, Cajeiri could not hear the answer, but Reijiri's guard was due to arrive by train this morning, so surely that was what it was. "We can send him."

That was entirely puzzling.

But then Uncle gave the phone back to Heisi-nadi.

"Well," Uncle said, "I had hoped to have you here, Nomari-nandi, to meet Lord Keimi, and various notables of Atageini, among other matters of the day, but it seems the Guild has urgent need of you in Ajiden. They are, it turns out, at the gates."

"At the gates," Nomari echoed, looking entirely dismayed. But he said nothing except, "Thank you, nandi."

"Is this the aishid he should have?" Mother asked, frowning. "Or is this the Guild's investigation? They have had no time to have come from Shejidan!"

"We are not, frankly, certain," Uncle said, "but I assure you we shall have it clear fairly shortly."

"Aiji-meni," Rieni said very quietly, at Cajeiri's elbow, "you might order us to ask Headquarters before this mission comes that far onto the grounds."

"Do!" Cajeiri said, and Rieni walked off across the conservatory, his back turned, and doubtless with communications engaged that Guild had not used in days.

"We should have asked," Mother said.

"We certainly have force enough here," Uncle said, and in a moment Rieni, his back still turned, made a Guild-sign with his free hand.

"Authorized," Haniri said, no faster than Cajeiri recognized it for himself. Rieni stayed in the exchange for a moment, then walked back to them and gave a little nod.

"The Guild-senior of the senior unit," Rieni said, "is Adiano. We know her. We are confident in the information. Her instruction comes from Headquarters, who report, unofficially, that the documents are filed and you are, though unofficially, Komaji-nandi's successor. You have an official escort, an assigned aishid."

"Well," Uncle said, "that is welcome news. You will of course go. And you will take your followers. If the Guild is seeking information, they may have some to give."

"I am overwhelmed," Nomari said. "I shall have no fear for myself, nandiin. But I hoped that I would be taking these people to a safe place."

"Guild will surely see to it," Uncle said, "if your people follow instructions. And one does suggest you state that firmly to them."

The phone was ringing. A servant picked it up, hastily brought it to Heisi, who said, "Nandi, the call is for our guest."

"Ha," Mother said, and they all watched as Nomari took that call.

"Yes," he said, and: "Yes, aiji-ma. Absolutely. One is so grateful, aiji-ma."

Then he looked uncertain, and looked at them, still holding the phone.

"Well," Mother asked. "Are you confirmed?"

"I am," Nomari said, seeming a little dazed. "He *said* I was. Is that it?"

"It certainly is," Uncle said, amused. "You are indeed, baji-naji, equal to myself—to Lord Keimi—to Lord Machigi."

"Not—for a time, nandi. I have years to learn a tenth of what you know."

"Well, well, Lord of Ajuri. Baji-naji, that is what you are, neighbor. And one assumes you will gather up all your people and take advantage of transportation. If you need advice, ask your aishid. Call me. I shall be very willing to advise you."

"What shall I do now? I need to advise my people. I need to change clothes."

"One hopes you will meet your aishid," Uncle said, "and certainly you will accept our gift of wardrobe, such as it is. You will offend us if not. My staff will pack for you. Heisi, see to it, both here and all the personal belongings that may be in the tents. All our Ajuri guests will go, as many trips of the bus as may be necessary. Eight seats for the aishid on the first trip."

"Nandi," Heisi said.

"See?" Uncle said. "A simple thing. You will need a major domo *you* can rely on. You must work that out. Guild will assist you. Very senior Guild. And of course, your neighbors. One suggests you attempt to rehabilitate staff such as you can, but do not trust too much. I would, were I asked, which I am not, first look to those staff who put out the fire, and perhaps look to those who have come forward to speak to the Guild. Were I in your place."

"Nandi, I—shall take your advice. Every scrap of it."

"The young aiji's aishid advises you your Guild-senior is known to them, and you may trust them. You may learn how extraordinary a recommendation that is. I would say the Guild is determined to install a presence in Ajiden that the Shadow Guild will neither subvert not surpass. Trust them."

There was the sound of motors, more than one, Cajeiri thought. Onami had retreated somewhat from the area and was speaking to someone not present.

It was happening. Heisi had gone off to direct staff. And news would be reaching Nomari's followers very soon.

"Nand' Reijiri," Uncle was saying, "may I beg your forgiveness—that we shall not be able to provide the bus until afternoon."

Something had arrived. One had no doubt of it when all four of his aishid suddenly stopped, listened to empty air, and Banichi and Algini both went immediately back to the rear of the apartment.

"There is a message," Jago said. She and Tano were still seated, waiting, as he was. "From Tabini-aiji," she added after a moment.

"Good news," Tano said then.

Good news was the sort they rarely got. Bren found his shoulders braced even against that, because it even more rarely meant good without a slight complication. He really, truly wanted not to have that call which meant charter a plane, go to the airport, fly straight to Shejidan.

Banichi and Algini came out of the back rooms with the expressions that might attend *fairly* good news.

"There is a new lord of Ajuri," Banichi said. "His name is Nomari, grandson of Nichono, approved by the aiji-consort, the young gentleman, and Lord Tatiseigi."

Lord Tatiseigi. "So the feud is ended?"

"Apparently. He is assembling a party at Tirnamardi and will take possession in person."

The Atageini-Ajuri feud had been part of the scenery not quite as long as the Taibeni feud with everybody, but it seemed, if there were no *but*—the geography of the midlands had just shifted.

"Dur is present, offering felicitations," Algini said, "and Geidaro-daja is confirmed dead, confirmed to be Shadow Guild action—none of them caught yet, but names are known. Ajiden suffered only minor damage. Guild units are now in Ajiden, and will remain in Ajiden looking for information, such as they can get, on Shishogi, on any other subject of interest. The new lord will be protected in Ajiden, and Headquarters has given him a very skilled senior aishid, one whose focus has been, for the last while, unraveling Shishogi's mischief and tracing Ajuri's connections to Kadagidi. They are investigators, and they may become permanent with this new lord, granted he can gain their man'chi. Certainly they are experts in the dealings of the Padi Valley Association, all of it, and there could be no one more qualified. This new lord has an asset that can keep him alive, if he will listen to them. There is that matter."

That was good news. That was unqualified good news.

"The aiji also wished to forewarn you, Bren-ji," Banichi said, "that the aiji-dowager is in residence at Najida. And that Machigi is her guest there."

Word had spread. And noise had begun, in the lower hall, a buzz of voices so urgent that Nomari begged leave to go down.

"When you have your aishid," Uncle said. "Wait. Take my advice and wait."

Nomari waited, and fretted.

But it was not that long before heavy engines rumbled up before the front doors, more than one motor, to be sure, and Rusani reported two trucks had arrived.

It took only a moment more before the lower doors opened and two units of Guild came up the two short flights to the hall.

They were not junior, that was clear by the scattered gray in the hair of one unit; and the other unit were no youngsters, either, Cajeiri was sure of that. They presented themselves respectfully to Lord Tatiseigi, and to him and Mother, to Reijiri, and then—then to Nomari.

"Nandi," the foremost said, a woman with a particularly fierce look. "We are here by assignment. I am Adiano. My partner Sadito, our teammates Kurali and Senami."

"We are assigned to you," Adiano said, "on what may become a life assignment, the center of which is keeping you safe, nandi, as your aishid, by your will and ours. We are directed by the aiji and the Guild Council to take you to Ajiden and see to your safety. Beyond that, we are at *your* orders."

"I am ready," Nomari said in a voice not quite steady. Nomari cleared his throat. "I hope you will extend that protection to the people who have supported me in coming here."

"If they stay close to you, nandi, we shall give it a high priority. We have two trucks. We are advised that we may have the use of the bus sitting at the front steps. That would let us accomplish this in one trip."

"You are most certainly welcome to use it," Lord Tatiseigi said, "provided its driver goes with it and returns forthwith."

"Nandi. Thank you. Let us set this operation in motion. How many shall we transport, and with what baggage?"

It was, shortly, as if a storm had blown through the front doors. "Will you be comfortable here, nandi," Adiano asked, "while we arrange transport?"

"Yes," Nomari said quietly, seeming a little overwhelmed. "We have two groups, nadiin, those in the house who gathered here with me, and those outside, who arrived from Ajiden last night—who have pledged man'chi. They are under my protection. But with caution, nadiin. With some caution."

"My aishid will assist," Uncle said dryly. "And there are a few uniformed Guild we shall send with you, who may have had a reconsideration of man'chi, wherever it may have resided."

"Nandi," Adiano said, and gave, Cajeiri thought, a slight nod toward him—but not him: toward Rieni and his unit, just behind him. "We shall deal with the problem. Your leave, nandiin."

She turned toward the stairs.

"Nandi," Rieni said, "give us leave to assist them."

"Go," Cajeiri said. "Thank you."

"Well, well," Uncle said, "a quiet seating and a cup of tea will do, before our parting."

"Nandi," Nomari said. "I shall never forget."

"Our houses have sat beside each other for a thousand years. During most of that we have been allies. Be it so again, nandi." There was a loud crash from belowstairs. "I am not going to ask what that was," Uncle said. "Nomari-nandi, as you leave our gates, you will pass through the Taibeni camp. Lord Keimi is, one understands, in residence. To set a tone, and for the good of peace in the region, consider pausing the bus there, debarking for a moment and introducing yourself to Lord Keimi. He is a very fine gentleman, uncle to these brave young people who guard my great-nephew, and you would greatly oblige me if you did that."

"I should be very happy to do it," Nomari said. "And thank you, nandi."

"Well, well," Uncle said, as noise and cheering broke out below. "Do restrain your people from all rushing out. The Taibeni mecheiti are a lively lot—one assumes they have not been left with war-caps, but still, recently excited, never penned, and one would wish no difficulty. Stay by the bus, and you will certainly be safe."

There began to be a crowd in the foyer, and out on the steps, all the people who had been sheltered in the lower hall going out into the sunlight and out to the trucks and the bus; and one assumed Guild was talking to Guild about what to do with the rest, some of whom would be reliable, some of whom had likely been persuaded of things that were not true, and some of whom had just been ordered to make mischief. But one could rest assured names were being taken and questions were being asked, and answers would be checked. Nomari might intercede for Guild caught in the situation, but they would still go to Head-quarters to be asked questions, Cajeiri was sure of that.

The racket died away, fading to a commotion out on the steps, as various people determined who would sit in fair comfort on the bus—there were some older folk in the original lot—and who would sit on storage boxes on the trucks—assuming they were market trucks, and typical. Likely one unit would divide themselves between the two trucks and assure that no discussion flew out of bounds on the way to Ajiden.

Cajeiri thought then—he truly hoped nothing happened to Nomari. He hoped they would see each other from time to time. And Nomari was so scared—trying not to show it, but he had good reason. Reijiri talked to him, made him laugh a little, and that was a good thing, because Reijiri was closer to Ajiden than to Tirnamardi, and it would be a good thing if Dur and Ajuri could get along, and visit one another for festivities. It would be an even better time if Atageini could join in, and someday maybe even Kadagidi, or whatever came next for that district. He liked to think that could happen.

He would like to make that happen.

And came the moment when Nomari's bodyguard came to bring *him* out to the bus, security would not let them go down. So they said their goodbyes and thank yous in the conservatory, and then Nomari's bodyguard escorted him away down the stairs, nicely dressed, compared to how he had arrived, a world of changes. He had Ajuri's ribbon to tie his queue, Mother's gift. And he went out the lower doors to a great cheer from his people, on the trucks and the bus.

It was a grand moment. A year ago even, he would have found a way to run down there and watch, but as it was—and sitting beside Mother and Uncle, he was just quietly happy, imagining how it was, imagining as the trucks fired up their engines and the bus did, and they all moved out.

"So long a road," Uncle said then, but it was not the road to

Ajuri he was talking about, Cajeiri was sure. "Peace," Uncle said. "Finally."

It was so quiet in the house without the Ajuri—one had hardly even heard the servants going about their business at all, but now they were busy down there, restoring order, putting supplies back in their right places, all those details, and preparing. Uncle asked nand' Reijiri to stay over a day for what Uncle called an extravagant festivity tomorrow—

It was the first Cajeiri had heard of it.

"I would be honored," was Reijiri's word. They had word that Reijiri's aishid *would* arrive shortly past noon, having been delayed last night by a Guild halt on all the region's rail transport, so he would have the comforts of his baggage and a more considered packing for travel than he had done when he had fueled the yellow plane and leapt into the air. "Is there an occasion?"

"There is," Uncle said, "but I have some formalities to manage. You will join us tonight for dinner, nandi, surely."

"With pleasure."

"And whether—" Uncle began to say, but just then staff announced that Lord Keimi had passed the gates and was riding in.

"And the lawn a muddy mess," Uncle sighed, "with the tents half down. What an appearance we shall make. Nephew. Be patient. You know Lord Keimi, surely."

"I have met him, Uncle. I was younger then. But he let Antaro and Jegari go with me."

"To our great good fortune. He is an excellent neighbor. I wish I had appreciated earlier what a wise man he is. Heisi."

"Nandi."

"Advise the stables riders are coming in. One trusts they will have someone with them to stay with their mecheiti."

"Uncle." The question of the festivity was buried in the matter. "What are we celebrating?"

"Why, the end of the feud with Ajuri. The resolution of a

matter that has had the midlands in chaos for three decades."
Uncle paused then, looking soberly at him. "The resolution of
a very dangerous state of affairs for Atageini clan, a very dangerous situation for us, for, indeed, all the aishidi'tat, and I beg you,
Nephew, very solemnly I ask you be favorable."

Grownups did not beg things of children. Especially Uncle
did not. It was scary, how anxious he suddenly seemed.

"What should I give you, Uncle? What can I do?"

"Support your sister as heir of Atageini. Will you agree to
that?"

He caught a breath. "What does my mother say?"

"She is willing," Uncle said.

"Then I am willing," he said, feeling his heart beating very
fast. "I think my sister will be smart, Uncle. Mother and Father
both are, and I am. So I think she will be a very good heir for
Atageini. And I will take care of her."

"You are a good lad, you truly are." Uncle had never seemed
so wrought, so anxious, or so hopeful. "I could not ask for better. My sister could not have asked a better granddaughter or a
better grandson."

"So there will be a festivity for her?"

"For everything. For an end to the feud. For a child to inherit
the lordship. For a new beginning in Ajuri, and an end to their
long troubles. For a day when the lord of Taiben visits our
grounds, at very least, in peace and alliance, and for Dur to be
with us, and, tomorrow, the mayors of Diegi and Heitisi and
Hegian, and Esien and Naien, with their families. This is a celebration decades delayed. And I would have Lord Nomari here,
except he has so much to do—I shall invite him, I certainly
shall invite him, but with the understanding there will be no
offense at all, should he stay where I am sure the Guild will
want him to stay tomorrow. I shall invite him to the Bujavid,
where your father may wish to invite him as well, and we shall
not slight him in courtesies, not in the least. I only wish your
great-grandmother were here . . . but this is your mother's

affair, indeed, indeed *her* moment, which she deserves to have all to herself—herself and her daughter, here, in Atageini, in Tirnamardi, as they always should have been. I know I cannot claim little Seimiro from your father, nor would it be right, but I do hope to have her on occasion, to teach her to ride . . ."

"And show her the great beast in the basement!"

"That, indeed."

"By lamplight."

"Maybe we shall, you and I. We can look forward to that."

He had mourned the fact their ages were so uselessly, frustratingly separate; but there was still the chance he *could* share things with her, things she had to see. She was not just for protecting and watching. She was going to be walking next year. She was going to talk. He could teach her kyo and Mosphei'. He could teach her the rhymes mani had taught him. When she started exploring things, he could show her all the good spots to hide—and *he* would know where to look when she used them. He would teach her to swim. And fish. And ride. "She will have her own mecheita, surely, Uncle."

"That she will."

His life was so pent about and watched and guarded that at the start of this trip he had felt he could hardly breathe. And then—everything started going right.

Baji-naji. Fortune and Chance. Order and chaos. Something had to go wrong. He had never seen so many things go right at once. The universe had the china all stacked up, fragile and tall, and there could not be this many good things.

His mind flashed, he could not help it, to the shuttle. The landing. Nand' Bren. And for a moment he felt cold fear.

No. One more good thing had to happen. That had to go right. It had to.

Fool, mani would say. She had said, on fortune and chance, Do not regard the 'counters. They bend the numbers any way they need to bend them.

And she had said, he well remembered it: Add your own

numbers and *make* them fortunate. That is at least as honest. And a great deal more comforting . . .

"Nephew?" Uncle asked. "Is there some concern?"

He looked up at Uncle, and superstition kept him from saying what it really was. He was afraid to say it; and it was stupid, and he hated it. But he could not for the moment shake the feeling. He was *not* mani. He had no power over things that mattered most to him. He depended on people. And he had *not* thought about the shuttle while everything was going on here, but now it kept popping back into his mind, a worry he could not shake off.

"No," he answered Uncle, an outright lie, but he felt better saying it. "Just—so many things here have gone right."

Uncle laughed a little. "I know the feeling," Uncle said. "But we have settled a few things. We still have Kadagidi to go."

"That is true." He was very willing to change the subject. "Do you have any idea for *that* lordship, Uncle?"

"We do not even know, yet, whether your father will not refuse to reinstate the clan."

"But there are Kadagidi townships all up and down the river. They have to have somebody."

"They may *have* somebody, but at the local level. Your father may appoint a hitherto landless clan to the honor and the manor house."

"He could give it to you."

"Gods, no. One of the sub-clans is likeliest. Ancheni, maybe, but whoever your father appoints will have an aishid very like the one assigned to Nomari . . . well-versed in the history and the misdeeds of Kadagidi, which in their case go deep into the age of iron. There has *never* been a reliable lord in charge. We have been their allies more than once, but we have not trusted them. Geidaro, Meisi—all that lot came of Kadagidi marriages. And there is, yes, a trace of Kadagidi blood in Atageini: we try zealously to forget it."

"And Atageini blood in Kadagidi?"

"More of it spilled on the floor than otherwise, but yes. Ancheni, twenty-two generations back, comes of an Atageini contract. I do not say that makes him virtuous. The Atageini in question was a scoundrel. Even we say it. So, well, maybe twenty-two generations have thinned the villainy sufficiently. Or perhaps your father will decide to elevate a sub-clan and let the name stand. I cannot guess. If he asks my opinion I shall give it, but I shall not press with it."

He could never leave a question lying. He could not bear it. "But what *do* you think, Uncle?"

"I would say Ancheni. We could build on a history, at least the fancy of a structure, that might work, given the right atmosphere. But you should form your own opinion, young gentleman. You should study all the issues, all the eligible and likely, and the unlikely, and form a theory, granted that I shall remain peaceful and so will Ajuri."

It worked out to a lesson to do. So many important things did. But it was also real. And the people were.

"Nandiin." The head of Uncle's aishid moved in quietly. "The Taibeni are arriving at the front steps. They express their willingness to come in. They know you are injured. They say they have no wish to risk your health."

Uncle drew a deep breath. "I would come down to them, but if they have offered, I shall not reject their courtesy. Say that I am able, and would, if they wish, but will gladly make them welcome here, where there are chairs."

"I shall relay that," Rusani said, and went off quietly.

In no long time the doors below and the outer doors both opened to a small group of Taibeni in riding clothes, who climbed up to the great hall—Lord Keimi, and Antaro and Jegari's parents, and four Cajeiri did not know, but took them for Lord Keimi's guard—carrying rifles and sidearms both, which nobody did, but Guild. And Taibeni.

Uncle met them standing, and Lord Keimi looked quite

unabashedly about at the tall pillars and the stairs and the gilt and marble, then gave a little bow. And Uncle did.

"Nand' Atageini." Keimi-nandi offered a gesture toward Deiso and Janiri. "My brother Janiri. My sister-by-marriage Deiso. Such a forest of stone you have here, Lord Atageini. Beautiful. I have rarely entered a hall but our own, but I heard such a story I had to see the man who took that ride. Truly. We had heard you and Malguri rode in the chases, but I wish I had been here to see the best of all."

"One is greatly flattered, nandi. I am this morning an old man who is feeling the bruises. I would have managed the stairs to honor your custom, but I would have been very slow about it."

"By no means should you. I wish someday to see more of your herd—in very fact I had been intending to approach you, in some quieter year, about a consideration of bloodlines."

"This line is East mixed with western plains. One understands the ancient southern line survives in Taiben, but I have never had one cross my path."

"They are smaller, with the faint leg striping—Nand' Tatiseigi, may I be so forward as to ask you to take a chair in your own hall?"

"Indeed you may." Uncle was feeling the strain. It was in his voice and in the grayness of his knuckles on the cane. "Tea, Hei-ji, if you please. I should be very happy if our visitors would sit a while." Uncle moved slowly, leaning on the cane, and servants moved quickly to arrange chairs before they arrived in the conservatory.

There was tea, there was quiet conversation which naturally turned toward mecheiti, and bloodlines. Cajeiri sat and listened, and thought it ironic that Antaro and Jegari, who ordinarily would sit, because they were limping about today, too, were standing by him, and not by their parents, but they had been very stiff and formal—because of Lord Keimi, perhaps; but perhaps, he thought, it was more that they wanted to be seen in their uniforms, on duty, proper and proud, too. He knew how the story about Uncle had gotten to Lord Keimi: through them, on the bus, on that ride home. And now Lord Keimi, who had always been remote and too stand-offish to attend the legislature in its sessions—was talking to Uncle as if they had not been technically at war during all their lives.

It was good. It was another perfect thing falling into place.

There was too much perfection.

His associates were landing. He was not sure when, but they were on their way. And whenever he thought about it, he worried. Today, when he thought about it, after so much that had gone right, he found the air short of oxygen, and his thoughts kept wandering to the gray concrete of the spaceport, and the fences, and now and again a half-remembered flash of the airport at Port Jackson, which had been so scary and brief a time he could not even call up the detail.

They have to be safe, he said to himself. Everything has to work. And they have to be safe.

20

Morning, and formal dress, a different coat than Bren had worn for the Committee on Linguistics . . . should the news services somehow notice: blue and green brocade, the paidhi's white ribbon of office, not the black of the Lord of the Heavens, not for this meeting.

Narani and Jeladi turned them out fit for a court appearance, black leather for his aishid, and full kit, which meant communications *and* weapons possibly in excess of what the Mospheiran government liked displayed, but he didn't argue the point with his aishid, not in the least.

A multitude of vans and a bus were waiting below—they and Shawn were getting underway at the same time.

"Well, safe landing, let us hope," Shawn said, with his own bodyguard standing by, and a number of cameras going—they shook hands, for the cameras. "See you at the stands, with the kids and their parents. Your drivers will know. Everything's arranged. We'll do a little presentation, a few words, and the same van and escort will take the people right over to Heyden Court, where Kate's waiting for them. And Ms. Johnson and family. The students, the tutors you arranged—they're here, already aboard. Their van will go with yours."

"How do they look?" Delicate question. One hated to have to ask.

"College students' best, not high fashion, but dress coats."

He nodded, gratified to know that, for the cameras, there

would not be anything to put the boys' faces into the evening news—no attractive images of atevi strangeness, nothing to raise issues.

"Good lads," he said. "They'll do. I want them to meet the kids and their parents, stay with them, in the background, all the way. Somebody who'll go with them to Heyden Court."

"You won't?"

"I don't intend to. The sooner normalcy sets in for them, the better. They've got a lot of newness to cope with and I'm not their new ordinary environment. They've been watching television, and they have some notion, but this is all just going to be a shock. Looking out a window is going to be a shock."

"Flowers are all right, I hope."

"They'll be pleased. Don't know if the parents have ever seen them except in pictures, but the kids have. It'll all be fine. The kids have been through the young gentleman's investiture and more than one full-blown security alert, so their idea of normalcy is fairly elastic."

"Just hope we can give them boredom," Shawn said.

"Sir." Shawn's bodyguard signaled him.

"They want us aboard," Bren said. "Are you going to be in your office this afternoon? I've called Toby in. My domestic staff will be shifting baggage—with the help of your security, and an unmarked truck. We'll be moving out soon as we get back. Thought I might drop by before I go."

"Do," Shawn said. "See you in a bit."

They moved off to their separate vans, with Mospheiran security driver and escort—a little low in the overhead for Banichi, who took the seat beside Bren—the smallest of the company.

And they were off, out onto the drive in the morning sun, trailing Shawn's van and two more, then diverging on Harbor Avenue, a right turn for them, left for Shawn.

Staff had taken up all the tents, spread them out to dry in the eastern pasture, somewhat beyond nand' Reijiri's plane, and gardeners worked to even the ground, spreading sand and earth and tamping it down—that from yesterday through part of the night and before full daylight.

The kitchen had likewise been busy all night, turning out both regular meals and confections, many, many confections, which Cajeiri had sampled. Even the seniors had had spiced tarts and slices of fruit roll, so that supper had been just a little spoiled.

Breakfast, however, was scant and quick, and it was back upstairs to dress for the event, before people began to arrive.

Mother and Beha-nadi stayed upstairs—keeping Seimei in a good mood, was his guess, that and the fact that Mother was in full court dress; Uncle was likewise in his chambers, preparing.

Cajeiri personally gave Boji a whole dish of eggs, with the hope that Boji, stuffed, would do what he usually did in such a state and simply curl up at the end of his favorite perch, wrap himself into a dark, furry ball, and sleep through all the commotion that was due to arrive.

The shuttle was on its way down. "Please tell me," he asked of all his bodyguard, "the moment you have any news, the moment it lands. I want to know. Please find out."

"They have not yet given out the precise time," Rieni said, "and may not until very close to the time. We are advised that there is a gathering of officials. We expect that nand' Bren will be among them."

"He will be meeting the shuttle," Cajeiri said. "I am certain he will go as close to where they will land as he can."

"We will find out as much as we can gather," Rieni said. "His aishid is not in direct contact with Headquarters, but they have relayed their intent to be there. They have also relayed a request for his brother-of-the-same-mother to bring his boat within reach of the harbor, which is the paidhi-aiji's intended means of departure."

That was somewhat good news, at least that everything was going as it ought.

"Lord Tatiseigi is going downstairs," Antaro said. "There are trucks at the gate."

The people from Diegi and Heitisi and all were due to arrive; and Lord Keimi had said he would come in, too, and that they would have riders move all their mecheiti back off the grounds and bring them in again when he left, precautions against any sort of infelicity, and, with the wind coming from the west this morning, it was a doubly good idea.

Nomari had called Uncle, personally, to say that *he* was not able to come, that his new aishid wanted him to stay close and safe within Ajiden until they could be absolutely certain of his safety. Nomari had called Mother, too, and asked Mother to convey his regrets, but there was no question. Nomari needed to be where he was, and he needed to avoid risks at least until his aishid could feel they were informed and in charge of the situation.

That order, Mother said, when Cajeiri visited her suite to hear what Nomari had said, had probably come from Guild Headquarters.

But—Mother said. But they *were* going to invite nand' Nomari to Shejidan when they all went home.

"We shall send the bus over to pick up Nomari and his aishid, if they agree, and then come back to Tirnamardi for all of us, including Uncle. That will be tomorrow."

"Tomorrow!" He had rather hoped, if things settled, that he might have a chance to ride. It was a small hope, but it was a hope.

"The bus will get us all safely to the train station, and the Red Train will take us all the way to the Bujavid, with no security exposure."

"Will Nomari's guard let him come?"

"He needs to meet your father. So he will get to offer his congratulations tomorrow, and maybe we will save him some of the sweets. Certainly a glass of wine."

But—Cajeiri thought. But—

"Nand' Bren will be coming back," he had said. "And we will have his bus."

"We *need* his bus," Mother said. "If he comes by sea, that will take a day. And I do not doubt but that nand' Bren will wish to spend a few days at Najida when he arrives. Your great-grandmother is there, as well, with her guard."

So is Machigi and his guard, he thought. It was *not* that safe.

"So we shall move fairly quickly," Mother said. "All of us. And the bus may not reach Najida in good repair, but it *will* be there for him, and *then* we shall patch the bullet holes."

"It is not a very good welcome," he said, a little upset at the notion. The bus looked a mess.

"Well, but it will be there for him," she said. Which he knew was true. Things were still chancy in the district. The Guild was still searching the basement at Ajiden, and some people might be very upset at what they would find.

"I do think we should make it up to him," he said.

"One does not in the least know how," Mother said. "Bren-nandi would never begrudge it to you, son of mine, nor ever to your father."

"Or you, Mother. He would not in the least. I know that. Nor to Uncle. He never would."

"He is a good person," Mother said. "And while I have blamed him in the past, I have become well aware that the peace we have in the house—we owe in some measure to him. He is a moderating influence, I will not say where, but he has stepped into some situations without partiality, where others certainly had it. I thought of that, on the train coming here, aware that, ordinarily, he would very likely have been involved, if only in keeping your great-grandmother at bay. I will say—*she* has shown a remarkable restraint, under circumstances I think she appreciated far better than I would have thought. Just tuck that into your pocket, son of mine, for some future time when we prove confusing. Or confused. Go back downstairs. Keep Uncle out of the kitchen, and make him sit down. I shall be down directly. I only do not want your sister in a bad mood. We shall let her have a good nap before the guests arrive, and then do things fairly expeditiously. Go. Be off with you. Take care with the door and do not wake your sister."

The shuttle's ground crew and security was set up toward the end of the main runway, which was longer than any other, and fairly well out toward the harborside, at least so that one could see the water from there. The several vans drew up together, and Banichi and Tano got out first, signaled all was well. Bren followed, down the single step, and Jago and Algini exited behind him. From the second van, the six-man Heyden Court security team emerged in gray business suits, not quite identical, but it took consideration to say so—suits, earbuds, and, one was sure, small arms under the coats. That was Jim A, Jim D, Ali, Maurice, Cohen, and Paul: he knew them all.

The third van gave up the three University lads, Karl, Evan, and Lyle, in their best, plain but neat, collars buttoned, all combed and with the queues hidden. They did hesitate at meeting him, but lest they be confused in protocol, Bren extended a hand in welcome, and introduced the young men to the security team, all under the open sky, and next to the massive length of concrete that was the runway. Granted, they had provided pictures, provided IDs, but today was the day it mattered. Today was the day it all became real.

"Excited?" he asked the students.

"God, I can't breathe," Karl said. "I don't think any of us slept."

"Are we going where the President is, sir?" Evan asked. "You want us to stay with them up there?"

"Every step of the way. Remember the one rule: don't get between the kids and their security and don't let them get separated from each other or their parents. There'll be new faces at every hand. We'll be with you through the business with the reviewing stand. But not to put a conspicuous atevi face on the operation, we'll stay well to the background. It's the President's operation. Then yours. You'll be with them all the way to Heyden Court. And we won't. We'll be on our way to the harbor, where I expect we'll find transport. I trust you've got your luggage."

"We took it up this morning, sir," Evan said. "We're moved in, well, at least, where we'll be. University is *not* happy with us. We have a summons to appear before the Committee."

"Ignore it. You're employees of the State Department. Salaried employees. If you need diplomas, we'll arrange it from Sagiadi University, on the mainland. And let them spin in the wind."

"Mr. Cameron. Sir." They had pulled up near a cluster of service vehicles, at a signaled spot, and two in the green jumpsuits of the Mospheiran space program had walked over to them, at an angle not crossing his aishid's presence. "Sir, they're over the western coast right now."

"Thank you," he said, and turned to look up the length of the runway. The reviewing stand, festooned in bunting, was up there, festooned in bunting, packed with news people and dignitaries, about at the first touch-down point.

"You've flown this approach before," the man said.

"I've been a nervous passenger, sir, but yes, thank you."

"That spot of sky, right there." The man from Mospheiran Space pointed to an area to the west, blue sky to the south of the city. "You know to stay clear, sir."

There would be the initial cooldown, various trucks moving in to hook up, and finally the personnel mover. "I do know. Thank you, sir."

He'd translated the manuals out of the Archive, watched the procedures develop, flown the route. He knew. And he was still anxious. The airport landing wasn't optimum, but it was what the Mospheirans had—which was why *most* of the landings were at the atevi spaceport.

But Mospheiran pride was deeply invested in this one. The

spaceport, they said, should be operational by spring. And there would be a second shuttle flying.

A good thing, for various reasons. A very good thing.

"There," he said, catching a pale dot in the sky. He pointed, and the young people beside him looked. His aishid—and to their credit, the other security team—was not distracted, not even by that. He watched, and what had been barely discernible became definite, a larger and larger dot, until it was clearly the shuttle, on course and coming fast.

It seemed forever. But it was coming way faster than any plane, large, nose high, and then on level, tires smoking, chute deploying to slow it down, all wheels down, now.

It grew larger in their sight, and slowed, and slowed. Is it going to have enough room? Bren wondered, holding his breath. There was scarily little runway left as it trundled to a stop, and sat there, the air around it rippling with heat, the smell of heating in the breeze that reached them.

"God," Lyle said shakily, and Evan and Karl just clung to each other's shoulders and breathed.

The cooldown had its procedures. Inside, crew would be shutting down systems, passengers would be gathering up whatever they had put in lockers, feeling Earth's gravity and experiencing the changes. And maybe thinking about Reunion, and Alpha, and asking themselves was being first down—such a great idea.

Trucks moved in. Finally came the personnel mover, which scissored up and extended a platform. Crew opened the hatch, and from this angle it was a little hard to see detail, but they were here, they were finally out and safely on Earth, as the module scissored down to ground level.

"They'll be a bit wobbly," he said. "Might suffer a bit of headache." He so hoped Irene hadn't been sick this trip. He hoped nobody had.

Doors opened on the personnel mover, and there they were, one of the shuttle crew in fatigues, then three adults, three children, all dressed Mospheiran-style. He walked toward them, and the youngsters all waved and grinned—Artur, red-headed as his father, with his father and mother behind him; Gene's mother, and Gene, dark-haired, but not so dark as Irene, who had grown a little more curl than her impromptu disguise had left her, a black and close-curling cap, still with blond ends here and there, like sparks Different from each other as they were, they were a set that neither Braddock's misdeeds nor Tillington's had ever fractured. And now they came with family. Artur took his parents by either hand and pulled them forward; Gene and Irene each put an arm about Gene's mother and they walked together.

The news and all the cameras were barred from this area. There was no record to be made, even by the Space Service. Bren flung his arms wide, let a welcoming smile reach his face and walked toward them as they came close.

"Hug," Bren said. "You're on Mospheira, and it's entirely different manners here. You're human. Enjoy it." He gave them each a gentle hug, one after the other, despite the hazard to starched lace, and offered his hand to their parents, one after the other. "Cajeiri can't be here, of course, but he sent me. These six gentlemen are your security, your aishid." The parents had lived this last while with Lord Geigi, and well knew what that was. "And these three earnest young fellows—" He waved the three translators forward. "These three are your tutors. They've given up careers in the Linguistics Department to devote themselves to teaching you, youngsters, so be good to them. They know a fair bit of Ragi, they know customs—and they know a very great deal about Mospheira and the local accent. They'll be staying in the same building, they'll be teaching you, answering questions, helping you. You'll live upstairs, they'll have a classroom on the floor below. You'll actually enjoy school, I think."

"Are you going to stay for a while, nand' Bren?"

That from Irene, who did not look to have been sick at all.

"I have to get back," he said gently. "I've been here for a

while setting this up, and I have to report to Tabini-aiji. I also have to report to Cajeiri, for one very major thing. You *will* get to visit for a couple of weeks as soon as you've had a chance to settle in and rest and learn a little about the house and Mospheira in general . . . I think Captain Jase might have explained some of it. We'll set up a phone connection for you in not too long—so you can talk to Cajeiri, at least. Visits come a little later. But they will come." He looked at the parents, at more sober faces. "It'll be good. You'll be wobbly for a few days. But it passes. If what you find at Heyden Court is anything short of good, any of you, you talk to someone, and if that doesn't work, you can just call me: pick up a phone and ask staff. We'll fix it."

"We'll have to depend on our children," Artur's mother said. "They've been filling us in. Telling us—all sorts of things. We'll do our best."

"We'll do our best for you, too. Let me be very frank: you know how Tillington felt. There *are* some few down here who are Tillington's sort and willing to act like him. It's a population. Some people aren't nice. Most people down here are just relieved that the kyo have agreed to a peace, they've had their own scare, they know you've been through terrible conditions, and they generally accept that you need to be down here so the station can recover from the damage it's had and everything can get back to normal. Ordinary folk just want you to have a fair deal. They want to see newcomers live nicely but not better than they do—you can understand that, I think."

"Absolutely," Artur's father said.

"You and your children, however, *need* security, because of your connection to the aiji's son, because of a history of war, and because of a handful of people of Tillington's bent. So you will be housed in what will become not only your residence, but also for outward appearance, the clerical and operational headquarters for the whole resettlement effort. So you won't *conspicuously* be living in a palace. You'll be our test cases, and people who'll deal with other Reunioners will be learning from you on a day to day basis. If you meet one who's a problem, there will be people to advise of that fact. I'm sure there will be problems we haven't thought of. We'll fix them. I know you're tired and under physical stress. But just get through this. We're going up the runway a bit to a ceremony welcoming you. Shake the President's hand. Smile, look friendly. He's a nice fellow. He means you well. Let the President make a speech, shake his hand, shake any hand offered to you. Then I solemnly promise we'll get you to your own residence, where you can sleep for a week if you want to."

"We'll be fine," Artur's mother said, her arm on her son's shoulders. "We'll really be fine. We were warned. We understand."

"Just don't look into the distance," Artur's father said. "That's fairly stomach-churning."

"Particularly don't look out the windows while we're moving," Bren said. "The youngsters were that way at first. Captain Graham was. It'll get better. Especially with the meds. Short views at first. We're going to take a short drive. You'll be able to sit down, your security will be with you, and it won't be a long lot of speeches."

Lord Keimi had come in first, with Deiso and Janiri, and other Taibeni had taken the mecheiti back to the camp, to prevent problems—because the next guests were arriving on trucks and in small vehicles: the mayor of Diegi, who had lent his car to Lord Tatiseigi, who had ample storage, had received it back again last night, and had taken aboard the mayors of Heitisi and Hegian, and the wife and son of the mayor of Heitisi, and the sister of the mayor of Hegian, followed by a number of trucks and vans. Nomari had sent good wishes, and a very felicitous gift, a porcelain bowl for Uncle's collection. Even two Kadagidi townships had sent gifts, a brass urn and a gazing-glass, a curious thing of blown glass with swirls inside, that sparkled in the light.

There had been food, mostly sweets, and most all the glass-ware was pressed into service, even some old, fragile things from storage. There were too many people, counting spouses and cousins and various village and township officials, and kin, for them ever to hope to serve at table, so people milled and mixed, and stared with great misgiving at the Taibeni, who had never come to an Atageini festivity.

But Uncle spoke with Lord Keimi and Antaro's and Jegari's parents, and introduced them to the mayors, who introduced them in turn to their spouses and cousins, and to the other no-tables, poets, and artisans of various sorts, who also had brought small gifts to the occasion—

Not to Uncle, these little gifts, but such things as toys and ribbons, and several nice little jackets for Sister.

Mother was not present, nor was she intended to be. Only after the party was well-advanced, and Uncle had told the story of the escaped mecheiti for at least the third time, and intro-duced everyone who could possibly be introduced—and after everybody had had a glass or mug of something a boy was not permitted to have.

Which was all right. He had tried it once. It had not been that much fun, especially in the morning. Slipping about . . . that had been fun.

Such moments were harder come by, now that he was obliged to be dignified. He stood by the potted orangelle mostly, and received felicitations.

And questions: "Will you be happy with your sister as lord of Atageini?" and "Has your great-uncle mentioned *anyone* for Kadagidi?" On the latter one, he swore he would make up a courteous card saying, No, nandi. I do not think he wishes to become involved in that question.

But he kept nodding and smiling, and he was very glad to have his aishid near him, simply because they were eight people *not* asking him questions.

And because they were keeping in touch with information.

"Jeri-ji," Antaro said in a lull, leaning very close to him. "The shuttle has landed safely. Everybody is there, everybody is safe, and nand' Bren is with them."

He heaved a great, deep sigh, and felt the tension that had gripped his chest unwind itself.

"Good," he said simply. "Good."

Then it was as if some great wind had risen and blown all the people instantly across the room, oblivious to him, all conversation stopped, everybody, including Uncle, looking up at the stairs.

Mother was coming down the steps, and Beha-nadi behind her was carrying Sister in her arms.

The vehicles that had gotten them to the end of the runway and two that had been waiting took them aboard, and the lead driver knew where he was going—a good thing, Bren thought: he'd not been this famous on his arrivals, and there'd been no reviewing stand and crowd to navigate. The massive stands were not a permanent feature. They were all planks and pipe, like a sports stand, made nicer by the Mospheiran colors, but the backside was a confusion of supports, with only numbers on placards to advise them where to park.

Their transportation would wait. They had to get out and climb. It was asking a bit to bring the kids and parents, fresh from zero gravity, up three flights of steps to reach the bunting-swathed box. He wished he'd considered *that* detail and had a scissor-lift for them or the like.

But they made it. They emerged into sunlight, with that—to spacefarer eyes—horrifying expanse of flatness beyond, but a crowd of people to give them something close-range to ground them. Shawn was there, with his security, with his aides, with the Justices, and the head of Science, the head of the University—looking a little grim—and the head of the Space Service, all there to shake hands quite solemnly, children and parents alike, while media from the pool hovered at the rail with their cameras and microphones and a massive screen showed the images to all the people in the stands.

Bren simply stood back a bit, as far out of camera range as he and his aishid could manage, and let it be Shawn's show, all of it.

And Shawn was in his element, being the common man for the visitors, asking how they fared, complimenting their courage, wishing them well. Karl and Evan and Lyle likewise put themselves as far to the back as they could, modest fellows, doing, Bren realized, what *he* was doing, taking their cues from him—not quite *with* the children, but not putting themselves in the spotlight, either.

It was all going according to program, until suddenly, from whatever direction, two, three nearby gunshots shocked the air and the world spun sideways amid deafening screams. Bren hit the carpet, lay there with one of his aishid pressing him to the ground, breath coming as best he could get it.

He was not hit. He was relatively sure of that. He tried to move, and then—it was Algini who had flattened him—Algini and Tano briskly lifted him to his feet, and he could see not a thing past Banichi and Jago except a wall of human bodies. He could tell nothing, except Artur's parents had him safe on the ground in a knot of security, Gene's mother was the same, hugging Gene and Irene both. The kids were all right. Their parents were.

"No, damn it, let me up!" Shawn's voice, as people began, amid the din of voices, shouting "Mr. President! Mr. President!"

"Give me a microphone!" Shawn ordered.

"Mr. President, stay down."

"The hell!" Shawn shoved himself to his feet, his coat sleeve soaked with blood, an aide trying to tie a scarf around it. "Give me a damn microphone!"

"He's hurt."

"I'm not damned dying! Give it to me!" Shawn grabbed the microphone from the stand and said, "Is this thing live?"

"Yes," someone said, and Shawn said, his voice ringing over the stands, while his blood-spattered face loomed on the giant screen beyond:

"Somebody doesn't want me to talk, somebody doesn't want us to be here today. Somebody doesn't want three innocent kids to come down here, because it's all a conspiracy launched two hundred years ago, when humankind had a *difference of opinion* about whether to go on with the ship or stay here and live under this sun. Well, *somebody's* wrong in the head! *Get over it!* What happened back then is not these kids' fault, it's not these parents' fault, it's not my fault, and it sure wasn't the atevi's fault! I'm not giving the speech I'd planned, about bright futures and our traditions and our family holidays, because we obviously have some work to do! We have these people on our doorstep who came here for help, who're being told by the ex-station director to go off to a barren moon and *die,* because somehow they're going to change us if they come down here. Well, my fellow citizens, *they're* not the ones bent on changing us. What will change us is not five thousand men, women, kids, and old people who've come to us for refuge. It's the notion that we're too fragile, too morally impoverished to give it. We *can* give it, we *should* give it, and by all we hold sacred, we're *going* to give it! We're not intimidated. We're not stupid. And we're not going to react in fear of each other. I'm done. I'm out of breath. Just *think,* for God's sake. What way of life do we want to show our new citizens? Give a cheer for them. Give a cheer. Let these two families hear what the *majority* of good people think!"

The uproar was massive, all about. Bren drew breath, went to the Reunioners, patted shoulders. "He means it," he said. "People here mean it. Tillington isn't going to win down here. Neither is Braddock." His aishid wasn't leaving him for an instant: they wanted him out of here, he well knew. A side glance caught the massive vid screen, and a trio in tight focus. It was Anna Parker, tears running down her ashen face, locked in an embrace with her olive-skinned son and her dark-skinned daughter. That image was up there. It was going out to a nation of human beings, not a word said, none needed.

"Sit down, Mr. President. An ambulance is trying to get through."

"My arm's bleeding. I'm not dead."

"The assassin is," one of the security team said. "Lone gunman, best we can figure."

"Random lunatic, maybe."

"Maybe," another of the team said.

"Get me up," Shawn said. "I'll *walk* down to the damn ambulance. I mean it."

"Let him," an aide said.

"But first thing," Shawn said, "I'm going to see these people get to their home. Excuse the left hand." He grasped hands of each of the parents, touched each of the kids. "Excuse us. We're going to fix this. You go with your security. They'll get you home. They'll keep you safe. —Mr. Cameron." Shawn was perfectly aware mikes were live, cameras full on them. "You'll be wanting to keep your schedule. Our regards to Tabini-aiji, and our firm promise that Mospheira is better than this. That we *all* are better than this. These families will be safe here. And *welcome* here. I'll be contacting you soon."

"Mr. President." Bren gave a little bow, and saw Shawn put a hand inside his coat, where there was disturbed thread in a pattern of beige brocade.

Thank God, he thought. Shawn had worn the damned vest. Shawn had taken the threat seriously. But *nobody* had expected such an event here, with the kids present.

That image, Anna Parker, the two kids, was going to haunt Mospheiran television over the next number of days. Maybe for years. Shawn had said it: Mospheirans weren't *like* that. That image was going to be on every screen, in every town, in every bar and every place people gathered to discuss what went on in the world.

"We shall go," he said to his aishid, and had a glimpse of the University kids, the three of them, shaken, standing aside. But Karl put out a hand as he came toward the steps, not touching him, aware of custom. Just delaying him to say:

"We're here, sir. Just—we'll do what we can."

"They've seen a lot worse. Very much worse. Just—help them see *better* in us. Be here. Do what I can't."

"Sir."

He gave a bow, a little one, a nod. And took his way quietly down the steps, his aishid before and behind him. It was not the paidhi-aiji's business now.

It was Shawn's. It was a Mospheiran matter, no matter how he wanted to sweep those kids up and get them to safety . . . on the continent, if he had his way.

But that was not the best way, even for the kids and the parents. The kids had to grow up human, first, cope with their own instincts, find out, first, what those instincts were. They had to have that, before they could be what Cajeiri needed them to be.

Down the stairs, behind Banichi and Jago, ahead of Tano and Algini. The ambulance had arrived, down below. Mospheirans had to sort this one out. He couldn't.

Everybody wanted to see Seimiro. That was no surprise at all. They crowded about, and Seimiro, who was usually in a good mood, behaved very well for the most part, as Mother held Seimiro in her arms, and walked about the hall, letting each group, starting with the mayor of Diegi, see Seimiro up close. Seimei even blinked at him and smiled, which the mayor took personally.

Group after group, however, was asking a lot of Seimiro, and especially she grimaced and fretted when people crowded close. It was the bodies shadowing the light, and then the lamps, Cajeiri thought.

But it was a felicitous day. All the numbers said so. Seimei's numbers and Uncle's agreed, which was, of course, complete nonsense, but Heisi explained the details of it, and explained how Seimei, born in spring, was the Lily of Atageini.

That was a bit much. Seimei screwed up her face and scowled as if she understood the notion, and Cajeiri simply kept an expressionless face and politely waited for the speeches.

"Her father and her brother," the mayor of Diegi said at one point, "will never fail her, and all her associations will benefit."

That was true, but it was a little excessive for a small bundle of pale silk and lace, who was starting to fret at the echoes in the hall.

It was, finally, down to the point of the gathering, and Mother held Seimiro in her arms while Uncle, who could not hold her properly with one arm in a sling, simply laid a hand ever so gently on Seimiro's head—and said the words:

"This is Seimiro, daughter of Tabini-aiji and Damiri-daja, sister of Cajeiri-nandi; granddaughter of my sister Muriyo. This is Seimiro-nandi, my heir, someday to be lord of Tirnamardi, lord of Atageini, heir to its privileges and duties, heir to its associations and obligations, and heir to its future in the heart of the aishidi'tat. This is my heir, nandiin! The lordship and the line are secure, and you are witnesses! The table has the document itself, and the ribbons and cards. I shall sign them—this hand will manage it, I promise you—and you shall sign as witnesses and associates. Wax is ready, for those of you who have brought ribbons and seals, and Tabini-aiji will receive a document heavy with the good will of our neighbors."

A murmur of approval echoed in the hall.

There would be one seal to come: that would be Father's.

Lord Keimi provided the ribbon of his own queue: the seal was his gold ring.

Uncle's, the impress of a lily in a special green wax, went on.

Reijiri's, a blue and white ribbon, likewise from his queue, and the mark of a sun and star.

And there was, which Mother affixed, a ribbon which had

arrived by Guild courier at dawn, the gold and blue of Ajuri, the impress of a sword.

The black and red of Father's seal would go on. That would be for him.

But now every witness would sign it, and for every attendee, even servants and Guild, there would be cards and ribbons, with Uncle's seal and, and Mother's, and his. Seimiro made her definitive progress about the room, in Beha-nadi's arms. Then Beha took her upstairs to have a nap, and they all settled at the table to sign cards for all the witnesses, of whatever station, things to be kept as family treasures—a record older than writing, so his tutor said. A treaty of acceptance.

An heir of Atageini. A lord of Ajuri. And his associates were down safely. Nand' Bren had promised they would make a phone call as soon as they were settled in, maybe in another day; and they had to be a little careful what they said, and only speak Ragi, for political reasons. He was anxious to hear their voices. They would make plans. But they could not set a date— for security reasons.

He was here—for family reasons. But he had no doubt when that call came through, the system would track him down.

He signed a card for Antaro's mother, and sealed and ribboned it himself. He had never quite felt the surrounds of *family* except with mani and nand' Bren and his three associates. He had never expected to feel it in the same room as his mother.

But he did.

21

*B*righter *Days* moved briskly past the breakwater, where the waters of the strait began. Bren sat on the locker by the transom, watching the wake, watching Port Jackson become a geometry in the distance, the hill of Francis House, the tall buildings, the few scattered constructions that were part of the airport.

Jeladi and Narani had gotten their luggage to the harbor, with the help of Shawn's security, and Toby and Barb had not failed their summons. They had still been fueling when Bren had come aboard, with Banichi and Jago, with Tano and Algini, and they had sat there a brief while, saying not that much, beyond just what had happened, and that the kids were safe.

Once fueling was complete, Toby and Barb had just let them be a while and gotten *Brighter Days* free of the dock and out into the harbor, under her engines. Now, Jeladi and Narani were belowdecks arranging things in the two cabins they would share. Banichi and the others just sat. The radio was audible, barely, to Bren's ears, and it was saying things like *an outrage* and *an attack against decency.* Shawn had released a copy of his intended speech, welcoming the children and their parents, and citing the Mospheiran traditions of family unity and family celebrations, while proposing a new holiday Shawn intended to call Reunion Day, a free day at all the nature reserves, reminding them all of the environment they had shared, and the fact that those who had come back from the long voyage had never felt natural gravity and never seen a tree. We have so much, he would have said, so very much it costs us nothing to share.

Now at least one commentator had quoted that, and said the name of the holiday should be a solemn reminder to what lengths some people could carry hate, and that Reunion Day should come to be a day of real reunion, a day of national reconsideration and reconciliation—*lest we repeat our mistakes*, the commentator said. *We have some sober thinking to do.*

If only they would, Bren thought.

And wished he had handled things better, that he had arranged things differently, that he had advised Shawn to meet the Reunioners in Francis House, in his office. But Shawn had not wanted the closed doors, the restricted meeting, about which detractors were sure to complain. Everything above board.

Thank God, he thought, Shawn had worn the vest.

"Bren," Barb said. She had picked up the phone, had it in hand, and spoke over the sound of the engine and rush of water. "Call from the President."

He got up immediately and went to take it, shielding the mouthpiece from the ambient. "This is Bren Cameron." He expected one of Shawn's aides, with, he hoped, a good report.

"*Bren. It's me. Sore as hell, but grateful. Real grateful. Wanted you to know—just had a report from Kate: the kids are in, the families are real impressed with the arrangements, they've now seen a tree, at least from the window, they're exhausted, but probably not going to sleep for hours. I'm back home, they are, and they tagged the gunman as an aide of John Woodenhouse, if that tells you anything. You remember him. Heritage Party, the legislative committee!*"

Unpleasant man. Who now had a problem on his hands.

"*My front hall, meanwhile, is starting to look like a florist shop, not to mention people sending donations and flowers for the children and their parents at Heyden Court. And not to mention offers of vacation cottages and plane tickets and requests for interviews—it's really quite overwhelming. Security didn't plan on a deluge of flowers. They're going to need cleri-cal staff. Or Kate will. But the kids and families are just going to take a rest for a few days. And so am I."*

"The arm, Shawn."

"Full recovery, given rehab. It'll be fine. If it weren't for you—a lot worse. Got to go now. My own doc wants me to lie flat. But I wanted you to know. Regards to everybody. You know who. I'm a little muzzy. Take care."

"Take care," he said, and Shawn broke the connection.

His aishid was looking at him, not in position to have heard any of it. "Good news," he said, "nandiin-ji. Shawn is back in his residence, in fair prospect of a complete recovery. People are offering expressions of regret and support, to him and to the children and their parents."

"Excellent," Banichi said.

"I think I'll change clothes," Bren said then to Toby and Barb. A wind was picking up off the port side, fair for the conti-nent and Najida. Very soon now Toby would shut down the engine and rely on canvas. "I'll help you with the sails. Give me a moment."